STALAG

Praise for Bill Walker

"Bill Walker is a consummate storyteller. Always inventive and always entertaining. You will have a great time with anything he writes."

—Richard Chizmar
Bestselling author of *Gwendy's Magic Feather*

"Walker is a hell of a writer!"

—Harlan Ellison

STALAG

BILL WALKER

DELARGE BOOKS

2021

DeLarge Books Edition 2021
ISBN-13: 978-1-7358796-1-1

This is a work of fiction.

Cover Design: Damonza Studios
Typesetting and Design: Bill Walker Designs
Printed in the United States of America

*To my wonderful wife, Debbie and my sons, Jeffrey and Brian,
whom I love without reservation.
Without your unflagging encouragement, and your steadfast
belief in me, this book would not exist.*

*And to my father
William A. Walker, Sr.
(1922-1996)
Veteran, friend, mentor.
An uncommon man, without whom I would not exist.*

PROLOGUE: 1978

The black semi had been following him for the last forty miles, ever since he'd left Cyberdyne. The euphoria from his sales meeting had still not worn off. After all, it wasn't every day one closed a five-million-dollar order. Frank Murphy allowed himself another self-satisfied grin and thought about the national sales manager job his boss had dangled in front of him. It was in the bag now. And while he loved being on the road, he wanted to be closer to home. God only knew Audrey had been begging him for years to take a desk job. Now, she would get her wish. Truth be told, Frank wanted it too. With Frank Junior turning twelve in a couple of days, Frank was all the more aware that his son's precious childhood was slipping past him.

Frank glanced in the rearview and saw the truck had drawn closer. It was an odd duck, that was for sure. Painted completely in a light-absorbing flat black paint, the truck had no markings. No big, splashy ads along the sides, no silhouettes of naked women cut out of shiny steel riveted to the mud flaps. Not even a license plate. How in the hell the driver or his employer got away with that, Frank had no idea.

The sun had gone down about two hours before, but he knew it was the same truck... pacing him.

Up ahead, Frank saw a flood of light off to the side of the road. A rest stop. He'd pull over and let the truck go on past.

Two minutes later, Frank pulled into the nearly empty parking lot of a small Airstream-style diner and waited. Seconds later, the black behemoth rolled on past, blatting its horn as if to say, "See ya later, sucker."

"Fat chance," Frank said. He smiled and breathed a sigh of relief and headed into the diner. The waitress, a blowsy woman in her late forties with blonde straw for hair and a gold front tooth, served him the hot coffee he craved and a slice of heaven they were calling cherry pie.

After he finished, he found the phone booth in the back. Audrey answered on the second ring, as always.

"How did it go?" she asked.

"How did you know I wasn't some heavy breather?"

Audrey laughed. "Because he always calls at six o'clock sharp, unlike my husband."

"Well, there you go. What would the world be without reliable cranks? It went fine. Closed the deal in record time."

Audrey let out a squeal of delight. "So, you're going to take the new job?"

"And what if I said no?"

"I'd brain you."

It was Frank's turn to laugh. "Yes, I'm taking it. This old warhorse has had enough."

They talked for a few more minutes about how their lives would soon change, and then Audrey said, "Frankie's been waiting up for you. He's so excited about his birthday, and now that you'll be home—"

"Put him on," Frank said, smiling again.

Frank heard the phone bonk onto the Formica counter, and his wife calling up the stairs. "Frankie? Your father's on the phone!"

A few seconds later, the boy picked up the extension in their bedroom. "Dad?"

"How's my number-one soldier?"

The boy laughed. "I'm fine, but Mom won't let me work on the model without you. So, when are you coming home?"

"Should be there late tonight. We can work on it all day tomorrow, if you like."

"That'd be great, Dad. You gonna be home for my birthday too?"

Frank smiled. "You bet. Anything you want to do?"

"Naw, we can just hang out and stuff."

The boy's casual tone belied his joy.

"You sure?" Frank said.

"Yeah, but I want to hear the Regensburg story again."

Frank laughed. "You never get tired of those old war stories, do you?"

"No, I don't."

"Sure, I'll tell 'em all again, if that's what you want."

"What about the camp?"

"You don't want to hear about that, Frankie."

"You promised, Dad. You promised you'd tell me someday. And I'm almost twelve."

Frank's smile turned bittersweet. "I know… but I'm not sure you're ready for that. It wasn't like on TV."

"But Mom said you were a hero there."

"Well, that's what some people say. But real heroes don't brag, Frankie, they just get the job done. I know I promised I'd tell you someday, and I will. Just not now. Okay?"

"Okay," the boy said. Frank could hear the disappointment, and his heart ached.

"All right, I'll see you tomorrow and we'll get that B-17 done. Okay?"

After saying his goodbyes, Frank paid his bill and got back on the road. He kept his eyes on the rearview, and after half an hour he began to relax. So, the truck had been following him. So what? It was a narrow two-lane road, and they were both going the same direction. He'd let his imagination get the better of him, started thinking of that old TV movie with Dennis Weaver being terrorized by a crazed truck driver. Frank laughed at the absurdity of it. In two hours, he'd be home in the bosom of his family with the promise of a brighter future for all of them.

Up ahead, Frank spotted a flashing red light marking a four-way intersection. He came to a stop and looked both ways. With no moon and no streetlights, he couldn't see anything either way, but no headlight certainly meant the way was clear.

Frank stepped on the gas and started through the intersection. A second later he was blinded by headlights snapping on, accompanied by the roar of a massive diesel engine barreling straight toward him. He had no time to react, no time to do anything before the black monster plowed into him head on. In the nanoseconds before his life ended, Frank Murphy Senior barely had time to wonder what the large "K" set into the truck's front grill signified.

Part I

ORPHANS OF THE STORM

1998

1

*W*here was Dean?

It was a question Frank Murphy found himself asking far too often, lately. And now, standing outside the Bridgeport Convention Center, with his hand shading his eyes from the early morning sun, Frank found his patience wearing thin.

His best friend and business partner, Dean Seger, was late—again.

Dean was always late.

From the time they'd first met in college, Dean ran at least an hour behind the world. He'd even been late for his own wedding, leaving his tearful bride, Marge, standing at the altar for over an hour and a half.

Frank wiped the sweat from his brow and walked through the glass doors into the convention center. He bypassed the lines of attendees gathered at the ticket booths, showed his exhibitor pass and headed into the auditorium, passing under a thirty-foot banner suspended from the rafters:

10th ANNUAL WORLD WAR CONVENTION

Welcome Vets & Buffs!

He reached his booth and nodded to the security guard standing watch. "Can you give me another five minutes? I've got to change," he said, grabbing his suit bag off one of his tables.

"Sure thing," the guard said.

Frank headed for the nearest restroom and changed into his father's old Army Air Corps uniform: khaki shirt, matching tie and olive-green trousers, and a well-worn leather A-2 flight jacket topped off with a rakish olive drab officer's crusher cap. He studied himself in the mirror and cracked a wistful smile.

"Almost fits, Dad. Too bad the shoes are still too big."

He sighed and gathered up his street clothes and headed back to the booth.

"Thanks for watching my stock."

The guard smiled. "No problem. You got some cool stuff. And I love the flyboy getup too."

The man sauntered off as Dean came running, his ever-present laptop clutched under his arm.

"Sorry, Shakespeare," he said, trying to catch his breath.

"What took you so long?" Frank asked.

With his sandy hair and easy smile, Dean Seger had the kind of face one instantly liked and trusted, which Frank found ironic, considering that he bore a remarkable resemblance to Eddie Haskell, the impish troublemaker from that old television show: *Leave it to Beaver*. Often Dean deliberately put on his "Eddie" facade at parties or when he wanted to rib Frank. It was all part of his devil-may-care attitude, an attitude Frank envied and wished he could emulate. Dean knew how to grab life by the scruff and shake it for all it was worth. And though there were some who thought he was a shallow jerk, Frank knew he could count on him as a true friend.

"Don't tell me—"

Dean shook his head. "Marge and I had a fight... I'd forgotten to tell her about the convention... What can I say? She hates it when I go to these shows, says I'm always bringing home 'tons of crap,' as she puts it. Had to promise her a night on the town before she'd let me out of the house. You know how it is."

Frank smiled in spite of his mood. Dean always had a way of making the worst situations humorous. "Yeah, I do, but I'm sure she likes it when we have a good payday. Let's finish setting up. They'll be letting in everyone in about twenty minutes."

They spent those minutes setting up their three tables with merchandise Frank had brought in from the van. When they were finished, Frank stood back and gave the booth a thorough inspection.

The *Murphy's Militaria* booth was fashioned from a dozen pre-fabricated pieces of aluminum tubing and custom-printed vinyl panels in red and black that snapped together and broke down in five minutes. It looked like it cost far more than it did, something for which Frank was grateful. He was straightening the overhead Murphy's Militaria banner as the public address system started blaring John Phillips Sousa music. A moment later the system crackled, and a voice called out, "Welcome everyone, the Tenth Annual World War Convention is now open!"

"Here we go," Dean said, grinning.

In moments, the room was under siege.

Never in his life had Frank seen so many people crammed into one space. Thousands choked the aisles between the hundreds of booths and stalls covering the twenty-five-thousand-square-foot expanse. The entire mass of them moved about like some giant, swarming hive, reminding Frank of the ant farm he'd had as a child.

And the noise...

The thousands of throats shouting, chattering, and laughing blended together into a deafening clamor like the roar of primeval beasts battling to the death in some forgotten rainforest, a rainforest redolent with the smells of Cosmoline, mothballs, roasting hot dogs, and stale beer.

Some of the people looked as if they *belonged* in a jungle: tattooed bikers strutted about in leather and denim, reeking of grease and gasoline. Their women, gum-snapping bimbos dressed in tight leather miniskirts and gobs of cheap makeup, hung on them like one of their ornamental chains. Skinheads wearing Doc Martens and nasty attitudes checked out the latest in Nazi chic. Good ol' boys from dirt water towns somewhere south of the Mason-Dixon line, with their ubiquitous Confederate flags, gun-racked pickups and potbellies, laughed, guzzled cheap beer, and traded war stories from nonexistent campaigns. There were glassy-eyed, slope-headed weirdos walking around dressed in full SS regalia, and straight-arrow mercenaries wearing mirrored sunglasses and the tensed attitudes of wary snakes. And among them walked Mr. and Mrs. America looking like shell-shocked refugees from the *Twilight Zone*.

I hope I brought enough inventory.

And then the first customer approached the booth and Frank got to work.

✻ ✻ ✻

"I'll give you three hundred for this," the heavyset man said, his voice hoarse from trying to yell over the noise.

After eight hours, it had become glaringly apparent to Frank that this convention was going to be a financial bust. It wasn't for lack of foot traffic. He and Dean had been busy, but the sales were few and far between. And this one was going south too.

"Three hundred is highway robbery, Ken."

"Not for a repaint."

Frank managed to hold his temper in check, his smile widening.

"It's original paint and decals, and you know it."

"And Forman's got a rack of these at their table for three fifty apiece. Come on, Frank, cut me some slack."

"I'm sorry, I can't."

The man sighed and nodded, handing the helmet back to Frank, who watched the man head back to Forman's crowded booth, one of the largest in the convention. He tried not to feel bitter, but it was getting harder and harder to swallow that pill.

Without taking his eyes off his laptop screen, Dean said, "Guy's a bozo. He wouldn't know a repaint if it was still wet, and Forman's crap is all fake."

"Yeah, but we could've used the sale."

"Not to worry, Shakespeare. I've got a guy who's drooling over that German Cross. Said he'd be back for it."

"Was he short and bald with a big red mustache?"

"Yeah, that's him."

"That's Farley Gibbons. Drool is all he's got."

Dean's laptop emitted a loud explosion, and "GAME OVER" appeared on the screen.

"Shit, dead again."

Frank laughed in spite of his sour mood. "I swear to God, you're never going to make that beachhead."

"It's not me," he said, pointing to the offending laptop. "It's this piece of crap."

Frank's grin widened. Same old Dean. He squeezed his friend's shoulder.

"I'm going to take a walk. Watch the booth, okay?"

Dean, already deep into another round of his game, gave him the thumbs up.

Frank bought a bottled water at a nearby concession stand and then wandered through the hall, stopping at various booths to check out the competition. He avoided Forman's. At the end of the room were a set of private rooms. A sign on an easel announced the times for a series of lectures. One of them caught his eye.

BERLIN: THE AFTERMATH
Lecture and Q&A at 3:00 p.m., Room 101

Frank glanced at his vintage Hamilton watch. The lecture was starting in five minutes. For a moment, he felt guilty about leaving Dean to his own devices but realized his friend would not let a potential sale escape his notice, despite his all-consuming fascination with his Normandy computer game.

"What the hell," Frank said, and strode into the lecture room.

※　※　※

The black Mercedes glided down the narrow side street, pausing at each building and then resuming its stately course. A moment later the car pulled up to a seedy-looking two-story brick building nestled between a dusty furniture store and a down-at-the-heels Chinese restaurant.

The sign above the display window and the front door spanned the entire width of the building and read: MURPHY'S MILITARIA in faded red block letters.

Inside the car, two men dressed in identical black suits gave the building a once-over, their hard, chiseled faces revealing nothing. The store's display window held all manner of militaria, with two tailor's dummies wearing full uniforms, one American and one German, along with an array of a dozen Riker cases chocked full of military awards, including those from the Third Reich and Soviet Union.

"Someone needs to clean the window," the man in the passenger seat commented in heavily accented English.

The man behind the wheel scowled. "Who cares about the *verdammt* window, Karl? Is this the last one?"

"*Ja*," Karl said, reaching for a briefcase at his feet. He snapped it open and pulled out a small flat package wrapped in plain brown paper, closed the briefcase, and placed it back on the floor. He then exited the Mercedes and walked up to the door, where he slid the package through the mail slot. Satisfied, Karl returned to the car.

"Let's go to the *Hofbrau*," Karl said in German. "I need a beer."

The other man chuckled, shook his head, and pulled away from the curb.

❋ ❋ ❋

The elderly gentleman stood in the glaring spotlight, gnarled hands clutching a stout cane of polished oak. He looked like a shabby scarecrow with all the stuffing knocked out of him, as if one good gust of wind would carry him away. Skin the color of dry parchment hung loosely from a hangdog face that spoke volumes about the hard life he'd lived, and his hair, a grayish-yellow, had thinned to the point where—with the hot light shining down on him—you could see the curvature of his skull. It looked as fragile as an egg. Oddly enough, the old man's eyebrows remained bushy, and shockingly black. When he spoke, his loose jowls wobbled and his voice, a reedy whisper, barely reached the back of the room. Yet the man held the audience in the palm of his hand.

"Well, enough about me," he said, coughing thickly. "Do any of you have any questions?"

Frank finished jotting in his notepad, then looked around as several hands went up. While the old man's stories had no bearing on his current book idea, one never knew when a tidbit of information might become useful. It was history, and history was a valuable commodity, especially for an author wanting to write historical novels about World War II. He watched the speaker point to a middle-aged man wearing a tan golf hat.

"Yes. Do you have a question?" he said.

The middle-aged man stood up, clearing his throat.

"Uh, yeah. I heard some of the German soldiers were disguising themselves as civilians in order to escape capture and prolong the street fighting. That true?"

The old man nodded slowly. "That happened, but not to a great extent. You have to realize at the war's end, especially in Berlin, things were not so clear-cut. People were sick of the years of fighting, and the Russians were committing all kinds of atrocities. Most Germans, soldiers included, surrendered quickly."

"We shoulda' killed the whole mess of 'em when we had the chance!"

Everyone turned toward the sound of the voice.

Frank spotted a young man near the back of the room, his shaved head gleaming dully. He was wearing faded fatigues and a ripped T-shirt emblazoned with "Give 'em Hell, Harry" in red, white, and blue. He looked no older than eighteen, as did the other two leering jokers seated on either side of him.

The room had fallen into a hush, and all eyes returned to the small stage. The speaker's eyes narrowed.

"*We* should have killed *them*?" he said, his voice growing surprisingly strong. "What do you know about it? What do *any* of you know?"

The old man scanned the crowd, his fiery gaze missing no one. He took a halting step forward.

"You all came to this convention to relive the past... Well, I've spent my life trying to forget it! You want to know what it was like? I'll tell you! One day, in a suburb outside Essen, my squad charged into a basement, firing like crazy. We didn't know what to expect. My God! We were just frightened kids. When the smoke cleared, we found we'd killed an entire family... civilians... Oh, God..."

He covered his face with his free hand and sobbed, his gaunt form trembling.

A convention staff member dressed as a WAC ran out, her walkie-talkie squawking in that awful silence.

The old man waved her off and faced the audience once more.

"You must forgive an old soldier's anger. These events are still so fresh to me. I can't expect you to understand. You had to be there."

Frank stared at the old man, his heart going out to him. Growing old was such a raw deal. You spent your entire life working toward a happy old age, only to find out when you got there that you were too old to enjoy it. If the thought weren't so tragic, it would be funny. Frank watched while the WAC helped the speaker offstage. He leaned heavily on his cane, shuffling toward the stairs leading to the floor, his face set in grim and painful determination.

And Frank realized something else. On top of it all, the old guy was right. How could Frank ever understand what it was like to have been there? How would he ever imbue the novel he'd been slaving over with that unmistakable aura of truth, when all he had were the secondhand recollections of frail old men?

Frank returned to the booth to find Dean finalizing the sale of an SS armband. When the convention closed, he and Dean broke down the booth, packed up all the stock and loaded it into the Murphy's Militaria van, a ten-year-old Ford Econoline that had seen better days.

"How'd we do?" Frank asked, slamming the van doors shut.

"We grossed about six fifty."

"For today?"

Dean flashed Frank a guilty look. "For the whole convention."

Frank sighed and leaned against the dusty van. "Shit, Dean, our booth space cost two grand! We can't keep going like this."

"I know, but I've got some ideas. Including a website. You know, Frank, we'd probably do a lot better if we sold online too." Dean paused for a moment, letting that thought sink in. "Forman's doing it."

Frank's expression clouded. "Call me old-fashioned." He shook his head, letting out a sigh of annoyance. "All right, I'll think about it. Who would we get to create a site for us?"

"Little old me. I've been reading up on it. Trust me, Shakespeare, I'll get us there."

They said their goodbyes and Dean went to his car and drove off. Frank climbed inside the van, his gaze falling on his flip phone lying in the center console.

"Crap, no wonder I didn't get any calls."

He picked up the phone, dialed a number, and listened to his messages.

It was Brenda.

"Frank? Did you leave your phone in the van again? I'm here at the game. Where are you? The kids are waiting. Call me ASAP, please!"

He slammed his hand onto the steering wheel. "Damn it!"

Tossing the phone onto the passenger seat, he started the van and screeched out of the parking lot and onto I-95. If traffic was light, he'd just make the end of the game.

It wasn't.

Frank arrived at the field as the last stragglers were leaving and the grounds crew were relining the field. Feeling like a prized jackass, Frank drove home, pulling the van into the driveway. He shut off the engine and tried to think of what he could say. As if it would make any difference anyway. Things were already about as bad as they could get. That wasn't quite true, though. Brenda had not yet uttered the "D" word.

He stared out the windshield, watching his family around the dinner table.

Brenda, her shoulder-length blonde hair framing that heart-shaped face he couldn't imagine living without—and yet he was— was serving Uncle John what was no doubt a second helping. Pete still wore his Pop Warner football uniform and was laughing at something John was saying, while baby Julie squealed in her highchair.

All in all, it was the quintessential scene of domestic bliss, and he missed it so much it fucking hurt.

Steeling his nerves, he climbed out of the car and trudged into the house.

At least his key still worked.

2

When Frank entered the kitchen, Brenda refused to look at him, her hands making short, abrupt movements as she scraped food off the dishes and placed them into the dishwasher. Other than the sounds of plates and cutlery clattering together, the silence was deafening.

Frank moved to the table and kissed Julie on the top of her head, then turned to Pete, whom he noticed was sporting a brand-new shiner under his right eye.

"I'm really sorry I missed the game, champ," he said. "I promise I'll be there for the next one."

"That's okay, Dad."

"How'd it go?"

The boy cracked an easy grin.

"We won."

For the moment, Frank forgot about his faux pas. "That's great, Pete." He reached up and touched the boy's black eye. "And how'd you get that?"

"Some big bruiser of a kid landed on him," Brenda said, her movements even more abrupt. "He's lucky he didn't break anything."

"Come on, Brenda, it's just a game."

She turned and fixed him with a level gaze.

"One you managed to miss."

Frank ignored the dig and turned back to Pete. "Those bigger kids are always going to be the ones that land on you. You just have to be quicker."

The boy nodded.

"Your dad's got a point, Petey," Riley said. "But next time one of those sonsabitches comes at you, butt him in the stomach with your head."

A spoon clattered in the sink. "Christ, John!" Brenda said.

Riley smiled and shrugged.

"Sorry, Bren, guess it's my killer instinct." He winked at Frank.

"You okay now?" Frank said, grasping the boy's shoulder.

"Yeah, Dad, I'm cool."

Frank smiled at the boy's nonchalance. "All right. Why don't you go on up and get ready for bed. I'll be up in a little bit."

Brenda finished cleaning up the kitchen, pulled Julie out of her highchair and exiting the room without another word.

Frank moved to the bay window and stared out at the dark. Riley stood up and moved to the fridge, pulling out two beers, handing one to Frank. He took a long draft, sighing with a pleasure he did not truly feel.

"Thanks for stepping in for me. Brenda seems to forget we do most of our business in the last couple of hours. I couldn't leave it all to Dean."

Riley grinned. "I'm happy to do it. Besides, it's one of the few chances I have to see my nephew." He gave Frank an appraising look. "You know, Frank, you need to tell him to hit back. It's football, for Christ's sake."

"Maybe I lack the killer instinct," Frank said, annoyed.

Riley put his arm around Frank's shoulder. "That's why I'm an investigator and you're..."

"Just a storekeeper?"

"Sorry, didn't mean it that way. But my offer's still open. I need a crackerjack researcher, and someone who can write. You're good at both. Brenda let me read that last article of yours. It was great stuff."

"Yeah, tell that to the two dozen magazines that rejected it."

"The point is what's left of your marriage is hanging by a thread. Brenda told me she wants to make the separation permanent."

Frank's expression turned from alarm to dejection.

"You need to show her you're willing to change, Frank. That moth-eaten store is dying and it's going to take your family with it. Just promise me you'll think about it."

"All right..." he said.

Frank drained his beer and tossed the empty bottle into the trash, said his goodbyes to Riley, and headed upstairs. He found Pete already dressed in his pajamas and in bed, the only light provided by a Darth Vader nightlight.

Pete saw him and his eyes widened. "You're still here."

His son's statement hit him like a sucker punch, and it was all he could do to keep his emotions in check. He moved into the room and took a seat on the boy's bed.

"I'm still here, champ."

"Did you sell a lot of stuff today?"

"A fair amount."

"But why do you always wear Grandpa Frank's uniform?"

Frank smiled and patted the boy's arm.

"The people at these shows get a kick out of it, but the truth is I guess it just makes me feel good. Makes me feel closer to my father."

"You miss him?"

"Every day..."

"When is Mom gonna let you come home?"

Blinking back tears of anger and frustration, Frank couldn't meet the boy's eyes.

"I don't know, Pete, I don't know..."

On the drive back to the shop, Frank's mind was awhirl. He kept hearing Pete say, "You're still here." Those three words cut him like a serrated-edge knife, reminding him that he was missing out on his son's precious years. And then there was Brenda. Despite what Uncle John had said, he couldn't fathom that she would actually divorce him. Yet he knew that Riley spoke the truth. He was a no-nonsense private investigator who didn't believe in soft-soaping anything. And his job offer was a generous one, and not born out of pity. He *knew* that. So why the hell wasn't he taking the goddamned job? Was his failing business worth the loss of his family? Of course it wasn't, but he couldn't just throw in the towel, either. He'd worked too hard to just give up—to *admit* he was a failure.

Frank pushed those thoughts from his mind as he pulled the van into his parking space in the alley behind the store. When he got out, he smelled the rot of garbage from the overflowing dumpster, reeking of Chinese food from the hole-in-the-wall restaurant next door. He'd lost count of how many takeout dinners he'd consumed from there, and now it made him want to retch.

Wasting no more time, he let himself into the store via the back door, locking it behind him. What light there was in the store came from fluorescent tubes in the display cases, which he rarely shut off. It was enough light to see that something lay on the floor underneath the mail slot.

Mail on a Sunday?

Shrugging, Frank walked to the front door, testing the doorknob out of habit, then bent down and picked up a small square package wrapped in brown paper and bearing just his name and nothing else. It was about the size of a CD—felt like one too. Frank imagined that Dean had whipped up a selection of tunes to while away his lonely hours in the store. Problem was there wasn't enough music for that.

He climbed the creaking stairs to the second level. Originally used for storing their inventory, Frank had turned half the space into a living area, a direct violation of his lease agreement, but he'd come clean with his landlord right off the bat and the man had been okay with it. Aside from the boxes that took up most of the room, Frank had a surplus Army cot, a small refrigerator and hot plate, a coffeemaker, and a desk, upon which rested his MAC PowerBook laptop. The only luxury missing was a shower. For that, he had to go to the YMCA a mile up the road.

Frank removed his father's uniform and placed it into its zippered suit bag and hung it on the pipe rack he used as a closet. Then he turned his attention to the package, ripping off the brown paper.

"What the hell is this?"

It wasn't a CD; it was a DVD, the artwork patterned after a World War Two recruiting poster. An American Army Air Corps officer stood back-to-back with a Luftwaffe colonel. Both had hard, stoic expressions. The headline read: RELIVE THE PAST—FIRST-HAND! Below the two officers the text read: CAMP STALAG: AN AUTHENTIC EXPERIENCE.

Pulling out the chair from the desk, Frank sat down, opened the DVD case, then slid the disk into his computer. A moment later the screen went black and music started playing. Frank recognized the tune as "The Horst Wessel Lied," also known as "Raise the Banner." It never failed to send a chill up his spine.

The screen faded up on a montage of a prisoner of war camp,

but the footage was in color and the structures looked brand new, rather than weathered, as he would have expected. And then a voice began narrating, a cultured voice with a distinct German accent.

"Are you a man who is thirsting for adventure? A man who wishes to test the limits of his endurance? Then welcome, gentlemen, to *Camp Stalag*, an exact replica of a German *Luftstalag* from World War Two, and the latest in reality television. You have been selected from an elite group. Together with three hundred like-minded men, you will spend two months in the wilds of New Hampshire, eating, sleeping, and breathing a unique piece of history for a primetime series to be aired next fall. The winner will receive one million dollars. We guarantee your experience will be authentic in every detail. Come, and experience the wonder of *Camp Stalag*. Come, and experience the thrill of a lifetime."

The screen faded to black, and titles in white block letters appeared:

**For further details and to complete your application,
please visit www.campstalag.com.**

Frank grabbed his flip phone, dropping it twice before he could open it and dial Dean's number.

"Hey, Frank, what's up? Did I leave the back door unlocked again?"

"No, but I need you to get over here right now. You're never going to believe what just dropped through our mail slot."

3

The large black BMW 750 IL slid gracefully through the traffic on the Mass Pike, slaloming past the slower cars as if they were standing still. Johann Schmidt glanced in his rearview mirror in time to see a driver in a battered Corvette give him the finger. He smiled, waved, and pressed the accelerator, feeling the 7.5-liter-engine's power. Then he thought better of it, bringing the car's speed down to an even seventy-five. No sense in risking another ticket. Heinrich would be displeased, and he wanted nothing more than to make his adopted father happy. A moment later, the guy in the Corvette passed him, shooting him a venomous glare before zooming off down the Pike. Again, Schmidt felt the contempt rise in his chest. These American fools and their arrogance. Soon, some of them would have cause to regret their arrogance.

Schmidt glanced down at the laptop computer on the passenger seat and smiled. Heinrich would indeed be pleased with what he was to show him.

Getting off the Pike in Wellesley, Schmidt cruised through the business district, past the women's college, and into an exclusive area dotted with stately homes. Moments later, he turned into a private drive that extended almost a quarter of a mile before it ended at a large, ornate wrought-iron gate.

From the glove compartment, he pulled out a small, rectangular box with a button in the center. He pressed it and saw the huge gate swing open.

When he pulled up in front of the Tudor-style mansion, the heavy mahogany front door opened, and a gaunt man in his fifties emerged. Schmidt alighted from the BMW, the laptop clutched to his chest.

"*Guten Tag*, Otto. Please have Dieter check the timing on the car. Cylinder eight is misfiring."

The older man bowed slightly and clicked his heels together.

"At once, *Herr* Schmidt."

Schmidt handed the butler his keys and entered the house. Picking up his pace, his boots smacked rhythmically against the oak parquet flooring, sending a thundering cadence echoing off the dark paneled walls of the large foyer. He took the hallway that led into the east wing, passing a fourteenth-century suit of armor guarding the vaulted archway. Its segmented arm, decorated with exquisite engravings, held a vicious-looking battle ax poised high above its slotted helmet, as if to strike off the head of all who would try to gain entry into the mansion's inner sanctum. He always smiled a greeting at the antiquated suit, wondering who the unlucky person might be who would be passing through the moment the deadly arm decided to fall.

Once beyond the suit of armor, the blond man marched past the long, narrow dining room, catching a glimpse of the minstrel's gallery and the array of hunting trophies hanging on the paneled wall just below it.

His destination lay at the far end of the corridor: the library with its set of double doors, hand carved with medieval designs. The doors stood slightly ajar, a warm slice of light spilling out into the hallway.

Schmidt halted when he heard the mournful tones of Pablo Casals's cello playing a familiar piece, the name of which he'd long forgotten. Classical music had never interested him, a fact that had irritated his benefactor. As a result, he was careful to keep his private opinions to himself. The sound of the cello swelled as the tone of the piece changed from sadness to one of unbridled passion. Knowing that his benefactor did not wish to be disturbed at such a time, he waited. The old man would be in one of his moods, a melancholia out of which only the most pressing business matters—or the best of news—would rouse him. Schmidt's heart raced. The news he bore would wrench the old man out of his despondency, of that he was sure.

A moment later, the Casals piece ended, followed by a cavernous silence that stretched into endless seconds.

It was time.

Straightening his shoulders and smoothing his clothes, he marched into the library.

A modestly proportioned room compared to the rest of the house, the library boasted solid mahogany bookcases that reached the full height of the twenty-foot ceiling and ringed the room on three sides. Halfway between the floor and the ornately carved ceiling ran a wrought-iron mezzanine that allowed one to peruse the upper shelves and was accessed by a circular stairway, also made of wrought iron.

The shelves themselves groaned under the weight of all manner of treatises on modern warfare and European history, all hand-bound in red morocco leather and embossed with intricate designs in 22-carat gold that incorporated the initials of their owner: H. K.

Schmidt scanned the room, his eyes coming to rest on the mahogany desk. Once the reputed property of *Reichsmarschall* Hermann Göring, it possessed an inlaid blotter of green lambskin, surrounded by the most delicate and ornate marquetry extending to the corners. The high-backed leather Eames chair behind it was empty for the moment.

The old man stood on the mezzanine, his back to the two-story Austrian-made stained-glass window depicting the coronation of Heinrich I, which emitted the only light in the room.

Schmidt squinted, trying to make out the expression on the old man's face, but the golden light of the afternoon sun arcing through the glass rendered his benefactor as a tall silhouette bathed in the colors of a thousand rainbows. He swallowed nervously, his voice suddenly lost to him.

"Well, *Hauptmann* Schmidt, have our endeavors borne fruit at last?" the old man asked, his sonorous baritone echoing off the walls. Schmidt felt the vibrations deep in the pit of his stomach, making his heart race even faster.

He clicked his heels and bowed stiffly from the waist. "Yes, *Herr Kommandant*. Nearly all of the sons have responded, as you predicted, as well as others who have stumbled upon the website through search engines. I believe we have more than enough candidates to fill the camp."

"*Ausgezeichnet*." The old man began walking toward the circular stairs, his immense shadow gliding across the floor. When he reached the floor, he strode rapidly to the desk, his features coming out of the shadows and into the pool of light cast by the stained-glass window.

Dressed in an expensively tailored charcoal-gray suit of conservative cut, Heinrich Koenig stood a fraction over six feet, his posture that of the old Prussian *Junkers*: imperious, arrogant, and straight as a lance. His face, though finely lined, had a narrow, ascetic appearance terminating in a jutting chin that held just the hint of a cleft. His hair also followed the Prussian tradition, shaved off at the sides, with a mat of iron-gray bristles on the top. Severe, and ultimately practical. Just like the man.

In spite of that severity, there was an air about Heinrich Koenig that bespoke a regal quality, the quality most associated with men who wielded immense power. But his two most arresting features, the ones most people never forgot, were the jagged white scar on his forehead, and the feral steel-gray eyes.

Those eyes shone now with an inner fire as Koenig drew close to the desk. A long-fingered hand reached out and caressed the computer Schmidt had placed on the blotter. Schmidt noticed a faint tremor in that elegant hand and frowned. Could the disease be getting worse already?

Koenig shattered the silence.

"Our dream is almost a reality, eh, Johann?" he said, his voice barely above a whisper. "Otto!"

The butler lurched forward, his jerky movements like that of a large windup toy. "*Jawohl, Herr* Koenig!" he said, cracking his heels together.

"Cognac! Bring us the Louis XIII. This is a celebration, an occasion that deserves only the finest!"

"At once, *Herr* Koenig."

The butler retreated the way he'd come.

Schmidt placed the laptop on the desk, plugging in the power and ethernet cables that discreetly poked out of a hole once occupied by an inkwell. The old man's eyes shone from the light of the screen as he took his place in the chair.

"Show me," Koenig said.

"I think you will be pleased with this one," Schmidt said, his fingers flying across the keyboard. In a moment, the blank screen was replaced by a document whose header read: CAMP STALAG APPLICATION. Schmidt reached over and scrolled down to the personal comments section. Koenig studied the screen, a sly smile turning up the corners of his mouth.

"'Dear Sirs,'" he read. "'Just wanted to say that I hope you'll consider me for your show. I've always been interested in the war, especially as my father fought in the European Theatre with his bomber group and was a prisoner in Stalag Luft I.'" Koenig's eyes narrowed. "What was his father's name and unit?"

Schmidt scrolled up the screen and said, "Franklin Murphy, 410th Bombardment Squadron."

Koenig let out an exhalation of triumph, the old man's eyes brimming with glee. "*Ausgezeichnet!*"

Schmidt smiled in return, saying nothing. He watched the old man, feeling a mixture of pride and love. To see him this happy was worth whatever the price.

"How is the construction progressing?" Koenig asked, without looking up from the screen.

Schmidt pulled a notebook from his pocket and turned to a marked page.

"Mannheim reports that everything is on schedule. The guard towers will go up on the fifteenth of May and the outer perimeter will be finished by the twentieth."

"Excellent. And what of the guards?"

"Those construction workers not returning to Germany will remain as guards. In addition, we have recruited thirty members of the Aryan Freedom Party, a right-wing group from Berlin. They are sympathetic to our cause and will follow orders. But they are not honorable. They are men without souls."

Koenig turned to face him, his jaw set firmly. "They are perfect. What about provisions and uniforms?"

"Everything shall be in place the week before the prisoners are due to arrive, *Herr Kommandant*."

"*Sehr gut*," Koenig said, smiling once again.

Otto returned bearing a Sheffield silver tray clutched in his spidery hands, on which sat two lead crystal snifters and a lead crystal bottle of Louis XIII Napoleon brandy.

Arguably the finest Cognac in the world, it had a special cachet due to the filigreed bottle, a bottle which the meddling American Food and Drug Administration had recently banned because it was rumored the lead contained in its crystal was leeching into the brandy. Upon hearing the news, Koenig had purchased the entire remaining supply, which now resided in a section of the mansion's labyrinthian cellars.

The butler placed the tray on the desk, careful to avoid the laptop. With exaggerated ceremony, he pulled out the bottle's stopper and poured a neat finger of the fiery golden liquid into each of the two snifters and left the room.

Koenig swirled the brandy around the inside of the snifter. "One of the few accomplishments those *idioten* Frenchmen can claim as their own," he said, watching the brandy's legs cascade down the inside of the glass. "We even had to teach the treacherous bastards how to make Champagne, and then they have the *Unverschämtheit*—the audacity—to go and take the credit. Hah!"

Koenig raised the snifter to his blade-like nose and inhaled sharply, his eyes closing briefly while he savored the aroma. Sighing with satisfaction, he said, "To our dream—to Camp Stalag!"

Schmidt clicked his heels. "Camp Stalag!" he echoed. They drank, taking the brandy in a single white-hot gulp.

With practiced ease, Koenig spun around and hurled the empty snifter into the maw of the fireplace, his eyes dancing with pleasure as it shattered against the soot-stained brickwork. Schmidt followed suit, amused at the archaic and wasteful custom.

"And now, then," Koenig said, rubbing his hands, "I am afraid we must 'burn the midnight oil,' as the Americans say."

Moving to the chair behind the desk, Koenig sat down at the laptop and began scrolling through the hundreds of applications with evident relish. Schmidt joined him, soon realizing that, with only the two of them, finalizing the list of prisoners would take considerable time.

Unfortunately, they could trust no one else with the job.

4

"How many Iron Crosses, Second Class?" Frank called out.

Dean, who was hunched over the store's desktop computer across the room, squinted at the screen. "I have twenty-two."

Frank mumbled a curse. "I've only got twenty in the drawer. What the hell, Dean? None of these numbers match!"

Dean stared at the floor. "I'm sorry, Frank, guess this kind of shit's not my strong suit."

"That makes two of us."

Frank slammed the drawer holding the Iron Crosses and moved to the next one. Just then the bell over the front door tinkled. Both men turned, looking hopeful.

It was Brenda, and when Frank saw the hard set of her jaw, he inwardly winced.

Christ, what now?

"Everything okay?" he asked, a part of him not really wanting to know the answer.

"We need to talk."

"Where are the kids?" he asked.

"Marge is watching Julie, and Pete's over at a friend's house."

"How about I come by the house later? Dean and I need to finish our inventory."

"We need to talk *now*, Frank."

She turned and headed up the stairs to the second floor, and Dean shot his friend a look that said: *What's up with her?*

Frank shrugged and followed his wife up the stairs. He found her standing in front of the desk, holding the *Camp Stalag* DVD.

"So, when were you going to tell me about this?"

Frank took the DVD out of her hands and set it down in front of his PowerBook. "Marge spill the beans?"

"You know Dean doesn't keep anything from her."

"Unlike me?"

Brenda stared back at him with a level gaze. Frank sighed.

"Okay, so you know."

"And that's all you have to say?"

"What do you *want* me to say, Bren?"

"Oh, I don't know. Maybe that you're not going off to some cockamamie summer camp for *two months* and leave your family to fend for themselves!"

"You kicked me out, remember?"

"Because you insist on clinging to these silly dreams of yours, like a child. Dreams don't pay the bills, and neither does this store, even when you're here."

Frank swallowed his anger. "Yeah, well, I guess I'm funny that way. Guess you've got three kids instead of two. Did you ever stop to think this store and my writing might just make me happy?"

Brenda's shoulders sagged, the fight leeching out of her. She moved closer to her husband and knelt next to his chair, her hand caressing the back of his neck.

"I know they do, Frank, I really do, but we have to do something. We can't keep living on hope. Would working for my uncle be so bad?"

"Yes... no... I don't know. Maybe I just don't want to admit that I've failed at everything that's ever meant anything to me." He stared into her cornflower-blue eyes. "I'm a good writer, Bren!"

"Yes, you are, and no one's asking you to give that up."

"No, but maybe that's what they're *telling* me..."

Frank turned and looked at the framed photo of his father on the desk. Frank Sr. stood with two of his war buddies wearing the uniform Frank wore to the convention. They were all laughing about something.

"Dad never failed at anything. Decorated war hero, top salesman for every company he ever worked for. If that damn truck hadn't rear-ended him..." Frank stops speaking, the pain overwhelming him.

"It's okay," Brenda said, giving his forearm a gentle squeeze.

"Now all I have are a few dusty photos and the war stories he told me when I was a kid. Like the time he and his buddies buzzed the latrine at the base, or when they almost got lost on the way back from bombing Regensburg..." Frank smiled. "But he would never talk about his time in Stalag Luft I. For some crazy reason, that place meant more to him than anything else. When I asked him, all he ever said was, 'It was something special, Frankie.'" Frank tossed the DVD onto the desk, where it landed with a clatter. "What hurts the most is I remember the stories more vividly than I remember him. He seems like a dream to me now, almost as if I'd made him up like one of my stories." He turned back to his wife, searching her face. "They never caught the truck driver, you know."

"I know... And I'm sorry you lost him so young. But wouldn't he want you to do what's best?"

"Maybe what's best is for you to file those divorce papers."

Brenda reared back in shock.

"John told me. Is that what you really want?"

"No... it's not," Brenda said, choking off a sob. "I want my husband back. And our children want their father."

Frank turned away, his lips trembling.

"And I want all of you back too—more than anything. But don't you see? This show could be the one chance we need. If I go—if I win—that money will solve all our problems. And maybe then my dad won't seem so much like a dream anymore..."

"What if you don't win, Frank? What then?"

He turned back to face his wife, his lips compressed into a tight line.

"I'll sell the store and take John's offer."

Brenda threw herself into Frank's arms, sobbing with relief. A moment later she pulled away.

"It's all so wacky, though. A POW reality show?"

Frank shrugged. "I'll admit it's a bit off the wall, but some of these shows become hits, and a million dollars is a million dollars."

"But how do you know this isn't some colossal joke?"

"Kind of a lot of trouble to go through for that. And I had Dean do a little research. It looks legit. But if it turns out to be a bust, I'll still sell the store. Win, lose, or draw, I'm done. Guess I just couldn't admit it, 'til now. I just don't know how Dean will take it."

Brenda nodded. "From what Marge has told me, he's only hanging on because of you."

Frank shot her a troubled glance. "Is that what she told you?"

"That and the fact that his old ad agency called him the other night. They desperately want him back."

Frank stared at the DVD. "He should take the job, though knowing Dean, he'll want in on this show. At least *someone* wants him."

"Uncle John wants you. He wants to hire you because you're really good and he *trusts* you."

"You're right—I know…." He stared back at his father's face in the photo. "You know what's really funny? Whoever's producing this show, whoever sent this DVD to me—it's as if they somehow knew, without a shred of doubt, that I'd grab for it like a drowning man."

Frank didn't see the glint of fear in his wife's eyes.

5

Brenda awoke the morning of Frank's departure with the sun streaming through the cracks in the blinds like God's fingers reaching through. Dust motes swam in the beams, and for some reason that warm, pleasant scene made her heart ache. Propping herself up on her elbows, she glanced at the clock on the nightstand. Next to it, the baby monitor emitted a soft white noise from its tiny speaker. No baby chatter, which meant Julie was still asleep. Brenda turned and looked down at her husband. She still had to pinch herself that he was back home, even after four weeks. When she'd kicked him out six months ago, his absence had felt like a prison sentence, more for her than it had for Frank, who'd looked like a wounded little boy as he trudged out the door with his suitcase. And now here he was about to traipse off again to spend two months in an actual prison—voluntarily.

The idea of this reality show still rankled, and she'd done her best to keep her own counsel once the decision had been made. She could live with it—she just didn't have to like it. And there it was. It still felt like some kind of sleazy bamboozle, yet there was no "fee" to be in the show, no up-front money to be risked and lost, and no travel costs other than getting to Boston. She remembered the email Frank received last week. She stood behind him as he eagerly scanned the message, his shoulders trembling with excitement.

CAMP STALAG

www.campstalag.com

May 12, 1998
Mr. Frank Murphy
10 Wilton Woods Rd.
Wilton, CT 06897

Dear Colonel Murphy:

Congratulations, you are privileged to be among the 300 men who will be our prisoners for Season One. As we have had an inordinate amount of requests for officer status, we have had to make some adjustments.

Fortunately, since we received your application in such a timely fashion, your request for the rank of colonel has been granted.

Be advised there has been a drawing from among the officers' names to determine who will be SENIOR POW OFFICER. The results of this drawing, as well as barracks assignments, will be announced upon everyone's arrival at Camp Stalag.

With regard to the travel arrangements: you will be met by the camp's buses at the Logan Airport Hilton in Boston, Massachusetts, on Saturday, June 1 for the drive to camp. The buses leave at precisely 3 p.m. Do *NOT* be late.

In addition, please find attached a list of articles we recommend that you bring, as well as ones we wish you to leave behind. This is to guarantee the authenticity of your experience. Your adherence to this list is a *must*.

STALAG

Sincerely,
Hauptmann Johann Schmidt
Adjutant to Kommandant Koenig

The *List of Prohibited Articles* came as a PDF that resembled cheap war-time paper replete with multiple folds and tatters, as if someone had carried it in his pocket for ages. The typography was in the traditional German *Fraktur* typeface and took some effort for the untrained eye to read. It was straightforward and of ingenious calculation, prohibiting the "prisoner" from bringing anything that could have been invented and/or manufactured after 1945. No disposable razors, no electric razors, no blow-dryers, no iPods, no portable televisions or radios of any kind…and no cell phones.

"What am I going to do about shaving?" Frank had asked.

"What about that old shaving mug, brush, and straight razor you insisted I buy you for your thirtieth birthday?"

"I thought you threw that out when the novelty wore off."

Brenda smirked. "You know I never throw anything out. It's in the attic."

The *List of Recommended Articles* was far shorter. Prisoners could bring their own toothbrushes, and other sundries, as long as they more or less conformed to the 1945 rule.

As the day of departure neared, Frank became more and more excited, while Brenda found her mood growing more and more gloomy. She rationalized that this stupid show was only going to last for two months, and if Frank won, they could finally think about renovating the house, something they'd talked about for years, but both had previously acknowledged as a pipe dream. Maybe, with a little luck, it wouldn't have to be one any longer.

Brenda glanced at the crib again and saw Julie was sitting up, staring at her through the padded bars. She played their daily game of peekaboo, eliciting a giggle from the little girl.

"Sssh, Button, we need to let Daddy sleep."

Brenda scooped up the child and headed downstairs into the kitchen, where she found Pete pouring milk into a bowl of Fruit Loops.

"Since your father's leaving today, I was going to make pancakes."

The look of sorrow and disappointment on the boy's face was too precious, and it was all Brenda could do to stifle her smile.

"I'll eat it," she said, placing Julie in her high chair and giving her a pacifier.

Relieved, Pete sat down at the counter, propping his head between his hands. "Is Dad coming back when the show's over?"

Brenda hesitated for only a moment. "Honey, everything is fine. Your dad's back for good."

The boy stared at her. "But you'd like it better if he didn't go."

Brenda frowned. What do you say to a perceptive kid like this that didn't sound patronizing? "Your father knows how I feel, but this is important to him."

"Because of Grandpa Frank?"

"Yes, and a few other grown-up reasons."

"You mean the million dollars."

Brenda didn't bother to suppress her smile this time. "There's nothing that gets by you, is there?"

The boy grinned. "Can I have six pancakes?"

Brenda laughed. "Coming right up."

❈   ❈   ❈

Upstairs, Frank eased himself out of bed, giving the suitcase lying open on the floor a quick check. As usual, Brenda had packed way more clothes than he would need, especially in light of the fact that the prisoners would be wearing period-correct uniforms. Shaking his head in mock annoyance, Frank made some last-minute clothing substitutions to his luggage, unpacking all the civvies Brenda insisted he take, and placing them back into the bureau, leaving the socks, white T-shirts and underwear. It was one thing to look right on the outside, but he had a feeling the period underwear, assuming they provided that, would not be as comfortable. He smiled when he placed the cashmere sweater she'd given him last Christmas back in the drawer, imagining the contrast of such luxury among the barbed wire and the mud. Aside from the silly image it evoked, there'd be no need for it—especially in June.

Remembering that he'd promised to give Dean a wake-up call, he picked up the phone and dialed. "Rise and shine, Sergeant Seger, time to move out."

The voice on the other end sounded thick with sleep. "Do you have to sound so chipper when you're rubbing it in?"

Dean's had been one of those requests for officer status that had been "adjusted."

"At least you're in my unit. And being a tail-gunner isn't so bad. They're usually the last ones tortured for military secrets."

"Oh, that's just beautiful, pal." Dean laughed. "And I owe it all to you."

"Absolutely," Frank said, suppressing his own chuckle. "Anyway, Brenda and I will be by at seven thirty. You'll be ready?"

"No *problema, Capitán*."

"That's Colonel to you."

"All right, already," Dean said, laughing again. "See you soon."

When Frank and Brenda pulled up in front of Dean's house, he was already outside waiting. The front door opened, and Marge Seger trudged out in her housecoat and curlers.

"Hi, Marge," Frank called out the car's window. "You want to come to the station and see us off?"

"You must be kidding," she said, looking shocked.

Dean kissed his wife, picked up his bag, and bounded over to the car.

On the way to the station, the two men reviewed their schedule.

"The train should get us into Grand Central by nine thirty," Frank said. "If it's on time, we should hit LaGuardia about ten twenty. And, if nothing screws up, that will put us on the eleven o'clock shuttle for a noon arrival at Logan."

"Just in time to sit and wait around for three hours," Dean said.

"Yeah, I know, but the next train was at two, and there's no way we would've made it."

"That's okay, Shakespeare," he said, grinning. "I was just busting your chops."

"I swear, being in the car with you two is like sending a couple of twelve-year-old boys off to camp," Brenda said, laughing. "I hope at least one of you guys brought the insect repellent."

They stopped talking and gaped at each other.

"God, I never even thought of it," Frank said.

She reached into her purse and pulled out a bottle of Woodsman's.

"I don't think you have to worry about them confiscating this," Brenda commented. "The stuff's been around forever, and the man at the store said it was the best."

Frank handed it to Dean, who uncapped the bottle and inhaled, wrinkling his nose at the pungent odor. "We definitely won't be winning friends and influencing people with this," he said.

Frank sat back and laughed. "Thanks, dear. I don't know what I'd do without you."

"How about remembering me in your will?"

"Don't do it, Colonel," Dean shouted in a mock hillbilly accent, and threw his arms around Frank, "she'll bleed you dry quicker than the skeeters!"

They laughed as the car made the turn into the train depot.

The 8:05 to New York was due in about ten minutes if it was on time, which was usually the case on a Saturday. Dean ambled into the depot, leaving Frank and Brenda to say their goodbyes.

"You take care of yourself, you hear?" she said, her eyes beginning to brim.

Frank held her long and hard.

"Stop it, or you'll have us both leaking like sieves. I'll be back before you know it. It's only two months."

"Which sounds like an eternity right now," she said, wiping her eyes and laughing at her own emotionalism.

She buttoned a button on his shirt that had come undone and smoothed the fabric with her hands. A lone tear escaped its prison and cascaded down her cheek. Frank wiped it away with his finger and kissed her, his lips a tender fire against hers.

"I don't suppose they have picture postcards of the guard towers?" she asked, finally breaking the kiss.

He laughed softly. "I doubt it, dear. Wouldn't be authentic."

The sound of the train's klaxon wailed in the distance. T h e 8:05 was arriving.

"I love you, sweetheart," Frank said.

"I love you, too, Frank."

They hugged one last time, and then broke away. Brenda headed back to the car. Frank waved and watched her drive away. She disappeared from view just as the train rounded the bend from Ridgefield and chugged into the station.

Dean popped his head out of the station house, two tickets waving in his fist. "Hey, Colonel! Last one to the bar car is a stoolie!"

"For cryin' out loud, Dean, it's eight o'clock in the morning!"

"Yeah, but we're not likely to get any booze where we're going."

True enough, Frank thought. If he was crazy enough to spend two months in a POW camp, he might as well have a drink or two on the way.

He laughed, shook his head, and hastened to the train.

6

While Schmidt drove to Logan Airport, he kept recalling the last moments he'd spent with Heinrich Koenig before leaving the grounds of the estate, the two of them standing by his BMW under the mansion's porte cochère. The old man had seemed edgy, his aristocratic face taut with emotion.

"Sir," Schmidt said, sensing the awkwardness of the moment, "everything is in readiness. Nothing has been left to chance."

Koenig put his hands on Schmidt's shoulders and stood gazing at him with the fondness a father has for his son.

"I know that, Johann, I know. It's just that I have waited so long for this—for the right time. Now, it has finally come. My dream is now reality." He stopped speaking and stared out toward the western horizon. After a moment, he looked back at Schmidt and squeezed his shoulders warmly. "As did the phoenix of myth, I have risen from the ashes. We shall show them all, won't we, Johann?"

"Yes, sir," he'd replied. And not sure what else to say or do, he drove away soon after.

Glancing in the rearview mirror, he watched Koenig recede into the distance, standing there, as always, majestically arrogant, and yet somehow sad and forlorn. Schmidt's heart ached, for he cared deeply for the old man. Heinrich had endured so much at the end

50

of the war and had never forgotten the hardships and humiliations suffered at the hands of the occupying Americans. But he'd finally triumphed, turning those bitter memories into a multibillion-dollar postwar empire rivaling those of the treacherous Japanese.

Never married, Heinrich Koenig nevertheless desired to pass on his great wealth and achievements to a son, a son who would keep his legacy and his dreams alive. After months of searching, Koenig found him in a crumbling orphanage in East Berlin in 1979 and adopted him soon after. That his benefactor was an unmarried middle-aged man did not matter. A few D-mark in the right hands always smoothed the way.

Young and impressionable, he was eager to learn everything Heinrich could teach him. The studies, rigorous and unrelenting, challenged Schmidt to strive on to ever higher plateaus of excellence. It was a proud day when the pupil surpassed the teacher in his knowledge of business and finance, of philosophy and psychology, and most especially, of Heinrich Koenig's vast knowledge of World War Two.

Throughout his youth, the old man taught him the "Koenig" version of the war: how the allies had robbed their country of its pride and glory, how they heaped humiliation after humiliation on a weary and demoralized populace. These were tales no one would ever find in the history books. They were the memories of a resentful man obsessed with a dead past, a past he wanted desperately to resurrect. Now, Heinrich Koenig's obsession became Johann Schmidt's obsession.

And yet there was one area of Heinrich Koenig's life the old man refused to discuss: that of his mother. Schmidt knew only that she had died in the waning days of the war. Her only memorial was an exquisite oil painting of her executed from the one surviving photograph Koenig had carried with him during his escape to the west. The painting showed an aristocratic woman approximately thirty-five years of age. There was a sadness around the eyes that the artist—an unknown genius—had managed to capture, a weariness for all the world's ills. And though they were of the same steel-gray color as her son's, they held none of the hate and ruthless ambition that Heinrich Koenig carried in his scarred and misbegotten soul.

As for his own past, Schmidt knew nothing other than what Koenig had told him. It was as alien to him as if read from some obscure novel. Heinrich Koenig's world was all he knew, and he owed him everything—even his life. Someday he planned to surprise the old man by taking his name, a final tribute to the benefactor who'd raised him up from the gutter to sit on Olympus with the gods.

And now there was Camp Stalag...

Conceived on a winter's night as they sat in the library sipping Louis XIII and watching the flames consuming the logs inside the fireplace, Koenig had suddenly sprung to his feet, his eyes burning with a fervor that Schmidt had never before seen, a fanatical gleam that made him shiver with fear, even as the old man's words wove their magical spell.

A replica of a *Luftstalag*! A place where the degradations of the past fifty years would no longer exist, a place where he and the old man could find peace of mind—a sanctuary.

The only bone of contention between them came when Heinrich suggested that each prisoner be required to pay a five-thousand-dollar fee to participate. Schmidt thought it ludicrous. They didn't need the money, and perhaps it would be better to let them come for free, or *to pay them*. It was then the idea came to him.

"Heinrich, what if we tell these men they are being invited to participate in a television show?"

"A television show?" Koenig said, his eyebrows arching. "Tell me more."

"As you know, one of our recent acquisitions is a television network. I've been told they are developing a show that would place average people into extraordinary situations, such as being stranded on a deserted island with the clothes on their backs and a limited supply of food. The object is to survive the trials and ordeals the show's producers set out for them—the winner receiving a million dollars. They are calling it reality television."

Koenig's eyes widened and he shot to his feet.

"*Ausgezeichnet!* It's brilliant, Johann! We can tell the prisoners there will be hidden cameras all over the camp. These American fools are so obsessed with celebrity and fame, they will flock to us like lemmings."

Schmidt's heart raced; Koenig's excitement was contagious.

From that moment on, Heinrich Koenig spent money lavishly. From the detailed architectural plans, to finding the original manufacturers of the wartime barbed wire used in the camps. No detail was too insignificant, and nothing was left to the imagination. The camp itself, now nearly complete, stood on a twenty-four-acre clearing surrounded by a dense pine forest, the nearest town over seven miles away. And it was perfect, a television producer's dream.

But it was all for naught.

Schmidt gripped the steering wheel until his knuckles turned white and his muscles screamed in pain. The tears that threatened to emerge from the corners of his eyes he held back with only the greatest effort.

Heinrich Koenig was dying.

They'd consulted every oncologist from New York to Zurich, tried every bizarre treatment from Laetrile to foul-tasting herbal teas and coffee enemas, but it was no use. The cancer in his brain spread inexorably. The doctors gave him, at best, another six months.

Cornering the doctor in Zurich, Schmidt had forced the bespectacled physician to tell him everything.

"He'll have blackouts, fugue states, seizures, and towards the end... motor dysfunctions." The young doctor, who looked as if he were still in high school, pulled off his bifocals and rubbed his eyes. "There will also be times he may not realize what day, or even what year it is."

Schmidt blanched. "At the end... will he... will he know me?"

The young specialist glanced down the hospital corridor a moment, then snapped his gaze back to Schmidt.

"Make sure his will is in order and his affairs are settled. Give him whatever he wishes, whatever will make his last days happy."

The young doctor, noting Schmidt's dazed expression, mumbled an apology and made a hasty retreat to the safety of some inner sanctum.

Later, after looking in on Koenig's sleeping form, Schmidt wandered the cold, windy streets of Zurich, trying to come to terms with all he'd heard.

What, he wondered, *will I do once the old man is gone?*

He passed restaurants and beer cellars full of laughing, happy crowds, and realized that aside from Koenig, he had no one. No wife, no children, no close friends. After Koenig's death, all he would have was Koenig Industries, an enormous yet empty inheritance. A conglomerate could never fill the void Heinrich Koenig's passing would create.

He tore himself from these thoughts. A tear finally crept out of the corner of his eye and ran down his cheek.

"These last days will be all you want them to be, Heinrich. This I promise you."

He wiped the tear and pressed the gas pedal, careening onto Massachusetts Avenue, his confident mood returning.

Entering the Back Bay, Schmidt weaved through the early morning rush, cruised onto Storrow Drive, and hit a wall of bumper-to-bumper traffic moving at a snail's pace. He cursed under his breath and snapped on the radio, tuning it to one of those idiotic talk shows.

Yes, he thought, *Camp Stalag will be run with ruthless efficiency, under realistic wartime conditions, for as long as Koenig lives.* He owed the old man his fantasy for all he had provided him in his life. A glorious monument to his benefactor.

He watched joggers running down the path toward some unknown mile marker. *Fools.* He could never understand the American mind-set. Everything for today, nothing for the long term.

Schmidt watched as a particularly taut specimen of womanhood ran by the car, followed by an obese man who looked as if he were about to have a coronary. Schmidt laughed. They all insisted on trying to keep fit while their leaders grew soft in mind, as well as body. When it was all over, America would find itself on the scrap heap of history, a two hundred-year-old dinosaur whose time had passed.

Finally reaching the entrance to the Southeast Expressway, Schmidt threaded his way through the moderate traffic, reaching Logan Airport ten minutes later. He found a slot in Central Parking and from there it was a short walk to the Hilton Hotel.

He smiled when he spotted the six black buses, lined end to end... waiting.

Excellent.

He had purchased the buses through one of Koenig Industries' dummy corporations in the Cayman Islands, the transactions airtight and untraceable. Once the buses had been delivered to a warehouse in East Boston, special teams of technicians carried out exacting and extensive alterations under his direct supervision. To the untrained eye, however, the buses appeared unchanged.

Going to the lead bus, Schmidt discovered all six drivers gathered by the front door, drinking coffee and talking animatedly.

"Gentlemen," he said as they turned to face him, "your attention, please. There are a few details you need to know and understand."

Schmidt then began speaking German, and the drivers listened intently, nodding without expression as the tall, blond man outlined the coming sequence of events. Schmidt had handpicked these men from all over the Fatherland for just this occasion, their loyalty and obedience without question.

Pleased with the preparations, Schmidt went inside the hotel to have breakfast and await the arrival of the prisoners.

Part II

CRUCIBLE

7

The train's relentless sway and the drone of its clacking wheels threatened to lull Frank to sleep in spite of the excitement he felt. While he watched the New York scenery pass by his window, he couldn't help feeling an odd mixture of apprehension and exhilaration.

It was really happening.

He was going to an actual World War Two POW camp.

He knew that all the movies, books, and even his father's vivid stories would pale beside the true experience.

It was something special, Frankie...

Draining his second beer, he reached into his bag and pulled out a small leather-bound book. Frank had decided to keep a journal of his experiences. Not only would it be an invaluable reference for his book, but it might make interesting reading later.

Opening the small volume to the first page, he took out a pencil and wrote:

June 1

I feel scared and happy all at once. Dean and I are off on our grand adventure! We'll be arriving in New York shortly. I hope this experience will be worth it in the end, but only time will tell. I miss you already, Brenda.

Unable to think of anything else to write, Frank closed the book and placed it back into the bag while Dean wobbled down the aisle carrying two more bottles of Budweiser.

"Jesus Christ, Dean, we're not going to be good for anything when we get to New York."

"That's the idea, Shakespeare," he said. "We wouldn't want to spoil the fun by being sober, would we?"

Rolling his eyes in mock disgust, Frank grabbed the beer out of his friend's hand. "All right, you win. Let 'em pour us on the plane."

"Now you're talking! Here's mud in your eye!" Dean clinked his bottle against Frank's and took a long gulp, his knobby Adam's apple bobbing rhythmically.

When they arrived at Grand Central, they grabbed their bags and bolted for the taxi stand. The cab ride to LaGuardia was swift, thanks to the lighter weekend traffic. When they pulled up to the United terminal, it was ten fifteen.

The flight to Boston was uneventful, except Dean was giddy and Frank wished he hadn't had the three beers on the train. They landed in Boston at 11:56.

"Now what?" Dean said, grabbing his bag.

"Well, I know a great little pizza joint right outside the airport," Frank offered. "They've got the best pizza and the ugliest waitresses in town. How about it?"

"Sounds great. Let's go."

After gorging themselves on two pepperoni pizzas and more beer, they returned to the airport to see if the bus had arrived. It was exactly two thirty p.m. when they stepped off the tram in front of the Hilton and spied the six large, commercial coaches parked in tandem outside the entrance. Each held a sign marked "CHARTER." Nothing indicated whether or not the buses had anything to do with Camp Stalag.

"You think that's them?" Frank asked.

Dean shook his head. "Hell, I don't know. Maybe."

"Well, I hate mysteries, so let's go ask," Frank said, moving toward the lead bus.

When they drew closer, Frank spotted a tall blond man dressed in a red Izod shirt and chinos standing next to the open door of the first bus. He carried a clipboard and was checking off the names of the men lined up in front of him.

This could only be *Hauptmann* Johann Schmidt, adjutant to the *Kommandant*. Frank's keen ears confirmed this as they advanced in the line. Schmidt had a pronounced German accent. Frank didn't know why that surprised him. He supposed that it was because he had assumed "Schmidt" to be a pseudonym and that the "Germans" were also Americans playing the game. This excited Frank even more.

After an interminable wait, they finally reached the head of the line.

"*Guten Tag*, gentlemen, good afternoon, I am *Hauptmann* Johann Schmidt. I will be accompanying you to the camp."

God only knew how many times the man had repeated those same words, yet they sounded as crisp as if he had said them only this once. Frank heard Dean slide into one of his "Eddie" routines.

"Hey, Adolf, what's with the civvies? Spill some kraut on your uniform?" He laughed dryly, his face molding itself into a self-satisfied smirk.

"Your name?" Schmidt asked, his demeanor icy.

Dean tried to ignore the man's riveting stare.

"Dean Seger, uhh, *Hauptmann*."

"Ah, yes, Sergeant Seger. Tail-gunner, 410th Bombardment Squadron." Schmidt checked Dean's name off the list. "Bus number two."

Dean sauntered off, and Schmidt turned to Frank.

"Colonel Frank Murphy, sir," Frank said, resisting the urge to salute.

"Yes, Colonel Murphy," Schmidt said, his tone less severe, "you are in the second bus with your friend."

Frank found Dean staring out a window at the back of the bus. He shook his head as he slid into the seat next to him.

"Nothing like starting out on the right foot," Frank said.

"Man, I thought that guy was going to spit nails. Did you see the way he looked at me?"

"Yeah, and I can't say I blame him. That was a pretty stupid thing to say."

"Well, I couldn't help it," Dean said, grinning. "He looked so out of place with those preppie clothes."

"And how out of place do you think he would've looked in a *Luftwaffe* uniform?"

Dean's expression changed as Frank's point became clear.

"Wouldn't have gone over big with the hotel crowd, huh?"

"Ahh... no, I don't think so," Frank replied.

They fell silent when more men got on the bus. Most of them looked to be in their late thirties and early forties and were chattering excitedly as they placed their bags in the overhead racks and took their seats. One of them, a tall, angular man with a tousled head of mousy-brown hair and an easygoing smile, stowed his bag and slid into the seat across the aisle from Frank. After a moment, he turned and introduced himself.

"Hi, I'm Bob Neff," he said, extending his hand.

"Hi, Bob, I'm Frank Murphy, and this is Dean Seger."

They shook hands and fell silent. Frank could tell Bob wanted to ask why they'd come but appeared reluctant to speak. Why was it that people always felt awkward after breaking the ice? After a few minutes, Frank's own curiosity got the better of him. "I'm a writer," he said.

"What?" Bob said, momentarily startled. "I'm sorry, I missed what you said."

"I'm a writer—a novelist. Dean and I also own a store called *Murphy's Militaria*."

Bob raised his eyebrows, his interest kindled.

"Really? Do you guys sell online?"

Dean shot Frank a knowing look, accompanied by one of his "Eddie" grins.

"What books have you published?"

Frank smiled wistfully. "Still working on that, I'm afraid."

Bob smiled in return and nodded. A kindred spirit.

"I'm an attorney," he said, "Corporate and tax. I'm with a firm that specializes in takeovers."

"Sort of like rape and pillage?" Dean asked.

Bob smiled again. "Some people look at it that way. Especially the ones who get taken over."

"You'll have to forgive Dean," Frank said, giving his friend a withering sidelong glance. "He was born without a mind."

"No, no—that's okay," Bob said, laughing. "It's kind of refreshing."

"So, Bob, why are *you* on this mad adventure?" Dean asked.

"I'm a member of a reenactment group. Some of my buddies are here with me. We get together every couple of months and hold maneuvers with a *Waffen-SS* group. We even took part in the Normandy Anniversary in France."

Dean's eyes widened. "That sounds a hell of a lot more exciting than going to prison."

"Maybe," Bob nodded, "but the excitement only lasts for a little while. It's all over in a couple of hours and I always feel a letdown, like something's missing."

"So why keep doing it?" Frank asked.

"Because for that brief time I really feel like I'm alive, like I could conquer the world, you know? This camp thing looked different right from the get-go, lasting two months and all. And a million dollars is nothing to sneeze at."

Frank smiled. "Guess we've all thought of that."

After another twenty minutes, when no other passengers got on, the driver climbed aboard, shut the door, and fired up the engine. A moment later, all the buses pulled onto route 1A and began the journey north.

✴ ✴ ✴

In the lead bus, Schmidt glanced at his watch. It was time. Nodding at the driver, they both reached under their seats and brought out small breathing apparatuses, consisting of a mask and a tiny tank no bigger than the CO2 cartridges used in air rifles. The apparatus would allow them to breathe uncontaminated air for five minutes—more than enough time to do the job. Taking care that none of the prisoners saw them, they clamped them over their noses and mouths. Schmidt nodded again, and the driver reached under his seat, grasping the valve attached to the pressurized tank fitted into a recess in the floor. The man twisted it open as far as it would go, then sat back and waited.

From the tank, a hose snaked down through a hole in the floor into a multiplexer. From the multiplexer, the gas flowed through hoses that ran up into the back of every seat.

The gas, odorless and colorless, acted quickly. Within seconds, all the men were unconscious.

Schmidt had seen rats drop in their tracks during the experiments in the Koenig labs, and the effects never ceased to amaze him.

Consulting his watch once more, Schmidt waited the prescribed time for the gas to dissipate. He then tore off his mask and strode up and down the aisle, checking to make sure that each man was unconscious. Pausing at the rear window, he caught the eye of the driver of the second bus. The man nodded, then gave a thumbs up, his expression unreadable through the breathing apparatus.

Schmidt allowed himself a thin smile. *Ausgezeichnet.*

Satisfied that all the other buses had followed suit, Schmidt returned to the front of the bus and took his seat. The men would be out for about thirty hours and would awake with no ill effects. Indeed, when the prisoners did awake, they would only think a few hours had passed. It was more than enough time to reach the camp's *real* location in Wisconsin.

There had been only one problem, a problem no one had anticipated at the time the Koenig chemists were formulating the gas: *men unconscious for over thirty hours would void their bladders and their bowels.* When they awakened, they would be upset, angry, embarrassed. They would begin to ask questions. And that could not be allowed under any circumstances.

When the chemists had mentioned this, Koenig had glared at these men with their goldfish eyes and their plastic pocket protectors and exploded into one of his rare, and much feared, rages. "*Idioten!* Fools!" he'd screamed. "This is unacceptable! Unacceptable! Solve the problem or you will find yourselves formulating pablum for the rest of your contemptible careers!"

The chemists had paled. They knew this was no idle threat, as one of Koenig Industries' many holdings was a well-known manufacturer of baby food. Fortunately, the problem had been solved by the ingenious inclusion in the gas of a mild muscle constrictor. Its only aftereffect would be aching bowels and bladders, and a mild tension headache. Of course, once they were inside the perimeter of the camp, these problems would become insignificant.

※　※　※

When the buses picked up speed, the butterflies in Frank's stomach worsened. Thinking of something, he turned to Dean and noticed he'd fallen asleep.

Strange, he thought, *Dean never sleeps while traveling.*

He looked around at the others and noticed that most of them were unconscious too.

This is weird.

All at once, Frank felt drowsy. In seconds, he was asleep as well. That Frank had lasted so long was a quirk in the formula the chemists at Koenig Labs had noted in some of the rats. The explanation still eluded them.

※　※　※

Frank awoke to the sounds of men talking and the bus bucking like an angry horse.

"Hey, Frank," Dean said, poking him into full consciousness, "wake up and smell the coffee. We're almost here."

Frank groaned and sat up in the seat. His head throbbed and his bladder felt as if it were filled with hot flaming needles. Turning around, he saw a long line of grumbling men waiting to get inside the tiny bathroom at the end of the bus. He turned back and gazed out the window. They were on a narrow, unpaved road that was little better than a cow path.

Glancing at his watch, Frank noted that they had been traveling for about three hours. Looking closer, he sighed in disgust.

"Damn it," he said, tapping his watch against the back of the seat in front of him. He put it to his ear and frowned. It was still running, yet the date read June 2 instead of June 1.

"What's wrong?" Dean asked.

"No big deal. I think my watch is screwed up."

Sighing, Frank got in the end of the line for the bathroom, the urgency growing with every bump of the bus's wheels. A few minutes later, after welcome relief in the coffin-like lavatory, he settled back in his seat and looked out the window once more. They were now traveling through a dense forest of thick pines and scrubby undergrowth. Though the time was just after six, the sun barely shone through the heavy branches scraping against the windows.

After another ten minutes, the buses came to a lurching stop. Frank looked toward the front but could only see the back of the lead vehicle through the windshield.

Soon, they began to move again, passing through a formidable chain link fence. Frank couldn't help noticing the signs:

"*NO TRESPASSING*" and "*INTRUDERS WILL BE SHOT.*"

After another half mile, the camp came into view. The pine forest, which completely surrounded it, had been cut back, creating a twenty-yard clearing that extended from the outer fence to the woods. Between the outer fence and the inner fence existed a no-man's-land, ten feet in width. Guards in full *Luftwaffe* uniform, with MP40 submachine guns slung across their backs, patrolled the area in slow, measured steps, accompanied by fearsome-looking Rottweilers.

The guard towers, eight-foot square huts perched on thirty-foot wooden scaffolds, were spaced every fifty yards. Each tower was equipped with a searchlight and an MG34 heavy machine gun mounted on a tripod.

The inner fence, much like the outer one, was constructed of four-by-fours almost nine feet high set into the ground every twelve feet. Between them, woven in a checkerboard pattern with strands placed every ten inches, was some of the meanest-looking barbed wire Frank had ever seen. The top of each post was tipped with angled barb-arms that faced back into the camp. Stretched between, and running the complete circumference of the camp, were three more rows of the same wire.

Rows of barracks, constructed of bare pine boards, bordered the quadrangle on two sides. Frank counted twenty.

The *Kommandant's* office and quarters stood at the other end of the camp near the rear fence. Close to it were the recreation hall, infirmary, mess hall, and cooler.

The movement of the buses interrupted his observations.

"Well, Shakespeare, it looks like the point of no return," Dean said.

The buses lined up in the quad, the doors opened, and a uniformed guard climbed aboard.

"*Raus! Raus!* Everyone out!" he said, his manner clipped and efficient. "Everyone will disembark and assemble in the quadrangle!"

"They don't waste any time, do they, Frank?" Bob said, grabbing his bag.

"No. I expect we'll get 'our money's worth.'"

Bag in hand, Frank marched down the aisle.

8

Frank followed the crowd spilling into the quadrangle. The men kept to the cliques they'd formed on the buses, standing around in knots of four or five, talking in low voices. Moments later, a contingent of guards marched into the quad, motioning with their weapons for everyone to line up along the front of the barracks.

Jabbering like excited children, the men formed two lines, one in front of the other, their eyes searching the grounds for what might happen next. Frank watched with a twinge of homesickness while the buses roared out through the gates, which locked behind the last of them with a discomforting finality.

Stop it, he said to himself. He'd chosen to be here, desired it with all of his heart.

Relaxing when that thought sank in, he scanned the quad, spotting two folding tables. Each had a placard tacked to its front. One read: *A-M* and the other: *N-Z*. After ten minutes, the men became restless and the lines began breaking up. The guards reacted instantly.

"Silence!" one of them screamed. "Fall in! The *Kommandant*!"

Everyone quieted down and formed ranks again. Frank looked toward the *Kommandant's* office, saw the front door open, and two men emerge: *Hauptmann* Schmidt, now in full uniform and, next to him, scanning the men with a hawklike gaze was none other than *Kommandant* Heinrich Koenig.

After a lengthy pause, Koenig strode toward the assembled men, halting at a point midway between them and the administration building. He stood ramrod straight, watching them, a paternal smile on his face.

At over six feet, he appeared to be in his late fifties, but Frank knew him to be at least ten years older. One thing was certain: the man exuded a commanding presence, a charismatic aura that was unmistakable. Even Frank felt it. He also noticed that the air had stilled, the only sounds the buzz saw of the cicadas and the soft sigh of a northerly breeze stirring up dust devils at their feet.

"*Achtung!* Attention!" *Hauptmann* Schmidt yelled.

Frank found himself snapping to with the rest of the men. Even Dean appeared serious, for once.

Kommandant Koenig swaggered down the line of men while Schmidt occasionally offered some comment Frank couldn't hear. Finally, Koenig strutted to a place in the middle of the quad. A guard rushed forward with a small wooden soapbox. He saluted the *Kommandant*, placed the box at his feet, and marched off the way he had come. Koenig stepped up onto the box and surveyed the men once again. At last he spoke.

"*Guten Abend*, gentlemen, good evening. Welcome to Camp Stalag. You have been granted the rare privilege of reliving a glorious chapter in history... a chapter well known to your fathers... a chapter we shall rewrite together. We guarantee your tenure here will be authentic in every detail. We shall treat you... clothe you... and feed you exactly as POWs were over fifty years ago. Tonight, we shall all settle in and get acquainted and then, starting tomorrow, our adventure begins."

He turned and nodded to *Hauptmann* Schmidt, who glanced down at his clipboard.

"Will Colonel Frank Murphy please step forward?"

"Uh-oh, what'd you do now?" Dean whispered.

"How the hell should I know?" Frank replied, breaking ranks.

He walked up to *Hauptmann* Schmidt.

"Please turn and face the men, Colonel," Schmidt said.

Feeling self-conscious, Frank turned, and Koenig spoke again.

"You may recall reading in the confirmation letter you received that we would be holding a drawing to determine the Senior POW Officer. This drawing was conducted utilizing the names of the five men awarded the rank of colonel. Colonel Frank Murphy is the winner of the drawing. He will liaise directly with *Hauptmann* Schmidt and me. The Senior POW Officer is the only one of you who will have access to my office. Any requests or complaints *must*, I repeat, *must* be given through him."

Koenig stopped speaking, his eyes raking across the line of men once more. Satisfied, he turned to Frank.

"Thank you, Colonel Murphy. You may return to the ranks. I will see you all at mess in one hour. Take over, *Hauptmann*."

"*Jawohl, Herr Kommandant*," Schmidt said, saluting.

Koenig stepped off the box and marched back to his quarters.

Frank's emotions were mixed. He wasn't at all sure that he wanted to be Senior POW Officer, that he wanted *any* responsibility. But then he realized that his book would benefit from that unique perspective, and reconsidered. As Koenig had stated, he would have access allowed to no other "prisoner." It was too good to turn down. Besides, how would it look if he did?

As Frank retook his place in line, Dean patted him on the back. "Way to go, Colonel."

Schmidt began issuing orders.

"All of you will now receive your barracks assignments. Please line up in front of the two tables behind me according to your place in the alphabet. Your uniforms are awaiting you in the barracks. You will deposit all civilian clothes in the boxes provided. They will be returned to you at the end of your stay with us. It is now twenty-fifteen. Mess will begin at precisely twenty-one hundred for this evening *only*."

While everyone lined up at the proper table, Schmidt took a position behind the two tables to supervise. The lines moved swiftly, and when Frank's turn came, the guard seated at the table asked his name, then thumbed through a card file, pulling out a crisp three-by-five index card. It was blank except for one line typed precisely in its center:

BARACKE 2

Frank stood off to one side and waited until Dean received his card. "What'd you get?" he asked when Dean caught up with him.

"Barracks Two."

"How about that, I was right. They're keeping the crews together."

They started towards the barracks.

"Did you get a load of that soapbox?" Dean laughed.

Frank smiled, recalling the scene. "Yeah, well, he's probably just enjoying his part."

"I don't know about that," Dean said. "He looked pretty serious to me."

"I'm sure he was," Frank said, "but all I could think of was Otto Preminger in *Stalag 17*."

Dean laughed. "Yeah? Well, all *I* can think about is what's for chow. I'm starved."

"Come on, Dean, look where you *are*."

"I know where I am, but my stomach doesn't give a damn."

Frank laughed, and the two of them continued walking the perimeter. Just as they finished their first lap, Dean noticed the far-off look in his friend's eyes. "How does it feel, Frank? Is this what you imagined?"

Frank sighed, turning his gaze toward one of the guard towers. Inside it, two guards smoked cigarettes, laughing over something he couldn't hear. "Yeah, it is. I felt something, almost from the moment I got off the bus, like I was coming home."

"Your Dad?"

Frank nodded. "I feel his presence here, Dean, as if he and some of his buddies were about to come walking out of one of those barracks any moment."

"Then it's all worth it."

"You think so?"

"Sure. I've known you for too long, Shakespeare."

They fell silent for a long moment, then Frank said, "Seeing all this makes me wonder, though... Maybe our generation made things worse, you know? Our fathers saved the world. What did we ever do?"

Dean laughed humorlessly. "Sex, Drugs, and Rock and Roll."

His expression turned thoughtful, and he reached into his pocket and pulled out a Lucky Strike cigarette, which he tossed between his lips with practiced ease. He patted his pockets, looking for a light.

Spotting a passing guard, Dean called out to him, "Hey, Fritzy, got a match?"

The guard slowed. "*Was ist los?*" he snapped.

"A match. You know, fire sticks?" Dean pantomimed lighting a match.

The guard shrugged. "*Ich verstehe Sie nicht.*"

"I don't think he understands English," Frank said.

Mildly surprised, Dean looked to Frank and then back to the guard, who continued scowling at them.

Turning to walk away, Dean spotted *Hauptmann* Schmidt marching toward the *Kommandant's* quarters.

"Hey, Smitty!" he yelled.

Schmidt stiffened, shot Dean a glare of cold contempt, then turned to Frank, his expression warming. "Yes, gentlemen, what can I do for you?"

"Your man here doesn't *sprechen Sie* English," Dean said, staring him down.

"None of them do," he replied. "All our guards are ex-border guards from what was once the German Democratic Republic. Unemployment is rampant in our reunited country, and because the *Kommandant* pays them all far more than they ever earned over there, they are grateful... and loyal."

"But I don't understand," Frank said. "The guard that ordered us off the bus—"

"Phonetics, Colonel," Schmidt interrupted. "They were taught rudimentary phrases phonetically to make it easier for the prisoners to follow orders. Only me, the *Kommandant,* and the sergeant of the guard speak English. Anything else, gentlemen? I have duties."

"Just one question," Frank said. "Where are the cameras?"

Schmidt smiled. "Ah, yes. The *Kommandant* wished them to be hidden, so as not to be obtrusive."

Frank didn't bother to hide his shock. "Hidden?"

"Yes, Colonel. Come with me," he said, motioning for them to follow.

Schmidt led them to the steps of the *Kommandantur*, where he pointed to a spot above the door. "One of them is right there above the doorway. Do you see it?"

Frank had to admit that it was tiny, but after staring at it for a moment, he could discern the glint of a lens along with a tiny red LED.

"There are hundreds all over camp. "The building marked as *Waffenlager* is the control room. Have I satisfied your curiosity?"

"Yes, *Hauptmann*," Frank said. "We'll see you later."

"Until mess, then," Schmidt said.

He clicked his heels, turned, and continued on his way.

"I hope they left them out of the latrines," Dean said.

"Yeah... right," Frank said, staring after Schmidt.

Dean frowned. "Hey, you okay?"

Frank shook his head, snapping out of his thoughts. "Yeah, I'm fine. Come on, let's go get settled."

Something bothered Frank. Nothing he could put his finger on, but it nagged at him nevertheless. He put it out of his mind when they pushed through the door of Barracks 2.

The barracks, a fifteen-by-thirty-foot shack constructed of weathered pine boards with no insulation, stood about one foot off the ground on heavy wooden pilings, presumably to prevent tunneling.

The room centered on the massive potbellied stove standing on a solid-looking mosaic tile base set into the floor and bordered by a beveled molding. Its dark, shiny exhaust pipe pushed through a jagged hole in the roof. Rough-hewn bunks, still smelling of pine sap, lined the walls and held a total of sixteen men. On the west side of the room, a door led to a closet-sized lavatory with a small sink. No shower and no toilet. Nature's calls required a trip to the outdoor latrines: a long, low-ceilinged building consisting of hard benches with holes cut in them, allowing the urine and feces to fall into deep limed pits. A quick look inside confirmed that Dean had nothing to worry about. No cameras.

Cramped quarters and smelly bodies.

That's exactly what they all had to look forward to in the coming two months.

A door at the east end of the room held a sign that read: OFFI-CERS' QUARTERS. Frank assumed they were meant for him. Several men, some of whom he recognized from the bus, were busily unpacking and changing into their uniforms.

Dean found his empty bunk. It had a placard with his name and a sergeant's uniform from the 410th Bombardment Squadron neatly folded on the pillow—all the insignia placed exactly right.

"Looks like I found my flop, Colonel," he said, jumping onto the bunk.

"Don't get too comfortable, Sergeant. We've got mess in twenty minutes."

Dean stretched and crossed his hands behind his head with a long sigh.

"Yeah, whatever."

Frank smiled at his friend and walked to his quarters. *So much for starvation*, he thought.

Inside, he found two bunks in a room about ten by fifteen. His bunkmate, Bob Neff, was already there.

"Hi, Frank. Guess we're roomies."

"Guess so. What rank did you pull?"

"Lieutenant. I forgot to put down a unit on the application, so they put me in the 331st Bombardment Squadron. Kind of funny, too. It was my dad's old unit."

"Like father, like son." Frank laughed.

"Looks like you got a great uniform," Bob said, pointing to the bed.

Frank looked it over. Like Dean's, all the insignia were in the correct places. The complete ensemble consisted of a khaki shirt and tie, olive-drab trousers, brown shoes, a russet-brown horse-hide leather A-2 flying jacket with leather colonel's birds sewn to the epaulets, topped off by a dark, olive-drab visored cap with polished russet-brown leather fittings and a gold-toned eagle badge. Everything looked and smelled brand new—and it was a dead ringer for his dad's old uniform.

"Christ, I'm going to look like Robert Mitchum with this on," Bob said, holding the uniform up against his body.

Frank grinned. "That's probably what they want."

Bob laughed and began changing his clothes, and Frank followed suit. When he finished dressing, he turned and looked at Bob.

"Well, what do you think? And don't laugh."

Bob gave him a thumbs up. "Pretty slick, Colonel. Pretty damned slick."

Dean burst into the room at that moment.

"Hey, Frank, what do you think of—"

He stopped short when he spotted Frank in uniform. His face cracked into a wide grin.

"Jeez, you look good enough to salute," he said, bursting into hysterical laughter.

Frank stared at Dean for a moment, a sly smile creasing his face.

"I do?"

"Definitely."

"Then stand at attention, soldier," Frank said.

"What?" Dean said, caught off guard.

"I said, 'Attention, Sergeant!'"

Although he had never been in the service, Dean snapped to attention professionally, his expression a mixture of surprise and amusement.

"Wipe that smile, soldier," Frank commanded.

Dean's face went slack.

"Next time you wish to come into my quarters you will knock, understood?"

"Understood, Sir!" Dean shouted as he saluted.

When Frank returned the salute, Dean dropped his arm, turned on his heels, and marched out of the room, the door slamming behind him. He reappeared a moment later, his head peering around the door.

"How'd I do?" he asked.

"Perfect, Dean, just perfect," Frank laughed.

A moment later, one of the other men knocked on the open door.

"Time for mess, guys," he said.

"That suits me," Bob said. "I'm starved."

Grabbing their jackets, they pushed out into the twilight, joining the throng headed for the mess hall.

9

The mess hall was laid out cafeteria-style in a cavernous building that could accommodate the entire population of the camp at one time. Frank knew that during the war, most camps doled out meager rations directly from the kitchen, expecting each barracks to cook its own food. Authenticity aside, it was obvious that *Kommandant* Koenig had his own ideas about running a POW camp.

Frank picked up a sectioned metal tray and advanced through a line that passed along an L-shaped counter holding steaming tubs of various foodstuffs. The kitchen staff, as brutal a bunch as any he had ever seen, stood behind the counter ladling the food onto the passing trays. They resembled men out of old Hollywood prison movies, with rough scowling faces no one could love. One in particular, a stocky man with sweaty black hair sprouting from his neck like moss, snarled at Frank as he passed.

The meal itself was meat loaf, mashed potatoes and gravy, green beans, and a fist-sized hunk of dark bread, possibly pumpernickel. There was even a dessert that looked like a passable strudel.

At the end of the line, guards directed the men to picnic-style tables according to barracks number.

Frank found the meal surprisingly good.

"How's yours?" he asked, pointing to Dean's tray.

"Man, I could get used to this," Dean said, his eyes lighting up.

About to offer a snappy comeback, Frank felt a tap on his shoulder. He turned and found a guard beckoning him with a wave of his MP40 machine pistol. The gesture was not a welcoming one.

"*Kommen Sie*," the guard said.

Frank stared back at the guard, whose expression remained impassive.

"Better go, Frank. This guy looks like he means business," Dean said, smirking. A man seated next to Dean giggled like a girl; the guard froze him with an icy glare and the man clammed up instantly.

"*Kommen Sie, bitte*," the guard repeated.

Frank stood up and the guard picked up Frank's tray, turned, and threaded his way through the tables, his MP40 bobbing against the small of his back. When Frank passed by the other tables, he heard some of the men murmuring his name. A knot of apprehension built in his gut.

What now?

It soon became clear where the guard was headed:

Kommandant Koenig's table.

The *Kommandant's* table stood apart from the others in a little alcove with shutters that could close it off from scrutiny. Covered in white linen and set with expensive silver utensils, the table's elegance belied its setting. Seated at the table were Koenig, Schmidt, and a third person Frank didn't recognize. The fourth place, he assumed, was meant for him.

"Good evening, Colonel Murphy," Koenig said. "Please join us."

Frank sat down and the guard began to lower the tray in front of him.

"*Nein!*" Koenig shouted.

The guard froze, his eyes bulging with fright. Koenig barked a series of orders Frank couldn't understand, and the guard immediately removed the tray and marched off, returning moments later with a plate he set down in front of Frank. The guard clicked his heels, saluted, and left. Frank stared at the plate in front of him, his mouth watering.

"I do hope you like *chateaubriand*, Colonel," Koenig said.

"Yes, *Herr Kommandant*, very much," he said, trying to get used to the German form of address.

"*Sehr gut*, excellent," Koenig replied.

Suddenly Koenig reacted as if he had forgotten something. "I am being remiss in my manners. You must please forgive me. You know *Hauptmann* Schmidt…"

Frank nodded, and Schmidt made a subtle bow from the shoulders.

Koenig continued. "Then allow me to present our sergeant of the guard, Hans Mannheim."

The sergeant also bowed from the shoulders, but any resemblance to Schmidt ended there. A human pit bull, Mannheim had the coarse features of someone who'd spent too much time in the ring. His face held a permanent scowl made worse by a mass of scar tissue and beady eyes Frank felt steadily boring into him. His skin crawled.

Koenig spoke again, breaking the spell.

"The reason I invited you to my table, Colonel, and I am sure you were wondering why, was so you and I could become better acquainted. Our paths will undoubtedly cross frequently."

"Thank you, *Herr Kommandant*, I appreciate that."

"Well, then, please, do tell us why you chose to be here?" Koenig asked.

Grateful for the chance to talk, Frank spoke about his writing, mentioning his novel about a POW camp.

"Fascinating," Koenig said. "I do hope to read it someday."

A look passed between Mannheim and Schmidt. Frank caught it but had no clue what it meant.

Koenig turned to a guard standing next to an old wind-up Victrola. "*Musik*," he ordered.

The guard clicked his heels, wound up the machine, then set the stylus onto the spinning record. Immediately the small room filled with a sprightly tune Frank recognized as "Who's Afraid of The Big Bad Wolf." It sounded bizarre in context with the surroundings, and he struggled to keep a straight face.

"Interesting choice," Frank said.

Koenig smiled. "Ahh, yes. It is the *Führer's* favorite. Who's afraid of the big bad wolf... we shall see."

Feeling uneasy, Frank returned to the previous subject.

"May I ask you a couple of questions?" he said.

"Please do."

"The biography that came with the mailing states that you were an industrialist and financier before you retired. I was just wondering what sorts of businesses you owned and invested in."

The *Kommandant's* eyes narrowed, and Frank could tell he was debating whether or not to say anything. Finally, Koenig spoke. "To put it as simply as possible, I own companies here and abroad that research and develop products in genetics, computers, electronics, aerospace, and defense."

"So you were able to retire from the fruits of your research?" Frank asked.

"Yes and no," Koenig said, relaxing a degree. "I find my *semi*-retirement busier than I would have expected."

"I'm curious about why you wanted to set up this camp."

Again, Koenig withdrew. When he spoke, his mood turned dark.

"Because, Colonel, as terrible as the war was for my country, I wanted to be a part of it. I wanted to be a flyer and defend my beloved *Deutschland* against the *Luftgangsters* who were bombing us into oblivion. Alas, I was too young. I spent my youth huddled in shelters, wondering if I would ever see the daylight again. As to your question, I suppose you could say I wanted to 'play war...' War is a funny thing... especially now, *Ja?* With the threat of nuclear annihilation still hanging over our heads, we tend to forget just how terrible conventional warfare truly is."

Koenig laughed without a trace of humor.

"Now there is a tidy euphemism. Conventional warfare. I assure you, there is no such thing. In war it is not just the weak soldier who breaks down..."

Koenig stared into the burning candles on the table, as if remembering something dark and disturbing. A moment later, he smiled, waving the mood away with a flick of his wrist.

"But enough of such things. Tonight... you are my guest."

Throughout Koenig's impassioned speech, Frank studied the man. He sensed a deep nationalistic pride in him, as well as a deep shame. But was it the shame of his country's excesses or that they'd lost the war? Frank refrained from asking, as if instinctively knowing he wouldn't like the answer.

"What can we expect tomorrow?" Frank asked finally.

Schmidt leaned forward, and Koenig motioned for him to take over.

"If you will permit me, Colonel Murphy," Schmidt said. "It is simple. Every morning the camp will awaken for roll call at precisely five thirty. During the course of the day, there will be two other roll calls, one at evening mess, and the other just prior to lights out. Occasionally, at the *Kommandant's* discretion, there also will be surprise bed checks. As for meals, there will be two a day in the mess hall."

"But the Geneva Convention—"

Schmidt raised his hand, cutting him off. "Yes, I know we are departing from the Convention in this regard, but it also states that we must safeguard against fire. The *Kommandant* feels that this is the best way. And, as Senior POW Officer, you will make the men understand this."

Frank nodded. He wondered just how easy *that* was going to be.

"Aside from the few restrictions I have mentioned," Schmidt continued, "the men are free to pursue whatever activities they care to. The recreation hall is open until evening mess, and there is a wide variety of sporting equipment they may use."

"What about the escape prize?" Frank asked.

Schmidt smiled, his eyes flicking toward Koenig.

"As advertised, the *Kommandant* will wire one million dollars into the bank account of the first man to elude capture. Of course, that assumes he is not shot while attempting his escape."

Frank paled. *Did he really hear that?*

Schmidt began to laugh, joined by Koenig and Mannheim. Finally, realizing that Schmidt had been joking, Frank began laughing, as well.

"We had you fooled for a moment, Colonel, did we not?" Koenig asked.

Frank smiled and nodded, all the while feeling like a first-class idiot. "You had me going, all right. I mean, after all, trying to escape is the whole point of the show, right?"

"Exactly… the show," Schmidt said, glancing at Koenig. "Now, gentlemen, I suggest we enjoy our meal."

The *chateaubriand* tasted as good as it looked. The only elements that spoiled the meal for Frank were Mannheim's relentless and unnerving stare and the unblinking eye of the camera mounted in a corner near the ceiling.

After mess, Frank took another walk around the perimeter. The sun had set, and the searchlights swept the grounds, dancing from spot to spot with unending precision. He took a deep breath and exhaled. *The air is definitely cleaner up here*, he thought. Glancing past the recreation hall, he spotted a small, squat cinderblock building he hadn't noticed before. Two guards stood on either side of the heavy steel door, their faces blank and unyielding. The words stenciled on the sign above it read: WAFFENLAGER.

From his rudimentary knowledge of German, Frank realized the sign meant the building was an armory. But that was in name only, as Schmidt had revealed that it housed the nerve center of the show.

I'd give an eyetooth for a look in there.

Continuing onward, he noted that the guard in the no man's land had doubled. He smiled, recalling the earlier conversation with Koenig. *What a way to spend a vacation.* Shaking his head, he walked on. He was just completing his first circuit of the perimeter when Dean caught up with him.

"So, how was the powwow with the brass?" he asked.

"Fine. They wanted to brief me on what the daily routine would be."

"And?"

Frank explained what the men could expect, leaving out the joke about being shot while escaping. Dean took it all in stride, until Frank got to the part about their meals.

"You've got to be kidding," Dean said.

"Yeah, I know, I don't like it much myself. But that's the way the Germans want it."

Dean started to say something, hesitated, and mumbled, "Hell, I could probably stand to lose a few." He patted his stomach. "When do you want to try for the million dollars?"

Frank and Dean had agreed that they would try to escape together but would split the money if either one was caught.

Frank glanced at his watch. "It's getting late. Why don't we turn in?" he suggested. "Tomorrow we can get the lay of the land, find their weak spot, then make our plans."

"Sounds good to me, man. I'm bushed."

When they got back to the barracks, they walked into the middle of a commotion. One of the guards was about to come to blows with Bill Jensen, a hulking black man from Dallas, Texas, over an electric razor.

"*Das ist verboten*," the guard said, grabbing the razor from the man.

"I don't give a hoot if it's fer boatin' or fer fishin'," Jensen said, grabbing it back. "This is mine!"

"*Nein*," the guard said, wrestling with the prisoner. The struggle became more violent when the guard smashed Jensen in the face with a back-handed slap. Instead of getting mad and throwing himself at the guard, Jensen shook his head and smiled, showing off two rows of perfect teeth. Judging from the black man's battered nose and the scar over his right eye, Frank guessed the teeth were capped. This strapping Texan was a man who loved his bar brawls, and brawlers were not commonly known for possessing attractive smiles.

The guard lunged for the razor again. Anticipating the move, Jensen grabbed the man's uniform tunic and hauled back a ham-sized fist, making ready to send the young German into next week.

"Hold it!" Frank shouted.

Jensen turned, noticed Frank, and the smile grew wider.

"Hey, Colonel! How about tellin' this here goon to lay off my stuff?"

Now, why had he done that? Frank wondered. He'd always avoided confrontation, and here he was getting ready to put himself right in the middle of one. Maybe the answer was simply that he hated to see a big guy beat up on a little guy, even if it was one of the guards.

Cursing his big mouth, Frank waded through the knot of men, halting a couple of feet in front of the hulking Texan. Jensen had a wide, angular face set squarely atop a hard linebacker's body that looked as if it had daily acquaintance with barbells and Nautilus machines. All eyes were riveted on him, even the guard, whose young European face was set in an expression of determined belligerence.

Frank suddenly wanted to be somewhere else, anywhere, rather than playing mediator for an overgrown schoolyard bully. Unfortunately, for better or worse, the Germans had made him Senior POW Officer, and it looked as if everyone else was going to take it seriously too.

Frank stared back at Jensen, measuring his words carefully. "Would you mind telling me what's going on here?"

Incredibly, Jensen's grin grew wider still. "Mind? Hell. This goddamn goon's tryin' to take away my razor," he said, shooting the guard a nasty look. The guard remained motionless.

Frank sighed inwardly. No matter how clear the rules were spelled out, there was always someone who either thought they didn't apply to them or didn't care.

"Did you bother to read the list they sent you, the one telling you not to bring stuff like this?"

Jensen tried to look tough.

"Yeah, so what?"

"So what? You applied to come here like the rest of us. I would assume that you'd want to play the game like the rest of us too."

"Yeah..."

"Then you should've left it at home, cowboy. Now let the guard have it."

Jensen's expression hardened, and then he laughed, the sharp sound echoing in the silence of the room.

"Oh, ho! Our new Senior Ass-kissin' Officer is sure gettin' into it just fine, ain't he, boys? Come on, ever'body... snap to it! Let's show Colonel Murphy the respect he deserves. Attention!"

Nobody moved, but Frank felt the tension in the room raise a few degrees along with the temperature. It felt like a broiler inside that tight little room.

Jensen spoke again. "They made me a colonel, too, Murphy. Maybe you can tell me why I didn't get the top job? Bet I know why. Give you three guesses, and the first two don't count."

The last words were spat out of his mouth, like a piece of bad meat.

Frank's reluctance faded as anger took over. It was one thing to have the Germans foist the job on him, and quite another to have some idiot making him look like a fool. Frank Sr. had always told him that bullies had to be put in their place, or they would make your life hell. It was now or never. Frank took a step closer, his eyes retaining their calm, even expression.

"Let me tell you something, cowboy. I didn't want this job—didn't ask for it. But as long as I've got it, I'm going to do my best. If you've got a problem with that, take it up with the *Kommandant*. Right now, we have another problem, and that problem is your lousy attitude. Give the guard the goddamned razor, and let's start enjoying our time here."

"Why the fuck should I?"

Jensen glared at Frank, the guard and the razor momentarily forgotten. It had become an issue of macho pride. He poked Frank in the chest, his meaty finger the size of an Italian sausage. "Come on, *big man*, tell me why I should!"

Frank met his gaze with a hard-eyed glare of his own. "Because it's the right thing to do. Because we'll all have a better time if we get along. So, how about it?"

For a moment it looked as if Jensen was going to haul off and slug him, but the moment passed, an easy grin creasing the black man's face. "Aw, what the hell," he said, shaking his head. "It ain't worth it, anyhow." He tossed the razor to the guard, who caught it with a contemptuous sneer.

"Good man," Frank said, patting Jensen on the shoulder.

Jensen laughed, and everyone else joined in. Unsettled by this sudden shift in moods, the guard edged toward the door, a puzzled frown on his jowly face.

"All right, you guys," Frank said when the laughter subsided. "Let's all say good night to Fritzy."

"Good night, Fritzy!" everyone sang out.

The goon, looking more unsettled than ever, scowled, muttered something unintelligible, and marched out.

Everyone roared.

A moment later the men surrounded Frank, clamoring to introduce themselves. There was Freddie Richards, an insurance salesman from Omaha, who kept muttering, "Ballsiest thing I ever saw." Roger Putnam, an electrician from Maine, wouldn't stop shaking Frank's hand, and Dana Webster, an actor from Los Angeles, wanted to give Frank's name to his agent. There were others, too, but after a while their names blurred together. Frank knew there would be plenty of time for them to get acquainted.

Bidding them all good night, Frank walked into his quarters. He smiled at Bob, who lay on his bunk, trying to read a book by the light of the bare forty-watt bulb hanging from the ceiling.

"You'll go blind doing that," Frank said.

"I know," he replied, "but they took away my reading lamp."

Frank's expression must have said it all, because Bob added, "Too modern."

"What are you reading?"

"A novel about Vietnam."

"And they let you keep that?" Frank asked.

Bob shrugged. "The goons must've thought it was about World War Two. Who knows?"

While Bob spoke, the lights winked out.

Frank peered at the glowing dial on his watch.

"Right on time," he said.

"What's that?" Bob asked.

"Lights out. Ten thirty sharp. Better get used to it. It'll be this way every night."

"Great," Bob replied as he got up and stumbled around, trying to undress.

Frank waited until his eyes got used to the dark. It really didn't matter because the windows had no shutters, and every few minutes the searchlights swept by their window, briefly illuminating the entire room.

"I gather we're gonna have to get used to that as well," Bob said, gesturing toward the window as he climbed back into his bunk.

"Be careful what you wish for..." Frank replied.

"You said it, Colonel. Sleep well."

"You too."

Frank lay awake for a while and thought of Brenda. He missed her so much already. He felt like a homesick kid on his first night in camp. He smiled, realizing that it *was* his first night in camp.

Remembering something he'd thought of earlier, he got up, padded over to his bag, and pulled out his journal. He tried to write down as much of the day's events and impressions as he could remember, but he soon tired from the effort of writing in the dark. And, he realized, he'd been awake since six that morning. Time to pack it in.

He placed the book under his mattress and slipped under the covers. The sheets were rough and stiff, and the single wool blanket irritated where it touched his skin.

Soon, however, the desire for sleep overcame all discomforts.

Sometime later, Frank awakened abruptly. Feeling disoriented, he glanced around and suddenly remembered where he was. The searchlights swept the room, and he watched the beam crawl across the wall, dust motes swirling. When it passed over Bob, Frank saw him snoring contentedly in his bunk, unaffected by its searing glare.

As tired as he felt, something continued to gnaw at Frank's mind, something that had bothered him since his arrival. His gut told him to watch his back; his mind tried to dismiss it. Whatever it turned out to be, Frank vowed to be ready.

After another few minutes, his eyelids drooped, and he drifted back to sleep.

Sometime later, Frank awoke again. The air had turned frigid. He pulled the thin wool blanket around his shoulders and debated whether to put on his A-2 jacket when the stillness was shattered by the clattering of jackboots.

"*Raus! Raus!* Roll call!" the goon yelled.

"What the hell?" Bob said, bolting upright in his bunk.

Frank rubbed his temples to relieve the dull throbbing just under the skin, the last vestiges of the trip and the beer he'd drunk. He felt like hell, as if he'd only gotten a couple of hours of sleep. When he grabbed his watch from the small night table next to his bunk, he saw the tiny glowing hands indicating it was nearly half past five.

"Oh, man," Bob said, burying his face in his pillow. "I am *not* gonna get used to *this*."

"Wait 'til you have kids," Frank said, grinning.

Through the window, Frank saw the sky turning a dull gray, the stars disappearing one by one.

Dawn was only minutes away.

Sighing heavily, he staggered out of bed as one of the goons burst into their room.

"*Raus!* Roll call."

"Yeah, yeah, hold your horses, pal, we'll be right out," Bob said, snatching his pants from where they'd fallen onto the floor.

The goon about-faced and left.

Grabbing socks, shirts, and shoes, they threw on their uniforms and hustled out of the barracks.

Outside, Frank's breath clouded in the chill, damp air, the dew settling on the ground around them. Lights still burned all over the camp, a hazy moonlike glow surrounding each bulb. It reminded him of a scene from an old black and white movie, with Basil Rathbone as Sherlock Holmes battling Professor Moriarty in the swirling fog.

"What now, Frank?" Bob asked.

"We wait and see."

Most of the men milled about, complaining about lack of sleep in loud, angry voices. Frank couldn't empathize with them too much. After all, this is what they'd asked for.

A movement farther down the quad caught Frank's attention.

Turning, he saw the door to the administration building swing open. Sergeant Mannheim strode out. He halted at the edge of the porch and eyed the prisoners with a hooded gaze.

"Doesn't that guy ever lighten up?" Dean said, from behind Frank.

"I doubt it," Bob replied.

"Fall in!" Mannheim commanded. "Form ranks for roll call!"

Everyone hurried to form lines as they had the previous night.

Mannheim strutted down the line, counting as he went. A few stragglers tried sneaking into the back row; Mannheim missed nothing.

"From now on, you will all have exactly five minutes to dress and form ranks for roll call," he shouted, giving the men a disdainful glance. "Any man who is late will spend two days in the cooler. Do I make myself clear?"

Without waiting for an answer, he resumed counting. He was just completing the task when *Hauptmann* Schmidt and *Komman-dant* Koenig emerged from Koenig's quarters.

They marched to a position roughly corresponding to the center of the quad and waited. The goon with the soapbox appeared shortly thereafter. Koenig stepped up, surveyed the men, then nodded to Schmidt.

"Report!" Schmidt shouted.

Mannheim snapped to attention and saluted. "All present and accounted for, *Herr Hauptmann*!" he said, dropping his arm when Schmidt returned the salute.

"*Ausgezeichnet*, Sergeant," *Kommandant* Koenig said.

He then turned his attention to the men.

"You men are now prisoners of the Third Reich. You will be treated well, in accordance with the Geneva Convention. When our glorious *Führer* has won the war, we will graciously return you to your families."

Frank smiled. It was almost quaint.

Somewhere in the ranks someone blew a raspberry; the men roared. The color rose in Koenig's face.

The *Kommandant* was not amused.

"Mannheim! Take that man to the cooler," he snapped, jabbing a finger toward the errant prisoner.

Mannheim screamed out an order, and two guards grabbed the man and dragged him towards the camp's jail. The man, amused at first, began struggling with his captors when it became obvious this was no joke.

Patience ran out for one of the guards, who struck him a brutal blow across the face with his rifle. He cried out in pain and terror, blood erupting from a gash in his cheek.

Several of the men broke ranks then, shouting curses at Koenig.

A quick glance from Schmidt was all Sergeant Mannheim needed. He grabbed an MP40 submachine gun from another of the guards, cocked it, and fired off a burst in front of the men.

The bullets stitched a line in the dust at their feet.

"Holy shit!" someone shouted. "They're using live ammo!"

Mannheim took a step toward the men, eyes blazing. "Silence! Only the Senior POW Officer may speak!"

Frank's heart lurched in his chest, his throat went dry, and every ounce of the confidence and conviction he'd gained since arriving at Camp Stalag leaked from his body like air escaping from a punctured tire. Every prisoner in camp now watched him. Why the hell had they picked him to be Senior POW Officer, anyhow? And what the hell could *he* do against Koenig and his goons? They had the guns...

"Do something, Frank," Dean whispered.

Frank snapped at his friend. "*You* do something!"

Dean's look of disappointment said it all.

Then, as if propelled by some force outside himself, Frank's feet moved a step out of the ranks. Koenig's eyes shifted to him and two of the guards aimed their rifles at him. Frank marched toward him, the blood roaring in his ears. With each plodding step, his feet felt heavier, as if he were wading through hardening concrete wearing boots of lead. At last, he halted ten feet in front of the *Kommandant* and waited, his mind racing. What should he say? What *could* he say?

Icy fingers of panic swept through his body and sweat popped out on his brow and trickled down the back of his neck. Nothing stirred, and Frank realized that even the birds had lapsed into silence.

Squaring his shoulders, he pulled himself to his full height, his eyes meeting Koenig's implacable gaze. The prisoners stared at the both of them, wide-eyed, breathless.

Koenig's lips curled in contempt. "Yes, Colonel Murphy?"

What saliva Frank had left instantly dried up. For a moment, he saw himself standing on some long-forgotten football field watching the bigger kids play without him, tears splashing his young cheeks. Why was he so goddamned afraid of putting himself on the line? Life was all about taking risks, wasn't it? He'd taken one last night in his confrontation with Jensen and had forced the big jerk to back down. So, why did his knees feel like jelly? Wasn't overcoming that inbred fear one of the reasons he'd come to Camp Stalag in the first place?

Screw it, he thought. *If I don't start taking control now, I never will.*

His voice, sounding somehow larger than himself, shattered the stillness.

"What the hell is going on here, *Kommandant?* Is clubbing some poor slob with a rifle and shooting at us with live ammunition your idea of fun?"

Someone shouted from the ranks. "Come on, Frank, tell the old kraut bastard to shove it!"

A few men laughed, but clammed up as Mannheim lurched toward them, his beady eyes scrutinizing the ranks like a bird of prey.

Frank saw a look of pure hatred pass over Koenig's face, immediately replaced by an expression of calm amusement.

"Why, no, Colonel Murphy," he said. "It is *your* idea of fun. This is what you came for."

Frank forgot his fear when Koenig smiled again, a smile that made his blood boil. Christ! The man was such a smug son of a bitch. Controlling his urge to scream mindless invective, Frank took another step forward, hesitating when he heard the sound of rifle bolts slamming home.

"Get back into the ranks, Colonel," Koenig said.

"Like hell! This was supposed to be for fun! This was supposed to be a game. You invited us here, lied to us, and then you shoot live ammunition at us like it's *nothing.* To hell with your authenticity and to hell with you!"

A rousing cheer went up from the prisoners, happy to see one of their number sticking up for them.

Instead of being angry, the *Kommandant* laughed, joined by Schmidt and a few of the guards, who undoubtedly thought they should laugh, though they had no idea why.

"You are most amusing, Colonel Murphy, most amusing," he said, chuckling. "We will forgive your impertinence this once..."

It was Frank's turn to laugh.

"Give me a break, Koenig. If you think any of us are going to stay here now and play your little sick game, then you're out of your goddamned mind!"

"You tell 'em, Colonel!" that same voice shouted.

Koenig's eyes narrowed, his jaw setting firmly.

"Get back into the ranks, Colonel," he repeated, his voice icy.

Frank stood his ground. He'd come too far to back down now. It was funny. Five minutes ago, he would have gladly let someone else confront Koenig. Now, he felt on top of the world. Give a man a little authority and before you knew it, he found himself trying to live up to it.

"Get back in line, now!"

Koenig stepped off his soapbox and slapped Frank hard with the back of his hand, knocking him down.

The prisoners gasped.

Stunned, Frank felt blood flowing into his mouth from a cut inside his cheek. He struggled to his feet, hot tears of shame burning his eyes, while two guards approached, their MP40s trained on him.

He'd played with the big boys... and lost.

With two machine pistols aimed at his back, Frank trudged back to the ranks. There was a long moment of silence while Koenig resumed his place on the box.

"You are *nothing*!" he shouted, voice booming across the quad. "You are prisoners. *My* prisoners. You have only the rights I allow you. Any insubordination, any infraction at all, shall result in severe punishment. If any of you try to escape, you will spend time in the cooler on half rations. If you attempt a second time, *you will be shot.*

"If this does not deter you, remember this. You have graciously supplied us with the names and addresses of your families. If you escape, we will hunt them down and slaughter them like the *filth* they are."

A hush fell over the quad.

No one talked back, no one *breathed*.

Savoring his victory, Koenig stepped off the soapbox and strutted back to his quarters.

"Oh my God!" someone moaned. "He can't mean it. He can't!"

Frank watched Koenig disappear into his quarters. The paralyzing fear that gripped him in that moment made him want to puke. They were all in the hands of a madman, a wealthy madman who could afford to set up his own private playground and people it with jerks like themselves stupid enough to go along for the ride.

He turned and studied the other men. Some of their faces held a blank stare, as if lost in the panic overwhelming their minds. Others struggled to hold back tears. Still more would have torn Koenig's head off were it not for the guards and their very *real* weapons.

Frank believed that Koenig would do exactly as he said. He also knew that he couldn't sit idly by and let him win, either.

"Frank!" Dean said, shaking him from his thoughts. "Did he mean it? Is this part of the game?"

Frank looked into his friend's eyes, seeing the fear that lived behind them.

He came to a decision.

"Pass the word around to the rest of the guys in the barracks. Tell them there's a meeting in my quarters before evening mess."

Before Dean could say anything, Frank walked away. He needed time to think, time to think up the brilliant idea that would get them all out of this madhouse—time to think of an idea that would wash away the shame and humiliation he knew would otherwise burn within his heart forever.

10

Schmidt watched the prisoners disperse, his chest swelling with pride. Heinrich Koenig had been magnificent. He had watched, transfixed, as those men changed from a defiant and arrogant mob to a group of dejected sheep. They could now do to them anything they wished.

Pulling himself out of his thoughts, Schmidt turned and walked back toward the *Kommandantur*, the building that served as both his and Heinrich Koenig's offices and quarters. Stepping onto the porch, he turned and scanned the quad once again. It was empty, save for a lone piece of paper skittering across the packed earth, propelled by a chilly breeze blowing in from the north.

Schmidt turned back and walked inside. Passing through the outer office that was his domain as adjutant, he entered the *Kommandant's* inner sanctum.

About fifteen by twelve feet, the *Kommandant's* office was painted a drab color of green and represented a militaria collector's wet dream. To the left side of the desk, against the back wall, stood a large swastika flag. It was rumored to be the legendary "Blood Banner" spattered with the gore of the *November Martyrs* killed in the Nazi Party's ill-fated "Beer-hall Putsch."

Directly behind the desk hung an original oil portrait of Adolf

Hitler. Koenig had spent years searching for it, and untold sums to secure its possession.

To the right of the desk was Koenig's pride and joy: a glass-fronted cabinet holding every major German military decoration from both world wars in mint condition.

The desk itself, a dark, richly varnished affair, had a luxuriant emerald-green leather blotter inset into its top, bordered by elaborate marquetry executed in abalone and gold.

Arrayed upon this opulent surface in a precise and meticulous fashion was a Mont Blanc executive fountain pen set, a banker's lamp, two in/out trays, a crystal decanter of brandy, four snifters, and a platinum-framed photograph of Koenig's mother.

Schmidt found Koenig staring out one of the two casement windows facing the quad, watching a change in the shift of guards, his regal countenance in repose. After a moment, he turned from the window and broke into a radiant smile when he spotted the younger man standing before him.

"Johann!" he said, embracing Schmidt at arm's length. "Was it not glorious? *Mein Gott*, it was just as I had imagined it would be—better, in fact! Did you see their faces? Did you see their hearts break when I threatened their families?"

Schmidt grinned; the old man's excitement was contagious. Moving farther into the room, he sat down on one of the chairs facing the desk, while Koenig took the leather upholstered swivel chair behind it.

"I cannot wait for the next step," the older man said, reaching across the desk for the crystal decanter. "A brandy, Johann?"

"*Bitte, mein Kommandant.*"

Koenig poured the Louis XIII into two of the snifters, then handed one of them across the desk.

Schmidt sipped it, the expensive brandy searing its way down his throat. It pooled in the pit of his stomach, smoldering like the embers of a dying fire. His heartbeat quickened, a question forming in his mind. "What *is* the next step, Heinrich?" he said, dropping the formality.

Koenig leaned back, his craggy brow knitting in thought, the chair's springs creaking as he moved. "We will let the prisoners make the next move," he said, swirling the brandy around the inside of the snifter, and then taking a sip. "My guess is some of them will try to escape... so, as a precaution, we will double the guard. In any event, it is paramount that we introduce them to the routine right away. Start with the bed checks tonight. The day after tomorrow we will begin regular searches of the barracks and their belongings. That, I assure you, will keep them off-balance."

Schmidt nodded and smiled again when he saw the glee in the old man's eyes. If playing this expensive game made him happy, then so be it. Both of them turned as a knock sounded on the office door.

"*Herein!*" Koenig said.

The door opened and Hans Mannheim marched in. He halted in front of the desk, stamped his feet, and froze at attention.

"Sergeant Mannheim reporting, *Herr Kommandant!*"

"At ease, Sergeant," Koenig said. "Please, sit down."

Bowing, the burly sergeant swiveled on his heel and took the one other empty chair, his stiff manner reminding Schmidt of a clockwork wind-up toy from his youth at the orphanage.

Mannheim was the one aspect of the camp Schmidt despised. He knew he should trust his adoptive father's judgment with regard to the personnel, but this man could only mean trouble of the worst kind.

Mannheim had been recruited from the dregs of society. Having spent most of his life in one prison or another, his cagey personality reflected a lifetime of fighting to survive. He was tough, hard, cold—all attributes necessary in a good sergeant of the guard. But could they trust him? Schmidt doubted it, and that worried him. Perhaps the cancer had already begun to corrupt the old man's judgement, after all? Schmidt pushed that unpleasant thought from his mind when Koenig began issuing orders to Mannheim.

"I want you to distribute the writing paper to the prisoners tomorrow evening after mess," he said, rising from the chair. "Have all of them write to their families. They are to tell them about how wonderful Camp Stalag is, how much fun they are having, and that because of the *Kommandant's* gracious invitation, they will be staying longer... and so on. Have them be deliberately vague about the length of their stay. Is that clear, Sergeant?"

Mannheim leapt to his feet, crashed his heels together, and saluted. "*Jawohl, mein Kommandant!*"

"Very well. Dismissed," Koenig said, returning the salute.

After Mannheim left, Schmidt turned to Koenig, his face reflecting his troubled heart. "Can we trust him, Heinrich?"

The old man retook his seat, a puzzled frown on his face.

"Who? Mannheim? Absolutely. If it had not been for me, he would be spending the remainder of his life behind bars in Germany. I managed to reach certain corrupt officials with the right amount of American currency."

"But why him, Heinrich?" Schmidt said. "The man is an animal."

"Because I needed someone with a great deal to lose. Someone whose loyalty was without question. With Mannheim, the choice was either life in prison or working for me."

Schmidt decided not to pursue the matter. Once Heinrich Koenig made up his mind, that was that. However, he felt it prudent to keep his eye on the sergeant.

Standing to leave, Schmidt remembered something else.

"Do you think these letters to the families are wise? These people will begin to wonder. An indefinite stay looks suspicious."

Koenig shook his head, a look of sadness in his eyes that broke Schmidt's heart.

"By then, it will not matter, Johann. It will not matter..."

※　※　※

"I'm tellin' you guys it's all Hollywood jive," Jensen said, eyeing his barracks mates. "Ain't none of it real! Christ, it's a goddamned TV show! What'd y'all expect? That they'd make it easy to get that dough?"

Everyone from Barracks 2 had crowded into Frank's quarters, sitting or standing wherever space permitted, their collective mood a mixture of fear, anger, and desperation. From his bunk, Frank watched them argue, seeing the questioning look in their eyes, eyes needing answers.

He ran his tongue over the raw spot inside his mouth, feeling a sharp sting. It was minor compared to the sting he felt in his soul. In that hidden place he still tasted the blood, still saw the contempt on Koenig's face, still felt like the scared little boy he used to be.

And he hated himself for it.

Frank broke out of his reverie when Dana Webster spoke. "I was standing right there when those bullets hit the ground," he said. "I could *feel* them. They were real!"

"Aw, shit," Jensen said. "Those were those itty-bitty explosives the special effects boys use. They can put 'em just about any place and fire 'em by radio. T'ain't nothin'. Hell, *you're* an actor, you should *know*."

"What about the guy those goons clobbered with the rifle?"

Everyone turned. It was Dean who'd spoken.

"Are you telling us they faked that?" he added.

"Hell, yes. I've seen those Hollywood guys shootin' movies in Dallas a hundred times. Those stunt boys know their stuff. They can make anything look real."

"Oh, come on, Tex," Dean said, his temper flaring, "You going to tell us that guy was a plant?"

Jensen let the Tex comment go by.

"Do any of you know the guy? Can anybody honestly tell me that guy was one of us, *for sure?*"

The room fell silent. Everyone's mind replayed the day's events again and again.

"What about the prize money?" Dana asked.

"What about it?" Jensen said. "I'll tell you what. I say Koenig and the Krauts are just whettin' our whistle, gettin' into the spirit of things. Makin' us sweat. Well, screw 'em. The sooner we try to escape—"

"The sooner we'll be dead," Frank said, cutting him off.

Jensen sneered. "Well, well, well. The Senior POW Officer speaks! The big man on campus has somethin' to say. You gonna show us your stuff, *Colonel?* You gonna be the big man again? He sure showed the *Kommandant* today, didn't he, boys?"

"Why don't you lay off?" Dean said, moving toward the big Texan, his fists clenched.

"You wanna take me on?" Jensen said, going nose to nose with Dean. "Come on, peckerwood, I'll turn you into dogmeat faster'n you can spit."

"That's enough!"

Everyone turned to Frank, who now stood in front of his bunk, his eyes blazing. "I don't claim to be the bravest man in the world, and maybe I proved it out there today. And maybe I didn't. But one thing I can be pretty sure of is that Koenig is playing this for real. Those bullets were *real*. That man's bloody face was *real*." *And so was that slap in the face, Frank*, he said to himself. "The only thing that isn't real is the prize money. It was a carrot on a stick to get us here. And like a bunch of jackasses, we fell for it." He turned to Jensen. "You think this is a TV show? Think again."

Frank moved over to the corner of the room, stood on Bob Neff's bunk and ripped the camera down from its mount. He walked back, tossed it onto the floor at Jensen's feet and stomped on it. The plastic housing cracked open, revealing nothing but a double-A battery powering the red LED, which flickered and went out.

"There's your TV show for you," Frank said.

Jensen's shocked expression said it all.

"And one thing we should get straight," Frank continued. "I'm not a colonel. I'm just a guy... like you."

Roger Putnam stood, his stocky frame straining the buttons of his first lieutenant's uniform. "Well, I say you're as fine a colonel as we deserve. And if it's all the same to you, we'd like you to stay on as the SPO. How 'bout it, men?"

Everyone nodded their head, except for Bill Jensen. "Well, now, ain't this cute," he said. "We got ourselves a shiny new hero. But even if our fair colonel is right—we're still in this rat hole, with no way a gettin' out until Koenig *lets* us out!"

"Bill's right," Frank said, receiving a curt nod from Jensen in return. "Maybe there's a slim chance that Koenig and the guards are playing their parts, the parts we asked them to play. But what if they're not?"

No one said anything, and Frank continued.

"What if Koenig has some hidden agenda, or is just plain crazy? It doesn't matter, because until we come up with a plan, here is where we're going to stay."

"You got any bright ideas, *Colonel*?" Jensen said with obvious sarcasm. Frank ignored it.

"Fair question. The answer is: no, I don't."

Jensen snorted and shook his head.

"But I do have a suggestion. We play along, keep our eyes open. Until we get the lay of the land, we're operating in the dark. Somewhere in Koenig's little kingdom there's a weak spot, and if we're smart, we'll find it. But we need to work together, or we're lost. What do you say?"

"I say we take a vote," Bob Neff announced. "Everyone in favor of Frank's suggestion, raise their hands."

Except for Bill Jensen, who stood sulking in the corner, the vote was unanimous.

Frank nodded, feeling a measure of confidence return. Together, they would find a way out, assuming that Jensen was wrong, and they wouldn't need one. But Frank had a sinking feeling they *would* need one—and soon.

"Anyone have anything to add?" Frank asked, looking directly at Jensen. The big man stared right back, the challenge unabated.

"We're with you, Colonel," Dana said.

Frank glanced at his watch.

"All right, then. Let's move out, guys. Time for mess."

❋   ❋   ❋

The chow line moved faster than it had the night before, because now there was far less to eat. The meat loaf, mashed potatoes, and beans from the previous night were gone, replaced by a watery gruel containing some bits of God only knew what, a small, hard chunk of black bread with a moldy rind, and weak lukewarm coffee with a strong aftertaste of burnt chicory.

When Frank passed before the kitchen goon, he noticed the man's perennial scowl had transformed itself into a sardonic grin.

"What *is* this crap?" Dean whispered.

"Breakfast," Frank replied, his eyes scanning the room. "Welcome to Camp Stalag."

They took their usual seats and Frank noticed that the boisterous atmosphere of the previous day had fled. In its place, silent men shoveled food into their mouths, their blank eyes focused on some distant place.

Frank picked up his spoon and took a bite. It was bland as hell, but it was edible.

"Man, this stuff sucks," Dean said.

"You really didn't expect food like that meat loaf every day, did you?"

"I don't know what I expected. You're the expert on POW camps."

Dean turned toward the *Kommandant's* table, now hidden behind its shutters.

"I'll bet those clowns in there aren't eating this," he said, stabbing the air with his spoon.

Frank stopped chewing when he noticed one of the guards staring at them.

"Knock it off," Frank warned.

"Yeah, right, knock it off."

He fell silent, unconcerned with who might be watching, and began swirling the gruel with his spoon. Frank was about to tell him to take it easy when a siren wailed. The guards in the room reacted as if someone had stuck them with pins. They rushed out the door, the gear hanging from their Sam Browne belts clattering as they ran. A second later the shutters hiding the *Kommandant's* table flew open. Koenig and Schmidt strode through the tables, two guards clearing the way for them. Some of the men hurried to the windows.

"Somebody's going over the wire!" one of them yelled.

The room erupted.

Everyone scrambled out the door, their voices melding into an excited roar.

Following the crowd, Frank and Dean spotted a man caught in the glare of two searchlights, halfway over the inner fence. He clung to the top strand, whimpering, his feet dangling three feet off the hard-packed earth of no-man's-land. Blood streamed from his hands in tiny rivulets.

The crowd parted when several guards shouldered their way through, making way for Koenig, Schmidt, and Mannheim.

"You there!" Koenig shouted. "You have nowhere to go. Climb back now and I will be merciful."

The man's eyes darted wildly about. He said nothing.

Koenig turned to Schmidt. "Who is this man?"

Schmidt consulted his clipboard. "Corporal Henry Blair, *mein Kommandant*."

Koenig moved closer to the wire, a paternal smile on his face. "Corporal Blair, you must come down. You have no hope of escaping. You *must* know that." His voice was softer now, almost gentle.

Slick with blood, Blair's hands slipped.

"I want to go home!" he cried.

Koenig smiled, but his eyes smoldered.

"Corporal. You've come a long way to be here. Why not enjoy it?"

"No! I want to go home—*now*!"

The men murmured, their voices growing angry.

"Let the guy go home!" someone shouted.

"Yeah, let him go!" another echoed.

A few started chanting, "Let him go. Let him go. Let him go..."

Koenig's jaw clenched. The situation was escalating. In a moment it would become unmanageable. He turned to Mannheim. "Get him down, Sergeant."

Stepping up to the wire, Mannheim pulled out his lead-lined truncheon—his piglike eyes dancing with sadistic joy—and poked at the man with swift, vicious jabs. Blair, more agile than anyone would have given him credit for under the circumstances, dodged the sergeant's blows, swinging his body back and forth. Their movements took on the aspects of a comic ballet that had everyone laughing at the silliness of it.

Everyone except Mannheim, Schmidt... and Koenig.

The *Kommandant's* face clouded. "*Hundführer!*" he screamed.

From behind them, Frank heard barking.

Dogs. Koenig had called for the dogs.

Frank turned toward the sound of the barking, as did the rest of the men. From behind a building, and within the no-man's-land, came two guards, each holding a leash pulled by a muscular Rottweiler. The dogs loped along, their long, fat tongues dripping saliva.

"Oh God," Frank muttered.

All the men began screaming for Blair to climb back over. Confused at first, he spotted the dogs rounding the corner of the fence and heading straight for him. Panicking, he began clambering back over. But his hands, slick with blood, slipped on the shiny wire. He fell into no-man's-land, landing with a dull thud that knocked the breath out of him. Before he could move, the dogs fell upon him.

"No! Help me! Get them off me!"

Blair's terrified screams turned to wordless cries of agony when the ravenous dogs tore into his flesh.

The spectacle horrified Frank, as did the potent coppery odor of the man's gore. He pushed through the crowd, his eyes intent on the *Kommandant*, but two guards grabbed him by the arms, restraining him. The rest of the men, cowed by the guards' machine guns, stood rooted to the earth.

As if noticing Frank out of the corner of his eye, Koenig turned toward him. *But something was wrong.* The old man stared at him—no, *through* him, as if he wasn't even there. And his eyes. They looked vacant, like those of a mannequin. Glancing towards Schmidt, Frank noted the younger man's fleeting look of alarm.

"*Halt Die Hunden!*" Schmidt shouted.

The two *Hundführers* grabbed their dogs by their collars and yanked them back from the wounded man. The Rottweilers howled in protest, their savage ululations sending a chill down Frank's spine. But what scared Frank more was that void behind Koenig's eyes. What did it mean?

Poor Blair lay in a ragged, bloody heap, moaning faintly, one leg barely held together by its sinews. Schmidt dispatched two guards to take him to the infirmary. However, since he could no longer walk, they were forced to drag him. A groan went through the men when the blood-soaked appendage separated from Blair's body. One of the guards, hesitating for a fraction of a second, picked it up by the boot, then followed the body around the corner and out of sight. Frank watched Koenig, Schmidt, and Mannheim strut back to the *Kommandantur*. The crowd, intimidated and horrified, began to disperse.

Any doubts regarding Camp Stalag were gone. They were all in terrible danger.

※   ※   ※

For the last two hours before lights out, no one spoke, unable to give voice to the horror they'd witnessed and the terror of what they feared the morning would bring. Even after the lights finally winked out, and darkness blanketing the barracks with an awful quiet, everyone lay in their bunks, their minds in turmoil.

Frank felt the tension from the outer room flowing into his quarters like some invisible, poisonous gas. Getting up, he padded out into the main room and stood there, staring into the darkness.

This had to end.

"Everyone in my quarters on the double," he said, his voice cracking the air like a rifle shot.

No reaction. It was as if he hadn't spoken. He stood there a moment longer, hoping someone would respond.

No one said a word, yet one by one, they filed into his quarters, sullen and despondent. He waited until everyone seated themselves.

"All right. We know our original fears were right. Let's not beat ourselves up over it. Anybody have any ideas since this morning? I'd be glad to hear them."

Nothing.

Frank could take no more. Their hopeless attitude grated on his nerves to the point where he wanted to slap some sense into each of them. "Look, goddamn it! It won't do us any good if we give up. That's what Koenig wants."

"How the hell do you expect to get out?" Jensen said. "Fly over the fence? It didn't help Blair!"

Jensen spoke the very thoughts running through all their minds.

"No, Bill, I don't expect to fly. But I do expect all of us to work together. We can't win if we've already surrendered."

"Well, so far, I've heard squat. 'Keep your eyes open, we'll find a weak spot,' blah, blah, blah! By the time we find their 'weak spot,' *Colonel*, we'll all be dead!" Jensen said, giving voice to everyone's deepest fear.

"Freddie?"

"Yeah, Frank?"

"Go stand outside the front door. If any goons come, knock on the wall as loud as you can. Two short, three long. Got it?"

"Got it, Frank."

No one spoke until Freddie had walked out and closed the door behind him.

"Maybe we can bribe our way out?" Dana offered.

"Aw, what the hell do you know? You're just a faggot actor," Jensen shot back.

Stung, Webster sprung off the floor and started pummeling the bigger man, his wide swings weak and ineffective. Afraid the scuffle would attract the guards, Frank jumped in with Dean and a couple of the others and pulled them apart.

"Stop it! Stop it *now*, goddamn it!" Frank said, his voice a harsh whisper. "Do you want the goons catching us?"

Frank's outburst had the desired effect. Assembling after lights out would mean additional sanctions the men had no stomach for. No one wanted any more trouble from the Krauts.

"It's not money they want," Frank said. "Koenig gets off on power. This whole setup is a sick fantasy."

"'Sick' ain't the word for it, bucko," Jensen said, staring daggers at Dana Webster.

Frank waited another moment for the air to clear. Everyone was scared and angry, lashing out at anything and everything. Frank couldn't blame them one damn bit.

"Like I said earlier today," Frank continued, "I don't have any brilliant ideas, but I'm willing to listen to any you guys might have, so let's stop screwing around and start thinking."

The room fell silent. The searchlights made several sweeps of the room before someone spoke. It was Roger Putnam, the electrician.

"If we had wire cutters, we could cut our way out."

Reaching into his pants, he pulled out something that looked like a pair of pliers. He held them up and clicked them twice. The searchlight glinted off the shiny nickel- plated metal.

"Seen a lot of prison movies," Putnam said, smiling sheepishly. "Thought they might come in handy."

The men erupted into excited whispers. The mood of the room had dramatically changed.

Frank clapped Roger on the shoulders, his eyes betraying their excitement. "Remind me to kiss you later."

Roger blushed and the rest of the men laughed. Suddenly, a knock sounded on the door. Two short, three long.

The goons!

Everyone scrambled out of Frank's quarters and into their bunks as if someone had tossed a grenade into the room. No more than five seconds after the last man closed his eyes in mock slumber, the door creaked open and Mannheim stepped in, followed by Schmidt. Carrying a large flashlight, Mannheim trained it on each of the men, making sure all were present.

Frank's heart pounded like a jackhammer. From his vantage point, he could see the flashlight through the cracks in the door. It danced back and forth with a brisk efficiency. Mannheim would be inside his quarters in seconds. He tore his eyes from the door and glanced over at Bob, taking a measure of comfort from his slow, regular snore. He then looked at the floor and froze.

The wire cutters lay near the door where Putnam had dropped

them in his haste to get to his bunk. There was no way the Krauts would miss them.

Throwing off the covers, Frank leaped onto the floor, wincing when a splinter shoved itself into his heel.

The flashlight drew closer.

He raced across the floor, grabbed the cutters, and dove back into the bunk just as Mannheim pushed open the door. With his heart hammering in his chest, Frank resisted the urge to gasp for breath, commanding his body to relax. He heard Schmidt whisper something in German to Mannheim. A second later, the sergeant's flashlight played across his face, halting a long, agonizing second directly into his closed eyes. It took every ounce of effort not to squeeze them tighter. After a moment, the light snapped off and the door closed with a muffled *click*. Only then did Frank let out the breath he'd been holding.

Another ten minutes went by before all the men filtered back into the room.

"That was close, guys," Frank said, sitting up.

"What happens now?" Dean asked, taking a seat on Frank's bunk.

"All right, listen up. Thanks to Roger's forethought, we have a way out."

Roger smiled when Bob Neff patted him on the back.

"But it's not going to be easy. There has to be at least one spot the goons in the towers can't see and the searchlights can't reach."

"What then?" Bob asked.

"Once we find it, two of us are going to cut our way out and make our way to the nearest police station."

All the men began talking at once.

"I don't like it," Jensen said.

The others groaned and the big Texan's eyes blazed.

"Hey! Why should fancy pants here get to go? For all we know, he'll keep going and leave us to rot."

That cut it. Seething, Frank marched over to Jensen. "It's one thing to call me a coward. Maybe I deserved that. And I really don't give a rat's ass about being a colonel, either, although you seem to find that awfully important."

Jensen blinked and looked away, his frown deepening.

"*Look* at me, goddamn it!" Frank snapped.

Jensen whirled, his nostrils flaring. Frank continued.

"I don't care about any of that, not anymore. But when you accuse me of wanting to run out on everyone, then I guess it's time we had it out, here and now." He poked the big man's massive chest with his index finger for emphasis. "And maybe you'll whip my ass too. But I'm not about to take any more of your crap. You got that?"

Jensen's eyes narrowed, and then suddenly he smiled. It was as if the sun had come out on a cloudy day. "All right, Colonel, you win," he said, saluting with a newfound respect. "And if anyone has a problem with that, they can answer to me!"

Everyone laughed.

"Who gets to go, Colonel?" Dana asked.

"I'd be proud to take any of you with me, but I think it's wise that there be only two of us. If all of us go, the goons'll know immediately and then our chances are just about nil. Does anyone want that?"

Frank scanned the room. No one spoke.

"Good. As for who goes, it's me and—"

"How about me?" Jensen asked. "I'm real good at hand-to-hand combat, and I can run like hell, if need be." For a change, his tone was calm, reasonable, and Frank found himself liking the big man.

"As much as I'd love to have you backing me up, Bill, I think *you* might be missed."

Jensen nodded, a knowing smile forming on his lips. "Yeah, you're right. I *am* a little tall."

"So, who goes besides you, Colonel?" Bob asked impatiently.

"Roger. Since he was smart enough to bring the wire cutters, I think he deserves to go. As for me, I'm the senior officer, and I'm not going to let anyone else take a risk that I'm unwilling to take myself. Anybody got a problem with that?"

"No, sir," Dana said.

Everyone nodded their assent.

Bob Neff still appeared dissatisfied.

"What about our families?" Bob said. "That nut said he'd hunt them down."

"There's one advantage we have that no one's thinking about," Frank said. "World War Two ended over fifty years ago. That's not Germany out there, that's New Hampshire. Two of us can bring all the help we need. There's no way he can make good on that threat, guys. *This is the United States!*"

This final fact galvanized the men. Frank smiled when he saw their fighting spirit return. All at once they began talking heatedly about how they were going to "shaft the goons." For the first time since morning, Frank felt real hope.

"One more thing. Over the next couple of days, I want everyone to check out the perimeter. Do it at different times, and for God's sake, don't make it obvious. Once we know their blind spot and the camp routine, we go."

"When, Frank?" someone asked.

"If everything goes well—one week from today, June tenth."

"All right!" Jensen said, pumping his fist in the air.

"Okay, guys, get some shut-eye," Frank said.

The men shuffled out of the room, but Dean hung back.

"You really handled that Jensen dude like a master, Shakespeare. For a moment I thought he was going to turn you into hamburger."

Frank clapped Dean on the back, a confident smile creasing his face. "So did I, Dean, so did I. But I think he's going to be okay from now on."

"I don't know... He makes me nervous."

Frank thought for a moment. "Why don't you keep an eye on him, then? Be his pal. Make sure he stays on the straight and narrow."

Dean looked shocked. "Me? Why me? What did I do?"

"We've all got to do our part. You're the one with the reservations. Now it's your responsibility to make sure he doesn't screw us up. Okay?"

He started to object, then nodded.

"You got it, Colonel," he said, saluting. "Good night."

"Good night, Sergeant," Frank said, smiling again.

After Dean left, Frank settled down in his bunk and went over his plan. If they got out and managed to get to a police station, would the cops believe them? More than likely these backwoods cops would take one look at their World War Two uniforms and call the wacko wagon.

"Hey, Frank," Bob whispered. "Do you really think we'll get out?"

"Yeah, I do. They can't keep us here forever."

"No... but they can kill us."

11

Heinrich Koenig awoke the next morning before the alarm went off, his eyes flashing open in the murky gloom of his living quarters. Momentarily disoriented, he leaned over and snatched the clock off the nightstand, squinting to make out the faint glow of the radium numerals on the dial.

4:05.

He still had twenty-five minutes.

He stood under the steaming shower for one minute before switching it to cold only. When the icy stream contacted his skin, invigorating his aging body, he took comfort in the fact that this was a response on which he could still rely. The basic senses were the last to go, the doctors had said.

Ever since Zurich, Koenig had lived in fear—fear of the inexorable deterioration of his mind. Fear that all he had accomplished would escape him in tiny, unnoticeable increments day by inexorable day.

He had already noticed lapses in time. *Drifting*, as he called it. They were blackouts, times when the disease took over and directed his mind and body to do God only knew what. And that loss of control was what scared him.

Toweling off, he dressed in a crisp white shirt and a freshly pressed uniform. He studied himself in the mirror, marveling at the skill of the reproduction: the custom-milled gabardine, the hand-woven bullion insignia, the exquisite tailoring. Everything was perfect. Koenig had quietly contracted with the original firms to make them. If any of them objected, his generous fees turned their protests into apologies. Only one had balked. The president of a *Lüdenscheid* firm threatened to call in the Federal authorities when asked to provide breast eagles featuring the constitutionally banned swastika. One week later, Koenig purchased the company through one of his blind corporations, then took consummate pleasure in tossing the flabby toad out on his pompous arse.

Heinrich smiled at the memory as he placed the visored cap at a jaunty angle on his head. Yes, money took care of most problems in life, one way or another. All except for the one inside his skull. His expression hardening, Koenig turned from the mirror and strutted from the room.

Pausing in the outer office to put on his greatcoat, he flung open the front door and marched out onto the porch, where he stood a moment, watching the searchlights make their graceful sweeps of the compound, and taking a measure of pride in his domain. Far to the east, he saw the sky beginning to lighten, turning from a deep umber to a dull, smoldering red.

Red sky at morning, sailor take warning.

Perhaps the old sea dogs were right, and there would be rain this day. It was hard to tell this far north. He glanced at his watch.

4:25. Time for action.

Striding across the quad, he passed two guards who stopped in their tracks and saluted, the click of their boot heels sounding like muffled rifle shots. Koenig returned the salute without slowing his pace and walked toward the recreation hall, veering left at the last moment. The two guards in front of the *Waffenlager* snapped to attention and brought their rifles up for inspection.

He ordered them to stand at ease, withdrew a key from his tunic's inside breast pocket, then placed it in the lock. The massive titanium deadbolt slid back with a loud metallic *clunk*, and the two-ton door swung open, aided by a small electric motor. Pulling the door shut behind him, he threw the bolt and switched on the lights.

The sight that greeted his eyes brought another smile to his lips. From every available spot on the walls hung every sort of small arm imaginable. Aside from the authentic World War Two weaponry the guards carried, there were 7.62mm NATO automatic rifles, 9mm Uzis, and grenade launchers. Stacked on the floor stood six cases of LAW rockets, five cases of assorted hand grenades and fragmentation devices, ten cases of antipersonnel mines, three cases of flares, and two of camouflaging smoke.

Passing these by, he moved to a steel trapdoor set into the center of the floor. He bent down, grabbed the lifting ring, and heaved it open with a soft grunt. Ten concrete steps descended into the dark expanse below. He started down, reaching over to a panel set into the cellar wall to switch on the lights. The room underneath the armory was about half its size and was taken up by a large, burnished steel box resting on a concrete platform, gleaming dully in the cold, fluorescent lighting. Moving around to the opposite side, Koenig approached the box and flipped open a hinged panel in its side. A bright-red digital readout greeted his eyes, casting its crimson glow over his face. The numbers raced toward zero, the last two digits a blur.

Only thirty seconds remained.

To the left of the digital readout was a ten-digit keypad, and a lock requiring the insertion of a barrel key.

Fifteen seconds...

Wasting no time, Koenig pulled out the key and inserted it, twisting it to the left.

Ten seconds...

And then he punched in his code, his slender tapered fingers moving with precision. When he completed the code sequence, the box beeped three times and then the readout reset itself. It now read: 24:00:00.

The box beeped two more times and the readout began counting down. Satisfied, Koenig closed the panel and returned to the upper level, leaving the mysterious box swathed in darkness.

Back outside, he stood in the middle of the quad and filled his lungs with the cold, clean air. Another day, another reprieve. No one else knew of the secret room underneath the *Waffenlager*, not even Johann. For though he cared for the young man like a son, the secret and its portents belonged to him alone.

And when the day came that his illness prevented him from resetting the timer, the device would begin a thirty-minute countdown that no one—not even God himself—could stop.

The explosion resulting from the small tactical nuclear device (fashioned from an atomic artillery shell secreted out from one of his own factories) would vaporize the camp and everything around it for seven city blocks.

Koenig hoped he would be able to warn Johann in time for him to get out and far away, but he could not be sure his mind would still be intact enough to remember. Many times, he'd had the urge to tell his adopted son about the device, but in the end decided to keep the secret. The boy was loyal, of that he was certain, but if faced with the knowledge of what lay underneath the armory, Koenig knew the young man's affection for him would triumph and the bomb would be disarmed. And that he could not allow.

He would die as a warrior on his own terms. He would never consent to lie in some hospital, rotting away while they pumped him full of drugs that stole away what dignity and lucidity he had left.

Never!

And if, by some miracle, the bomb did not deter whatever outside forces might be marshaling to rescue the prisoners, he had the means and the men to fight them. And fight them he would. For a fleeting moment, he pictured a pitched battle: the FBI and ATF storming the camp.

No, he thought confidently. *Those blithering fools will come nowhere near this place.* They would stay away because Heinrich Koenig knew "where all the bodies were buried," as the Americans were fond of saying. In his dealings with their government, he'd made sure to learn more about *them* than they were able to learn about him.

Once he had the crucial knowledge that would paralyze them, he'd sent them copies of their files. Koenig smiled as he strolled back to the *Kommandantur*. How he would have loved to have seen their faces. But, alas, this was not to be, for time was running out.

And when it did, it would be *Götterdämmerung*, and Heinrich Koenig would fly home to Valhalla on the wings of the Valkyries.

12

"This is slop!" the man from Barracks 5 screamed. "This is the same fuckin' *shit* as yesterday!"

The goon behind the mess counter—the one everyone now called Scarface—scowled, his face turning a deep crimson. Scarface didn't understand a word of English, but Frank knew anger when he saw it. Anger and, just maybe, a touch of cruel satisfaction.

The mouth-watering fare from two nights before was now a bittersweet memory. For the second morning in a row, they got a breakfast gruel of indeterminate composition, a piece of stale, moldy black bread, and a watered-down ersatz coffee to round out the meal.

"Give me something else besides this fucking slop!" the man yelled again, flipping his tray at Scarface, who sidestepped the flying mess. Behind him, the other men grumbled, their petulant murmurs turning to angry shouts. It was plain to see that future meals would likely be as bad. Farther back in line, men cried out when the guards shoved them aside. Behind them strutted Sergeant Mannheim. Seeing him, the men moved out of his way like some pathetic imitation of the parting of the Red Sea. He never once acknowledged anyone in his path, his steely gaze locked on the loudmouth from Barracks 5.

When he reached the head of the line, Mannheim grabbed the

man by the collar of his khaki jumpsuit and pulled him so close, their noses nearly touched.

"You do not like the food, Private?" he asked. His voice was so soft, Frank had to strain to hear.

The man—whose name was George Crouse, Frank later found out—gulped audibly, his eyes darting to the other prisoners in a useless plea for help. Mannheim shook him like a doll.

"You still have not answered my question, Private." The last word was uttered with unmistakable menace.

"Ahh, well, it l—looks a—" Crouse's frightened stammer cut off abruptly as Mannheim shook him again.

"You would like something better, *Ja?*" Mannheim asked, his voice a gravelly hiss.

"Well, maybe some scrambled eggs... some bacon..." His voice trailed off, a weak smile turning up the corners of his thin-lipped mouth.

Mannheim smiled then, too, projecting a surprising amount of warmth and humor. Seeing that his situation was not so bad after all, Crouse relaxed. It was exactly what the sergeant was waiting for. With a move that would impress a professional fighter, Mannheim balled up his fist and smashed it into the man's gut with a lightning-quick jab. Crouse doubled over, his breath exploding from his lungs, followed by a deep groan of shock and pain.

Grinning with malignant relish, Mannheim grabbed the man's head and shoved him toward the counter, the blunt steel edge slamming into his gut in the same place the beefy sergeant had hit him. Before Crouse could move, Mannheim caught him by his longish brown hair and thrust his head into the large pot of steaming gruel. He began to struggle at once, flailing like a fish on a hook, his burning lungs already starved for oxygen.

Holding the squirming man with ease, Mannheim turned to the rest of the men. "All of you will eat what we give you... or starve!" he shouted. "Anyone who complains will spend three days in the cooler with nothing to eat but the cockroaches! Do I make myself clear?"

Frank's throat choked with panic, watching the submerged man thrash about, spattering the counter with thick dollops of gruel. Mannheim waited for an answer, his evil smile widening with each passing second.

He wants *the man to drown*, Frank thought.

"Do... I... make... myself... clear?" Mannheim repeated, slowly enunciating each word while Crouse's struggling grew more and more feeble.

"Yes!" Frank blurted out. "Yes, you're clear! You're clear!"

Without another word, Mannheim let Crouse slip out of the pot and crumple to the floor. He leaned back against the counter, gulping air and sobbing uncontrollably, while several of his barracks mates moved to help him to a nearby table. Frank noticed the skin on Crouse's face and neck had turned beet red. Second-degree burns, at the very least.

Mannheim stood firm, his ham-sized fists perched on his hips in a show of arrogant contempt. "Next in line!" Mannheim shouted.

No one moved, feeling a little queasy at the prospect of eating gruel someone almost drowned in.

"Next in line, *schnell!*"

Grabbing a tray, Frank walked to the head of the line, thrust it at Scarface, and waited. Smirking, the goon ladled a huge portion onto the tray, looked Frank square in the eye, then spit into the gruel. Frank held his emotions in check, staring back at the goon, whose smile widened, revealing a mouthful of black, rotted stubs.

Frank smiled back, blew Scarface a kiss, and then moved down the line. The men cheered as the smile fled from the ugly goon's startled mug.

Later that afternoon, while Barracks 2 and 4 held an impromptu softball game, Frank found a moment to stroll the perimeter. He walked twice around before he thought he saw the perfect place. Right under the northeast tower.

Of course!

The mess hall blocked the area directly under that tower from the view of the two adjacent towers. All they had to do was run alongside the barracks. When they reached the blind spot, they would cut the fence, crawl through, and scurry across ten feet of open space. Next they would cut the second fence, and then run the last twenty yards to the woods. After that, they were home free. There were only two problems. That ten feet of open space between the two fences could be seen by two of the towers simultaneously. Since they could never be sure that the searchlights from one wouldn't catch them, they would have to time it precisely. That was the easy problem.

The second was the patrols. Guards patrolled both inside the camp and between the fences. The inside patrols marched about the camp in what appeared to be a random pattern. After watching them carefully, Frank realized their movements formed a lazy figure eight. Strange, yet predictable.

Next came no-man's-land.

Once they had cut through the first fence, they were at the mercy of the *Hundführers* and their perpetually hungry Rottweilers. The *Hundführers* passed any given spot every ten minutes. Frank, and several other men, timed them. The timing *never* varied. The *Hundführers* marched at the same consistent, plodding cadence day and night. Ten minutes was not a lot of time to cut through two fences and make it to the woods, but it *had* to be enough.

Frank sighed as he thought about all the problems. Individually, they could solve them. Taken together, they presented formidable obstacles that would either see them get clean away or turned into steak tartare.

Returning to the game, Frank noticed a group of men huddled around Barracks 6. Dean was among them.

"What's going on?" Frank asked him.

"Goons are searching the barracks," he replied.

Immediately Frank thought of the wire cutters. Turning quickly, he nearly ran into Schmidt.

"Well, Colonel Murphy, I trust you and your men are settled in?"

The man's patronizing tone ticked Frank off.

"Just what the hell are they searching for, Schmidt?"

"*Hauptmann* Schmidt," he said, his tone glacial.

Frank's temper flared, but he let it go. No sense in flying off the handle about a situation of which he knew nothing.

"What's the idea, *Hauptmann* Schmidt?"

"Contraband, Colonel. We can't be too careful, now, can we?"

"You've got to be kidding. We've only been here two days. We haven't had time to *get* any contraband. And, besides, where would we, anyway? It's not as if we can bribe the guards with nylon stockings and Hershey Bars from our nonexistent Red Cross packages."

"Come now, Colonel, we wouldn't want to rob you of your full experience. How you Americans say, 'Getting your money's worth.'"

Frank stalked off, his emotions boiling over. It wasn't the searches that pissed him off. It was the fact that he let that smarmy bastard Schmidt get the better of him, and he very *definitely* did not like that.

Back at the softball game, Frank motioned for everyone to gather round.

"Schmidt is searching the barracks," he said. "If any of you have anything you don't want found, stick it down your pants. If it's too big for that, forget it—the goons'll find it. Roger?"

"Yeah, Frank?" he said.

"Where are the cutters?"

Roger smiled conspiratorially and patted his crotch.

"You didn't, by chance, slide into home plate today, did you?" Frank asked, a tiny smile on his lips.

Everyone laughed, including Roger, who crossed his eyes in mock pain.

Frank's smile widened. "Come on, you guys, let's show 'em we don't give a damn. Play ball!"

❋   ❋   ❋

When Frank sat down to evening mess, he noticed that Dean looked disturbed about something. He sat staring at his tray, a faraway look in his eye.

"What's up? You look like hell."

Dean didn't react at first. Slowly, he lifted his gaze from the food and stared at Frank for a long, pregnant moment. His eyes held a hopeless expression that rang alarm bells in Frank's head.

"We're not in New Hampshire," he said.

Frank frowned, shaking his head. "What? What are you talking about?

"We're not in New Hampshire, Frank," he repeated, his voice becoming intense. "*I know it.*"

"Where the hell else would we be?"

Dean leaned closer, his eyes matching the intensity of his voice. "Have you noticed that it's been getting dark a little early? I have. About an hour earlier than it should."

With a sudden chill, Frank realized that Dean was right. It was early June and should remain light out until well after seven thirty. Frank hadn't given it much thought, but sunsets here occurred around six thirty.

We are on Central Time!

Dean's voice broke through his thoughts.

"I talked with a guy from Barracks Seven this afternoon. He told me that we're most likely somewhere in the upper Midwest—maybe Wisconsin."

"How does he know that?"

"The guy's a bird watcher. He practically flipped when he saw this certain kind of woodpecker—*a Black-Backed Three-Toed something or other.*" Dean paused, noting his friend's puzzled expression. "Frank, they don't exist in New Hampshire—only the upper Midwest and Canada."

"But how, Dean? How could they have done it?"

"Do you *really* know how long we slept on the bus?"

Frank glowered, then he remembered. "My watch! *That's* why it said June second. There was absolutely nothing wrong with it! We were on that bus for over twenty-four hours!"

"Bingo," Dean said.

The frantic murmur of Frank's thoughts now became a howling mob. In the jumble of his mind, the one thought that remained crystalline clear held the worst portents of all. Anyone looking for them would be looking in the *wrong* state. Shaking the thought from his mind, Frank came to a decision. "I'm moving up the timetable," he whispered. "Two of us are going tonight. I think I've found the blind spot."

Dean grabbed Frank's arm, the sparkle coming back into his eyes, along with his infamous Eddie Haskell grin. "Let's stick it to 'em, Shakespeare."

Frank's spirits soared. They were going to *beat* these bastards.

❈   ❈   ❈

Dear Brenda,

Just wanted to write you a quick line to tell you how much fun Dean and I are

having. You'd think being in a prison would be boring. It's anything but.

We have lots of sports equipment and we spend our days playing baseball and

volleyball. The wildlife is plentiful too and noisy as hell at night. Make sure to tell Pete that one of the guys saw a Black-Backed Three-Toed Woodpecker. I know how much he loves his birds.

The food is great, too, and Kommandant Koenig has graciously allowed us to stay longer than the allotted two months free of charge, so I'll probably stay at least another couple of weeks or so. Don't worry, I'll be back in time for Julie's first birthday.

Love you and I miss you.

Love,

Frank

13

"We've got an hour to go before lights out," Frank said. "We wait 'til the goons do bed check and then another hour after that. Then we go."

"What if they don't do bed check at the same time tonight?" Roger asked.

Good question. Once again, everyone had crowded into Frank's quarters for a final briefing. Their faces showed the same expressions of fear and hope. All day long they walked the perimeter, lay on their bunks, talked about their wives and children, played baseball and poker—anything to keep their minds from dwelling on the coming night.

Their anticipation reached such a fever pitch the men swore the guards were paying them more attention than usual. Maybe they were. Mannheim stalked through the barracks not once, but twice, scowling more than ever. What if they knew? What if, tonight, they were waiting outside the wire with the dogs... and the machine guns?

"If they haven't come by two o'clock this morning, we go anyway," Frank said.

Frank had made one miscalculation in moving up the escape.

The moon hadn't fully waned, making it especially dangerous. The only thing worse would have been a fresh layer of snow on the ground, making them perfect targets for the trigger-happy goons in the towers.

The rest of that final hour they spent playing poker with a deck missing three cards. To Frank, that deck symbolized the whole crazy mess they were in. Who could have imagined being held prisoner by a nutcase who missed the glories of the Second World War? And who could have imagined anyone being crazy enough to put himself in his hands?

But what really nagged at the edges of Frank's mind was how in the hell Koenig could hide this place from prying eyes. A prison camp in Wisconsin, or wherever the hell they were, covering over twenty acres was not something that could be covered with a tarpaulin, or even the old camouflage netting used to hide artillery and tank formations. It was just too damn big.

Then again, Frank had heard that white supremacist groups like the Aryan Brotherhood had secret enclaves buried deep in the woods of Wisconsin and nobody bothered *them*. And even when they *knew* where they were, the government could be quite cowardly when it came to confronting an armed foe, even one less well-armed than themselves. One only had to recall the standoff with the Montana Freemen to see the truth in that. They could be here for weeks, months, years, or until Koenig tired of his little game. But what lay beyond that thought, Frank did not want to contemplate.

As always, the lights winked out at precisely ten thirty, or was it nine thirty? He hadn't bothered to change his watch. It didn't matter much. Lying on his bunk, Frank thought about what lay ahead, not the least bit surprised to feel a twinge of the butterflies in his stomach. After all, it was not every day that a man cut his way out of a

German POW camp in the middle of the United States and made a mad dash for God knew where in the middle of the night.

He checked his watch again, finding that only ten minutes had passed. It was going to be a long night. A few moments later, Frank grew drowsy. He shook his head to clear it, then sat up and stared out the window. As he saw it, they had to get to a road as fast as possible, preferably a well-traveled one. Once there, they'd flag someone down and get a ride to the nearest town. It sounded right, but he had no way of knowing how far away the road would be, or how well-traveled. That dirt lane leading into camp could be one mile long or twenty. Frank knew they would only have until the five thirty roll call before the guards discovered them missing. Not a lot of time.

After midnight, Mannheim and one of the guards made the bed-check rounds. It was earlier than usual. Frank didn't know whether to feel good about that or not. They hadn't done two in one night yet, but he wouldn't put it past them.

But they have to sleep sometime, he thought.

The minutes crawled by, the next hour feeling like ten. He used the time to write in his journal, keeping the entry short and nondescript. Putting anything in it about their escape plans would be idiotic. The guards might find it.

A frightening thought struck him: the goons had *already* found it in their search of the barracks earlier that day. And read it. Who the hell was he kidding to think they wouldn't look under his mattress?

Frank slammed the book closed, feeling the anger rising in his chest. He saw it all in his mind's eye: Mannheim and a couple of the others slapping their thighs, laughing in contempt at his homesick outpourings to his wife, laughing themselves silly and putting it back *exactly* where he'd left it.

He sighed, letting the anger slip away. There was no way to know for sure, and what could he do about it, anyway?

"Screw them," he muttered.

"Wha—What?"

Frank turned and saw a bleary-eyed Bob Neff, his head poking out above the coarse blanket. "Nothing... Go back to sleep."

Bob mumbled something unintelligible, rolled over, and was soon snoring again.

At least you *can sleep*, Frank mused.

Just after one o'clock, Roger knocked lightly on Frank's door, waking Bob Neff again. He swung out of his bunk, looking as fresh and as eager as a Boy Scout on his first overnight. Frank wanted to throttle him.

"Come in," Frank called out.

The door creaked open and Roger slipped inside.

"Don't know about you, Colonel, but I think I'm 'bout ready to puke," he said.

Frank smiled sympathetically, the man's heavy down-east accent a welcome respite from the silence of the room and the chaos of his thoughts. As for his own stomach, it had become progressively more upset as the time for them to move out approached, until it felt as unstable as a boiling pot.

"I know what you mean," Frank said. "Helen Hayes used to throw up before every performance."

"Who?"

Frank smiled again. "Never mind. I must be getting old."

Walking out into the main room, they found everyone awake and as nervous as they were. Jensen approached Frank, his meaty hand extended. "You give 'em hell, you hear?"

Frank shook his hand, glad to have the big man as an ally.

With everyone's encouraging words ringing in their ears, Frank and Roger stole out of the barracks.

"Stick close to the walls," Frank whispered. "And watch the towers. If a light comes our way, duck around the side of the building. Keep moving as fast as you can. Once we make it to the mess hall, we'll be safe for a while."

Their timing of the searchlights over the past several days revealed a sweep pattern that repeated in intervals every twenty seconds. That meant they had about that much time to go from one barracks building to the next before the ensuing sweep.

If they weren't safely hidden by then—they were dead meat.

The light from the nearest tower swept by them, the incandescent spot passing within ten yards. Too close for comfort. Frank waited an extra beat, then tapped Roger on the shoulder. They dashed from the shadows of Barracks 2, managing to make it to the next barracks with time to spare. They waited only a moment before scurrying to the next one, flattening themselves along the wall, hidden from the towers' view. Both of them gasped for breath, their fear and anxiety at fever pitch. Two more barracks to go. Then they would have to cross open ground between the last barracks and the mess hall.

The searchlights swept near their hiding spot twice before they felt ready enough to move. "I think we can make the last two in one shot," Frank said.

The other man's eyes widened, and he shook his head.

"We can't stay here too long," Frank said. "The faster we get to the wire, the sooner we'll be out of here. Okay?"

Roger nodded and poked his head around the corner. Snapping his head back, he flatted himself against the building. "Goons!" he whispered, his eyes bulging.

They held their breaths and waited the interminable moments

for the two guards to walk by. They came into view, passing only a few feet from where they stood. Suddenly, they stopped moving, and one of them, a tall one with hooded eyes and a crewcut under his field cap, said something that made the shorter one laugh. All those two guards needed to do was turn a few degrees and they would be staring right at them.

Sweat popped out on Frank's forehead and trickled down his face. It made his skin itch like crazy, but he couldn't risk a movement to scratch it, a movement one of the guards might catch out of the corner of his eye. The shorter of the two guards pulled out a pack of cigarettes, extending it toward his compatriot.

"*Amerikanisch*," he said.

"Ahh, *Ausgezeichnet*," the tall one replied.

Accepting a cigarette, the tall guard pulled out his lighter and lit them both.

Frank thought he would scream when the light from the lighter illuminated them against the wall like a spotlight. A moment later, the guards moved off, talking animatedly, their laughter echoing through the compound.

After they disappeared, both Frank and Roger exhaled.

"Christ," Roger whispered. "I thought we were goners."

Moving away from the wall, Frank stuck his head out and looked. The quad stood empty. "It's clear. Let's go," he said.

Sprinting, they made it to the last barracks building well before the searchlight swung back their way. They hid behind a rain barrel, and Frank took the time to survey the next leg of their torturous journey. It was twenty feet to the side of the mess hall and another thirty to the base of the tower. If they hid behind the wall closest to the rear fence, they would be invisible to the towers.

It was this last twenty feet of open ground that promised to be the most dangerous, that is until they reached no-man's-land. They would be in perfect view from both the northeast and northwest towers. The timing would have to be perfect, with no margin for error. Any screw-ups and it would be the cooler for three days and their hopes of freedom dashed completely. That is, if they weren't shot.

Frank wiped the sweat from his brow with the woven cuff of his A-2 flight jacket. He'd always wanted one while growing up, and now he wished he'd left it in the barracks. The damn thing was hot. "When I say go, run your ass off and duck behind the mess hall. Okay?"

Roger nodded. Even in the dim light, Frank could tell that Roger was as scared as he was. There was no turning back. If they screwed it up—so be it. Frank said a silent prayer. This had been the easy part. Once they reached the base of the tower, they would have to time the patrols in no-man's-land, cut a hole through both fences, and run for the woods. Snapping out of his thoughts, Frank watched the lights. It was time.

"Move it. Now!" he whispered.

Both of them scrambled across the open space. Hearing a muffled cry behind him, Frank turned and saw Roger sprawled upon the ground. He'd tripped. His heart racing, Frank grabbed him and pulled him around the side of the mess hall.

"Oh, shit," Roger said, his chest heaving as he gulped for air. "We gotta go back."

Frank looked at the other man, not quite sure what he heard. "What do you mean?"

"We gotta go back, Frank. I dropped the cutters."

Frank inched his way around the building and peered out onto the quad. He could just make out the wire cutters lying directly in the center of the area between the barracks and the mess hall—right where Roger had fallen. Frank timed the lights again, then noticed movement about fifty yards away. The guards were coming back—right toward the cutters.

Now he was *really* sweating. If he stayed where he was, the guards would spot him. On the other hand, they were sure to spot the cutters. Returning the way he'd come, he told Roger what was happening.

Instead of panicking, as Frank had expected, the other man looked around their immediate area then picked up a sizable stone. Frank smiled as he figured out Roger's train of thought.

Motioning Frank back to his observation post, Roger went the opposite way around the mess hall and waited. Seconds later, a loud clatter came from somewhere behind the guards.

Good job, Frank thought.

The two guards spun around, their rifles at the ready.

"*Was ist los*," one of them said.

Not taking any chances, they ran off the way they'd come. As soon as they disappeared around one of the barracks, Frank began timing the lights. The opportunity came quickly. He bolted out onto the quad, snatched the cutters off the ground, and darted back behind the mess hall.

"Nice going, Colonel," Roger said, slapping him on the back. Frank managed a smile as the two men crouched behind the rain barrel and watched for the no-man's-land patrols.

Soon, one of the *Hundführers* passed directly in front of them. Were it not for the fragrant garbage left out behind the mess hall, Frank knew the dogs would have alerted the guards to their presence. He watched the Rottweiler sniffing the air when it passed. Growling softly, it searched the complex odors tantalizing its olfactory nerve, searching for anything unusual. It hesitated for a second, cocking its massive head sideways. Frank held his breath, praying for a miracle. It came a moment later when the impatient guard yanked on the leash, propelling the dog forward.

Turning the corner, the guard passed his counterpart coming the other way. Once the second guard and his dog passed their location, Frank watched them march slowly along the perimeter until they disappeared around the southeast tower. They now had about ten minutes to make it through both fences. "Go," Frank said.

They streaked across the last thirty feet and stopped at the fence directly under the northeast tower. Roger handed him the cutters, and Frank found they cut the fence wire like it was made of butter. Folding back the small flap, Frank passed Roger the cutters and signaled for him to go. He squirmed through the hole and scurried to the outer fence. Frank followed, replacing the flap and making the fence look as pristine as possible.

Four minutes remained until the patrol returned.

Roger was already cutting through the outer fence when Frank joined him. Three more snips and the flap was large enough.

Freedom.

"Which way?" Roger whispered, his voice tight with anticipation.

Frank's stomach growled and he swallowed, tasting a brackish coppery taste that made him want to puke. For a fleeting moment, he almost considered giving up, like those crazy compulsions people got when looking down from a great height. You could almost feel your body willing itself to jump, as if all it would take was some small part of yourself letting go. But just as quickly as it came, the thought evaporated. It was time to move.

He grabbed Roger by the shoulder. "We'll head into the woods and follow the perimeter until we hit the dirt road."

Roger nodded and crawled through the jagged hole. Frank followed him, freezing in his tracks when the searchlight from the nearest tower snapped around, catching them in its bright, unyielding glare.

"*Halt!*" the guard screamed. "*Halt, oder ich schiessen!*"

Frank looked past Roger's panic-stricken face to the woods beyond and his heart sank. *God, no. Not now. Not when we're so goddamn close.*

The guard screamed again, and this time Frank heard the unmistakable sound of an MG34 machine gun bolt slamming home. In spite of the paralyzing fear that gripped him, something inside Frank clicked into place.

"Run!" he screamed.

Frank streaked past Roger, his expression a mixture of panic and grim determination. A split second later, Roger found his own feet and raced off after him.

The guard in the tower, perhaps more surprised at being disobeyed then at the escape itself, fired his machine gun, screaming hysterically. The noise of the MG34 drowned him out, its high cyclic rate sounding like the roar of a Harley at full throttle. Next, the siren wailed, guards shouted, and Frank's heart crashed against his ribcage. He ran faster, his feet thudding against the soft earth, his eyes focused on that black line of trees that never seemed to grow any closer. He prayed there were no rabbit or gopher holes ahead. If he hit one now, it would break his leg.

Behind them, the barking of the dogs joined the din as well as another of the MG34s. Tracer rounds whined past him, their phosphor trails leaving white-hot streaks on his retinas. Other bullets kicked up small puffs of dirt, stitching across the ground at his heels. Still more smacked into the trees just ahead, snapping branches and punching holes in the trunks. They sounded like slaps. He felt one rip past his head as he dived into the woods into a darkness so total, it scared him more than what he'd left behind. He stopped running and waited for Roger to catch up. The other man slammed into him, sending them both tumbling into the sharp undergrowth.

Scrambling to their feet, they turned to see a squad of guards armed with MP40s and Mauser 98k rifles barreling through the main gate. Mannheim waved them on, stamping his feet and bellowing orders. Bringing up the rear, two *Hundführers* tore past the burly sergeant, each with two of the husky Rottweilers on leashes.

"Come on," Frank said, pulling at Roger.

They plunged further into the woods.

Staggering blindly forward, Frank kept his hands outstretched, hoping some stray branch wouldn't find its way into an eye. He nearly tripped several times when his feet stumbled over fallen trees and thick, vinelike roots. He stopped again and turned. The guards had switched on flashlights; their sharp, brilliant beams stabbed through the darkness. As frightening as that image was, Frank realized he could now see what lay in front of him.

The dogs howled.

Frank ran on. That coppery taste was back, and his lungs felt raw, like someone had scraped them with coarse-grained sandpaper. If he didn't stop running soon, he'd drop.

The dogs drew closer, their barking intermixed with hungry growls.

Where was the goddamned road? How much further could it be?

Frank stumbled again, cursed, then realized the ground had begun sloping downward. Pushing himself to his feet, he let his momentum carry him down the gentle grade. Through the pines ahead, he saw a faint greenish light.

Mercury vapor lamps! The road!

A giddy feeling overtook him, the endorphins flooding his body giving him renewed energy. He pushed on, the light from that lonely streetlamp like a beacon to a storm-wracked ship.

An MP40 chattered and a bullet tugged the sleeve of Frank's leather flight jacket.

The road loomed closer.

He could see the blacktop glistening from the early morning dew, its smooth, obsidian surface sparkling like a billion sapphires.

The machine gun roared again as Frank and Roger broke out of the woods and onto the small two-lane road—right into the path of an oncoming car.

Frank gasped. It was too late—they were dead.

The car, a souped-up GTO, blared its horn, shrieking to a halt no more than six inches from them. The driver sat there frozen, his eyes bulging in fright.

"Are you guys crazy, jumpin' out in front of me like that?" he yelled out his window. "I coulda killed you!"

Frank ran around to the passenger side.

"We need your help. Someone's after us!"

The driver, a young man with long black hair and a leather vest, stared at Frank, taking in the World War Two uniform. His companion, a slim-hipped young blonde, gazed at him with equal incredulity.

The baying of the dogs grew louder, and the young man peered past Frank toward the woods. Following his gaze, Frank saw one of the guards emerging from the woods.

The young man's jaw dropped. "Get in!"

The door flew open, and both Frank and Roger dived in, barely making it inside before the driver popped the clutch. The car's powerful 400 cubic-inch engine roared, the rear tires screamed, and they shot off down the road at an incredible rate of speed. Frank spun around and looked out the rear windshield, seeing Mannheim emerge with the other guards, screaming his ugly head off. Frank sighed and slid down into the seat, his heart pounding like crazy.

Christ. It would just be his luck to get clean away only to keel over with a heart attack. Wiping his eyes, Frank glanced into the rearview mirror and saw the young man gawking at him again, his eyes even wider than before.

"What the hell is goin' on?" he yelled, his voice cracking. "Those looked like soldiers!"

Frank shot a look at Roger, who shrugged, as if to say, "you tell him." Frank leaned forward.

"How far is the nearest town?"

The young man shifted gears and tromped on the gas. The car roared again.

"In this baby... about a minute or so," he said, grinning proudly.

Frank grabbed the front seat, trying to counteract the G-forces that wanted to smash him back into his seat. "Have they got a police station?"

The young man's eyes narrowed.

"They got a sheriff, if that's what you're needin'."

Frank sank back in his seat and smiled for the first time.

"So, what was all that about?"

Frank sighed again. This kid wasn't about to let it go, and he supposed that he owed him some kind of explanation, even if it was a bald-faced lie. But what could he tell him that would make any sense? He smiled again, an idea popping into his head. It was just crazy enough to sound believable, and close enough to the truth not to be a lie.

"We're reenactors," Frank said, remembering Bob Neff's story from the bus. "We get together every now and then with a German group and play army. I guess they got a little overzealous this time. You know how it is."

Roger raised his eyebrows and Frank shot him a dirty look.

The young man laughed. "Lordy. I sure do. My Uncle Renny used to do that, seemed like every weekend. He used to tell me about the Civil War group he was with. Time and time again he—"

The car swerved as the young man's companion grabbed the wheel.

"Watch the road, Harlan!" she snapped. "My momma's gonna skin me as it is."

The young man cackled. "Thelma, honey, your momma and me is just like this. She loves my ass."

Thelma scowled. "You'll be lucky if she don't fill your skinny butt with buckshot."

"So where are you guys from, anyway?" Harlan said, ignoring his girlfriend's comment.

Before Frank could answer, the town came into view. A tiny thrill coursed through Frank when he spotted the sign:

Derleth, Wisconsin: Home of Cadby Dairy.

Dean was right. They *were* in Wisconsin.

From what he could see, the town had a single main street, consisting of about a dozen small shops. The garage/filling station looked as if it had popped right out of the 1950s. And like almost everything else in town, it was closed. The Sheriff's office, however, was definitely open. The amber light from its big plate-glass window spilled out onto the street, looking warm and inviting.

Harlan pulled the GTO up to the curb in front of the Sheriff's office and opened the driver's door, allowing Frank and Roger to climb out. Frank leaned down to the window.

"Listen, I sure would appreciate it if you would come in and tell them what you saw."

Harlan glanced at Thelma, then turned back, a sad smile on his face. "Sorry, boys. Thelma here is a bit shy of her majority, if you get my drift."

It was Frank's turn to smile. "That's okay. I appreciate the ride."

Harlan nodded back, a look of understanding in his eyes. "Give 'em hell, soldier."

With that said, Harlan stomped on the gas and the black GTO streaked away.

Frank turned and stared through the sheriff's front window, letting his eyes scan the small, sparsely furnished front room. The lawman dozed fitfully, his feet propped on the big oak desk, and his dark brown ranger hat pulled low over his eyes.

"I guess they don't get much action around here," Roger said.

Frank smiled wryly. "I think that's about to change."

14

When Sheriff Harry Dickson saw the two men enter his office, he knew trouble had come to his town. It was bad enough that he'd been awakened out of a sound sleep. He'd been having a delicious pornographic dream about Hilda, the new waitress at Gordon's Diner, the one with the giant hooters. He'd been drooling over her curvaceous form ever since she'd blown into town a month ago—him and every other male in town with blood pressure higher than zero.

Now with these two characters standing in front of him, he'd have to go to work, a prospect he avoided at all costs. And Dickson *hated* to work. That's why he'd taken the sheriff's job in the first place, after Lem Dibble died. That senile old fart had conked off right there in the office with his feet up on his desk.

Yep. That was the way to go, sittin' down easy and takin' it slow.

At thirty-nine years old, and a hair under six feet, Dickson could best be described as the Pillsbury Doughboy gone to seed. His receding hairline and round eyes gave him an owlish appearance completely at odds with the requirements of his job. Not that he ever had to get tough in a town like Derleth.

No, more than likely he'd throw Farley Thompson in the tank

every Friday night until he sobered up, or break up the occasional domestic squabble, and that was about it. The two men who stood in front of him now, dressed like World War Two flyboys, spelled nothing but trouble.

Heaving himself upright, Dickson pushed back his hat and tried to look businesslike.

"What can I do for you two?" he said, his gaze finally focusing.

Taking one of the seats in front of the desk, Frank plunged right in. "Sheriff, I know this is going to sound crazy, but my friend and I just escaped from a camp about seven miles from here. There are about three hundred of us being held there against our will. You've got to call and get some help down here."

Frank now had the man's full attention.

"A what?"

"It's like a German POW camp. We just broke out."

"And that explains what you're doin' decked out in these flyboy uniforms?" Dickson asked.

"That's right. You've got to help us, Sheriff. The man running the place is a lunatic."

Dickson frowned. This was beginning to sound like somebody's idea of a bad joke. Probably ol' Jess Rivers who owned the roadhouse two miles out of town. He could just see that toothless, old goat slapping his thighs, the tears streaming out the corners of his eyes as he turned red from laughing. This wouldn't be the first time Jess and his cronies had tried to put one over on Dickson. One of these days he would teach him a lesson, throw the fat tub into one of the cells and go fishing for a week. That would teach him, yes indeedy.

Dickson turned at the sound of the high-pitched laughter coming from the desk next to his. Toby Lennart, his deputy, sat there grinning like some stupid farm boy who'd figured out what his pud was for. Dim bulb.

"What's so funny?" Dickson asked, his tone making it plain that he didn't really want an answer.

Lennart guffawed, his hat tumbling off his head. It hit the floor, where a good-sized dust bunny attached itself to the brim. "Hell, Harry. Don't you know when someone's yankin' your chain? These boys came in Harlan Cutter's jalopy."

Dickson gave his deputy what he hoped was an appropriately withering glare, then turned back to Frank and Roger. He frowned again, his mouth curling into a contemptuous sneer. Yep. Ol' Jess was at it again.

❈   ❈   ❈

Frank gazed into the sheriff's disbelieving face and saw all his hopes evaporating. These two hicks thought that they were a couple of jerks out to play a joke. When he thought about all he'd gone through, including his harrowing flight through the woods, his emotions boiled over.

"Look! There are lives at stake here! The least you could do is go there and check it out."

The sheriff studied Frank for a moment, then acknowledged the challenge with a curt nod. He turned to the deputy.

"Toby, get on the horn to Bill Mathers downstate. See if you can get anything on two white males dressed in World War Two getups."

"Phone's out again."

The sheriff snatched up the receiver, listened, then slammed it down. "Can't keep nothin' running in this one-horse town. Go in the back and use the shortwave."

Toby's jaw dropped. "Harry, you're not buyin' into this crap, are you?"

147

Dickson slammed his palm onto the desk. "Goddamn it! Shut up and get on the radio! And use the headset. I can't stand that squawky thing."

Toby scowled and stalked out of the room. Dickson turned back to Frank.

"Okay, boys. I'm gonna give you one more chance. But you better talk straight with me."

Frank stared back, saying nothing, the silence broken only by the ticking wall clock and Lennart's voice mumbling into the radio's microphone. The sheriff shifted in his chair, then tore his gaze from Frank when his deputy returned.

Dickson raised his eyebrows in annoyance. "Well? Don't sit there with your thumb up your butt, Toby. What'd he say?"

"Bill said they're all tied up with some undercover op. Said to go ahead on your own and to file a report."

The sheriff nodded. "All right, then. We'll drive out to this POW place in the mornin'. Until then, I think it's wise you boys bunk down here for the night."

Frank smiled, relieved. "Thank you, Sheriff. We're obliged. By the way, is there a payphone I can use? I'd like to call my wife."

"Phone company took 'em out about two years ago. Didn't pay." Dickson stood up, his swivel chair squealing in protest. "Come on in the back and we'll fix you up."

Rising, they followed the rotund sheriff into the back where the holding cells were located. Pulling a ring of keys off his belt, the sheriff unlocked one of the cells, and Frank moved past him, seating himself on one of the iron-framed bunks. Roger hesitated a moment, his eyes scanning the bars, then joined Frank, taking the other bunk.

"Thanks again for your help, Sheriff. We don't know what we would've done if you hadn't believed us."

The sheriff cracked a dry smile. "I don't know that I do. Guess I should make that plain."

"But you'll check it out?" Frank asked, worried again.

The sheriff nodded, his eyes twinkling. "Like I said, fellas, we'll drive out there in the mornin'. Meantime, get some rest. War's over for tonight."

The sheriff wandered back to his desk, leaving them alone. Frank stared at the bars of the holding cell and chuckled. A moment later, he burst out laughing.

Roger looked at him, puzzled. "What's so funny?" he asked.

"I was just thinking. We escaped from one prison to spend the night in another."

When Roger didn't laugh, Frank knew something was wrong. "What is it?"

Roger turned his head so that he faced the ceiling. "My daddy was what you would call the town drunk. Every Friday night he'd drink himself silly, get beaten to a pretty pulp, and end up in a cell a lot like this one, most of the money from his job at the shoe factory pickling his liver. My mom would bring me and my younger brother down to the jail the next mornin' and she'd make us stand there watchin' him snore, his great big blubber belly hangin' out, and she'd say, 'You lookee there, boys. There's your future if you don't mind your Ps and Qs.' Never forgot that. When that sheriff brought us back here, it all came back."

Frank felt terrible. All he'd tried to do was break the tension with a little humor, and he'd put his foot in it instead. "I'm sorry, Roger, I had no idea—"

Roger shook his head and shrugged. "It's okay, no reason you should."

"Is he still alive?"

"Old cuss died of liver rot before I was ten... I miss him." He paused for a moment while old emotions held sway, then continued. "Funny thing was, even at that young age, I knew something was eating at him, something he couldn't—or wouldn't—let go of. I wanted to ask him what it was. I even went down to the neighborhood dive where he hung out, hoping he'd be in a jolly mood and would tell me. But when I asked him, his eyes got all weird, like a cloud had passed behind 'em. He just looked at me with those blank, watery eyes of his and told me to get the hell out."

Frank shook his head. "Jesus, that's tough. You ever find out what it was?"

"Not 'til the day he died, when I finally got up the courage to ask my mom. She told me he kept having nightmares every night about all the women and babies he'd killed dropping bombs out of his B-17 and would wake up sweating and screaming. He was a bombardier."

"What unit was he in?"

"The 333rd. Same one they assigned *me* to."

"Good unit. They flew out of the same base as my dad's—" Frank stopped talking as another thought flashed through his mind. "Say, that's funny..."

"What?"

"Most everyone I've talked to lost their fathers when they were real young. Me, you, Bob Neff. And all of us have been assigned to the squadrons they served in, whether we requested them or not. I wouldn't be a bit surprised to find out that it's the same with a lot of the other guys."

"What about Dana? I know for a fact that his father didn't even serve in World War Two."

Frank conceded the point with a shrug. "Obviously, he's a wild card. So is Dean, for that matter. His father served in the infantry and is alive and well and on his third wife."

"And Jensen? He's not exactly what I would call *authentic*."

"Not true. There were a number of blacks who served in the Army Air Corps. Some with distinction. No, I think there's a core group of us whom Koenig has handpicked to be here. The rest are filler, you might say."

"But why? What's his game?"

"I don't know..." Frank said. "It doesn't make much sense."

And then again, maybe it did. Perhaps someone in Koenig's past, someone he loved deeply, had been killed as a result of a mission flown by a unit within the 94th Bombardment Group, a group consisting of all the squadrons represented in the camp. Maybe it was something else entirely. Who the hell knew? But it did bear further thought.

"You may have something there, Frank," Roger said, nodding his head. "Of course, it really doesn't help us much at this point."

He had to laugh at that. Leave it to a pragmatic, hard-headed Yankee to cut through the crap right to the heart of the matter. This odd and disturbing coincidence, if that was what it truly was, really *didn't* help them in their current situation. But maybe, just maybe, it was the key to Koenig's madness.

"We should get some shut-eye, Colonel," Roger suggested. "To-morrow's likely to be a doozy."

The two of them fell silent, and Frank lay back on his bunk, his mind racing over the day's events. Using his bunched-up A-2 jacket as a pillow, he turned over on his side and closed his eyes, blotting out the glaring light from the fluorescent lights out in the hall. Some-time later, right before sleep stole over him, he heard Roger crying. His sobs cut Frank's heart like a scalpel, sounding like the weeping of a sad and frightened little boy.

The next morning, Frank and Roger awoke to the heavenly smell of brewing coffee—*real* coffee. Frank's mouth watered.

"Good mornin', fellas," Dickson said, carrying two steaming mugs into the cell. "I thought we'd go over to the diner and get us some breakfast 'fore we drive out to this camp of yours. How's that sound?"

"Terrific, Sheriff," Frank said, sipping the piquant brew. "This coffee's terrific, too, by the way."

"Why, thank you. It's one of my few skills," he said, chuckling.

After washing up in the closet-sized bathroom, Frank and Roger climbed into the sheriff's cruiser and they drove the quarter mile to Gordon's Diner.

Set catty-corner to the road, the diner was the embodiment of classic 1950s architecture: one-part railroad car, another part Airstream trailer, the interior had a cheery tackiness comprised of red Naugahyde upholstery and lots of metal-flake Formica. Seeing it brought a smile to Frank's face and, for the first time in God only knew how long, a feeling of security. A second later, the odors of frying eggs and sizzling bacon slapped him in the face like a physical force, making his stomach growl.

"Man, that smells good," Frank said.

"You said it," Roger replied, nodding appreciatively.

They took a booth in the corner and tried avoiding the open-mouthed stares from the other patrons. Frank snatched the hat off his head, feeling a little foolish; Roger followed suit.

A moment later, the waitress approached with the menus. All three of them stared unabashedly at the sultry young girl's magnificent 40-inch bust and the vicious curves of her hourglass figure.

"Hi there, Hilda," the sheriff said, a shy grin on his face. "How are you this fine mornin'?"

"Why, Harry, you gonna have another breakfast?"

Looking flustered for a moment, Dickson quickly recovered. "No, no. But my out-of-town friends wanted to sample some of Sam's fine cookin', and I just had to bring 'em by."

The girl gave him a saucy smile, knowing the real reason he'd stopped by. And then she frowned, her plucked brows diving toward her pert nose. She'd noticed the uniforms.

"You guys goin' to a costume party?" she asked.

"That's right, honey," the sheriff said, trying to move things along, "Now how about three orders of steak and eggs with toast and Sam's fresh-squeezed OJ."

"Comin' right up."

She walked away, her gait a marvel of biomechanics no one ever taught in school.

The sheriff turned to Frank and Roger, who watched Hilda swivel her way back behind the counter.

"Yep," he said. "I'd eat burnt toast and a rotten egg if she served it."

Frank and Roger swallowed. "Definitely," they replied in unison.

After breakfast, they got on the road. Retracing their steps from the previous night, Frank wondered if they'd be able to find the road to the camp again. Everything looked different in the daytime. Trees, road—everything. Apparently, the sheriff read his mind.

"Where'd you say this turnoff is?" he said, yelling to be heard through the bullet-proof partition.

"I think it's just around this bend," Frank said, hoping he was right.

When the cruiser made the turn, Frank bolted upright in his seat.

"Oh, no."

Stretched across the narrow blacktop blocking their way stood a cordon of half a dozen guards, armed with MP40s. In front of them, with a nasty grin of triumph smeared across his pockmarked face, stood Sergeant Mannheim.

The cruiser screeched to a halt, throwing Frank and Roger against the partition.

"What the hell?" the sheriff said, his eyes bulging in surprise. He shook his head as if to clear his mind of a mirage, then squinted as if that would somehow reconcile the incongruity of having armed *Luftwaffe* soldiers standing on a road in rural Wisconsin.

Roger grabbed his arm. "The deputy sold us out," he said.

Frank banged on the partition. "Get us out of here!"

Amazingly, Sheriff Dickson waved the comment off, smiling with misplaced confidence. "Relax, boys. Let me handle this."

Opening the cruiser door, Dickson heaved his bulk out of the car and waddled toward the Germans.

"What does he think he's gonna do, Frank?" Roger asked.

A moment later, they got their answer when the Germans raised their weapons and fired. In an instant, the sheriff's tubby body turned into a bloody pulp as dozens of rounds riddled him. His corpse, dead on its feet, danced like a spastic marionette. A second later, the firing stopped, and the sheriff collapsed onto the road, smacking the pavement with a wet slap.

"Out!" Frank screamed.

He reached for a doorknob, suddenly realizing that, like most police vehicles, the rear doors could only be opened from the outside. They were trapped.

"Goddamn son of a bitch!"

Frank battered his fists uselessly against the partition and slumped into the seat.

"How can they kill a sheriff, Frank? Someone will miss him!"

Frank met Roger's eyes and saw the horror in them.

"I don't think they care," he said.

Through the windows, Frank saw the guards coming for them. He didn't even bother to fight back when they dragged them out of the cruiser and marched them up that dusty road, through the gates to the *Kommandantur*. Koenig and Schmidt stood outside, waiting, their manner cool. With them stood Deputy Toby Lennart, a cocky smile on his hawkish face. Frank wanted to kill him. The guards halted them in front of the steps.

"What's gonna happen to us now?" Roger said.

Frank shook his head. "I don't know."

"Silence!" Mannheim shouted.

Koenig eyed them, then turned to the sergeant. "Take them to my office."

Mannheim clicked his heels, barked out the order, and four guards grabbed Frank and Roger and hustled them up the steps and into the *Kommandantur*.

Koenig turned to Lennart, his voice pregnant with menace. "They should have been here an hour ago. What delayed them?"

The deputy fidgeted, stammering out a reply. "H-Harry wanted to go to breakfast. He took 'em along. I tried to stop him, but—"

Koenig nodded to Mannheim, who hauled off and delivered a roundhouse punch to the deputy's gut. He folded like a limp rag, collapsing on the porch, gasping for breath.

"Idiot!" Koenig screamed. "You *never* show these men in public. Never! You return them to the camp immediately!"

"But, but—how could I?" Lennart whined, "with Harry wantin' to handle everything? He woulda suspected somethin'!"

Mannheim drew back his fist again and Koenig waved him off.

"Perhaps now that circumstance has smiled on you, you will make a better sheriff than Harry, *ja?*"

Lennart nodded rapidly, anything to appease Koenig. "Our deal... is it—"

"—still in effect? Quite. Only now you are to detain and report any suspicious people who arrive in town. Is that clear?"

"Yes, sir. Perfectly clear."

Koenig nodded to Schmidt, who pulled out an envelope fat with cash and tossed it to Lennart. The deputy's eyes lit up when he riffled through the thick stack of hundred- dollar bills. Then his expression clouded, an unpleasant thought occurring to him.

"What about Harry?"

Koenig smiled. "Let us worry about the late sheriff. Take the cruiser back into town, wait two days, and report him missing to the state police."

Lennart brightened again. "Yeah! I can do that!"

The deputy climbed to his feet, stuffed the envelope into his jacket pocket, and trotted across the quad and out the main gate.

Koenig watched him leave, then turned to Schmidt.

"I do not think we can entirely trust our new sheriff to... how do the Americans say it, 'mind the store?' Tell Hilda to seduce the *dummkopf*. Maybe then we will know *before* he does something stupid."

Schmidt started to leave, then turned back, his face troubled. "Did we have to kill the sheriff? Was it *really* necessary?"

Koenig stared at his adopted son, his eyes growing cold. "Nothing must stop us, Johann. Nothing. The war will only be won with eternal vigilance and merciless retaliation. We... cannot... falter..."

Koenig's voice trailed off and his face again became like that of a department store mannequin: blank and featureless. His mouth hung open and a thin string of drool oozed out of the corner. Alarmed,

Schmidt stepped forward and grasped Koenig's arm, shaking him gently.

"Heinrich! Heinrich, please."

Just as quickly as he drifted off, the light returned to the old man's eyes. Eerily, his conversation picked up exactly where it had left off, as if nothing had interrupted it.

"Have the guards bury our dear, departed sheriff in the woods, and wash the road."

A look of sadness crossed Schmidt's face; he bowed and clicked his heels. "I shall attend to it at once, *mein Kommandant*."

Koenig nodded curtly, turned on his heels, and strode into the *Kommandantur*.

※　※　※

Frank and Roger sat in the *Kommandant's* office, trying to avoid the intimidating glare of the guard watching them. He stood unmoving, his finger curled around the trigger of the MP40 aimed at them.

Behind them, Frank heard the stomp of boots in the outer office. The guard immediately snapped to.

"*Achtung, der Kommandant!*"

The door swung open and Frank and Roger stood. Koenig crossed the room and sat behind the desk. Mannheim entered a moment later, taking a position to his right.

Koenig stared first at Frank and then at Roger. Frank wondered just what it was he was thinking. After another minute, when the tension in the room peaked, Koenig's face broke into an easy grin.

"Well, Colonel Murphy. I see you have gotten into the spirit of Camp Stalag. Here two whole days and already you have tried to escape."

"Yeah, and I'd do it *again*. Except this time, I wouldn't go to your stooge."

"I'm sure you can agree that a facility such as this must have its friends on the outside, *ja?* Deputy Lennart is but one of many my largesse has established."

"Yeah, I'll bet," Frank said, disgusted.

"Nevertheless," Koenig said, "an example must be made. You and your comrade will spend five days in the cooler on one-quarter rations."

Frank stood up and looked Koenig straight in the eye.

"Piece of cake, *Kommandant.*"

Koenig smiled, his eyes glittering like malignant jewels.

"Maybe so, Colonel. Next time you will wish you had stayed put. Or rather, your family will."

Frank exploded. "You touch them and I'll kill you, you crazy old man!"

Koenig's expression hardened.

"Take them," he said.

"He's going to be trouble," Schmidt said, after the door had closed.

"I would not worry about it. After five days on one hundred calories a day, he will be in no shape to cause any."

15

Brenda Murphy lay on the bed, watching the shadows of the trees outside her bedroom window dance across the opposite wall. The lace curtains added snowflake patterns that undulated with the soft breeze wafting through window, accompanied by the buzz saw whine of the cicadas. It had been almost a week since Frank had left, a week that stretched into untold hours of loneliness.

Not that she hadn't kept busy. With little Julie becoming ever more mobile and demanding of her attention, she scarcely had time to think, much less worry. Still, there were the lazy times, the quiet moments in the dark when she would climb under the sheets and suddenly realize Frank wasn't there, that he wasn't about to come out of the bathroom in his pajama bottoms—those tacky red silk ones she both loved and hated—talking about some juicy tidbit from his day at the store. Moments like those made her feel that her life was complete.

And now, lying there watching the morning sun twinkle through the maples, she felt that hollowness deep inside, as if half of her soul had been ripped away. *My better half*, she thought. And though the phrase was a hoary cliché, Brenda knew it was true in her case. Frank was so much more easygoing, so quick to forgive, while she held grudges lasting for years. He blew a fuse and it would all be over, while she would stew for hours. Some people, her parents includ-ed, thought they complemented each other perfectly. Yin and Yang. And so she believed, more so now that he was gone.

The baby monitor sitting on her nightstand squawked with a stream of static. And then Julie's soft cries pierced her thoughts, bringing her back to reality. *I don't know how single mothers manage,* she said to herself for the thousandth time, and in the same breath she hoped she never had to find out.

Brenda threw off the bedclothes, pulled on her robe, then went into the nursery. Julie was still asleep, her cries the momentary stress of an infantile dream. Tears flooded Brenda's eyes. Poor little But-ton. Ever since Frank left, Julie had cried and fussed, as if sensing her father was not going to come back.

And there it was—the thought she dared not think.

Frank would see that life without her was great, and he would skip out on her with some young bimbo. Of course, the idea was preposterous. Frank was as loyal a husband as one could ask for, but she couldn't shake it from her mind.

She returned to the bedroom, shed her nightgown, and padded into the bathroom. Staring at herself in the full-length mirror, she turned first one way then the other. Nothing sagged—yet—nothing wrinkled, and her tush and thighs were still creamy smooth. "You still got it, girl," she said, smiling to herself.

Reaching into the shower, she turned it on, adjusted the tem-perature, and stepped inside, letting the hot, stinging spray cleanse her mind as well as her body.

Obviously, she couldn't expect a grown man to want to be with his wife every minute. She remembered plenty of times when Frank had been underfoot, and she'd banished him from the house while she got her chores done. And though the house still rang with the shouts and laughter of rambunctious children for hours at a time, it felt empty with him gone.

Out of the shower, Brenda toweled off, making herself relax and remember that he would be home in only a few more weeks. Besides, Uncle John was looking to have Frank start his new job as soon as he got back. He had no choice.

After feeding the Julie and seeing Pete off to school, she cleaned out the master bedroom closet of clothes they had decided to give away. That left more space for new clothes—hers. Brenda smiled, thinking of Frank's mock dismay over his shrinking allotment of hanger space.

At noon, she spotted the mailman arrive, stuff the mailbox, and drive away. She made sure Julie was secure in her playpen, then walked out and retrieved the contents. There was a flyer from the local PTA about an upcoming meeting, the phone bill, the gas bill, and a letter—one of those funny-looking flimsy ones they used in Europe. She held it closer, and her heart fluttered. The address was in Frank's handwriting, and it was stamped with a New Hampshire postmark.

Brenda tore it open and read it quickly, hungry for anything from him. At first, what he had written made no sense. *"Make sure to tell Pete that one of the guys saw a Black-Backed Three-Toed Woodpecker... I know he loves his birds..."*

Was Frank losing his mind up there in the wilderness? He knew damn well that Pete cared little about anything other than sports, computer games, and cartoons. She read it again, coming to the part about staying at the camp longer. She could just imagine Frank having the time of his life and deciding—on impulse—to change his plans. It wouldn't be the first time. There was only one problem with that. Frank would not let Uncle John down and jeopardize his financial future over something like this. Something was wrong—she felt it. And yet, she resisted the urge to panic.

And then her eyes found the letter's last line.

She stared at it, a part of her mind unwilling to digest the awful implications couched in that innocuous sentence: "*...I'll be back in time for Julie's first birthday.*"

Julie was thirteen months old. She'd had her first birthday *last* month. There was no way Frank would *ever* forget that. Something had happened, something terrible, and Frank was trying to warn her the only way he could.

Brenda stood frozen by the mailbox for several minutes, letting all this sink in. She tried reading the letter once more to convince herself she was imagining it, that maybe this was a gag he and Dean had cooked up, but she couldn't see the words through the veil of her tears. A small whimper escaped from her while she ran back into the house.

In Frank's office, she turned on the Power Book and waited for it to boot up.

"Come on, come on," she said, smacking her thigh with her hand. "Hurry the hell up."

When the computer finished booting, she brought up Internet Explorer for Mac and typed in: *www.campstalag.com* in the command line. A moment later, a 404 page came up:

SORRY, THE PAGE YOU REQUESTED WAS NOT FOUND.

"Oh, God."

In the kitchen, she fumbled for her address book, trying to keep from dissolving into a blubbering mess. Julie began to wail in her playpen, as if sensing her mother's distress.

When she found the number she wanted, Brenda punched it into the phone, misdialing it twice before getting it right. The phone rang six times—an eternity.

"Marge?" she said.

"Brenda, honey, is that you? You sound all funny."

"It's me," she said, her voice breaking.

"What's wrong? Is it the kids? Are they okay?"

"They're fine, Marge."

"Well, I'm glad. You know I keep pestering Dean that we oughta have them while I'm able. You know I'm not getting any younger..."

Brenda wanted to scream into the phone, tell Marge to shut up and listen, but she let the other woman prattle on for another two minutes until a momentary lull in the other woman's monologue gave her an opening. She made her voice sound as calm as possible. "Have you gotten a letter from Dean?"

Marge sighed. "Is that all? You had me worried, honey. Yes, I got one just this morning. Can you imagine? Those men are going to stay another two weeks. I swear I don't know how they can run a business that way—"

Brenda squeezed her eyes shut and slammed down the phone, cutting off Marge Seger in mid-chatter.

She held herself, rocking back and forth in the chair. "Oh, God. Oh, God. Oh, God!" She had to get a grip on herself; she was flying apart. She had to think.

He's not coming home.

Another anguished cry escaped her throat, the thought refusing to be banished. She knew that damned DVD was trouble from the moment she saw it. Why hadn't Frank listened to her intuition? Why did men always have to be so damned stubborn?

"Shit!" she screamed, knocking a cutting board off the counter.

It clattered to the floor, rebounding off the refrigerator, finally coming to rest near the garbage compactor.

Julie cried harder.

"Sorry, Button," she said. "Mommy's just a little upset right now."

She went to the phone again and dialed her parents in Boston. As usual, her mother picked up after the first ring. "Hello?"

The voice had a slight quaver to it now, but it still sounded warm, loving—safe.

"Hello, Mom."

"Sweetheart!" she said, her tone brightening. "How are you?"

In spite of the panic she felt, her mother's soft contralto calmed her, allowing her to think. "I'm fine, Mom. I was wondering if you and Dad could take the kids for a little while."

"Is everything all right? Did you and Frank have a fight?" she said, her voice taking on an edge.

If it had only been that, Brenda thought. She swallowed and continued. "No, Mother. In fact, Frank wants me to join him in New York. He's finishing up a convention, and he wants to make it a second honeymoon."

She hated lying to her mother, but the truth would only upset her and complicate an already insane situation.

"That sounds so romantic, dear. Of course we'll take the children. Lord knows, your father certainly loves to spoil Pete and Julie."

"As soon as I have my flight information, I'll call you and let you know."

"All right, dear. Give my love to Frank."

She hesitated a moment before answering. "I will, Mother. Love you."

Hanging up the phone, Brenda realized she no longer felt frightened. Anger and rage replaced it—anger at Frank for putting her in this situation, and rage at these crazy people who would kidnap three hundred men for their own perverse pleasure. "Damn it!" she said.

Looking at her daughter, she realized Julie had stopped crying and was staring at her mother with wide, curious eyes.

"You pissed off, too, Button?" she asked, smiling when her child's mouth split into a wide gap-toothed grin. "No? Well, we're going to go get your daddy from that bad old stalag. How about that?"

"Gaaaahhh!" Julie screamed.

Scooping the child out of the playpen, Brenda brought Julie upstairs and put her down for her nap. Then she began to pack. Normally fastidious when it came to preparing for a trip, she stuffed items into her suitcase, not caring if they were color-coordinated or if they got wrinkled. The anger she felt before returned with a vengeance, but now she controlled it, rather than having it control her. It smoldered under the surface, waiting for the moment to burst forth in all its fury.

She imagined a moment where she could wrap her hands around the neck of this Johann Schmidt, whoever he was. Oh, how she relished that thought.

With the suitcase stuffed full, she carried it down to the front hall, then went into Frank's office to call the airline. She was placed on hold, and while she waited, her eyes found the portrait of Frank's father sitting on the desk in its silver frame. Part of her wanted to grab it, smash the glass, and rip the old photo to scraps, while screaming, "*It's all your fault!*"

But blaming a dead man for the mistakes made by his son was

silly. Almost as silly as blaming the son for his father's transgressions, as if sin was something one could inherit. She'd never held with that aspect of her Catholic upbringing. Original Sin. What nonsense. It was dogma designed by a privileged few to hold power over the many. No one who looked into the innocent eyes of their own child could *ever* believe that.

"I just wish you hadn't made that awful war seem so damned glorious," she said to the man in the photo. "Couldn't you see what you were doing to him? Couldn't you see that he worshipped you?"

But the picture remained mute, a ghost captured in silver nitrate. And it was just as well, for her husband hadn't heard her, either.

A moment later, the airline reservationist came on the line. The only flight available departed from Hartford at six o'clock in the evening. She booked two tickets, one each for herself and Pete. Because Julie was still under two, she would fly free, as long as Brenda held her in her lap the whole way.

When Pete got home, he squealed with excitement when told he would be missing school and flying to see his grandparents. Brenda smiled while he ran around the living room yelling at the top of his lungs. At least someone would be having a good time.

After scrambling to get Pete and Julie packed, she put them all in the Volvo, drove to Hartford, leaving the car in the public parking lot just outside the airport. From there, they boarded the shuttle bus that would take them to the terminal. Brenda's apprehensions rose when the bus made stop after stop. She passed the time by studying the faces of her fellow travelers, wondering what sort of problems they worried about. Could any be as crazy as hers?

The shuttle dropped them at their terminal, a little over an hour ahead of their scheduled departure time, and Brenda tried to figure out a way to tell Pete about his dad, a way to cushion the blow. She decided to tell him the truth; she owed him that. Besides, she couldn't bear the thought of lying to him as she had to her mother.

"Pete," she said. "I want you to listen for a moment, okay?"

He nodded and looked at her expectantly.

"The men who run the camp your daddy's staying at have decided to play their game for real—"

"You mean they won't let him go?" Pete asked.

There was no pulling punches with this one. "Yes," she said, expecting him to burst into tears.

"Wow," Pete said, his eyes wide.

Looking at his rapt expression, Brenda couldn't decide if she wanted to laugh, cry, or both. "You're going to have to promise me something, okay?"

Pete nodded again, his blond head bobbing. Brenda suppressed a smile.

"Your grandma thinks I'm going to New York to meet your Daddy for a vacation. But I'm really going to try and help him. You've got to promise me that you won't tell Grandma or Grandpa what I've told you. Promise?"

"But, Mom, isn't the truth better?" Pete asked.

For once, Brenda wished she hadn't been so scrupulous with her children's upbringing. "Yes, the truth *is* better... but I don't want your grandparents to worry, honey," she said, putting her arms around her brood. "They've had a hard life and want to think their family is all right. You see what I mean?"

Pete nodded.

She hugged him tight against her, tears stinging her eyes. He squirmed in her arms, having now entered the phase where his mother's affection caused embarrassment in public.

Breaking the embrace, Brenda glanced toward the gate. A uniformed attendant had arrived to check in the passengers.

"Okay, I'm going to check us in. Stay here and watch your sister, okay?"

"Okay, Mom," Pete said.

She got up and walked toward the desk.

"Mom?"

She turned and looked at her son.

"I promise," Pete said.

Brenda beamed. She was not happy at the situation, but she was very proud of her son.

On the short flight to Boston, Julie slept while Pete became engrossed in his Game Boy, the beeps and buzzes thankfully silenced by earphones. The landing into Logan was swift and without incident. Brenda said a silent prayer when the wheels touched the runway. She hated flying.

Carry-on luggage in hand, they waited until most of the passengers left the plane before making their way down the aisle and into the terminal. Brenda's mother and father waited just inside.

Herb and June Lewis were in their late sixties and had lived in Boston all their lives. Brenda recalled the first time she brought Frank home to dinner during their junior year at Boston University—a lifetime ago. Seeing them standing there brought tears to her eyes. They looked so old. Had her father shrunk, or had she somehow grown bigger? She used to find him so imposing, a big man with a bigger heart.

When Pete saw them, he cried out and ran to them, his nascent self-consciousness already forgotten.

Brenda, cradling Julie in one arm and the stroller in the other, hung back for a moment.

"How are you, you little dickens?" June said, hugging the boy.

Herb folded his arms in mock indignation. "What? No hugs for Grandpa? I guess I'll have to take your surprise back to the store."

"Surprise?" the boy yelled.

"Yessiree. I can't get you one every time," he said, opening his arms.

"You always say that, Grampa!" Pete said, hugging his grandfather. The older man laughed and squeezed the boy with his spindly arms.

June turned to her daughter and embraced her. "Oh, sweetheart. It's been too long."

At those words, Brenda's carefully constructed facade crumbled like an old tenement. Clutching her mother for dear life, she cried, her body quaking with each heartrending sob. Herb, sensing it was time for women's talk, herded little Julie and Pete off into a corner.

June let her daughter cry herself out and then took her aside and sat down.

"It's Frank, isn't it? Is it another woman? Has that man been unfaithful to—"

"Oh, Mother, I wish it were that. I really wish to God it were that."

Brenda stared off into space for a moment, trying to fit all the pieces together so they would make sense. Signaling her father, she waited until he and the children were settled around her before explaining. She told them the whole story from the moment Frank received the DVD until his letter arrived in the mail. Somehow, recounting the story helped her regain the hold on her anger, something she both wanted and needed.

"I wasn't going to tell you because I didn't want to worry you. But I just realized I have nowhere else to turn. I need you to look after the kids while Uncle John and I look for him. Of course, that's assuming he'll help me."

June placed her hand over her daughter's.

"Brenda, honey, we're glad you told us, and of course we'll help, any way we can."

Brenda felt the oppressive weight lift off her shoulders for the first time all day.

"John's a good man," Herb said. "He was the best cop I ever worked with. If anybody can find him, he can. And don't you worry, he'll help, or I'll brain him."

Her father shook his fist and grinned. Brenda threw her arms around him. "You're the best, Daddy," she said, another tear escaping from the corner of her eye.

Herb pulled back, his expression that of a hard-nosed cop on a case. "Do you have any evidence, anything for John to go on?"

"I brought everything. The DVD and copies of all the emails from the people responsible for this," she said.

He patted her thigh. "Good. You sit tight and I'll go call him."

He rose and walked over to the bank of pay phones, his hands groping his pockets in search of coins.

Brenda glanced at her mother and caught her staring. The older woman had a questioning look. "Tell me something, dear. Why did Frank do this? It sounds kind of—"

"Crazy?" Brenda said, giving voice to the word her mother had obviously wanted to avoid. "I've thought about that a lot, Mom. I think Frank needed to prove something to himself."

Her mother nodded. "Your father was the same way, always volunteering for extra details that scared me green for half my life. He kept saying we needed the money, but I knew better." She nodded, looking to her husband with a twinkle in her eyes.

"My God, Mom, I never had any idea. Why didn't you tell me?"

June grasped her daughter's hand and squeezed, a tiny smile turning up the corners of her mouth. "We didn't want to worry you, sweetheart."

Touché, Brenda thought.

Her father came back, his face flushed with excitement. "He'll see us tomorrow at eleven."

Later that evening, after a home-cooked meal of meat loaf and mashed potatoes, she put the children to bed and spent the rest of the evening watching an old Humphrey Bogart movie with her parents, finally going to bed just after two.

It felt odd and confining to lie in her old twin bed with its lacy canopy and frilly pillows, listening to the familiar creaks and groans the house made at night. And yet, it was all somehow warm and comforting.

The next morning, Brenda and her father rode from her parents' home in Newton to downtown Boston. She yawned continuously as they headed down the Mass Pike. Her old room still held all the knickknacks and memories of childhood, but the bed seemed lumpier than she remembered. Then again, maybe she was just getting old. She smiled, recalling the teddy bear that had mysteriously appeared sometime in the night. Remarkably, what little sleep she had gotten occurred after its appearance.

Mother knew best.

Her father's late-model LeBaron cruised down Boylston Street, passing the Public Library with its hideous modern extension, and the newly renovated Copley Park. Turning right onto Clarendon, he slowed when the street became bottle-necked from one of the ever-present road crews tearing up the streets. She looked out her window and watched Trinity Church in all its Romanesque beauty glide by. As always, it took her breath away. Up ahead lay the entrance to the John Hancock Building's parking garage.

After parking the car, they rode the swift, silent elevator to the thirtieth floor. Tucked into the northeast corner suite were the offices of John Riley Investigations. When they walked into the reception area, Brenda didn't know whether to be impressed or disappointed. She supposed that, like a lot of other people, she fell victim to all the romantic notions of Dashiell Hammett and Hollywood, expecting frosted glass doors with something like "Spade and Archer" painted on them.

Instead, the offices were decorated in a modern and masculine style. Exquisite Oriental throw rugs covered the thick beige Berber carpeting, each reflecting the eclectic, yet harmonious color scheme. The paintings and metallic sculptures adorning the walls were high-lighted by a soft, warm lighting that seemed to grow out of the pieces themselves. The receptionist's desk was a thick slab of malachite supported by trunks of dark mahogany carved with African tribal designs.

"Good morning," the receptionist said, greeting them with a warm smile, "you must be Brenda. Please come with me. Mr. Riley is expecting you."

The woman led them down a long corridor lined with the stuffed heads of African game, each accompanied by a picture from the matching safari. Reaching a large mahogany door, the woman knocked softly then pushed it open.

The office itself was over six hundred square feet, and maintained the decor exemplified by the outer offices. The desk was an immense piece of burled walnut, its top inlaid with tooled leather. Behind it, through a tinted picture window forming the entire wall, stretched the most spectacular view of the Boston skyline she had ever seen. The effect was both stunning and intimidating.

Riley looked up from his work, grinned, and rose from behind the desk. "Herb!" he said, grabbing the older man in a bear hug. "You old dog. You look great. Retirement agrees with you."

Herb laughed. "Retirement, hell. I can still run down a perp with the best of 'em." He paused, his eyes scanning the room. "You've done well, Johnny, but I think you'd best lay off the Guinness at Clancy's."

Riley glanced down at his paunch and laughed, then he clapped the older man on the shoulders. "You always had a way with words, Herb."

"Hello, Uncle John," Brenda said.

Riley turned to Brenda, sweeping her up in his arms. "And how are you, Short Stuff?"

At the sound of her old tomboy nickname, Brenda broke into tears.

"Hey, hey. What is this, what's wrong? What's Frank done now? Has he hurt you—"

Brenda shook her head. "He's missing, John. I don't know what to do. I—" She fell silent and stared out the window, tears streaming from her red-rimmed eyes.

"It's gonna sound crazy, Johnny," Herb said. "I hardly believed it myself. And after forty years on the force, that's saying a lot."

Riley frowned. "Let's talk about it," he said, easing into the chair behind his desk. "Tell me everything."

Brenda sat in the butter-soft leather chair opposite the desk and retold the strange and incredible story she'd come to look upon as her personal nightmare. Riley took notes while she spoke, his expression growing more intense as detail followed detail.

"May I see the DVD and the emails?" he asked.

Brenda handed them over.

Hefting the DVD in his callused hands, Riley stood up, strode over to an entertainment center adjacent to the wet bar, and inserted the disk into a high-priced DVD player. Moments later, the room filled with the sights and sounds of Camp Stalag.

Hearing that German accent again sent a chill down her spine. She turned away from the screen, unable to bear watching it again.

Riley studied the screen, his piercing, blue eyes darting back and forth, missing nothing. After the DVD ended, he watched it again, then turned his attention to the emails and then the DVD booklet. When he saw Heinrich Koenig's biography, his mood shifted from concern to dread.

"Have either of you been watching the news lately?" he asked.

Brenda and Herb looked at each other and shrugged.

"No. Why do you ask?" Brenda said.

"Heinrich Koenig has been reported missing after failing to show up for the annual Koenig Industries board of directors meeting in New York City a week ago."

Brenda shook her head, confused.

"Brenda," Riley said, "Heinrich Koenig is one of the five richest men in the world. He's worth billions and has connections to the highest levels of our government. I'd be willing to bet those billions that he's the same Heinrich Koenig mentioned in these materials and your husband's letter."

"How can you be sure, Uncle John? The name might be just a coincidence."

Riley hesitated only a moment before dropping in the final piece of the puzzle.

"His adopted son, *Johann Schmidt*, is also missing."

"Oh my God!" Brenda said, her carefully controlled composure cracking apart.

"What can we do, John?" Herb asked, putting his arm around his daughter.

"As much as I hate to throw business to a competitor, so to speak, I think we should call the FBI. This is a kidnapping, plain and simple. Solving this kind of crime is what they do best."

"You'll help?" Herb said.

"Absolutely. I'll do whatever I can. In fact, I know someone in their Boston office."

Brenda got up out of the chair and walked over to the window. It was midday, and she could see traffic building up in Copley Square. Looking northward, her eyes followed Route 93 toward New Hampshire.

Hang on, Frank, she thought. *Please hang on.*

She turned from the window, a glint of steel in her gaze.

"Call them," she said.

16

Bob Neff lay on his bunk, staring at the ceiling, the faces of his wife and two kids dancing in front of his eyes. Would he ever see them again? That thought chilled him. And what's more, he didn't know if he could just sit around anymore waiting to find out.

And what about my business? he thought. He'd taken time out to come on this trip just after completing the grueling negotiations on a major merger. There was nothing unusual in that; he usually took time out afterward to recharge his batteries. He *needed* to get away. And yet he could tell his partner wasn't happy about the timing on this one, for there'd been a rush of smaller, yet equally lucrative deals that rode in on the coattails of the major one. He'd promised to be back in time to sort everything out. And now here he was, rotting away in this godforsaken camp. He had to get out. But how?

Sitting up, he swung his feet onto the floor, slipped into his brown lace-up shoes, and crossed to the door. He paused, listening to the laughter and chatter from the others in the main room. How could they laugh like that when Frank and Roger were still in the cooler?

He pushed the door open, walked into the main room of the barracks, and met a thick haze of cigarette smoke. Bill Jensen, Freddie

Richards, Dean Seger, and Dana Webster sat playing poker, using non-filtered cigarettes in place of regulation chips. Judging by the huge pile in front of Jensen, it looked as if the big Texan was winning. Some of the other men stood around kibitzing, while the rest either lounged or dozed on their bunks.

Jensen spotted him out of the corner of his eye and looked up from his cards. "Where you going?" he asked.

"Out for a walk. What difference does that make to you?" Bob replied, irritated. He started for the door.

Jensen shrugged, pulled out two cards, and threw them face down on the table. "Gimme two," he said to Dana, who was currently acting as dealer. He collected his cards, placing them in his hand. A flicker of annoyance crossed his face. "It don't make a particle of difference to me," he said to Bob. "But you might wanna watch your butt, since it'll be lights out in about fifteen minutes."

Bob gave him a flippant salute. "Yes, sir! I'll be sure to give your regards to the goons." And then he walked out.

Jensen shook his head. "That boy's gonna get his ass shot off, fer sure." He threw down his cards with a loud guffaw. "Full boat, boys!" His hand consisted of three aces and two kings.

"Aw, damn," Freddie said, throwing down his cards in disgust.

Dean said nothing, his mind obviously preoccupied with his friend.

Dana smiled, watching the last of his cigarettes disappear into Jensen's pile. "It's a good thing I don't smoke."

"Yeah, well, it's a good thing you can't play cards, either."

Dana smoldered, prompting another loud burst of laughter from Bill Jensen. "Oh, come on, kid, lighten up. There's a few trick's you gotta learn, that's all. And it's a good thing you got the master to teach you." With that said, the big Texan divided up his pile of cigarettes into four smaller mounds, sliding one each to Dean, Dana, and Freddie. Then he grabbed the deck, shuffling the cards with professional aplomb. A wicked grin spread across his face. "Now, boys, let's play cards!"

❋ ❋ ❋

Outside the barracks, Bob stood watching the searchlights, feeling lonelier and more frightened than ever. He turned up the collar of his A-2 against the night air, thrust his hands into the pockets of his khaki trousers, and struck out across the quad, intending to make a fast circuit of the camp. Maybe that way he'd be able to clear his mind, think of something. The letter he'd written home, or rather the letter he'd been forced to write, was filled with platitudes and innocuous phrases. Mannheim made him rewrite it three times, until it said exactly what the bastards wanted it to say. Other than that missive, his family would hear nothing.

He stared at the section of the perimeter fence where Frank and Roger had cut through and made their getaway. It had been repaired and a permanent guard posted. Now that the goons knew of the blind spot, they had decided to get rid of the no-man's-land altogether, filling the empty space between the fences with a jumbled mass of loose barbed wire. That avenue of escape was now closed off forever.

As for the *Hundführers*, they now roamed throughout the camp at will, taking great delight when their Rottweilers decided to snap at one of the prisoners. It made for a lot of tension in the ranks, as if things weren't bad enough with the extra roll calls and the surprise bed checks at all hours of the night.

Coming abreast of the *Kommandantur*, Bob halted in his tracks. A light burned in the *Kommandant's* office, the golden glow spilling onto the ground outside the barred window looking warm and inviting. He could see Koenig bent over his desk, writing briskly. Was he actually sitting there pretending to do fifty-year-old paperwork?

Suddenly, Bob had a crazy idea. He struck out toward the *Kommandantur*, his heart in his throat. It *was* a crazy idea, nuts in fact. But his feet kept going, taking step after step, drawing closer to the glowering guard standing outside the front door. The guard's eyes flicked toward him when his left foot touched the bottom step leading to the porch.

"*Halt! Was ist los?*" the guard said, bringing up his MP40.

Bob saw the goon's finger tighten on the trigger and his bowels loosened. Why the hell was he doing this?

"I wish to speak with the *Kommandant*," he said in perfect German.

The guard, surprised to hear the mother tongue spoken so fluently by an American, nodded curtly. "Wait here," he replied. He turned on his heels and marched through the door. A moment later he returned and beckoned with the barrel of the machine pistol.

Bob followed the guard through the antechamber and into the *Kommandant's* office. Koenig sat behind a great carved desk, his uniform as crisp as if it were just donned. He smiled and motioned for Bob to take a seat.

"Normally, I would not have allowed this visit, as you are not the Senior POW Officer. However, since Colonel Murphy cannot be here, I decided to grant your request. Tell me, where did you learn to speak German? You took my guard quite by surprise."

Bob shifted nervously under the man's hawkish gaze, aware of all the expensive trappings of the room. His eyes glanced over Koenig's shoulder, taking in the ice-blue stare of Adolf Hitler's portrait.

"My grandmother taught me. She was from the old country."

Koenig nodded and smiled. "Ahh, yes. Have you ever been there, *Leutnant...*"

"Neff, Bob Neff. And no, I haven't."

"A pity. And please, do forgive me, *Leutnant*. We have only just begun our adventure, and I do not as yet know the names of all the prisoners. But there is ample time."

There was that smile again, like a serpent.

Bob coughed. "Uhh, that's sort of why I came, *Herr Kommandant*."

"Yes?"

"I need— Well, you see how it is. I've got commitments at home, and well, I need to get back as soon as possible."

Koenig's smile turned brittle at the edges, his eyes narrowing slightly. "I understand, *Leutnant*. I understand very well, indeed. But you must know that repatriation in time of war requires special circumstances."

Bob shook his head. "Time of war?"

Koenig stared at him.

"Oh, yeah, right, time of war, sure. What *are* special circumstances?"

Koenig reached for the decanter on his desk. "Brandy, *Leutnant*?"

"Sure, why not?" Bob said. He followed it with a smile. If this old coot wanted to continue the game, who was he to argue? Koenig nodded and poured the amber liquor into two snifters, handed one of them to Bob, then leaned back in his swivel chair. He paused, the snifter halfway to his lips. *He's waiting for me*, Bob thought as a fleeting thought of arsenic poisoning passed through his brain. Realizing how silly that thought was, Bob raised the snifter to his lips and took a swallow, nearly choking as it burned its way down his throat.

"Nice," he said, nodding appreciatively.

"Now, as to your question, *Leutnant* Neff. Repatriation would occur if the prisoner were either incapacitated, or dead. And you look quite healthy. Of course, one never knows in these trying times."

Bob's anger rose. This old fart was playing him like a prize fiddle. Well, no more. "Listen," he said, rising from his chair. "It's been real fun, but I've got to get home. My family and my business need me. Now, I intend to pack my things and get a good night's sleep. Tomorrow, I'm going to walk out that gate, and all the way home, if I have to."

He started for the door, when suddenly it burst open, and there stood Sergeant Mannheim, his eyes blazing with hateful glee.

"Mannheim, show our guest back to his chair," Koenig said.

Bob whirled on Koenig, his finger jabbing the air accusingly. "Now, wait one damn—"

He never got to finish the sentence. Mannheim spun him around and smashed him in the solar plexus, doubling him over.

"Careful, Sergeant, we do not want him marked."

Tears streamed from Bob's eyes as he fell back into the chair, gasping for breath. Koenig came out from around the desk and stood over him, gazing down with contempt.

"I will make a deal with you, *Leutnant*. You will keep me informed of the prisoners' plans, and I will allow you to leave Camp Stalag—and your family to live. If you fail to 'deliver the goods,' as you Americans say, I will have them killed—one by one."

Bob could hardly believe his ears, and yet through all the pain, tears, and humiliation, he found he still had an ounce of defiance left to fight back. Raising his head, he glared at Koenig. "You can't do that, this is a free country."

Koenig roared, and Mannheim allowed himself a sardonic grin. "I most assuredly can, my dear *Leutnant*. And it is all so simple, really, precisely *because* your country is free. Your strengths are also your Achilles heel. A few paltry dollars in the right grubby hands and suddenly those brakes on the family Buick give out on a steep grade, little Amy is raped and murdered on the way home from school by assailants unknown, your wife disappears without a trace... Shall I go on?"

"H-How did you know my daughter's name?"

Koenig leaned in toward Bob's face, his voice becoming a seductive caress. "I know everything, *Leutnant. Everything.*"

Bob hung his head and wept, his slumped shoulders shaking uncontrollably. He was beaten. No matter what Frank had said, he knew that nothing could protect Helen and the kids if some maniac—this maniac—wanted to harm them. "All right," he sobbed, wiping his runny nose with the back of his hand. "I'll do it. I'll do it, damn you!"

"*Ausgezeichnet, Leutnant, sehr gut.*" Koenig placed an understanding hand on Bob's shoulder, perched there like some flesh-colored parasite.

"Serve me well, and those gates will open for you, *Leutnant* Neff, as they will for no other. You will walk out a free man, safe in the bosom of your loving family." Koenig's grip tightened on his shoulder, his hateful voice becoming a whisper in Bob's ear, making him flinch with loathing. "Your father would be so proud."

Bob's anger renewed itself. He knew that his father would hate him for what he'd agreed to do. And yet, he also knew with a dreadful certainty that unless some miracle occurred, he would never see his family again.

17

For the umpteenth time, Frank wondered what time it was—what *day* it was, for that matter. After the first "day" in the cooler, all the familiar landmarks marking the passage of time became a jumble. Cooler. Now there was an oxymoron of epic proportions. Aside from historical origins, the name bore no relation to the reality of the temperature. A windowless concrete cubicle, it retained most of the day's searing heat long after the sun dropped below the horizon, leaving him just this side of delirium.

And as near as he could tell, he'd been in there four days. It might even be the fifth; he didn't know. Food consisted of a few chunks of black bread and a thin, watery soup. The guards supplied water spottily and only to stave off acute dehydration.

Kommandant Koenig did not wish him to die, only to suffer.

At first, Frank played word and number games while whistling tunelessly in that dark little room. He spent part of the first day calculating the exact dimensions of the room he could not see. He then catalogued all its physical blemishes by touch. The concrete felt slick from the bodily fluids leeching out from his pores.

The room measured exactly six by six by seven. Stretching himself, he could just touch the ceiling, which consisted of rough-hewn

183

beams of pine overlaid by tightly fitted boards. The cracks, he surmised, were caulked with some sort of tar or pitch. After exhausting all his mental exercises, Frank let his mind wander.

That's when time slipped away. That's when he began to lose it. He couldn't even count on the regularity of the food and water that appeared through a tiny slot in the bottom of the door. He would be daydreaming and the slot would shoot open, blinding him with the bright artificial light streaming through. He always had to take a moment for the spots to stop swimming in front of his eyes before he could grab the meager portions sitting in the battered tin bowl.

The food, barely enough to sustain him, left his body progressively weaker until he lay sprawled near the door, too listless to move.

Yes, Frank thought, *my sentence must be nearly over.*

Feeling drowsy, he let sleep steal over him. It passed the time more quickly. Sometime later, it could have been a minute or several hours, Frank awoke when two pairs of arms yanked him to his feet. He tried opening his eyes, but the light hurt too much, and he ended up with a blinding headache right behind each orb. Staggering drunkenly when a spell of dizziness struck him, he tried in vain to keep his legs moving while the two guards dragged him out of the building.

Everyone stood at attention in quad.

Roll call.

The two guards hauled him to a spot near the *Kommandant's* soapbox and held him there. That was okay with him. Frank knew he would fall over if they didn't.   Two more guards dragged Roger Putnam alongside. He stared off into some point in space, acknowledging nothing.

Christ, he looks like shit.

And then Frank realized he probably looked just as bad.

"*Achtung!*" Mannheim screamed. "*Der Kommandant!*"

Koenig emerged from his quarters and took his place on the soapbox, surveying the prisoners with an icy glare. Schmidt followed swiftly in his wake, taking a position just to his right.

"All present and accounted for, *Herr Kommandant!*" Mannheim said, saluting.

Koenig returned the salute. "At ease, Sergeant." He fell silent for a moment, relishing the prisoners' despair, and then he spoke, his voice booming across the flat, dusty ground. "I have just heard on Radio Berlin that our glorious forces have repelled an Allied attack at Remagen Bridge. Rommel is moving like lightning in North Africa, and the Russians are fleeing in the face of our tanks. We will soon be victorious."

Even in Frank's depleted condition, he knew none of what he heard made sense. These events had occurred in different years. If the Germans were trying to pretend that World War Two still raged, wouldn't they at least have the facts straight?

Staring at the *Kommandant*, Frank saw the queer light in the old man's eyes and felt a bone-deep chill. Koenig really *believed* the war was on and that they were somewhere in Germany.

The look of worry etched into Schmidt's face told him something else: *the old man is losing his mind... and Schmidt* knows *it!*

"All of you men," Koenig continued, "must now realize the futility of further resistance or escape. The two men you see before you are examples of what each and every one of you can expect if you try to escape. We will not tolerate a second attempt. Mannheim! Dismiss the men."

Mannheim saluted, turned on his heels, and screamed, "Dismissed!"

The four guards holding Frank and Roger upright let them collapse to the ground and marched off. Immediately, a group of prisoners, led by Dean and Bob Neff, lifted them up and carried them back to Barracks 2. Once inside, they stretched them out on their bunks and fed them scraps hoarded from previous meals.

"Here, Frank, eat this," Dean said, holding his friend's head. It was the same old stale black bread, but it tasted like manna from heaven. Frank wolfed it down; his stomach growled for more.

"After that, you get this," Bob said, pulling a bruised apple out of his pocket.

"Oh, God," Frank said, his mouth watering. "That looks great."

"Don't talk," Dean said. "Eat!"

After the apple and a chocolate bar someone bribed from one of the guards, Frank felt his strength returning. They left him alone, and he realized that he could no longer keep his eyes open. In seconds, he fell into a deep, dreamless sleep.

When he finally awoke, he discovered that he'd slept right through to the following morning's roll call. He eased out of his bunk, walked outside the barracks, and took a quick tour around the camp, noting the heavier guard and the coils of barbed wire filling no-man's-land. He also noted the general malaise.

But it was while he watched the men play softball that he formulated an idea, and the more he thought about it, the better it sounded.

After the game, while everyone relaxed in the barracks, Frank emerged from his quarters. He'd shaved and washed in the barracks' small lavatory as best as he could and changed into his one spare uniform. He felt better today—still shaky, but better. Taking a deep breath, he strode into the room, a look of grim determination on his face.

"Listen up, everyone," he said, scanning the room. "We're not giving up. I've got another idea, and, if we work together, I promise you all we'll make it out."

No one said a word. He should have known better. The blank, apathetic stares greeting his statement only proved how hopeless they all felt. He couldn't blame them. He'd given them hope, and he'd let them down.

"Look, I know we blew it, I know it looks hopeless, but I've got another idea."

"Look, Colonel, *you* blew it, not us," Jensen said. "I, for one, am sick and goddamned tired of this shit. No matter what Koenig says, he's gonna have to let us out of here sooner or later, so let's just enjoy ourselves and not sweat it."

Frank couldn't believe what he'd heard. The man's stupidity would have been laughable had their situation not been so critical. "Do the rest of you feel this way?"

"Not all of us," Dean said, after a moment. "But we've been talking to some of the men in the other barracks and they're all for sitting it out."

"Sitting it out? Did you guys hear that little speech out there? Koenig's round the bend. He's nuts." He strolled down the length of the room, looking at each man and shaking his head. "You know, I'll bet you all have yourselves convinced that this is part of Koenig's little game. Well, I'll tell you what his game is. Power. Power to do whatever he wants, whenever he wants to do it. You think he was still playing the game with that grandiose little speech of his? Well, I've got news for you guys, Koenig really *believes* the war is still on."

"Oh, come on, give us a freakin' break!" Jensen said, standing up from the table where he'd been practicing card tricks.

"I mean it. I was watching Schmidt while Koenig spoke. He looked *worried*, like he couldn't believe it was happening."

"Hell, that don't mean shit. Maybe you ain't screwed on so tight, either?"

Frank's even temper boiled over. He launched himself at the bigger man, shoving him against one of the walls. He was still weak, but the surprised expression on Jensen's face let Frank know that he wouldn't fight back.

"I've just spent five days in the goddamn cooler with nothing but the roaches and a bucket of my own crap to keep me company!" he said, nose to nose with the startled man. "You think *that* was a little game? Then *you* try it! And while you're in there, you can stew on this! They've kidnapped three hundred men and moved them across state lines. That's a felony with multiple life sentences for all involved. If you think they're just going to let us walk out of here, then you're in worse shape than Koenig." Frank let go of Jensen and turned to face the rest of the men, his voice deadly calm. "When this little game is through, and you all know it will be, sooner or later, they're going to use those guns—*on us*."

The truth behind Frank's words finally pierced everyone's mind. Now, there was no doubt they had to get out before Koenig ended his game. More than likely, as the old man sank ever deeper into his fantasy world, circumstances would force Schmidt to give the order, and Frank did not like that prospect at all.

"What do you have in mind?" Roger said from his bunk.

Frank smiled. After five days in the cooler, Roger's spirit had not dimmed.

"We're going to dig a tunnel."

"What?" someone said.

"Did he just say a tunnel?" someone else blurted out.

Everyone began jabbering and shouting questions.

Frank held up his arms. "Guys! Guys! Hold it down a minute."

"Frank," Bob said. "How are we gonna dig it? We've got no tools."

"I know it sounds crazy, but we *can* do it. I've thought the whole thing out."

Frank went on to explain his plan in detail. The camp would begin cultivating vegetable gardens in front of all the barracks. This would give them the cover needed to get rid of the dirt.

"As for tools, we'll have to improvise, make them ourselves."

"What about shoring?" Dean asked.

"Come on, you guys, am I the only one watching the late show?"

Walking over to a bunk, he threw off the flimsy mattress, revealing the bed boards underneath.

"We've got three hundred bunks in camp. If we get a few boards from all of them, we'll have enough."

"Yes!" Freddie said, clenching his fists.

"How far do we have to dig it, Frank?" Dana said.

Striding to the back wall, Frank pointed through the window to the woods beyond. "From the barracks to the fence is about ten feet, another ninety to the woods. Add it up."

"It'll take us six months to dig that far!" Jensen said.

"Hold on a second," Dean said. "I've known Frank for a long time. He's had some kooky ideas, and this probably tops them. But what choice do we have, guys? What else are we going to do?"

Dean's words reminded them all of what Frank had told them moments before. Their fate now rested with them.

"I'll make it easier for us," Frank said. "We'll come up halfway between the woods and the fence."

"That's nuts! They'll catch us," Jensen said.

"Maybe. But if we time it right, we can duck out one at a time while the searchlights and the patrols are focused elsewhere."

"There's another idea," Dean said.

Everyone turned toward him.

"When we're ready to go, we'll have someone in the barracks across the quad stage a diversion, light a fire or something."

"That's it!" Frank said, delighted with his friend's ingenuity. "But it's got to be a *big* diversion, enough to pull *all* the goons over to one side of the camp. Dean?"

"Yeah, Shakespeare?"

"Can I leave this in your capable hands?"

"Count on it," he said, giving Frank a thumbs up, along with his Eddie Haskell grin.

"Who all is goin' this time, Colonel?" Jensen asked.

"*All* of us."

Everyone chattered at once, their voices blending into a low-pitched roar while they planned, schemed, and dreamed of getting out—of seeing the last of Camp Stalag and all it represented. In all the excitement, however, no one noticed Bob Neff slipping quietly out the front door, a look of despair etched into his face.

✠   ✠   ✠

Schmidt watched the old man while he listened to the vintage Blaupunkt radio for news of the war. Increasingly, Heinrich Koenig lost touch with the here and now, preferring to believe that Adolf Hitler lived, and the *Wehrmacht* triumphed. The *Führer's* raspy bellow poured out of the old radio's speaker sounding vital and intense, as if he were speaking right at that moment, rather than fifty-odd years in the past. The old man listened raptly, and every once in a while, would comment on something Hitler said in a feverish murmur reminding Schmidt of the homeless beggars he recalled seeing on the streets of Boston. It broke his heart.

After the speech came several announcements and then a program of Wagner. Annoyed with the music, Koenig switched off the radio and sat back in the large leather chair that dominated his living quarters, lost in thought. Schmidt, taking this as his cue, walked out of the room and into the *Kommandant's* office, closing the door softly. He moved to the closet along the same wall, opened it, felt for the secret button, and pressed it. A small panel slid open with a soft hiss. Inside an area the size of a common wall safe sat a compact disc player and a small stack of CDs. He opened the player, extracted the disc, and replaced it in its plastic jewel box.

He reached for another, studying the plain white label:

RADIO BERLIN: June 8–15, 1942.

Schmidt had taken hundreds of hours of the old wire and wax recordings and had them transferred to compact disc in preparation for the day when Koenig would begin confusing the present with the past. It was better to humor the old man rather than have him listening to static.

He recalled the first time back in Wellesley when he found Heinrich trying to tune in Radio Berlin. He'd looked so lost and bereft. Schmidt couldn't stand seeing him like that. With Koenig's money, it had been easy to make the CDs. With enough money, anything was possible.

Placing the new disc in the player, he closed the panel, then the closet door, and walked back into the living quarters. He found Koenig pacing the floor.

"If the allies think they can invade us, they are mistaken, Johann. The *Wehrmacht* will crush their feeble army. We must expand the camp. There will be hundreds of new prisoners to contend with, and there will be no time to lose."

Schmidt was at a loss for words while he watched the pathetic display before him. The old man was worse than he thought. How much time did he have left? It was a question that nagged at him night and day, and yet he pushed it from his mind each time, unwilling to face the inevitable.

"Yes, *Herr Kommandant*. I will begin construction immediately," he said, not knowing what else to say.

"*Ausgezeichnet*," Koenig said, rubbing his hands together with glee. "Announce to the prisoners that anyone volunteering for work detail will receive double rations..."

The old man stopped in his tracks, a look of confusion crossing his face. He looked to Schmidt, his eyes filled with anguish. "I—I have been drifting again, haven't I, Johann?" he said, holding up his trembling hands.

Schmidt tried to think of something to say that would ease the old man's heart, but nothing sounded right.

"Maybe you should rest, Heinrich. It has been a great strain with the escape attempt."

"No!" he said, jumping to his feet. "We have to be vigilant, Johann. They will try again. You can be sure of that. The Inspector General may arrive at any time. We *will* show him a model camp. Order the work details at once."

"Yes, *Herr Kommandant*," Schmidt said, his heart sinking. "It shall be done."

***

Frank waited until the afternoon before going to the *Kommandant's* office. He wanted to make sure that the Koenig would be in a good enough mood to grant his request. Their whole plan depended on it. Truthfully, he had waited because he was afraid to see the man. There was no way to predict whether he would be magnanimous or maniacal. That he was dangerous, there was not a shred of doubt.

Crossing the quad, Frank saw a lot of the men seated outside their barracks, sunning themselves and talking. Others played volleyball, and still more were engaged in a spirited game of touch football, laughing and shouting as one team crossed the makeshift goal line. Ever since he'd revealed his plan to the men, their mood had skyrocketed. That gave Frank the confidence to face Koenig.

He would do this for them.

Stepping onto the *Kommandant's* porch, he ignored the menacing glare of the guard and knocked on the door. A voice called out from inside.

"*Herein!*"

Frank opened and walked in, coming face to face with Schmidt.

"Ahh, Colonel Murphy," he said, his jocular air an obvious front. "What may I do for you?"

"I have a request from the men."

"Yes?"

"I need to speak with the *Kommandant.*"

Schmidt's face clouded. "I am sorry, but I cannot allow you to disturb the *Kommandant*. Give your request to me."

This was not what Frank had counted on. He couldn't be sure Schmidt would relay it.

"Maybe I should come back later—"

The door behind Schmidt opened, and Koenig stepped out.

"Johann, I need to— Ahh, Colonel Murphy, what a pleasant surprise."

"I have a request from the men, *Kommandant.*"

"Very good, Colonel. It just so happens that I wish to speak with you. Please, come into my office. Johann, accompany us."

Inside the office, Frank took the chair opposite the desk, his nervousness returning. Behind Koenig, the portrait of Hitler glared down at him with haughty contempt, making him even more uneasy.

"What may we do for you, Colonel?" Koenig asked. He had an amused expression on his face, as if he took great pleasure from some secret that only he knew. Oddly enough, this calmed Frank down.

"The men were wondering if we could start a vegetable garden in the quad. As I'm sure you know, the food is sometimes less than inspiring, and a few vegetables might keep us from getting scurvy."

Frank tried to gauge Koenig's reaction, but the man's face was a mask, betraying nothing of what he thought. Finally, he broke the silence. "I think that is an excellent idea, Colonel. It also will keep your men occupied and not thinking about escape."

Frank smiled thinly. "Thank you, *Kommandant*. The men will appreciate that. Of course, we'll need some tools and some seeds."

"You shall have the tools. We also will count them every night and keep them under lock and key."

Frank nodded.

"As for the seeds," Koenig continued. "*Hauptmann* Schmidt will procure them for you."

"Great. Now, you said you wanted to speak with me?"

"Yes. I would like you to tell me where the 410th Bombardment Squadron is based," Koenig said, all lightness gone from his voice.

"What?" Frank couldn't believe what the man had just said. What the hell was going on?

Koenig smiled patiently, though his eyes retained a cold, unbalanced gleam. "I want to know where your bomber group is based, Colonel. They are doing great damage to our munitions factories, and Berlin wants answers. So, I ask you again. Where is it based?"

Frank turned to Schmidt, looking for some kind of explanation, but the younger man continued staring straight ahead, refusing to meet his gaze. Frank decided to be brash, to see just how far gone the old man was.

"Why don't you look it up in the history books?"

Koenig's eyes narrowed. The room became deathly quiet. The only sounds remaining: the ticking desk clock, a small fly buzzing angrily against the window, the tap of Koenig's pencil, as well as his own breathing, filled his ears with a roaring cacophony.

"Your name, rank, and serial number will only get you so far, Colonel," he said. That infuriating look of amusement returned. "We will continue this another time. Dismissed."

Frank trudged out of the *Kommandant's* office in a daze. The man hadn't heard what he'd said. *The man heard me recite my name, rank, and serial number!*

Gazing out over the quad, the confidence he'd fought so hard to attain evaporated, replaced by a gnawing anger and despair. He knew his plan would work; the question was whether any of them would live long enough to dig their way out.

18

Two days had passed since Riley placed the call to the FBI's Boston office, and he was growing concerned. He was not concerned for his friend, whom he figured was busy with his caseload, but for Brenda, who kept calling him every hour, it seemed, looking for any scrap of information.

When he returned from lunch late that afternoon and checked his messages, he discovered that his old friend, Special Agent Tony Carter, had finally called back. *Thank God*, he said to himself.

"Becky? Would you get Tony back on the line, please?"

"Yes, Mister Riley," she said.

Scooping up the mail, he strode into his office, closed the door, and sat behind his desk. A quick sort separated the checks from the dross, which he left for his secretary. His intercom buzzed.

"I've got Special Agent Carter on the line for you, sir."

"Thanks, Becky. Put him through."

"Well, Sport," the raspy voice said, "when are you going to let me win back some of that money?"

"As soon as I have some to lose," Riley said.

There was a deep chuckle on the other end of the line, acknowledging their long-standing ritual.

"How are Rachel and the kids?" Tony asked.

"They're fine. Tommy got his scholarship to Harvard, and Lisa's all excited about entering high school. Rachel's still chairing the Women's League Fine Arts Committee."

"Uh-oh. Sounds like you get dragged around to too many gallery openings."

Riley laughed. "Yeah, after a while, they all begin to run together. I swear if I have to drink one more glass of champagne and eat one more canapé, I'm gonna throw up."

"Well, we can't have that... Listen, I'm sorry for not calling back sooner. I was out of town on a case. Got promoted to the Anti-Terrorist Unit."

"Hey, you hit the big time! Congratulations!"

"Don't congratulate me yet. The case is ongoing, and it's a real ball-breaker."

"Bad, huh?"

"Believe me, you don't want to hear about it. So, what can I do for you?" Tony said, bringing the small talk to a close.

"Tony, I've got a really strange case. I think it's a little more in your line than mine."

"I've seen some bizarre ones in my time. What's up?"

"An old friend of mine brought his daughter in. She was about to fly apart at the seams. Said her husband was being held against his will in a German POW camp somewhere in New Hampshire."

"What?" Tony laughed, but there was an edge to his laughter, something indefinable.

"I know, I know, but listen to me for a sec. I know these people—have for many years. They wouldn't waste my time making up stories."

"I believe you," he said, turning businesslike. "Give me the rundown."

Riley then related Brenda's story, leaving nothing out. When Riley mentioned that Heinrich Koenig might be behind it, that edge in Tony's voice reappeared.

"Koenig is big stuff, John. His board of directors is going a little nuts trying to find him. Koenig Industries stock took a big nosedive when it leaked out that he didn't show for their monthly meeting and might be missing. They called us right away. What makes you think it's him?"

"I'm not sure, but I think it bears looking into. According to my client, he may be holding more than three hundred men. To me that spells kidnapping—*big* time."

"Well, you're right about that," he said.

There was a significant pause before the FBI agent spoke again. "Let me look into this and call you back. It might take a couple of days."

"That's okay. Anything you can find out I'd appreciate."

"No problem. Give your family my best," he said.

"I will, my friend. Take care."

Riley hung up the phone feeling significantly better about the situation. He resisted the urge to pick up the phone to call Brenda, but there was no sense in calling her back until he knew more.

One point nagged at his mind, however: that cautious edge in Tony's voice. To Riley, it sounded like fear. Of course, he could have imagined it. Tony was a pretty tough guy who'd seen his fair share of field action. Still, Riley had long ago learned to trust his gut instincts. They'd saved his ass on more than one occasion.

He left the office at five and drove into Wellesley, searching for Koenig's estate. He knew it was a waste of time, his gut was telling him that, and yet his years of experience also told him that leaving any lead hanging was a big mistake. He'd broken many a case simply because he refused to ignore any detail, no matter how insignificant.

As for Koenig's home, Becky had found the address in the mailing list of one of the local civic charities. It had taken her five minutes to sweet talk it out of one of the male staffers. Koenig may not have listed his name in the phone book, but anyone donating the kinds of sums that he did soon found their addresses appearing on lists sold and distributed to other needy causes all across the country.

Riley recalled the sheer hell he went through trying to get the post office to stop delivering requests for money to his house and office. If there was ever a law needed, he thought, it was one restricting junk mail.

He spotted the narrow driveway leading to the estate when he passed it. Cursing, Riley swung his late-model Lexus LS 400 around and headed back toward the house. He marveled at the length of the driveway as it wound its way through blossoming dogwoods and stately oaks. Unfortunately, he soon found the way barred by a wrought-iron gate set into a formidable stone fence topped by jagged pieces of broken glass. The house itself was hidden from sight by a grove of ancient fir trees, standing in formation like resolute sentinels.

"Damn. Now what?" he said.

He looked closely at the gate and noticed an intercom system recessed into one of the granite posts. Climbing out of his car, he approached it, spotting a video camera mounted high overhead tracking him while he moved. Concluding that he was already being watched, he relaxed and pushed the buzzer on the polished brass plate.

He waited five minutes before someone answered.

"Yes?"

The voice, cold and clipped, sounded machinelike through the small, tinny speaker.

"Yeah, I'm looking for Mr. Heinrich Koenig. I have a delivery for him."

"*Herr* Koenig is not in residence," came the response.

"Oh. Well, maybe you could tell me when he'll be back," Riley said, beginning to lose his patience. "It's real important that he receive this package. It's from the Board of Directors."

"Where is the package?"

Riley frowned and then remembered the camera. "It's in the car," he said. "Can I at least bring it up to the house? It doesn't matter who signs for it."

Even with Koenig gone, one could never tell what might turn up at his house, perhaps the very clue it took to bring the case to a speedy close. Riley waited, his request greeted by the silent hiss coming from the speaker. After a few more seconds elapsed with no response, he grew annoyed.

"Hello?" he said, pressing the buzzer again.

Finally, a crackling noise issued from the intercom followed by the equally useless reply. "*Herr* Koenig is away on business. I have been instructed to let no one on the premises until he returns."

Riley sighed. He was getting nowhere with this single-minded chump. "All right, thanks," he said.

"...For nothing," he muttered, climbing back into his car.

He made it back to the office in twenty minutes, grabbed his mail and messages off Becky's desk, and walked into his private office. There were two from Tony Carter and one from Brenda Murphy. Riley sighed. He could sense her desperation, even through the innocuous phone message. He wished he had something to tell her, but there just wasn't anything they hadn't already considered.

And the immediate future looked no brighter.

He was about to pick up the phone when he saw that both of

Tony's messages said not to call the office—*no matter what*. Becky had underlined the last three words.

Strange. Why would Tony care if he called him at his office? He'd done so countless times before.

Deciding to play along with his friend, Riley opted to try him at home; he was about to dial the number when Becky buzzed him.

"Excuse me, Mr. Riley. I've got Tony Carter on the line."

"Thanks, Becky," he said, snatching up the phone. "Hey, Tony, what's up? You sound like you're calling from the Callahan Tunnel."

The street noises filtering through the handset pointed out the obvious: Tony was calling from a pay phone and he sounded worried—*very worried*.

"John, I haven't got much time, so listen to me carefully. Get off this case!"

The vehemence with which those words were spoken shocked Riley.

"What the hell are you talking about? I just can't dump a client."

"For your own good, you'd better," he said.

"What's going on? Talk to me."

Riley heard Tony let out a long, protracted sigh.

"All right. But we've got to meet. I can't tell you this stuff on the phone."

"Where?" Riley asked.

"You remember that spot up north we visited last summer?"

"Yeah."

"Meet me there tonight—nine o'clock."

"What the—"

The phone clicked and buzzed. Was Tony cracking up? Maybe the pressure of the job and his recent promotion had finally taken its toll. Riley knew what that was like. One day you're on top of your game, and the next thing you know you're a basket case... or dead. Yeah, Riley knew all about that. He'd seen too many good men become casualties of their jobs. At least he'd had the sense to retire when he did, before it all came apart at the seams. Now he could pick his own cases, set his own hours. Rachel still complained, but at least she didn't have to fear that dreaded phone call in the middle of the night.

Now he had the same jittery feeling he had during those last days on the force: that the world was about to fall on his head.

❋ ❋ ❋

The 4x4 jounced along the lonely dirt road, transmitting the shock from every rut, stone, and chuckhole up through Riley's tired bones. With every twisted mile that passed, he became more and more apprehensive. Tony had sounded scared, really scared. And that did nothing to alter Riley's growing dread. What could be so bad that it would frighten a man of Tony's skill and training? Riley wasn't so sure he wanted to know. But he couldn't let down Herb and Brenda. That would be worse.

Riley braked when he came to a familiar bend in the road, and the 4x4 rolled to a stop. His ears filled with the incessant, nocturnal sounds of the New Hampshire wilderness: crickets, frogs, and the eerie call of a loon from the nearby lake. *Am I too early*, he thought? He stared into the woods, thankful for the moonlight streaming through the trees.

Then, like a pair of monstrous, glowing eyes, two headlights blinked on and off. For a fleeting moment, he wondered if it was really his friend out there. Christ! He had to stop thinking like that. Thoughts like that got you killed. Then again, so did curiosity. But he couldn't turn back now; he was in too damn deep.

Throwing the 4x4 into gear, Riley roared off into the woods, crashing through the underbrush, nearly hitting a tree in his haste. Soon, he reached a small clearing, surrounded by lofty pine trees and carpeted in wild grass. It lay empty, save for one other vehicle: a familiar Jeep Cherokee with a dent in the right front fender. Tony stood by the driver's side door, his expression unreadable.

Shaking his head, Riley shut off the engine and stepped out of the 4x4, feeling the soggy ground squish beneath his boots. While he walked the short distance to the other man, his stomach heaved when he caught the stench of some dead animal. He and Tony stared at each other a moment, and Riley saw fresh lines etched on his friend's face. He looked about ten years older.

"You okay?" Riley asked, extending his hand.

Tony grasped it, his manner remaining grim.

"I've been better," he said.

"Well, you certainly have a flair for the dramatic. What've you got?"

Tony's expression hardened and his eyes darted off into the woods, as if he were expecting unwanted company.

"You sure you wanna hear this?"

Riley nodded.

"All right, then. But I hope the hell you have the sense to *listen* to what I'm going to tell you."

Riley's eyebrows shot up. "I'm standing out in the middle of nowhere, and you ask me that?"

"I'm sorry for that, John. Believe me, I wouldn't do this if I didn't think it was necessary."

"It's okay. Don't sweat it."

Tony sighed and rubbed his eyes. "This thing is big, really big—"

"You've known about this all along, haven't you? That case that took you out of town..."

Tony nodded, looking off into the dark. "I couldn't say anything to you over the phone. And if my superiors were to learn I was talking to you now—"

"Come on, we've known each other too long. Spill it."

"Koenig's always been a loose cannon. It's no secret he hates Americans, but that didn't stop him from coming here after the war and making billions manufacturing high-tech weaponry."

"But how could he just disappear with three hundred guys?"

"He didn't. We know exactly where he is."

"So, you're going in?

Tony's looked away, embarrassed. "We can't," he said.

"What do you mean, you can't?"

"Look, I've told you more than I should. Trust me. This is bigger than you can handle."

Tony started back to his Jeep Cherokee. Angered, Riley grabbed him by the arm. "So that's it? You drag me out into this field, feed me a bunch of bullshit, then tell me to stay out of it?"

"Sorry. It's the best I can do."

Tony opened the door to his Jeep, and once again, Riley grabbed him, this time spinning him around. "Sorry doesn't cut it. Damn it, Tony, you owe me!"

Tony met Riley's angry glare, his own eyes narrowing. "All right, then, have it your way. But this makes us even."

Riley nodded, acknowledging that a line had been irrevocably crossed, perhaps even ending their friendship. *The hell with it*, he thought.

"Koenig's got a tactical nuclear device," Tony began. "The same kind he supplies to the military."

"Where did he get the plutonium?" Riley asked, keeping his emotions in check.

"You remember hearing about that nuclear accident in Krasnoyarsk?"

"Yeah."

"As near as we can tell, the Russians concocted the story to cover up a theft of weapons-grade plutonium, enough for several bombs. We think Koenig bought some of it on the black market. But we can't be sure."

"How do you know he's got it, then?"

In spite of the chill in the air, Tony wiped a film of sweat off his brow. "Satellite recon photos of the camp. We can tell if there's any radioactivity beyond the normal background."

"And..."

"It's right smack in the middle of it. And what's worse is Koenig's threatening to blow the damn thing if we come within twenty miles of his precious camp. No troops, no flybys, no presence."

"He can't be everywhere. How would he know?"

The FBI agent grimaced, as if he'd tasted something vile. "He's got his own satellite, John—"

"Jesus!"

"We're tracking him... and he's tracking us—a goddamn Mexican standoff."

"How big's the bomb?"

Tony hesitated.

"How big, damn it?"

"An MK-57 has a blast yield of five kilotons, can vaporize a couple of city blocks, and leave everything around it lightly damaged, with minimal radioactive residue. It's designed so soldiers can move in immediately afterward."

Riley paled.

"Christ."

Tony placed a comforting hand on his shoulder. Riley wanted to shake it off.

"We're doing the best we can," Tony said. "Besides, in addition to his eye in the sky, Koenig has his own security force, plus a wide network of highly paid informants. We can't afford to tip our hand."

"What *is* your hand, Tony? What are you going to do?"

Tony stared back, saying nothing. Riley nodded, understanding his friend all too well. "You're going to sacrifice those men."

"They're dead, John. And so is Koenig. He's got brain cancer. We checked with his doctors in Zurich. Koenig's never coming out, not without a fight. And you can't fight someone with nothing to lose! If we do *anything*—it'll turn into another Waco, or a Ruby Ridge. And the Bureau can't take another hit like that. Not again."

Disgusted with his friend, Riley turned away. Tony grabbed him. "I'm sorry about your nephew, John, I *really* am, but do you know what we're dealing with here? A group of Nazi terrorists holding hostages in the middle of the United States! The only thing the government is interested in is damage control."

A flicker of guilt passed over Tony's face. Riley ignored it. "You *want* the place to blow. And if Koenig doesn't finish the job, you bastards will burn the trimmings."

Tony nodded, his expression hardening. "That's right... The story ends here. And if you get in the way, I won't be able to help you... You'll burn with the trimmings. Go home, John... Forget you ever heard about this."

"Maybe you'd like to tell that to my client and her two kids."

Again, Tony was silent.

"I thought so," Riley said, retracing his steps to his 4x4.

Tony called out to him, his voice tinged with urgency. "Don't you see, John? A military leader with the means and the acumen to take on the United States. A madman with no fear."

Riley slammed the door to the 4x4, pushing his key into the ignition and twisting it. "Yeah," he mumbled. "Just like World War Two."

※　※　※

Tony watched Riley's 4x4 retrace its route back through the woods, knowing in his heart that he'd lost a friend—perhaps the best friend he'd ever had. It felt, he realized, a little like death.

The 4x4 shimmied and shook as it climbed over a fallen tree, and Tony kept watching until the red of the 4x4's taillights winked out in the darkness, then he turned back to his Jeep.

From out of the woods a sharpshooter team appeared, dressed in camouflage fatigues, their stolid faces smeared black with greasepaint. Each carried a semiautomatic .50 caliber Barrett Sniper rifle. Matte black on every surface, the rifle boasted an 11-shot magazine, laser sights, and pinpoint accuracy to one thousand yards. The men could place a half-inch group at that distance with iron sights on their worst day.

The team leader, a stocky redhead from Idaho, approached him, his radio headset faintly squawking with Bureau traffic. "We can take him before he reaches the main road," he said, cold and professional.

Tony shook his head, again looking back toward the area where Riley's 4x4 had disappeared. "No," he said, smiling sadly. "Let him go. He's no danger to us now."

※　※　※

While Riley drove back to Boston, he couldn't stop thinking about what Tony had told him. If he'd been nervous before, he now felt a relentless, gnawing anger. But that anger had nothing to do with

Koenig and his doomsday machine. What pissed Riley off now was that three hundred men were hoping and praying for help that would never come. The end result would be that sooner or later, Koenig would end his game and take everyone with him. Of that, Riley was dead sure.

Someone had to get in there and warn them, give them a fighting chance on their own. By the time he pulled into his parking space in the basement of the Hancock Tower, Riley had the makings of a plan. It was audacious, maybe even crazy, but in his heart, he knew it held the only chance Frank and the others would have.

But where the hell are they? That was the one question he'd neglected to ask Tony, and after what had just happened between them, it was unlikely that he'd tell him now. Tony wanted Riley to stay the hell out of the FBI's business—had made that plain. But the way Riley saw it, Tony and the rest of them were a bunch of lily-livered cowards, deserving of everyone's righteous anger. And as far as staying out of it was concerned, well, Tony could shove it. Riley would find them without his help.

"Damn it!" he said, slamming the steering wheel. "Where are you, Frank? Where the hell are you?"

※　※　※

Riley watched the sun creep over the State House dome and drank his tenth cup of coffee. It tasted bitter and did nothing but make his stomach burn with excess acid. He poured it down the sink, stared at his bleary-eyed reflection in the mirror, and almost laughed. With the salt-and-pepper stubble on his face and those rheumy, bloodshot eyes, he looked like some kind of crazed derelict.

"You aren't winning any beauty contests today, pal," he said to his reflection. "Too bad you're not a genius, either."

And there it was. After an all-night session that recalled his days studying for the sergeant's exam, he'd come up with nothing. The Big Zip.

He turned on the sink's faucet, threw some cold water on his face and returned to his desk. He stared at the contents of the Murphy file and marveled at how little he really had. Disgusted, he leaned back in his chair and stared out the window, trying to come up with something—anything at all. He watched a flock of gulls gliding on the air currents, heading toward the ocean, and wished he could join them. Christ, he needed a vacation.

And then it hit him.

Bolting upright in his chair, he grabbed Frank's letter, reread it, and burst out laughing.

"You son of a bitch!" he yelled, jumping to his feet. "You beautiful, gorgeous son of a bitch!"

There, in Frank's studied scrawl, lay the answer. It had been right in front of his face the whole time. He glanced at his watch. The bookstores would not be open for at least another four hours. Frustrated, he sat back and forced himself to attend to a few outstanding cases, agonizing over the snail's pace at which the hours passed. At five minutes to ten, he could stand it no longer.

He stuffed Frank's letter into his pocket, told Becky that he would be out for half an hour, and dashed for the elevators.

He darted through the traffic on Boylston, oblivious to the angry calls of drivers and the odd stares from his fellow pedestrians. He headed to the bookstore across from the Prudential Center. Instead of browsing, as was his normal custom, he went straight for the nature section. He was afraid they might not have the book he was looking for and was about to leave, when he spied it sticking out from between two much larger volumes:

The Audubon Society Field Guide to North American Birds.

He looked at the letter again, checked the book's index and flipped to the proper page. There it was, right on page 683: *The Black-Backed Three-Toed Woodpecker favored coniferous forests and ventured as far south as the northern*

tip of Wisconsin.

"God bless you, Frank Murphy," Riley whispered as he copied down the information. Not only had Frank cleverly told them he was being held against his will, he had practically given them the address. For the first time since taking the case, Riley felt like he was earning the obscene amount of money he was charging. Now, at least he had something to go on.

Back in his office, Riley dialed Herb's number.

"Hello, Herb," he said, trying to contain his excitement. "Put Brenda on."

Riley heard the phone clunk down on something hard and Herb's voice echoing through their house. After a moment, Brenda came on the line. "What's up, Uncle John?"

"I know where he is." He held the phone away from his ear when she started shrieking with joy.

"Hold on a second," he said, laughing.

When she quieted down, he continued. "We're not out of the woods yet, but I have a plan."

"What is it?"

"Stay where you are. I'm going to come over and we'll go over it together."

"Okay," she said, her voice brimming with excitement. "I'll see you soon."

Riley hung up, grabbed a legal pad and, for the second time that day, ran past his bewildered secretary.

19

"God, this stuff itches," Dean said as Frank looped the two-pound bags of dirt over Dean's shoulders. Each set of bags were made from the legs of sliced-up long johns connected by a strip of burlap sacking and hung around the neck under the shirt. They continued down into the pants, ending just below the knee. The burlap itched terribly, but they hadn't much choice.

Frank smiled at his friend and signaled for one of the other guys to go down in the hole. It would be Frank's turn next, a prospect he dreaded. He'd already been down twice and discovered he was claustrophobic.

Dean pulled his pants up over the bags and tucked in his shirt.

"How do I look?" he said, to no one in particular.

"Like a goddamned filthy idiot," Jensen said.

Dean smiled. They were *all* filthy. When someone had expressed concern that the guards would notice the dirt on their clothes from digging, a couple of guys organized an impromptu game of tackle football with Barracks 6. Now they all looked like refugees from a detergent commercial. And since the camp had no laundry facilities for the prisoners, they would stay that way until they escaped.

Frank suggested that everyone wear his long johns during stints in the tunnel, changing in and out of them underground. This way, grubbiness would be held to a minimum. Of course, when the tunnel had to be closed up in a hurry, this made for some hair-raising moments while the diggers frantically pulled on their clothes over the long johns.

God, what I wouldn't give for a bath, Frank thought, scratching himself. The showers, if one could call them that, were barely more than weak trickles, like a gardener's watering can. It got the dirt off, but it was not the steamy, luxurious experience Frank and all the others dreamed about.

He watched Dean saunter out the door, thankful for the baggy trouser styles of the 1940s. With modern fashions they would never have been able to put their pants on over the bags, much less hide them.

The idea for the trouser bags was a direct steal from *The Great Escape*, a favorite movie of many, and a constant source of inspiration. A guy from Barracks 1, a tailor by trade, made enough of the bags to keep a steady stream of men taking the dirt out without arousing suspicion.

Once outside, a man carrying a load of dirt would stroll about for a while and then head to one of the gardens, where he would pull strings attached to nails holding the bags closed and, voilà, the soil would flow out around his ankles to mix in with the fresh dirt in the garden. It was simple and unobtrusive, and the guards saw only innocent men walking about with their hands in their pockets.

When Koenig granted Frank's request for vegetable gardens, Schmidt had gone into town dressed in his preppie civvies and brought back all manner of seeds and fertilizers, along with dozens of rakes and hoes. Frank was almost sorry they wouldn't get to grow the stuff.

On the first day, Mannheim had distributed the tools then stood with his fists on his hips, scrutinizing the prisoners while they worked. Soon he grew bored and wandered off. Frank had men from every barracks tilling the soil in front of Barracks 2, as well as several of the other barracks. He guessed that they would have about a week or so before the guards became suspicious. It was not a lot of time.

Frank turned his attention back to the tunnel. Already five days old, and worked nearly twenty-four hours a day, the shaft descended more than fifteen feet. From there it expanded to a small room hollowed out to accommodate the man operating the air pump, those men packing the trouser bags, and the man prepping the bed boards for shoring. Beyond this "utility room," the shaft extended ten feet laterally.

In his estimation, they would have dug a third of the way by the time the guards became suspicious of the gardens. Beyond that, Frank planned to have various sporting events occurring continuously every day until dark. With the clouds of dust these activities produced, there would be no problems disposing of the dirt. Plus, the latrines and the deep holes beneath them provided another ready-made disposal site.

After careful consideration, Frank placed the trapdoor under the potbellied stove. Because the area underneath it had a cinder block foundation to hold the stove's weight, it made an ideal place to dig without anyone being able to observe them from the outside. The hole inside the foundation was exactly two feet square. It was perfect.

Although an insurance salesman by trade, Freddie Richards turned out to be a talented carpenter, a skill he'd honed from many hours in his garage workshop making furniture. Using tools he'd created, and nails pilfered during work details in the new compound under construction, as well as those pulled from the barracks walls, Freddie created all sorts of digging tools.

He made it so two men could lift off the stove utilizing two re-worked bed boards and then the tiled platform underneath via four concealable lifting lugs, allowing access to the tunnel.

Frank saw they had one hour left until mess. After dark, the work became riskier. Koenig had stepped up the surprise inspections, and the guards, ever on the alert, took to making random visits to the barracks. This meant creating an unobtrusive system of lookouts whose job consisted of reporting anyone coming within fifty yards of Barracks 2. If one of the guards penetrated the "safe zone," then that fifty yards gave them just enough time to pull everyone out of the hole and pack up, sometimes for the rest of the night. All this made the night work nerve-wracking, as well as dirty and grueling.

As a solution, someone suggested the idea of placing dummies in the beds of those working, allowing them to stay underground during the guards' visits. But Frank had nixed that idea. Once one of the dummies was discovered, even by accident, their whole plan would be endangered. The risk was too great to take.

"Your turn, Colonel," Dana said, popping out of the hole.

Frank sighed and climbed down the bed board ladder.

Reaching bottom, he stared upward toward the entrance, feeling his testicles contract. The bed boards glowed with the warm light cast from the home-made candles placed every ten feet. The guards issued two candles per barracks in case of a power outage. This initial supply soon ran out.

Dean devised a virtually endless supply by boiling the water out of margarine stolen from mess and using unraveled burlap as wicks. A partially snipped-out tin can became a holder/reflector they could then nail to the tunnel walls. It gave off a soft, yellow light that quickly fouled the air. With the tunnel completed, those soft pools of light would extend more than sixty feet.

Frank shivered when he imagined staring down that lengthy expanse. He reminded himself, though, that at the end of that forbidding passageway would lie freedom. And freedom meant Brenda and the kids. If he kept that thought in the forefront of his mind, he knew he would make it.

He got down on his belly and pushed himself forward, sliding toward the face of the shaft like a soldier creeping toward his enemy. The tight confines of the tunnel made it necessary for everyone to "combat crawl," or risk bumping their head, or worse—collapsing the roof.

The panicky feeling returned, tightening his chest like an asthma attack. The air smelled stale, and his head felt as if a large vise squeezed against his temples. Fighting these sensations, he made it to the tunnel's end, where Bob Neff chopped away at the hard-packed earth with his home-made shovel.

"Take a break. I'll spell you," Frank said.

Sweaty, filthy, and looking like some crazed raccoon, Bob handed him the shovel and eased by him. The width of the bed boards used for shoring barely allowed two reasonably thin men to squeeze by each other.

"Have fun, Frank," he said, crawling off into the gloom.

"Yeah, thanks a lot."

After Bob left him alone, Frank squeezed his eyes shut, took several deep breaths, and began. The shovel, constructed from a split bed board and a tin can, did not allow for very efficient digging, but through his determination and his fear, he quickly filled two buckets with dirt.

Backing toward the pumping area, he passed the buckets to Roger, who filled more trouser bags from the large pile at his side. The work was hard. Frank had to use muscles that hadn't seen action for years to make any headway in the densely packed earth.

Even fifteen feet down, the soil, a curious mixture of sand and earth, was highly compressed, making the digging a thankless chore. By hacking away with the flimsy shovel, he managed to dig another two feet, placing eighteen more bed boards. He banged them into place with the rock they used for a hammer, feeling a real sense of accomplishment. With only a few nails, they had to make sure the bed boards were wedged together as tightly as possible. The dovetail joints suggested by Freddie worked wonders in that department. Once the ground settled, they would be impossible to move. God only knew if they would hold the weight of the dirt for any appreciable length of time.

"Frank!"

It was Dean's voice echoing down from above. Frank stopped digging long enough to hear the next word Dean said. It was loud, clear—unmistakable.

"Mannheim!"

"Oh, Jesus!" Frank said.

Scrambling backwards as fast as he could, he shot up the ladder and out the hole in seconds.

Immediately, Jensen and Dana put the tiled platform and stove back in place and connected the exhaust pipe, while Frank pulled on his uniform over his filthy long johns.

When he finished buttoning the shirt, Dean threw him a damp rag. He snatched it out of the air and wiped his face, neck, and hands.

"Hurry it up, guys," Roger said from his position at the door. "He's about twenty feet from the door, moving fast."

Everyone rushed to get into natural-looking positions. Frank,

Dean, Jensen, and Bob Neff took up the poker hands that always stood in readiness on the picnic-style table in the middle of the room. Dana and everyone else lay down on their bunks, pretending to read or nap.

The front door banged open and Mannheim strutted in accompanied by one of the other guards. Scanning the room, he swaggered over to the game, looked at Frank's hand and the growing pot of cigarettes.

"You should never bluff with only a pair, Colonel. It is suicide," he said, smiling menacingly.

Frank threw down his hand in disgust. "What do you want, Sergeant? Or do you just like popping our balloons?"

Mannheim offered no comment. Instead, he nodded to the other guard, and the two of them walked around the room, pawing through the men's personal effects. Frank watched in horror when Mannheim approached the stove.

Deliberately turning his attention away from Mannheim, Frank's glance settled on Dana Webster, who sat on his bunk pretending to read a tattered World War Two era paperback, one foot resting on the floor. Frank's blood froze when he noticed a small pile of dirt accumulating next to his shoe. Dana was still wearing the goddamned trouser bags.

And it's leaking!

Frank's upper lip beaded with sweat when Mannheim moved closer to Dana's bunk, the sergeant's beady eyes absorbing every detail. In a matter of seconds, he would see the dirt, and it would all be over. Frank envisioned the tunnel destroyed, and Mannheim laughing while he placed his pistol against each man's head and pulled the trigger.

Thinking fast, Frank threw his cards at Jensen.

"You're cheating, goddamn it!"

Jensen looked at him, his expression a mixture of anger and confusion. Having no time to wait for him to get the picture, Frank threw a cup of cold coffee in his face.

"I'm sick and fucking tired of your shit, Jensen!"

The big man from Dallas roared, upended the table, and grabbed Frank by his shirt, his massive fist pulling back to strike. Frank wondered if, maybe, he should have picked on Bob instead.

"Halt!" Mannheim bellowed.

Everyone froze while the stocky sergeant wedged himself between the two men, easily pushing them apart with his muscular arms.

"I do not care if you pigs wish to wallow in filth. And I do not care if you squabble among yourselves. You will, however, refrain from doing so while I am conducting an inspection. Do I make myself clear?"

No one spoke.

"*Sehr Gut.* Now, *Colonel* Murphy, the *Kommandant* requests your squalid presence in his office."

Seizing Frank by his shirt, he shoved him in the direction of the door, where he stumbled into the other guard.

"The rest of you may carry on with your trivial games," Mannheim said. He marched out to the quad while the other guard grabbed Frank and hustled him out the door.

Jensen shook his head in bewilderment, his anger abating. "What the fuck was that all about?"

"Oh, no!" Dana shouted.

Everyone turned, their eyes drawn to the dirt cascading from his trouser leg. The bag had finally broken and the full load now lay heaped on the floor.

"Do you think Frank was trying to—" Jensen asked.

Dean nodded his head solemnly.

"Christ," Bob said. "If Mannheim had spotted that—"

"We'd all be in front of a firing squad," Dean finished.

❋　❋　❋

Relieved beyond imagining, Frank let Mannheim and the other guard prod him toward the *Kommandant's* office. He stumbled up the steps onto the porch, wincing when the sergeant jabbed him in the small of his back with his truncheon. Laughing, Mannheim moved ahead and went through the door. The other guard shoved Frank inside, causing him to stumble again. He regained his footing, shooting the guard an angry look.

The outer office stood empty and quiet, indicating that Schmidt was also in Koenig's office.

Mannheim stepped up to the door and rapped twice.

"*Herein,*" came the reply.

When the door opened, Frank's fears and suspicions about Koenig's condition were confirmed. He sat slouched in his chair staring into space, eyes red-rimmed and puffy. His tunic was unbuttoned, his tie pulled down, and there was a two-day growth of graying beard on his face. In the background, the Blaupunkt radio played martial music at a modest volume.

Frank glanced over at Schmidt. The younger man's worried expression betrayed his growing concern.

It was Schmidt who finally spoke. "Sit, Colonel Murphy," he said, his eyes never leaving Koenig's face.

Frank took the last empty chair and waited. The music stopped after a few minutes and an announcer, speaking German, made an introduction. Crowds cheered. Then, after a pregnant pause, came a raspy, hypnotic voice Frank had no trouble recognizing.

Adolf Hitler.

For the first time since he'd entered the room, Koenig stirred. His eyes closed and his breathing became deeper and more regular. After a few more agonizing moments, Koenig opened his eyes and leveled his gaze at Frank.

"Will you now tell us where your base is located, Colonel?" he said.

Christ, not this crap again.

"If you cooperate," Koenig went on, "I can assure you that you and your men will be accorded new privileges, better food." He smiled paternally. "Surely this information is not so dear as that of your compatriots' well-being."

Frank forced himself to look out the casement window over Koenig's shoulder. Through it, he could see the men tending the gardens, and a dusty game of rugby between Barracks 7 and 10 going on in the quad. He also saw the *Hundführers* and their Rottweilers, and the guards manning the machine guns in the towers, and the barbed wire. A moment later, he came to a decision: If Koenig wanted to play out this little charade, he might as well humor the crazy old bird. And by doing so he would be safeguarding the tunnel.

It was doubly fortunate that Frank's father had served in the 410th Bombardment Squadron, for he knew almost all there was to know about the unit, including where it was based. That it now might make the difference between freedom and imprisonment was an irony not lost on him.

"Where is it, Colonel?" Koenig said, his voice taking on an unpleasant edge.

Frank shook his head. "About sixty miles northeast of London, *Kommandant*, in a little hamlet called Bury St. Edmunds, for all the good it'll do you."

Koenig smiled thinly.

"Clever, my dear Colonel. We were sure you might try a ruse, but you see, we know you are lying."

This is absurd. Completely nuts.

"Listen, *Kommandant*. My men and I have just about had enough—"

The door banged open behind him, and Mannheim entered with the same guard as before. This time they had Dean between them. Frank hadn't even realized the sergeant had left the room.

Schmidt immediately stood up, vacating the chair. The guard holding Dean dragged him over and pushed him down into it. And though he put up his usual wise guy front, Frank saw fear in his eyes.

"Welcome, Sergeant Seger," Koenig said, his voice silken with menace.

"Hey, Frank. What the hell is this cr—"

"Silence!" Mannheim screamed, swatting Dean across the jaw. Dean glared at the sergeant and rubbed his face, the skin of which now blazed an angry red.

Koenig continued without missing a beat. "Your colonel and I were just having a pleasant little chat about your unit. And since his memory is faulty on this particular point, we were wondering if you could tell us where it is located?"

Dean frowned and reached up to his face again. His hand came away smeared with blood leaking from the corner of his mouth. He wiped it on the arm of the chair, defiant. "Sorry, Adolf, no can do."

"Tell him, Dean, it's not a game anymore—it's not worth it."

Dean grinned at his friend. "I know that, Shakespeare. But the truth is, you never told me where the hell it was."

Koenig's mouth became a tight line of anger. "You may find this all very amusing, Sergeant Seger," he said, "but *I* do not. You shall learn respect... the hard way."

Dean laughed. "Respect you? Fat chance. Go ahead, I can take anything you dish out."

"We shall see, Sergeant, we shall see." Koenig's expression hardened. "Mannheim."

The sergeant balled up his fists and began beating Dean senseless. His fists were like hammers slamming into Dean's face, making a sound like someone beating a rug with a baseball bat. Dean gamely tried to ward off the blows, but the sergeant's years as a street fighter gave him the supreme advantage. Frank wanted to vomit.

"Stop it! Stop this now!" Frank yelled.

Moving to get up, he found the barrel of an MP40 jammed against his temple. He collapsed into his chair, helpless to do anything but watch. And that was somehow much worse than being on the receiving end of those crushing blows.

A moment later, Koenig motioned for Mannheim to cease, and the sergeant backed off. The beating had only lasted seconds, but Dean's face and upper body were already covered with a blanket of blood gushing from his nose and mouth. Both lips were split, and his left eye had swollen completely shut.

"Where is the bomber squadron located, Sergeant?" Koenig repeated, each word dripping with venom.

Dazed and groggy, Dean shook his head, flinging a spray of blood against the nearest wall. He then fixed Koenig with a level stare from his one good eye, and said in a tight whisper, "Fuck you, you crazy old Kraut."

Mannheim drew back to punch him again. Koenig held up his hand.

"It is time we used other methods," he said.

Nodding, Mannheim left the room, returning a short time later with a third guard. In the sergeant's hands was an object Frank didn't recognize until Mannheim flicked a switch and a low hum filled the room.

An electric cattle prod.

"No, goddammit! I told you where it is!" Frank screamed.

Koenig ignored him and motioned for Mannheim to proceed. The new guard grabbed Dean's pants and yanked them down, while the second guard held him in the chair with a belt around his chest. Almost as an afterthought, Mannheim walked over to the old Victrola standing in the corner, cranked it up, and put on the record.

Once again Frank heard the cheery strains of "Who's Afraid of The Big Bad Wolf." This time it chilled him to the bone.

"Oh, God, please! Don't let them do this, Frank!" Dean said, his voice breaking. "Tell him the goddamn location!"

Frank looked helplessly into his friend's eyes. "I already have!"

Koenig nodded, and Mannheim placed the prod against Dean's testicles and pressed the button. The hum became a low, throaty roar as Dean screamed, the voltage twisting and jerking his body off the chair.

Tears streamed down Frank's face while he watched his friend writhe in excruciating pain. He had to fight back the nausea twisting his guts when the odor of singed hair and flesh reached his nostrils.

Schmidt stared at the floor, his hands gripping the arms of the chair with white-knuckled intensity. For that fleeting moment of silence between his friend's agonized screams, only Frank and Schmidt existed. He stared at the young German, willing him to look up. And when he finally lifted his gaze and met his own, Frank saw the battle going on behind them—the utter torment.

"Take off the music," Koenig commanded in German.

One of the guards not occupied with holding Dean down ran over and pulled off the needle. There was a loud scratch followed by a cavernous silence.

"Will you tell us now, Sergeant Seger?" Koenig asked, deadly calm.

Dean breathed in ragged sobs as he struggled to get the words out. "Stick it!"

Koenig nodded.

Mannheim turned to the guard near the Victrola and said, "Music."

The music started over and, once again, the sergeant lowered the prod into Dean's crotch. His scream went for a long, endless, agonizing moment, ending in a wracking cough that caused him to vomit up his meager lunch.

"Enough!" Schmidt cried, leaping to his feet. "This is pointless! Take them both to the cooler."

Startled, Mannheim looked to Koenig, but the *Kommandant* had again lapsed into catatonia. He stared into some inner void, a gluey stream of drool hanging from the point of his chin.

"That is an order, Sergeant. *Schnell!*"

Mannheim shot Schmidt an evil glare, then signaled the two guards, who picked Dean up from the chair and dragged him out of the office.

Prodded from behind by the last guard, Frank followed.

Barely conscious of where they were headed, Frank's mind reeled. Koenig was deteriorating fast. Whatever was wrong with him was holding sway for longer periods of time and with increasing frequency. How soon would it be before he existed totally in his dream world, a world where World War Two was still being fought? The thought held a certain irony for Frank. How much different had *he* been, hanging on to old memories like a lifeline? Was this the end result?

When they approached the cooler, Frank looked back toward

the *Kommandantur*, spotting Schmidt standing alone on the porch, a look of profound guilt on his face.

In spite of the horror of the last half hour, Frank now knew Schmidt was the key to their freedom, that he was torn between his misplaced loyalty and some small amount of decency. Somehow, Frank had to exploit that chink in the armor, to persuade the man to end this lunacy. He only hoped it wasn't already too late.

20

"WBZ," the receptionist said into her headset. She paused, listening to the frantic voice of the caller. "I'm sorry, but Bart is out on assignment. May I take a message?"

The caller started screaming, and the receptionist winced, her patient smile tightening. "I'm very sorry, sir, but the best I can do is have him paged. I can't guarantee he'll return your call."

The caller hung up after another string of invective. Without a moment's hesitation, she punched another button on her blinking console. "WBZ... Yes, I'll put you through immediately..."

Riley waited patiently in front of her station and couldn't help stealing glances at her lithe form while she scribbled one of the hundreds of messages she wrote every day. He admired her cool professionalism too. With the amount of idiotic callers she had to deal with every day, he found it amazing that she could maintain that soft, mellifluous tone and unruffled poise. He imagined himself in that role, suppressing a smile when thoughts of wholesale slaughter entered his mind.

"Yes, Mr. Simpson, I'll see that Bart gets the message right away."

Turning away from her flashing console, the receptionist smiled and said, "May I help you?"

"Yes, I'm John Riley. I'm here to see Chuck Weathers."

She glanced downward into her appointment calendar.

"Yes, Mr. Riley. You may go on back. It's just through—"

"Thanks, I know the way."

Smiling again, she went back to her phone.

Riley walked through the door, strolled past the offices and into the area where Chuck Weathers held court. Ever since moving into the Boston market from Omaha, "Weathers' Weather" was a popular segment of the evening news. Chuck's reasonably accurate forecasts were given in a friendly and accessible manner, popular with young and old alike. And when he wasn't preparing his broadcasts, he gave talks about meteorology to rapt students at various elementary and secondary schools in the area.

Riley spotted him hunched over his computer wedged between several larger companions of the small PC he worked on.

"So, where are my Sox tickets?" Riley said.

"Same place as my forecast. Up in the air," he said, a twinkle in his dark brown eyes. He was tall and lanky, and his salt-and-pepper hair and his tanned, wizened face made him look older than his thirty-five years.

"I can't believe you came all the way down here looking for those tickets. So, what can I do for you, or are you dying for another tour of our grand facilities?"

"All right." Riley laughed. "I deserve that."

Riley recalled the last time he was there. Chuck gave him a tour, and he'd accidentally pushed a button he shouldn't have touched. The minor panic that ensued when an unscheduled commercial began running during a steamy scene on a popular soap sent the crew into a frenzy. Riley didn't think he would ever live that one down.

"Seriously. What're you up to?" Chuck asked.

"I've got a problem that I thought you might be able to help me with."

"Shoot."

"Can your weather satellites spot buildings on the ground?"

"Somebody lose their house?" Chuck asked.

When Riley didn't laugh, Chuck squirmed in his chair.

"I'm sorry. I couldn't resist. Tell me what's going on, that is, if it's not confidential."

"I have a client whose husband is lost somewhere in the Wisconsin wilderness. It could really shorten the search if we could spot him via satellite. I know it's technologically possible, and you were my first thought. Can you do it from here?"

Chuck's smile dimmed. "Shit, John, I wish I could help you, but this system won't do that."

"Why?"

"The GOES system—"

"Goes?"

"Sorry. It's an acronym that stands for *Geo-Synchronous Orbital Environmental System*. The GOES system takes measurements such as temperature, moisture, wind speed, and other related information, converts it into digital information that our computers then turn into the images you see on our forecast. There's really nothing optical about it. What you need are *spy* satellites using high-resolution optics like the ones produced by Itek. Those babies can pick out license plate numbers from hundreds of miles up."

Riley stood up and shook hands with his friend.

Noting his sad expression, Chuck added, "Look, if I can still be of help to you in any way, call me, okay?"

"Thanks, kiddo, I appreciate it."

When Riley started to walk out, Chuck called after him.

"Hey, why not try the military? Who knows, they might even help."

Riley shook his head, remembering Tony Carter's ominous warning. "They're exactly the people I *can't* go to. I'll see you."

Driving back to his office, he knew he had only one choice. It was like finding that proverbial needle, but nothing else was going to do the job. By the time he reached his office, the final phase of his plan fell into place.

He went to his bookshelf, pulled out the atlas, and took it to his desk. From the index, he flipped to the page highlighting the northeast corner of Wisconsin, the part of the state bordering Michigan, and where he was convinced Koenig had placed his camp.

"I know you're up there somewhere, Frank Murphy," he muttered.

He found what he was looking for in Marinette. A small city right on Green Bay, it boasted a small passenger airport perfectly situated for what he planned.

He picked up the phone and dialed Herb Lewis's number.

"Hi, Herb."

"Let me guess," he said, laughing.

Riley grinned. "Yeah. Put her on."

The phone made the familiar clunking sound when Herb went to get his daughter.

"So how did it go with Weathers' Weather?" she said brightly.

"Not good."

"Damn it," she said, her mood changing abruptly. "Why? What happened? Wouldn't he help?"

"More like *couldn't*. Weather satellites aren't designed for that purpose. I'm sorry."

"I'm sorry too. It's not your fault. It was stupid letting my hopes get too high."

She fell silent, and Riley wished he had something more to give her, something other than what he planned to do. He decided to tell her anyway. "There is one other idea."

"What?"

"I have a pilot's license and my own twin-engine Cessna."

"Don't tell me you're going to fly around up there hoping you'll spot them?"

"Exactly. I know you think it's crazy, but—"

"Crazy? I think it's wonderful," she said, her mood brightening once again.

Riley was surprised by her enthusiasm for what he thought was a last-ditch, hare-brained idea.

"Wait a minute, Brenda, there's no guarantee I'll find him this way. I could fly around there for weeks and not spot a damn thing."

"Maybe if you had two pairs of eyes instead of one, you'd stand a better chance."

"Oh, no you don't," he said, realizing where this was leading. "You're staying right where you are."

"John," she said, her manner becoming businesslike, "I'll just fire you and hire someone else who *will* take me."

Riley sighed, knowing that she might very well do that. No, he thought. She *would* do it.

"All right, you win. But if we *do* spot them, you're staying back behind the lines. I am not going to take responsibility for you getting your ass shot off. Mine's going to be in enough danger. Agreed?"

"Agreed," she said, no doubt beaming at her victory.

"Okay. I'll call you tomorrow or the next day when I've got everything worked out."

"Thanks, John. I knew you were the right man for this."

"Yeah, right, and I should probably have my head examined too. Take care."

Riley hung up the phone and swore. He hadn't wanted her to come because he hadn't told her about the bomb.

...Koenig's threatening to blow the damn thing if we come within twenty miles of his precious camp!

His friend's words still frightened him. Telling Brenda would have solved nothing and would have pushed her already frayed nerves over the edge. If he had insisted on going alone, and she fired him, she would have gone in with someone who knew nothing about the real situation. Riley knew he couldn't allow that. He hoped like hell that taking her along wouldn't be a worse mistake.

"You really got your balls in a sling this time, ol' boy," he said to himself.

21

My eyes must *be getting used to the dark*, Frank thought. Holding his hands up in front of his face, he could just make them out in the gloom. It was either that, or his mind playing tricks, something all too common in an environment much like a sensory-deprivation tank. He felt something scuttle across his other arm, and he batted it away with a muffled curse.

"You okay, Frank?" came the faint cry from the adjoining cell. The walls, although made of poured, reinforced concrete just over two feet thick, would transmit the sound of their voices if they stayed close enough to them. If he put his head against its slick surface, the sound of Dean's voice became even clearer. Even still, one had to have sharp hearing to catch the low frequencies canceled out by the concrete.

"Yeah, I'm fine," he replied. "How about you?"

"Still a little sore, but the swelling's gone down. It feels like I've been to a bad dentist."

Dean laughed, making Frank feel even worse.

"I just wish I could have done something, I—"

"It's okay... Nothing you *could've* done."

"I know, but I still feel I should've tried."

"Then we'd both look like palookas. And where's the sense in that?"

Frank smiled, remembering a thought that had formed in his mind not long after the heavy steel door clanged shut, plunging him into an endless night.

"Hey, Dean? This is going to sound a little screwy, but did you ever have anything you regret *not* doing?"

"A *little* screwy?" Dean laughed. "No, not really, what about you?"

Frank had thought about little else, the time stretching out in front of him like a limitless void. By his own estimation, they'd been in the cooler for just over four days. Schmidt had not given them a specific sentence, and Frank wondered if they would ever see the sky again.

"Yeah, I do... I love Brenda like no woman I've ever known, and I wouldn't change my life with her for anything, but there's this one moment I keep thinking about, one moment I wish I could live over again, just so I could see what would happen."

Dean coughed. It was a deep, racking cough, wet with phlegm—like pneumonia.

"That sounds bad," Frank said.

"I'm okay, just a touch of bronchitis, I think," he said, clearing his throat of mucus. "Sounds worse than it feels. Anyway, what's this grand moment of regret? I want to hear all the dirt."

Frank grinned. "It was about six months before I met Brenda, and I was kind of going with this woman on a strictly casual basis—"

"Casual for you, or her?"

"Both. I didn't really like her all that much, and for all I know she felt the same about me, but she was good in the sack, a real screamer, if you get my drift."

"Yeah... Was she cute?"

"Are you going to let me tell this?"

"Okay, okay. Go ahead."

"Thanks. No. She had a big nose and a laugh that sounded like a donkey. The sound of that laugh about drove me crazy—but I was horny, so what can I say? Anyway, we were at this movie in Harvard Square, two seats in from the aisle. The movie was a real dog, and I found myself looking around the theater after a while. Just curious to see who else was there, you know?"

"Yeah?" Dean said.

Frank smiled at his friend's anticipation. "Apparently this woman had come in after the beginning, and had taken the aisle seat, one seat away from me." He paused for effect, letting the silence drag out.

"Come on, Shakespeare, spill it, or I'm going to strangle you when we get out of here."

Frank chuckled. "I'll tell you, Dean, I looked at her, and just at that moment she looked at me and turned on the most dazzling smile I had ever seen. She was absolutely gorgeous... and *alone*."

"Oh, man. What did you do?"

Frank smiled wistfully. "Nothing."

"Nothing? Jesus."

"Yeah... As a gentleman, I felt honor-bound to finish out my date with Shirley. I never saw that other girl again. I even went back to the theater a couple of times, hoping she'd come back."

"Aw, man that sucks. So..."

"...So, if I had to do it again, I would find some way of telling this woman to go out into the lobby, meet her there, and get her phone number. At least then I would've had a shot. Hell, my whole life might've been different."

"Or she might have been some psychotic bitch who liked to pick up men in movie theaters and castrate them once she got them alone." Dean howled.

"I never thought about that," Frank said, catching the infectious nature of his friend's raucous laugh. "So, pal o' mine, you sure you haven't got one tiny little experience you wish you'd done different?"

"You mean, besides coming here?"

"*Touché.*"

"Actually, I *do* remember something. This was just after New Year's, 1991, I think. I was in this disco for a private party, and I'd been eyeballing this girl all night. She was dancing with her girlfriend, so I figured, well, she's either a lesbian, and you have no chance in hell, or she's available. So, with that thought in mind, I finally got up the nerve to ask her to dance. I walked up to her and popped the question, and then she turned and looked at me. It was like one of those Hollywood moments, like Elizabeth Taylor and Monty Clift in *A Place in the Sun*. When she turned, Frank, when she saw me, her eyes went real wide and her whole body jerked, as if someone had juiced her. I actually *felt* it. To make a long story short, we spent the rest of the night laughing, dancing, drinking, and smooching like crazy. It was one of the best nights of my life."

"So, what's wrong with that?" Frank asked.

Dean sighed. "Turns out she was married."

"Ahh, crap."

"Yeah. And what made it worse is that we actually met one last time, a few days later. She was *this* close to having an affair with me, this freaking close, but instead, she chose to be loyal to her husband. I really admired her for that, you know? At the same time, I was dying inside because in that short amount of time, I was already madly in love with her."

"What could you have done?"

"I think if I knew she was wavering so much, I would have grabbed her by the hand that first night, run to the nearest motel, torn her clothes off, and given us *both* something to remember. She probably still would have broken it off, but at least we'd have that one torrid memory."

Frank fought back the tears that stung his eyes, wiping them with the back of his hand. Every man and woman must have similar stories, he realized, episodes they reran in their minds over and over again, remaking that crucial choice that had sent their lives down a different path.

He was glad he and Dean had shared their stories. Besides passing the time, he'd never felt closer to his friend than he did right at that moment. It made for a poignant counterpoint to the horror in which they found themselves.

Frank was about to offer a rejoinder when he heard the main door to the cooler bang open, the clump of boots and the jangle of keys in the lock.

The guards were releasing them.

An instant later, the door swung open, and the bright light of the bare bulb in the corridor flooded inside, blinding him.

"*Raus!*" the voice said.

Squeezing his eyes shut against the light, Frank made the effort to get up, finding that his legs had turned to rubber and that he could only get to his knees.

The guard grabbed him by his shirt collar and yanked him to his feet. Opening his eyes slightly, Frank saw Mannheim standing in front of him. "*Hauptmann* Schmidt wishes to see you," he said. "*Kommen Sie.*"

Once they were moving, Frank felt stronger, and his vision cleared quicker than it had after his previous stint in the dark. *I must be getting used to this*, he thought. *Wonderful.*

Quick-marched across the quad and shoved roughly through the door of the *Kommandant's* quarters, Frank and Dean were soon seated in front of a troubled *Hauptmann* Schmidt.

"You may return to your duties, Sergeant Mannheim," Schmidt said, barely acknowledging the man.

"The *Kommandant* would want me to—"

"Leave us!" Schmidt shouted, slapping the desk with his open palm.

The sergeant stiffened, his face turning a healthy pink. "*Jawohl, Hauptmann*," he hissed through clenched teeth.

Turning on his heels, he marched out the door, slamming it behind him.

Schmidt leaned back in his chair, steepling his fingers in front of his mouth. He stared hard at both Frank and Dean, his blue eyes unblinking.

Frank suppressed a smile and stared back, determined not to be intimidated. The moment dragged out for another two agonizing minutes before Schmidt moved.

"The *Kommandant* is ill," he said finally, dropping his hands into his lap.

"No kidding," Frank replied.

"You do not understand." Schmidt leaned forward, his voice fraught with anxiety. "He has a tumor in his brain. That is what is causing this wild belief that the war is still on."

Frank's anger came close to the boiling point. "You knew, and you let him torture my friend! You encourage him, and you have the power to stop it!"

Schmidt looked stricken, as if all his accumulated guilt were piling up in his mind like sand in an hourglass.

"I am sorry. I—"

"Fuck you, you're sorry. It's too late for that. He killed Blair, and his blood is on *your* hands too! You've got to end this insanity now, before he kills somebody else!"

Schmidt looked at Frank with eyes that burned with shame, and something else. Was it love for an old man who had lost control, or was it fear of what would happen to them when this was all over?

"I am sorry for this. I will try and prevent it from happening again, but I regret that you must stay." He turned to the door. "*Unteroffizier!*"

The door opened, and one of the guards entered.

"Feed these men double rations from the officers' mess, and return them to their barracks," Schmidt said in German.

"*Jawohl,*" the guard replied, saluting.

"Have it your way, Schmidt," Frank said, lurching to his feet. "I hope you can live with yourself."

Without waiting to be pushed or prodded by the guard, Frank turned and stalked out, with Dean following close behind.

When they got back to the barracks, Frank found Jensen dealing the cards to Bob, Dana, and Freddie. Some of the others lounged on their bunks—the usual tableaux that signified tunnel work was in progress. Upon seeing them enter, everyone dropped their poses and crowded around, throwing out a barrage of questions.

"Hold it a minute, guys. Hold it!" Frank said. "One at a time. Bob?"

Bob looked flustered.

"What happened, Frank? Some of the guys in the quad thought they heard screaming coming from the *Kommandant's* office the other day. When you two didn't come back, we didn't know what to think."

Frank tried to find words that would not inflame them, then realized it was exactly what they needed. "Koenig ordered Mannheim to use a cattle prod on Dean. He wanted to know where our bomber base is located."

Most of the men looked bewildered.

"And after Frank told him, the son of a bitch turned Mannheim loose on me anyway," Dean added.

"Oh, shit," Jensen said. "We're fucked."

Ignoring the big man's remark, Frank continued, "We've got to finish the tunnel and get out of here—or we're dead. Someone give me a progress report. Where are we?"

Roger raised his hand.

"As best as we can estimate, the tunnel is about thirty-five feet long, give or take a foot. But the shorin's runnin' out, and I don't know if anyone can spare any more bed boards."

Frank walked over and sat down on a bunk, his brow knitted in concentration. He looked up a moment later. "All right, see what you can scrounge up. Beg, borrow, or steal what you can. If we have to, we'll space them out. We've got to go full bore on this." He stood up and faced the men, a steely-eyed look of determination in his eyes. "No matter what happens, we're out of here a week from today!"

22

Riley knew that something was wrong the moment he walked into his office. It was as if the atmosphere inside had thickened. He knew it because instead of greeting him with her characteristic warmth and mild sarcasm, Becky shot him a worried glance, her lips compressed into a tight line.

"Have a fight with Harold or something?" he teased.

Becky was having none of it. She tilted her head toward his office, her frown deepening. The door stood ajar.

"Hell, Becky, why didn't you tell me a client was waiting," he said, starting for the door. Before she could warn him, he was already through it.

His effusive apologies died on his lips the moment he entered the room. Two men sat on the leather chairs opposite his desk. They stood at his approach, appraising him as if he were a fly on a wedding cake. Identically dressed in expensive blue suits, with white shirts and striped regimental ties, they looked bland, nondescript. It was their eyes that gave them away. Hard and bright like diamonds, they glittered with menace and suspicion.

"Mr. John Riley?" one of them asked.

"Yes," Riley said, not sure if doing so was the smart move to make.

240

The one who asked the question, a phlegmatic type with brown hair and a mild facial tick, pulled out an ID and flipped it open. "Special Agent George Harrens, Federal Bureau of Investigation. This is my associate, Special Agent Adam Stern," he said, nodding toward the shorter blond-haired man next to him. "We were wondering if you could answer some questions for us?"

Still wary, Riley pasted a smile on his face, sat down at his desk, and bade the two agents to retake their chairs.

"Ask away. I'm always anxious to aid the FBI whenever I can."

Harrens smiled thinly and flipped open a small notebook. "You know a Special Agent Anthony Carter?"

"Yes, I do," Riley said, suddenly worried again. "Is he all right?"

"Has he been in contact with you recently?" Harrens asked, ignoring his question.

Riley's palms started itching, a sure sign that something *was* wrong.

"No, he hasn't, actually," he lied. "I haven't heard from him in a month. I expect he's been busy."

"Do you spend leisure time together?"

Riley's blood pressure rose. He didn't like this sanctimonious twit one bit. What had Tony done to set these two assholes loose? One group Riley always hated in the department were the Internal Affairs types. Always skulking around trying to dig up dirt on otherwise decent guys. He squelched the urge to throw them out and smiled.

"We do play some poker, now and then. If you see him, tell him he still owes me twenty bucks from last time."

Harrens's face twitched twice, the only expression on his otherwise impassive face. He flipped his notebook closed and stood, Agent Stern following suit.

"I'm afraid you're going to have to accompany us, Mr. Riley," he said.

Riley spread his hands. "I'd like nothing better, gentlemen, but I have a full schedule today and—"

"No, you don't."

"Excuse me?"

"Your secretary informed us that your first appointment isn't until eleven thirty."

"My secretary never informs anyone of anything without my permission."

Harrens and Stern stared back, saying nothing. Somehow, this made Riley angrier than if they'd offered some lame excuse. "Now, wait one minute, guys, you have no right to go snooping around in my business. Let me see your warrant."

Harrens smiled coldly. "You can come with us cooperatively, Mr. Riley, or by force. The choice is yours."

Riley stabbed the intercom button. "Becky? Get me the FBI on the phone."

He was greeted by a silent hiss. "Becky?"

Nothing.

Riley suddenly felt cold all over. He straightened up, keeping his facial expression neutral. "Do you mind if I go to the men's room first?"

"Sure, but make it quick. Agent Stern will accompany you."

"*Danke Schön*," Riley said.

"*Bitte*," Harrens replied.

Before the agent could react, Riley smashed him in the face with one of his ham-sized fists, knocking him back over a chair. He sprawled, unconscious, onto the carpet, blood pouring from his shattered nose.

Stern, grunting something in German, vaulted over the low coffee table and landed on Riley's back, the agent's weight sending the two of them stumbling toward the large plate glass window. Riley saw that if he didn't do something, they would both go through it.

Using their combined momentum, Riley planted his right leg and bent forward, grasping the agent by his head. The inertia sent Stern flying over Riley's back into the window. It shattered with an ear-splitting crash, and the agent plummeted out of sight, screaming like a frightened girl. Wind howled through the hole, whipping papers off the desk and sending them whirling about the room.

Riley heard a coughing sound behind him and felt something hot whiz by his right ear. Reacting by instinct, he dived over the desk, reached into his top drawer, and pulled out his .40 caliber Glock pistol. He held it over the desktop and emptied the magazine, spreading the shots in a fan-shaped pattern. He was rewarded with the sound of someone groaning in pain. But whether the man was really hit or just faking it to draw Riley out, he didn't know. And it really didn't matter. He had to move.

He dumped the empty magazine, snatched a loaded one from the drawer, and slapped it in place. Then he racked a round into the chamber. Mentally, he counted to three and sprang to his feet, the Glock held out in front of him grasped in both hands. Harrens lay crumpled on the carpet, a dark pool of blood spreading out from his midsection. Gut shot.

Riley crept toward the dying man, ready at any moment to pepper the bastard. But when he drew closer, it was clear Harrens, or whatever his name was, was beyond any further action. Harrens saw him then, his glazed eyes focusing into a glare of hatred. "*Irisch schweine*," he hissed.

"Love you, too, pal," Riley replied, taking a last look out the window. He saw Stern far below, splayed out on the sidewalk, a growing knot of people surrounding him. A siren screamed toward the building from somewhere to the north.

Retracing his steps through the office, he went to the front door and peered out. No one in the hall. But that didn't mean there wasn't a backup team somewhere waiting to finish the job. And where was Becky? Had she run away, sensing the danger he'd walked right into? Riley prayed that was the case. But he couldn't shake the thought that another of Harrens's men—or rather, Koenig's men—had done something to her. And now that Koenig's security force was onto him, what did that mean for Brenda? It was this last thought, coupled with the rising tide of voices coming down the hall, that propelled him out the door and down the back stairs. He had no desire to try and explain all this to a bunch of rent-a-cops, not when Brenda could be in danger.

He raced down the stairs, blood pounding in his temples and his breath coming in short gasps. *I've got to stop eating like a pig*, he thought, wheezing. *Start exercising again too.* He wouldn't be much good to anyone if he dropped dead of a heart attack.

Riley reached the parking garage, and his Lexus five minutes later. He started the engine and slammed the car into reverse in one sweeping motion. He tried to catch sight of whoever might be tailing him, but nothing appeared out of the ordinary. There were too many cars for a positive make one way or the other. If they had the parking garage covered at all, they could be anywhere. Patting the Glock in its shoulder holster, Riley pulled out his monthly pass and smiled at the pretty parking attendant sitting in her air-conditioned kiosk.

If something's going to happen, it'll be now.

He glanced in his rearview mirror and spotted a man sitting in a Toyota Tercel right behind him. The guy looked bored and half-asleep. Behind him was a middle-aged woman in a dusty brown Mercedes. Neither of them appeared to be likely assassins; however, one could never be sure. It was possible that Koenig's operatives were arrogant and overconfident enough to believe one team was enough to take him out. Now that they had failed, all hell would break loose.

He arrived at Brenda's parents twenty minutes later, hiding the Lexus behind the toolshed. In this strictly workingman's neighborhood, it wouldn't pay to have prying eyes ogling his luxury car.

He rang the bell and waited, his nerves making his hands shake. Herb answered the door a few moments later, a frown of concern on his face. "Johnny, you look winded. Everything all right?"

"Something's come up, Herb. Everyone here?"

"Sure, come in, come in."

Riley brushed past him, his eyes taking in the empty living room, and headed directly for the kitchen. Herb followed on his heels. Riley found Brenda, her mother, and the two kids having their lunch. Brenda looked up from the peanut butter and jelly sandwiches she was preparing, her eyes widening. "Uncle John?"

"How long will it take all of you to pack?" he asked.

June looked confused. "Pack? Whatever for?"

Riley found his patience wearing thin but checked his emotions when he realized that he had to explain the problem if he wanted their cooperation, even if it meant momentary panic. He could deal with that.

"We've all got to leave here, as soon as possible. Koenig's onto us. Two of his assassins just tried to kill me."

June Lewis gasped, her hands flying to her mouth, eyes wide with fear. Brenda, on the other hand, remained calm. "How *could* he know, John?"

As briefly as he could, leaving out the part about the bomb and the government's despicable hands-off policy, Riley told them about his meeting with Tony. "...And according to their intelligence, Koenig's got his own security force. They're well-paid, thorough, and fanatical in their devotion to him."

Herb broke his silence. "If they're that good, Johnny, where could we possibly hide from them?"

Riley nodded and dropped into one of the empty chairs around the kitchen table. God, he was tired. Glancing at the children, he noted their wide-eyed looks, envying them their innocence. "I've thought about that," he said, wiping his face with the back of his hand. June placed a tall glass of iced tea on the table in front of him, and he took a long, frigid gulp, nodded his thanks, and continued. "My wife and I own a cabin deep in the Maine wilderness. I bought it lock, stock, and logs under an assumed name ten years ago after I retired from the force, stayed there for a year to clear out the cobwebs. No one, and I mean *no one* knows about it, but my wife, my son... and me. There's a phone, a short-wave radio, a fresh-water well, a wood-burning stove, and a full pantry of canned goods that should last you all at least a month."

"What about us, John? When are we going after Frank?" Brenda asked.

"Tonight."

⁂

The small four-seater Cessna 310 sailed into the sky and banked westward, leaving Hanscom Field behind. Brenda watched the ground recede, feeling her stomach twisting itself into knots. Ever since childhood, she feared flying; she really couldn't remember why she felt that way. No relatives had died in crashes, she'd had no close brushes with death herself, nothing that would create this lifelong, irrational fear. Yet it persisted.

She recalled all those news stories about private planes crashing and killing everyone aboard. Commercial airliners were one thing, but with a small, light plane like the Cessna, anything could happen—and often did. Still, Frank needed her, and that was enough to make her overcome anything.

Closing her eyes when the plane dipped from a sudden downdraft, Brenda felt another wave of nausea. She gritted her teeth and thought about their destination. According to John, the flight to Marinette, Wisconsin would take four hours by normal jetliner. In this small plane, with a maximum range of five hundred miles and a top speed of one hundred and eighty, the flight would take the better part of twenty-four hours with frequent landings and refueling. And some of the control towers at the fields where they would need to refuel would be shutting down about the time they landed, creating even longer delays, and necessitating an overnight stay in a nearby motel. For without tower clearance, there could be no takeoffs and landings.

Brenda turned away from the window and watched Riley at the controls. Unlike the gruff professional he appeared to be on the ground, in the air he took on a free-spirited air she found both amusing and annoying. She also realized his carefree attitude made her jealous and resentful. Jealous, because he did not have a loved one in the hands of a madman; resentful, because this flight was a rescue mission, not a joyride. Then again, Koenig's men *had* tried to kill him. Maybe his attitude was a defense mechanism, a way of coping.

"So, John, are you going to tell me the rest of what your FBI friend had to say?"

Riley shot her a puzzled look. "What do you mean? I told you everything."

"That might work with your wife, but it won't wash with me. I could tell you were leaving something out, something you thought would worry me. I've come this far, I can take it."

Riley nodded, a rueful smile creasing his face. "No fooling you, is there?"

"Not a chance in hell."

Riley sighed, flipped on the autopilot, and turned to face her. "You're right, I didn't tell you everything. The government knows where the camp is located."

Brenda sat up in her seat, and Riley held up his hand. "Hold it. Let me finish." He paused, shaking his head. "There's no right way to put this, so here it is: They know where they are, but they're not going in. They're too scared of another Waco—"

"But—"

Riley grabbed her arm. "Listen," he said gently. "Koenig has possession of a tactical nuclear device, and it's inside the camp. He says he'll blow it if anyone comes near the place."

Brenda's expression remained impassive, but her eyes began to moisten.

"Maybe they're mistaken, John. Maybe they're trying to scare you off."

"I don't believe so. With what I've learned about Koenig, it doesn't surprise me at all. He's one crafty son of a bitch. And ballsy, too. Those two goons of his had picture-perfect FBI credentials."

"What can we do?" she said, her emotions rising with the pitch of her voice. "We can't just stand by and let that monster kill my husband and all those other men. My God!"

Riley took her in his arms and held her while she sobbed into his shoulder. He felt the hot wetness of her tears and wished he hadn't told her, after all. Still, he'd come to know the adult Brenda very well over these last couple of weeks and, even if she didn't know it herself, she was one strong lady. She would not only get over this moment, she would probably want to storm the gates herself.

"How far are we flying tonight?" she said, calming down.

"Johnstown. It's about sixty miles east of Pittsburgh. We'll stay the night, refuel, and take off at first light. We should make Chicago by ten o'clock in the morning."

She nodded, suddenly feeling very tired. Leaning against the window, she used her jacket as a pillow and fell asleep in moments. Maybe it was a way to escape the horror of what Riley had just told her. Maybe in her dreams she would find a way to cope.

23

Dean had a bad feeling when Frank entered the tunnel that morning. They'd exhausted the supply of bed boards that could be spared. If they used any more of them, the men would be falling through their bunk frames to the floor. Frank insisted they keep digging but would only accept volunteers after he'd made it clear that the risk was greater. Everyone raised their hands. Everyone wanted to contribute. That still did nothing to allay the fear Dean felt for his best friend.

At random times during the day, the Germans had taken to driving heavy earth-moving equipment over and around the area under which the tunnel lay. Ostensibly this equipment was being used to construct the new compound, which grew ominously closer to completion every day. But the prisoners knew the real reason: the Germans suspected something, and that made everyone nervous, and the need for success all the more imperative.

When Frank descended into the hole, Roger Putnam made ready to follow. In that instant, Dean made a decision.

"Hold it a second," he said, grabbing Roger's arm. "Let *me* go."

Roger shrugged and said, "Hey, be my guest."

Quickly descending, he caught up with Frank at the face of the tunnel. Dean looked over the meager shoring and shivered. Bed boards were placed about every other foot instead of right next to each other. Dean could see by the feeble light of the fat lamps that the air was hazy.

Dust.

The heat of their bodies and the fat lamps had dried out the dirt on the inside. There was only a handful of boards left and twenty feet left to dig.

When Frank picked up the makeshift shovel, he turned and smiled. "I see we have a glutton for punishment. I thought you'd had enough of this for a while."

But Dean wasn't in the mood for repartee.

"Maybe we ought to figure out something better for the shoring," he said, his eyes searching intently for cracks in the wood. "I don't like the way it feels down here."

Frank shook his head. "We can't afford to waste the time. Every day that goes by—every *minute*—we give those bastards that much more time to find the tunnel. You saw what they're doing up there—"

"Yes, I did. And some of the guys think there's a leak."

"There's no proof of that. Besides, if there was a leak, the goons would have dropped on our heads like a ton of bricks."

"Maybe you're right, Frank, maybe the goons don't know. But this tunnel is still unsafe. If we die down here, where's the good in that?"

"We'll die if we *don't* get out!"

His vehemence startled Dean. It also frightened him. But he knew his friend was right.

Frank turned back to the tunnel's face and began digging. He gouged huge chunks of earth out of the wall. They fell to the floor, crumbling like dry muffins. Dean scraped the fallen dirt into a bucket and crawled back to the pumping station.

Freddie, slick with sweat and breathing hard from operating the pump, gave him a nod. "You okay?" he asked.

"No, I'm not. That shaft is dangerous. There's no telling what—"

Dean heard a rumbling overhead. Mannheim was at it again. In his mind's eye, he saw the huge backhoe lumbering back and forth over the tunnel, and he gritted his teeth, seething. "Damn that pizza-faced son of a bitch!"

CRACK!

In that confined space, the breaking bed board sounded like a gunshot.

"Oh, no," he said, his head whipping around.

CRAAAACK!

Another bed board snapped.

The tunnel's caving in!

He scurried back down the shaft, barely able to see anything because most of the fat lamps had blown out. The air, thick with dust, clogged his eyes and coated his tongue with fine grit. His eyes adjusted and he realized the tunnel was shorter by at least a dozen feet. The exact length supported by the scanty shoring. Frank was nowhere in sight.

"Freddie! Somebody!" Dean screamed. "Get down here, now!"

He didn't wait for a response and started frantically scooping away the newly fallen dirt with his bare hands, tears streaming down his face. Unnoticed in his frenzy, several areas of the tunnel back toward the entrance also began buckling.

While he was digging, Roger came up behind him.

"Oh, God," Roger said. "How much? How far back?"

"I don't know! Twelve feet maybe. DIG!"

Both of them began throwing the dirt behind them. Seconds ticked by like hours.

How long can Frank hold out? Is he already dead?
Dean pushed those thoughts out of his mind and dug faster.
Frank's alive! He's alive, goddamn it!

❈   ❈   ❈

The air was all but gone, and Frank's mind teetered on the abyss. Though there was no light, he could feel it growing blacker. *I'm sorry, Brenda*, he thought. *I'm sorry I didn't make it.*

His mind conjured up strange images when the cells of his brain, starved for oxygen, began to die. What they said about dying wasn't true. Your whole life didn't flash before your eyes, just the parts you wished you could have changed. There was the time he'd walked out of the house during a terrible fight and stayed away the entire night. Later, when he saw the hurt in Brenda's eyes, he'd wanted to kick himself.

It was blacker now.

The images had a tunnel-vision quality to them, as if the world would end in a giant iris-out.

To hell with it. Might as well just give in to it. Let go. Float away...

Suddenly, in his last gasp of sentience, Frank felt hands grasping his legs. Like some bizarre breach birth, he was pulled out into the light. *He couldn't open his eyes. Why couldn't he open his eyes?*

Voices... He heard voices.

They sounded far off and reverberant.

"Breathe, goddammit!" he heard someone say as a great pain erupted in his chest.

Breathe? Why? There's no need to breathe in heaven, is there?

Another blow pounded his chest, causing him to cough up the dirt he'd swallowed. It came out between his gasps for breath, like some evil bile. When the fresh oxygen flooded his lungs and then into his brain, his mind cleared. It was then he realized the voices belonged to Dean and Roger.

"He's gonna make it!" Roger said.

Frank opened his eyes and stared at Dean, a weak smile on his lips. "You're late again, Seger."

Dean laughed. "Not late enough, you sorry bastard. Now do us both a favor and shut the hell up." Turning to Roger, he said, "Give me a hand. We've got to get him topside. I think this whole shaft's going to go."

As fast as the tight space would allow, Dean and Roger dragged Frank to the entrance and hoisted him out. Once back inside the barracks, they carried him into his quarters and laid him out on his bunk.

"Stay with him," Dean said. "We've got a few hours 'til roll call. He'll have to be up and around by then. For now, let him sleep."

Roger nodded and moved over to Bob's bunk. Going to the door, Dean paused, gazing steadily at his friend.

"It wouldn't have been worth it, Frank," he said quietly.

He paused for another moment and then left the room, softly closing the door behind him.

※　※　※

Dean saw that the trapdoor was shut, and the room had been put back in order. As usual, there was no trace of dirt or anything that might give the tunnel away. He opened the front door and stood outside, leaning wearily against the building's outer wall.

Closing his eyes, he tilted his head up and let the sun's rays bathe his face. In another week or so, it would be July. Then the heat would turn vicious. Then again, because they were so far north, maybe it wouldn't be so bad.

"*Achtung!*" a voice called out.

Dean's eyes snapped open.

"*Achtung!*"

Looking around, he saw one of the guards gesturing toward Barracks 2.

"Shit," Dean said. He ran around the side of the building, stopping short when he saw what the commotion was all about.

His heart sank.

The backhoe was parked directly over the tunnel, which had now caved in along its entire length, leaving a depression running straight back to Barracks 2. Mannheim stood atop the backhoe bellowing in triumph, like a bull that had beaten the matador, for once.

Rat bastard.

A siren went off somewhere in the camp, and more guards came running, along with a contingent of *Hundführers* and their Rottweilers.

"What's wrong, Seger? What's happened?" Jensen said, coming up behind him. Dean said nothing; he didn't need to.

"Oh, God. No," Jensen moaned.

Dean got no comfort from the big man's misery, for it boded ill for all of them. Others crowded in behind him, their groans and curses depressing him further.

Dean turned to face them. "Get back inside, now!" he ordered. Surprisingly, no one questioned his authority. For the moment, everyone was too stunned. When they rounded the corner of Barracks 2, they saw Schmidt marching toward them. Mannheim fell in beside him, his gravelly voice screaming, "Roll call! Into formation, *schnell*! Roll call!"

The cry was taken up by the other guards as they rousted everyone from their barracks. Those who protested or dawdled received a savage kick or the butt of a rifle in the back.

The siren died while they fell into their accustomed ranks. As usual, Mannheim counted everyone personally. When he passed those of Barracks 2, he sneered at them. Dean glanced over at Frank and noticed that he at least appeared to be steady on his feet.

Kommandant Koenig emerged from his quarters moments later. Pausing briefly on the porch, he surveyed the formation. Then he started forward, losing his footing on the steps. For a moment, it looked as if his limbs had refused to work, his upper body moving while his legs remained rooted to the porch. Schmidt ran to his aid, reaching for the old man's arm to steady him. Koenig knocked the younger man's hand away, straightened his spine, and marched to the spot where his accursed soapbox awaited.

"All present and accounted for, *Herr Kommandant*," Mannheim said.

Koenig returned the sergeant's salute and then turned his attention to the men. "We seem to have a group of moles among us," he said, his eyes glittering oddly in the midday sun. "We seem to have a group who thinks this is a game."

He paused, his eyes riveting on the men of Barracks 2.

"This is not a game!" he screamed, a bit of spittle forming at the corners of his mouth.

"Your armies think they can wade ashore at Normandy and just dance their way to Berlin? We will stop them!" he screamed.

Dean glanced at the other men, all of whom looked badly spooked.

Koenig continued.

"All but one of you from Barracks Two will spend the next month in the cooler on one-quarter rations. You *will* learn that escapes will not be tolerated!"

The men from Barracks 2 looked bewildered.

"*Leutnant* Robert Neff! Please step forward."

It was Schmidt who had spoken. And now everyone in camp was buzzing.

"Silence!" Mannheim screamed. The talking ceased, the only sound the wind soughing through the pines and the clatter of hammer blows from the new compound under construction.

"*Leutnant* Neff! Step forward!" Mannheim repeated.

Looking as nervous as a high school girl waiting for her prom date, Bob Neff broke ranks and worked his way to a position midway between the men and Koenig. He heard someone whisper, "What's going on, Bob?"

Bob kept silent.

Koenig studied Bob with a paternal smile, then spoke, his voice reverberating like a cannonade. "Your foolish attempt at escape has failed. It has failed because of the commendable and forthright service of *Leutnant* Robert Neff, who kept me personally informed as to your progress."

There was an audible gasp from the men.

"Lousy traitor!" someone shouted.

Bob closed his eyes and hung his head, tears of shame running down his cheeks.

Dean couldn't believe his ears. Bob Neff had ratted them out, had told Koenig everything! The goons had let them dig their merry way, all the time waiting for the right moment to shove their faces in the shit. The bastards had waited until freedom was within reach, and then snatched it away. Dean wanted to kill them: Koenig, Mannheim, Schmidt—every last one of them. Bob, too. Why had he done it? Why?

Koenig continued, his buoyant mood apparent to all. "...And as a reward for his service to the Reich, *Leutnant* Robert Neff is hereby repatriated." He lowered his eyes to Bob, who now openly wept. A sneer crossed his lips, gone instantly. "You may go, *Leutnant* Neff. As promised, freedom awaits."

Koenig motioned toward the gates, which, unbelievably, were

opening. Bob raised his eyes toward them, and then back at the prisoners. Nearly to a man, they stared back at him with unconcealed hatred. Turning back to face the gates, he took his first halting step toward freedom.

All at once the prisoners started screaming, their voices a gabble of vile invective. Crying harder, he picked up his pace, his breathing coming in halting sobs. The walk turned into a trot, which then became an all-out run.

Dean watched with mixed emotions. Bob had been a bit of a nerd, but the decent sort, so Koenig must have gotten to him somehow. Nevertheless, the man *had* betrayed his compatriots. And that could not be so easily forgiven

"Good riddance, you fucking piece of shit!" a man from Barracks 10 yelled. It was followed by hoots of derision from several of his barracks mates. But as Bob drew closer to the gates, Dean found his hopes going with him. He was leaving; he was getting out. Soon he'd be home with his family.

And then the shot rang out.

Bob halted in his tracks, turned to face the men one last time, then dropped to the dirt, unmoving.

"No!" Freddie cried.

Dean caught Frank's eye. His friend stared back at him, his expression a mixture of shock and anger. Dean knew exactly what he was thinking.

We're all doomed.

Two guards ran over, picked up Bob's body, and dragged it off. Koenig continued staring at the men for a moment, then turned and walked back to his quarters, his steps slow and measured.

Schmidt, looking shell-shocked and weary, stepped onto the box.

"Dismissed," he said in a quiet voice.

Everyone filtered back to their own barracks. No one came for the men of Barracks 2, the month-long sentence either forgotten or rescinded.

No one cared.

24

Riley and Brenda spent the night in a small motel near the Johnstown field, then took off at six o'clock in the morning. Their next stop, Chicago. Refueled and in the air again by eleven o'clock, they turned northward for the leg into Marinette. By one o'clock they were circling the field.

"Marinette tower," Riley said into the mike, "this is November, eight, three, five, six, Zulu, requesting a landing vector, over."

There was some momentary static and then a reply came through the radio's tinny four-inch speaker.

"Roger, November, eight, three, five, six, Zulu. This is Marinette tower. Please turn northwest two degrees and decrease your altitude to two thousand feet. You may vector in on runway three-alpha. You are cleared to land, over."

"Roger, Marinette tower, over."

Riley banked the plane and made the two-degree course correction to bring the Cessna down to the required altitude. Descending slowly, he throttled back when the wheels screeched against the tarmac.

He taxied to the terminal and signaled the ground crew to begin refueling. The crew chief, a grizzled veteran wearing a checked cap with tie flaps, gave him a toothy grin and a thumbs up.

"Why don't we grab some grub and stretch our legs?"

"Sounds great. I'm sick of bologna sandwiches," Brenda said.

In the small coffee shop, Riley waited until the waitress took their orders before pulling out his aeronautical chart of the Green Bay area.

"This is where we're going to search," he said, spreading the chart out on their small table. "I'm convinced that the camp is located somewhere in Marinette or Florence counties."

"What about farther west?"

Riley shook his head.

"Those counties are bordered by national forest land. Not likely they'd be there. Farther west it gets more populated. Isolation is Koenig's schtick. No, they're right in here somewhere," he said, placing his finger on the chart.

Brenda stared at the spot Riley's finger touched and prayed he was right. She picked up a glass of water with a trembling hand and took a sip. Her heart was racing.

Riley folded the chart when the waitress brought their orders.

"So, how do we do this?" Brenda said.

Riley stared out through the tinted floor-to-ceiling window that looked out over the airport.

"It won't be easy. We've got more than eighteen hundred square miles to cover, and that's quite a haystack. Even something as big as that camp won't be easy to spot in all of that. It's a big needle, but it's still a needle."

Brenda had stopped listening, her thoughts a jumble. There was something nagging at her mind, something just below the surface, something that just might give them the edge.

It came to her.

"Postcards," she muttered.

"What?" Riley said, his furrowed brows betraying his confusion and worry.

"Postcards, John. I don't know why I didn't think of it earlier!"

"Wait a minute. You're not making any sense. What're you talking about?"

She flashed him an indulgent smile and patted his hand. "Don't worry, Uncle John, I haven't lost it yet." She paused a moment, then continued. "When Frank left, I asked him, half-jokingly, if they had any picture postcards of the guard towers."

Riley frowned, still confused and anxious.

"John... Guard towers have searchlights. At night the camp will be lit up like a Christmas tree!"

Brenda smiled even wider, both proud of herself and tickled by Riley's thunderstruck expression.

"Remind me to hire you when we get back to Boston," he said, his smile matching hers.

With more than six hours of daylight left, Riley and Brenda planned their first night's route. They would take the plane in an ever-widening zigzag course, working their way northward. With luck, they would spot them that night.

※ ※ ※

Riley pulled back on the stick, and the 310 shot up into the sky with an effortless grace. The sun, an enormous crimson ball, slipped below the horizon as they banked westward. At their present airspeed, he estimated that they would have about four hours' flying time. However, if they hadn't spotted anything after three, they would have to head back to Marinette. Leveling out, he began a systematic sweep of the landscape below.

At an altitude just above twelve hundred feet, they could spot anything down to the size of a campfire. After two hours, Riley sensed Brenda's impatience.

"You okay?" he asked.

"Yes, but my eyes are killing me," she said, not taking her eyes from the moving landscape below. "Where are we?"

Riley flicked on the autopilot and consulted his chart, cross-referencing the chart's location with the same one on an ordinary road map.

"We're near Middle Inlet. About twenty miles northeast of the field."

"Damn it," she said. "We're never going to find them."

Riley hated to see her lose hope so soon. It wasn't like her.

"I know you hate to hear 'I told you so,' but look, we've got another hour of flying time before we have to return to Marinette. We might see something between now and then."

She turned from the window for the first time, a small tear cascading down her cheek.

"Thanks," she said. "I guess I'm just tired and feeling overwhelmed with everything. Let's keep going."

Riley smiled and patted her on the shoulder.

"That's my girl."

After the hour passed, they'd flown to just north of Wausaukee, covering nearly seven hundred square miles.

Nothing.

Nothing but small towns and lakes reflecting the pale moonlight.

Returning to Marinette, Riley noticed Brenda's face now bore a look of grim determination. He knew there was no turning back for her.

✳   ✳   ✳

After retrieving their keys at the motel's front desk, Riley walked Brenda to her room. "Do you want to fly during daylight tomorrow?" he asked.

She shook her head.

"No. I know we'll find them faster this way, and I need the sleep. Thanks anyway. Sleep well."

She kissed him gently on the cheek and entered her room, closing the door behind her.

Striding to his own room down the hall, Riley sat down on the king-size bed, picked up the phone, and called his wife. He knew something was wrong as soon as she came on the line.

"John," she said. "I'm so glad you called."

Her fearful tone sent icy daggers into his heart.

"What's wrong, Rachel? Is it the kids?"

"No, no. Thank God. Penny Carter called."

"Tony's wife? What did she want?" he said, not sure if he should feel relieved or annoyed.

There was a long pause...

"Tony's dead, John."

Riley felt a hammer blow in his chest.

"John? John? Are you there?"

He found his voice a moment later, clearing his throat with a loud cough.

"What happened?"

"Oh, God, Penny was such a mess, she hardly made sense—"

"Tell me."

"As near as I could understand her, one of the other agents found him in the garage... sitting in his car... He'd shot himself—"

Rachel started crying, and Riley tried to comfort her, but his words felt useless, like a gearshift on a horse.

"Tonight was their anniversary. They had plans, reservations at L'Espalier. Why did he do it, John? Why?"

As much as he'd lost respect for his friend, Riley knew one thing without a shred of doubt. Tony Carter had been a dedicated FBI agent, had believed in the cause wholeheartedly, as misguided as he was over this Koenig mess.

Tony would never have killed himself.

Period.

Especially with a new promotion, a hot case, and a wedding anniversary. There was only one explanation.

Koenig.

And that spelled trouble with a capital T.

"Rachel, calm down and listen to me. You've got to do exactly as I tell you. Get the kids and put them in the car and drive to our spot. Okay?"

"You mean the—"

"Don't say it! Yes, go there immediately and wait to hear from me. And don't answer the phone unless it's our signal. Do you remember what that is?"

"Yes," she said, her voice steadying.

"Good. By the way, Brenda's parents and the kids are there already, so it shouldn't be too lonely."

"That's good, they're nice people."

Riley smiled. Rachel was already coping.

"All right. Get going and drive safely. I love you."

"I love you too," she said. "John?"

"Yes?"

"Please be careful."

"I will."

Knowing he'd be unable to sleep, he left the room and went downstairs to the bar. It sat tucked into the far corner of the motel's "family" restaurant, boasting eight Naugahyde stools fronting an oak-topped bar crisscrossed by ancient glass rings and cigarette burns. A vestigial dance floor, left over from the days when disco was king, sat off to the side. The place smelled of stale beer and staler memories. At least it was empty, save for the lone bartender wiping glasses with bored, lazy strokes. And that suited Riley just fine.

He eased himself into the first stool and nodded to the bartender, a whippet-thin man, just nudging into middle age and doing his best not to show it.

"What'll it be?" the bartender said, flashing him a gap-toothed grin.

"What have you got for beer?"

"Bud, Bud Light, Beck's, and Molson Golden."

"Molson."

Taking a long gulp of the ice-cold Canadian beer, Riley reviewed everything Rachel had told him. Koenig's assassins had been busy boys. He knew that the Bureau would see through the suicide for the thinly disguised ploy it was. They might be running after the wrong political football these days, but they knew their business when it came to examining the evidence. And when they did, they would see that it didn't hold up. But would that be enough to make them disobey the hands-off edict from on high?

Maybe not.

Maybe now, more than ever, the government would wish to see Koenig go up in flames. Once he did, the government would tear his holdings apart and confiscate the billions in spoils. But the real crime was in letting all those innocent men die. And if Riley had his way, he'd make damn sure that didn't happen.

The other question burning in his mind was whether or not Koenig's security people would have someone at his house, someone who would simply follow Rachel up to their retreat in Maine, killing everyone there.

He closed his eyes, praying that his family had gotten the jump on them. There were very few people left alive who could boast that particular trick.

He downed the beer and ordered another, lifting the foamy glass in a silent toast to Tony.

Keep the game going for me, ol' buddy, wherever you are. I might be dealing in real soon.

Part III
GÖTTERDÄMMERUNG

25

The shells blasted overhead, shaking the old mansion to its foundations and bringing chunks of brick and mortar down on his head. Dust swirled in the murky air, making the cellar room appear like a night filled with fog.

Those godless Russian bastards ringed the outskirts of the city, pounding them day and night with their artillery. Hundreds of guns sent thousands of shells into their midst, sounding like the never-ending roar of some gigantic wounded beast.

Heinrich held his mother against his body, feeling her warmth and her trembling. She lay curled into a fetal ball, whimpering softly into his shoulder, jerking every time a shell exploded.

Not much was left of the ancestral home above their heads. Heinrich and his mother now lived in the cellar permanently, only venturing above when the shelling ceased long enough for him to scrounge whatever food and clean water existed. The supplies dwindled more every day. On his last foray, he'd asked for any news of the fighting. But the old men and women, all who were left in the dying city, scurried away, their heads hung low and their eyes darting about like frightened mice.

Cowards!

Let them all die. And let those who chose to live under the Russian boot regret the day they'd been born, for he knew they surely would. As surely as he knew the red hordes were coming. As for him and his mother, Heinrich had every intention that they should survive—by whatever means necessary. That is, if she did not go mad from the shelling. The constant pounding was enough to test even the strongest of men.

He looked at her now. Once beautiful, Marta Koenig's golden hair now hung in lank, greasy strings—her clothes in filthy tatters. He imagined his own appearance was little better.

CARRUMP!

Another hit, this one almost directly above. The shock wave brought down a section of the wall. He covered his mother as best as he could, feeling the bits of brick glancing off his back like hailstones. On the other side, he saw the skeletons of the Mueller family. All five of them. He thought they'd gone west months ago.

CAAARRRRUMP!

Farther away this time. It might mean the Russian line had advanced. If only he had been two years older like his brother Albert. He would have given those fiends a taste of German bravery. But Albert now lay in some nameless grave somewhere outside Stalingrad. Not the casualty of glorious combat, but a starved and frozen corpse left to litter the path of their ignominious retreat from those Communist bastards!

Heinrich cocked his head, sensing that something had changed. It took him a moment to realize what it was.

Silence.

The shelling had stopped.

Leaving his mother's side with a few whispered endearments, he scrambled through the rubble to the stone steps leading to the surface. She cried out for him not to leave her, but he *had* to see what was out there. Besides, their meager larder, such as it was, was almost depleted. He needed to find something for that night's supper.

Reaching the top step, he found the door to what had been the main house still passable. Even still, he had to throw all his weight against it to make it move.

Squeezing through the narrow opening, he stepped out into the cool open air, squinting to keep the red ball of the sun from dazzling his eyes. The quiet was preternatural, like the inside of a coffin. And no telling how long it would last. Seconds... minutes... hours? Only God knew—or maybe the devil.

Emerging from the wreckage of the house, he stepped onto the ravaged street. It stretched before him, dotted with small fires from open gas mains, exploded cars, and the occasional bloated corpse. The burial parties came through infrequently now. He smelled the sickly-sweet odor of death constantly. He saw an old man scrounging through the pockets of a dead *Waffen-SS* soldier. No one else moved on the street. So few people left.

He started to make his way toward the square when he stopped in midstride.

What was that?

A sound, a low rumble, drifted through the air. When he turned and glanced up the street, the sound intensified, vibrating the ground beneath his feet. He moved to an overturned *Kübelwagen* and hid behind it.

A moment later a tank turned the corner, a column of soldiers following in its wake. He spotted the large red star emblazoned on the turret's side.

Russians!

Trying to stay hidden, he ran back through the door to the cellar, bolting it behind him.

"Mother! Mother! We must go!" he said, running to her side. "They are here!"

She smiled up at him, a wild look in her eyes. "Albert is here? My Bertie is here?"

He saw, to his horror, that she was completely unaware of what was happening around them.

"The Russians, Mother, the Russians are here."

She frowned, not knowing quite how to process that information. A second later, her serene smile returned.

"Bertie will protect us," she said.

The sounds of the approaching tank now shook the cellar. Suddenly, its engine cut. The silence frightened him even more than its horrid rumbling.

Shaking her, he tried to get her to move. "Come. We must go. Now!" he whispered.

Finally realizing something was wrong, she started screaming. Panicked, Heinrich clamped his hand over her mouth.

Too late.

He heard men shouting orders and someone pounded on the door, making it shriek and groan. They would be through it in moments.

He scanned the room, grabbed a piece of wrought iron scavenged several days before, and returned to his hiding place behind an old piano crate. Three feet long and fashioned into an ornate arrowhead at one end, the spike came from the fence that had bordered their property. He'd picked it up almost as an afterthought. Now, it was all he had to defend himself against the Russians and their machine guns.

The hammering on the door grew more insistent and Heinrich's pulse pounded in rhythmic counterpoint.

With a loud crack, the door exploded inward, ripping off its hinges and clattering down the steps. A squad of six Russian soldiers lunged through the opening, eyes flashing, their weapons at the ready. Heinrich clutched the spike harder, feeling the iron's rough texture against his tender skin. He'd have one chance to kill one of them before they killed him. Better to die fighting...

The Russians fanned out and began to search the basement. Heinrich counted to three, then leaped to his feet and ran at the soldier closest to him.

The squad leader spotted him and raised his SPD-38 submachine gun. "*Stoy!*" he screamed, his finger tightening on the trigger.

Poised to strike, Heinrich hesitated long enough for one of the soldiers to snatch the spike out of his hands. The squad leader stepped up to him, his cold, black eyes boring into him.

"SS?" he asked in heavily accented German.

Heinrich looked bewildered.

Impatient, the Russian squad leader slapped him to the ground.

"SS?" he shouted.

"No!" Heinrich said. "No SS here."

The squad leader looked at him, as if seeing his youth for the first time, and then turned his attentions to Heinrich's mother.

"Ahh, *Fräulein*," he said, leering.

"She's my mother, you pig!"

The squad leader looked first at Marta Koenig then back to Heinrich, and then burst into laughter. "*Sie ist meine Mutter, Schwein,*" he said, mimicking Heinrich's adolescent squeak.

Still laughing, the soldier said something Heinrich could not understand. Two of his cohorts ran to the woman and dragged her to her feet. She gazed at them impassively. The squad leader turned to Heinrich and smiled again.

Reaching upwards, the squad leader took hold of his mother's blouse and ripped it off, exposing her large, pendulous breasts.

"Ahh, *Ausgezeichnet, ja?*" he said, fondling them roughly.

His mother, reacting for the first time, kicked the squad leader squarely in the testicles. He doubled over in pain, vomit spewing out his mouth. One of the other soldiers brought up his rifle and stabbed her squarely in the gut with his bayonet.

"You fucking pigs!" Heinrich yelled, throwing himself at the man, his hands reaching instinctively for the rifle. They fought, the Russian trying to wrench the rifle out of Heinrich's hands. The boy held on, prompting the Russian to yell for help.

The squad leader, barely recovered from his mother's well-placed kick, grabbed his weapon and crossed the room, his mad Tartar eyes narrowing. He knocked Heinrich to the ground and bashed him in the head with the machine gun's wooden butt.

Heinrich's vision turned a sickly gray, pain exploding in his head. *He would not die. He would not!*

Through eyes half-blinded by blood, he watched the squad leader smile and aim the machine gun, preparing to deliver the *coup de grace.* His finger tightened on the trigger, when someone cried out from above. The squad leader lowered his weapon and looked toward the steps where another soldier beckoned.

Forgetting the boy, the soldiers dashed up the stairs and out into the twilight. Heinrich crawled to his mother's side and held her in his arms, the tears streaming down his face mixing with her blood. A thin layer of dust lay on her unblinking eyes. She was dead.

He waited until he was sure the Russians were gone and then crawled out of the cellar. The air outside smelled of burning petrol and charred meat. Looking around, he saw that the Russians were long gone, but they'd left their mark. A new body lay atop a pile of rubble. It was Frau Knebel, their neighbor. Her blank eyes stared heavenward, already clouding with decay, her clothes ripped to shreds and her throat cut from ear to ear. Heinrich stared at her, dry-eyed and numb. He had no more tears left to cry.

It was then he heard the drone of engines and looked skyward. A fleet of American B-17s flew overhead, so low, he could see the winged Pegasus painted on their fuselages. Shaking with fury, he raised his fist and screamed.

"*Amerikanische Bastarde!* Why did you leave us to these animals?"

Heinrich Koenig awoke with a start, his body bathed in sweat and the scream dying on his lips. He sat up, breathing hard, his lungs burning for air. The dream came frequently now. He saw his mother die every night, over and over again, the Russian soldier's bayonet piercing her belly, the belly that had held his unborn sibling.

And the planes.

The American planes.

It wasn't until he was grown that he'd discovered those planes were a part of the 94th Bombardment group and that those particular planes that awful day belonged to the 410th Bombardment Squadron.

Heinrich sat up in bed and sighed. The relief of waking was soon outweighed by the pain in his head. It had grown worse. The pain and disorientation left him weak and confused in those few moments of lucidity. Koenig glanced at the clock.

4:25.

"*Mein Gott!*"

He vaulted out of bed, his vision swimming while he struggled into his shirt and tunic. The jodhpur pants, so handsome and stylish, presented more difficulty than usual. Pulling on his boots, he left his cap behind and dashed out of the room, through his office and out onto the porch.

The key! He'd forgotten the key!

Running back inside, he grabbed his keys off the bureau, glancing at the clock once more.

4:28.

A small whimper escaped his throat when he tore out of the building and sprinted across the quad. His heart pounded and his lungs burned. His body, long out of shape, resisted the demands he now placed on it.

The men guarding the *Waffenlager* watched with growing unease at the disheveled specter of their *Kommandant* fumbling with the keys in the lock. Their anxiety increased when they saw the flash of panic in the old man's eyes. What could be so urgent?

Koenig flung open the door and darted inside, not bothering to bolt it behind him. Instead, he ran directly to the trapdoor and lifted it up with the ease of someone on an adrenaline rush. Descending the steps two at a time, he darted over to the bomb and tore open the panel.

00:00:30, 00:00:29, 00:00:28, 00:00:27...

He yanked the chain holding the barrel key out of his shirt, slammed the key into the lock on the panel, and twisted it.

The code! What was the code?

Koenig began panicking as the numbers he sought eluded his ravaged mind.

00:00:24, 00:00:23, 00:00:22...

A sharp pain ripped through his head, and he moaned in agony. Was this a stroke? Had something finally given way? The pain increased, driving him to his knees. Inhaling huge gulps of air, he felt the pain lessening.

He looked at the timer.

00:00:08, 00:00:07, 00:00:06, 00:00:05…

"*Nein!*" he said, panic welling up in his chest.

The code! Yes! The code was his and Johann's birth dates!

He punched in the numbers on the keypad and saw, to his infinite relief, the timer reset itself and begin counting:

24:00:00, 23:59:59, 23:59:58, 23:59:57…

Drained, he pulled out the barrel key, closed the panel, and trudged wearily up the steps and into the armory. He closed the trapdoor and stood staring at it.

What was he doing here?

Baffled, he strolled out of the *Waffenlager*, passing the bewildered guards, ignoring them completely.

"*Herr Kommandant?*" one of them said.

Koenig turned. "*Ja?*" he said.

The guard pointed to the door of the armory. Koenig was puzzled for a moment. The door. He'd forgotten to lock it.

"Ach!" he said, returning to the door. "*Ich bin ein dummkopf!*"

He locked it, then smiled at the guard, patting him paternally on the shoulder. "*Danke schön*," he said.

"*Bitte, Mein Kommandant,*" the guard said, bowing.

Koenig bowed in response, turned on his heels, and marched smartly back to his quarters.

� ✕ ✕

From the shadows beside the nearest barracks, Frank Murphy watched Koenig return the way he'd come. Ever since the guards had discovered the tunnel, Frank had been unable to sleep. He'd taken to solitary walks outside the barracks after lights out in direct violation of the regulations. If he were caught, it would mean the cooler. Not that he gave a damn anymore. After the last two times, he could do it standing on his head.

It was funny. Now that he didn't care about being caught, he found it easier than ever to take his "constitutionals" without being noticed. Of course, he didn't walk brazenly across the quad giving the guards a smart salute, either. He still had to be careful, but his state of mind had advanced far beyond where it had been.

After Dean dragged him out of the collapsing tunnel, Frank's mood went from the happiness of being alive to the despair of one whose only hopes lay cruelly dashed. The tunnel had been Frank's last hurrah, his last plan—until now.

Koenig's mad dash to the armory had given Frank one more idea. It was reckless, dangerous, and probably doomed to fail. But what choices did they have? There were no more options. They would overpower the two guards posted at the *Waffenlager*, change into their uniforms, and wait for Koenig to appear. Once the armory was open, they would take whatever was inside and shoot their way out.

Frank waited until a patrol passed by, then snuck back to the barracks and slipped into bed. He was dog tired. But now that his mind found refuge in his new plan, his body found refuge in sleep. A precious hour of oblivion before roll call.

※　　※　　※

"Are you out of your mind?" Dean said when Frank confided his plan to him after morning mess.

"Hold it down," Frank whispered, glancing about as they walked around the quad. "Just listen to me and act like you're hearing a joke, for Christ's sake."

"That shouldn't be too hard," Dean said, his exasperation overcoming his ability to act.

Frank ignored the crack and continued. "I've been thinking about this for a while. Koenig makes this little pilgrimage every morning."

"How do you know? You haven't been watching him every day, have you?"

"No, but others have been."

"Who?" Dean said, his annoyance growing.

"It doesn't matter. The point is, he does it. All we have to do is be there the next time and we're out of here."

"Frank," Dean said, halting in his tracks, "let me ask you something. You ever fire a gun?"

Frank looked at him as if he were crazy.

"No, but—"

"No buts. You listen to *me* for a change. I have fired weapons, mostly rifles and shotguns that my dad collected. I have *never* operated a machine gun. Chances are most of the other guys haven't either."

"So what? They'll learn."

Dean sighed, trying to figure out a way to get through to his friend, a friend who was becoming obsessed.

"Not fast enough! They're gonna have ex-border guards firing at them. Men experienced at killing. It'll be a goddamn bloodbath."

Frank looked at him, his eyes burning with purpose and, at the same time, filled with utter sadness.

"What do you think it'll be if we don't get out?"

Frank turned and walked away.

Dean knew Frank was right. With Koenig sinking more and more into his delusions every day, their chances of survival diminished. Maybe, with this last dash at freedom, they would succeed. Either that or die like men, rather than helpless sheep led to the slaughter.

Another image came into Dean's mind, an image of open pits filled with the bodies of executed men and women while leering

SS soldiers placed pistols against the heads of those waiting their turn to die. He saw them slam forward, the bullets plowing through their brains. He watched while the soldiers, giddy with the slaughter, kicked the bodies into the pit and raked them with machine gun fire.

Dean's breath caught in his throat. The image, which had begun as a scratchy black and white movie in his mind, now attained color and vividness. The SS soldiers transformed into Mannheim and the guards, and—he noted with mounting horror—the bodies in that awful pit now bore the faces of every prisoner in camp.

26

Riley took off just after sunset the next day and flew directly to the Wausaukee area, then began a slow zigzag over the landscape. Brenda was silent for most of the first hour, preferring to watch the tops of the tall, dark pines moving swiftly by, not allowing herself the luxury of doubt. Frank was down there, somewhere. She could feel it. She knew they would find him soon. If not tonight, then the next night, or the night after that. She knew Riley might want to throw in the towel after a while, but she wouldn't. *Not ever.*

"Where are we?" she asked.

"We're passing over Clarkville. Derleth should be up ahead."

So many small towns. She passed the time by making up imaginary families inhabiting the doll-like houses they flew over. In her mind, the husbands were safely home, and everyone was warm, happy, and well fed. It was silly. Small towns were like any other place, filled with murders, divorces, and broken families with husbands who would never come home.

"Penny for your thoughts," Riley said.

"Just feeling sentimental."

Riley nodded. "Yeah. It'll get you every time."

A few minutes later they passed over Derleth. Brenda could see Gordon's Diner, its neon sign flashing a cheery red. The parking lot surrounding it was peppered by a few pickups and the odd Buick or Ford. Nothing Japanese, not here. The plane shot over, leaving the town behind. A few minutes later, they were flying over several small lakes and ponds and then, once again, like a familiar and tiresome friend, came the dense black of the Wisconsin wilderness.

Brenda squinted her eyes at something over the horizon.

"John? Is there another town up ahead?"

He flicked on the autopilot and turned on a small goose-necked reading light. Consulting his chart, he shook his head.

"Nope. Nothing for another ten, fifteen statute miles."

Brenda's heart raced. She stared ahead, the glow growing brighter. In seconds, the trees broke and right below them lay Camp Stalag.

"Oh my God!" she said. "We found it."

Riley banked the plane and circled the camp in a wide arc. Far below, Brenda saw men in uniform scurrying about, pointing toward the plane. Were they too low? Would the soldiers start shooting? Not waiting to find out, Riley marked the position on his chart and finished the turn.

Brenda stared ahead through the windscreen, tears coursing down her face.

"I guess a part of me really didn't believe all this until I saw that awful place," she said, turning to Riley. "Maybe we should call the State Police and let them handle this."

Riley rubbed her shoulders affectionately.

"You know I wish we could. If we contact anyone—"

"I know," she said, remembering everything Riley told her about Koenig's security force, and his friend's death. He was right. They could trust no one but themselves. "I just wish I could *do* something. I can't sit and wait in that motel, John."

Brenda hated feeling helpless. But they had no other choice other than to go ahead with their plan. It might be crazy. It might not even work, but it was all they had.

"I need you to be there," Riley said. "In case something goes wrong."

"What?" she asked, exasperated. "What could I possibly do if something *does* go wrong?"

"Tell the world the truth."

"Would the world really care?"

He smiled wearily. "Maybe. Maybe not. But you have to stay clear of this."

� � ✳

After roll call the next morning, Frank called a meeting in the barracks. The mood of the men, still somber in the aftermath of Bob Neff's brutal murder, was made all the more depressing by the callous disposal of his body in the nearby woods. Frank couldn't help thinking of the wife, and the children whose father would never return.

He leaned on the pot-bellied stove, watching the men. Dana Webster lay on his bunk, doodling on some writing paper, while Roger Putnam stared at the floor. Even Dean, always the joker of the bunch, sat at the picnic table, his eyes an opaque glaze.

Frank grabbed a pan off the stove and banged it hard against its cast-iron flank. The loud clatter made everyone jump.

"Jesus!" Dana said.

"That's right, guys," Frank said. "You'd better start praying because you're all but dead."

Angered, Roger got up and walked over to where Frank stood.

"Fuck you!" he said. "I'm sick of your 'we're dead if we don't get out' speech. Why don't you just let it be?"

Frank met his gaze, his expression unyielding.

"Good. Get mad. Get real mad, because without that, you'll all end up the way Bob did!"

"He was a traitor. He got what he deserved," Dana said, and flopped back onto his bunk.

Frank ran over and grabbed him, pulling him to his feet. "No, he wasn't," Frank said, his eyes blazing. "He was just a guy caught up in something crazy—like the rest of us. Koenig got to him, pushed the right buttons. It could've happened to any of us!"

Bill Jensen stood up, his massive physique even more intimidating than usual. "Colonel's right. Bob was okay. And I'm sorry he's dead."

"Me too," Freddie echoed from his bunk across the room.

Frank looked to the others. "Anybody have anything else to say?"

There was only silence. Nodding once, he turned back to Dana, loosening his grip when he saw the contrite expression on the young actor's face. "I'm sorry, Frank. We're all a little freaked out."

Frank clapped him on the shoulder. "It's okay. I just don't want to stay here one minute longer than I have to. And I don't want us to give up, either. I think I've found a way out. It's been staring us in the face the whole damn time."

"So, what *masterful* plan does Colonel Miraculous have for us now?" Roger asked, unmollified.

Dean stood up. "Wait a minute," he said. "I know how everyone here is feeling, but I think we should listen to Frank."

"Oh great! Now we're getting advice from Eddie Haskell," Roger snapped.

His emotions finally boiling over, Dean slugged Roger, knocking him back onto his bunk. Instead of retaliating, he remained motionless, paralyzed with shock.

"You," Dean said, jabbing his finger at Roger's nose, "shut the fuck up and listen." He turned and shot the room an angry glare. "All of you just shut the fuck up! Look at you! You're sitting around like a bunch of fucking old ladies. I, for one, am sick and goddamn tired of feeling sorry for myself. If you don't want to listen, fine! You can rot here for all I care. But do us all a favor and can it!"

"All right, then," Frank said, winking at Dean. "For those of you who are interested, this is the plan."

Frank launched into his scheme, outlining his strategy step by step: how they would take possession of the armory, grab the weapons, distribute as many as possible before someone sounded the alarm, and then kill as many of the bastards as they could.

As Frank's excitement transferred to the men, he saw the fire in their eyes once more, a fire he knew could not be quenched with anything less than their freedom. But he also saw something else: *fear*. And he couldn't blame them; he was scared shitless.

"I can't make you guys do this," Frank said. "If any of you want out, raise your hands. They'll be no hard feelings."

He waited. No one moved.

Frank felt a flood of warmth and love for these men. They would win, or all go down together. Koenig would not have passive sheep for his slaughter.

"Thanks, guys," Frank said, placing his hand on Dean's shoulder. "I know I've let you down these last couple of times, but this time we'll take them on together. This time we're gonna get the sons of bitches!"

All of them cheered.

It was a sound Frank would cherish forever.

"Okay," he continued. "I want each of you to approach men from the neighboring barracks. Keep it low-key. The more we have ready to fight, the better—"

Frank stopped speaking, a strange noise intruding.

"What the hell is that?" Jensen said, his dark features twisting into a puzzled frown.

The noise grew louder, sounding like a giant fly.

Roger hopped off his bunk, a smile spreading across his face. "It's a plane!" Roger said, his voice cracking with excitement. "It's a goddamn fucking plane!"

"Come on!" Frank said, running to the door.

The men pushed through the door, spilling out into the quad where other men from other barracks milled about in a happy pandemonium. The plane, a twin-engine Cessna, circled the camp in a wide, lazy arc.

"Maybe he'll go for help," someone said.

"Hell, maybe he'll drop a brick on Koenig's fat head," someone else said. Everyone who heard it hooted with laughter. By now every man in camp stood in the quad waving and cheering. The guards, confused and nervous, began herding the prisoners back toward their barracks, trying to make them disperse.

Frank watched the plane circle. The pilot waved and wagged his wings, causing another happy roar from the crowd.

"What's he doing now?" Dean asked.

The plane climbed abruptly, picking up speed.

"I think he's leaving," Frank replied.

He heard the engines cough and sputter, then cut out.

"Oh, no," Dean said. "He's gonna crash."

They all watched in horror when the plane started to fall. Frank heard the pilot trying to restart the engines to no avail.

Koenig and Schmidt watched from the porch of the *Kommandantur*. When it became apparent that the plane was going down, Koenig strode out into the quad, barking orders.

"Sound the alarm!" he screamed in German.

The siren wailed, and a squad of guards double-timed out through the gates. The plane, finally under control, glided down into the new compound, barely missing a pile of lumber when it touched down. The rocky soil, still bristling with tree stumps, caused it to bounce several times. Each time the plane's wheels slammed into the earth, the men gasped, certain it would roll over and explode. It finally came to rest, listing ominously to one side about twenty feet from the outer fence.

The pilot was climbing out of the cockpit when the guards fell upon him. They grabbed him by the arms and quick-marched him around the perimeter and in through the gates.

"Aw, nuts," Roger said. "This poor slob's in for a real, fine welcome."

Frank pushed his way through the crowd, a smile breaking out on his face. He wanted to scream with joy. It was Riley! With his heart pounding, Frank raced towards the prisoner who, with prodding from the guards, marched toward Koenig and Schmidt.

Dean caught up with Frank as he neared the *Kommandantur*, his voice a breathless whisper. "What's going on?"

"Brenda's found us," Frank said, his pace quickening.

Dean's startled expression said it all. "You *know* that guy?"

Frank nodded and leaned toward his friend. "I haven't got time to explain. Let's just say I'm a better letter writer than the Krauts'll give me credit for."

Dean beamed. "You crafty sonofabitch! What're you going to do?"

"Put all that historical research to good use. Keep everyone cool 'til you hear from me, okay?"

"Got it, *Colonel*," Dean said, saluting.

Frank caught up with Riley when he and the contingent of guards halted in front of the *Kommandantur*. Koenig towered over them, radiating haughty assurance.

Schmidt looked on, uneasy.

"Welcome to Camp Stalag," Koenig said, his voice suffused with false bonhomie. Turning to the guards, he said, "Take him into my office."

"Hold it, *Kommandant*," Frank said. "According to the Geneva Convention, the Senior POW Officer is to be present at all interrogations."

Koenig nodded. "Quite right, Colonel Murphy. Come. Please join us."

Koenig turned and headed into the building, followed by Schmidt. When the guards shoved him through the door, Riley turned and gave Frank a conspiratorial wink. It did little to overcome his growing unease.

Inside, Frank took the chair next to Riley and waited while Koenig sat down behind his desk. The old man reached for the crystal decanter of brandy and poured himself a generous drink.

"Well," Koenig said, swishing the brandy. "To what do we owe the pleasure of this surprise visit?"

Riley maintained his cool demeanor, as if finding himself back in World War Two were an everyday occurrence. "I was on my way to Iron Mountain and, as I'm sure your men could attest to, my engine conked out and I was forced to land in your field. Lucky for me there *was* a field."

"Liar!" Koenig screamed, his face purple with rage. "Who are you, and what are you doing flying over German territory out of uniform?"

Riley looked around the room, first at Schmidt, whose face remained unreadable, and then at Mannheim, who stood blocking the exit, his hands curled into fists.

Frank took this as his cue.

"I would advise that you only tell him your name rank and serial number."

"Silence!" Koenig said, pounding the desk for emphasis.

Riley glanced at Frank, who returned the wink.

"My name is Captain John Riley, United States Army Air Forces, serial number 16084006."

Koenig leaned back in his chair, a smug expression spreading over his face. "Well, *Captain* Riley. Do you realize that your precious Geneva Convention allows me to shoot you as a spy?"

For the first time Frank saw a look of worry cross Riley's face.

"Now, *Kommandant*," Frank interrupted, "what good would that do? If this man were a spy, he sure as hell picked a lousy place to infiltrate, now didn't he?"

Koenig roared. The apparent silliness of the situation spread even to Mannheim's normally dour face. Frank shot a glance at Riley, noting the man's calm.

"For once, I agree with you, Colonel," Koenig said. "Now that the good captain is here, he should become better acquainted with our facilities. Mannheim!"

The sergeant snapped to attention. "*Jawohl, mein Kommandant!*"

"Take Captain Riley to the cooler so he may reconsider his reluctance to speak with us."

Koenig then turned to Frank, his mirth evaporating.

"You may join him there, Colonel Murphy. Convince him of his folly. You have until tomorrow."

Frank sneered when the guards grabbed them and shoved them toward the door.

"Colonel!" Koenig said.

Frank shook himself loose from the grasp of the guards and stared defiantly back at the old man.

Koenig's eyes drilled into him. "Tomorrow..."

✵ ✵ ✵

The door of the cell slammed shut, leaving them both in the abyssal gloom. Koenig was either getting careless, or he actually expected Frank to talk John into divulging non-existent military secrets. Either way it was a screwed-up situation, no matter how you sliced it.

"That's *my* spot," Frank said, his grin hidden in the dark.

"Sorry, my mistake," Riley said, sliding over. "Is it always this cheerful?"

Frank settled down onto his haunches, preferring to squat rather than sit on the hard, cold concrete.

"Oh, it gets better," he said. "Slick job with the name, rank, and serial number, by the way. I was afraid you wouldn't pick up on it."

The other man chuckled. "Yeah, well. It was my dad's. They drummed it into his head night and day for seventeen weeks in basic training. He never forgot it. I don't even know why *I* remember it; it just came out."

"Lucky for you it did. Koenig's losing his mind. Spends half the day living in the past."

"Sounds like someone I know."

Frank sighed. "I deserved that. How's Brenda?"

There was silence for a moment. Frank held his breath.

"She's fine. Worried sick, but fine. She's waiting for us at the local motel. She's one hell of a headstrong lady."

Now it was Frank's turn to laugh. "For once, I'm glad. I *knew* my letter would work," he said, slapping his thigh. "I *knew* she would find me. So, what happened to your plane?"

"Nothing."

"What? You mean you—"

"Faked it? Yeah."

"But why? Now you're in the same mess we're in."

Riley placed his hand on Frank's shoulder. "I had to get in here and warn you."

"Warn me. About what? That I'm in the hands of a lunatic? Believe me, I know it all too well." He paused, another thought occurring to him. "When is help arriving?"

Another long silence.

"It's not..."

"Maybe you'd better tell me what the hell's going on," Frank said.

By the time Riley had filled him in on Koenig's complete background, his private assassins, and the government's wait-and-see attitude, Frank fumed.

"You mean to tell me those jerks know all about this place and they're just sitting on their goddamned asses? Why, for God's sake?"

Riley exhaled. There was no easy way with this.

"Koenig's hidden a tactical nuclear device somewhere in this camp."

"What!"

"The weapon is his insurance. The government is keeping their hands off until—"

"Until this mad fuck blows us all to hell and then they'll come in and cover it up with some toxic spill story."

"That's about the size of it."

"Goddamn motherfucker!" Frank said, kicking the door.

There came the sound of hurried steps and the peephole in the steel door slid open.

"*Was ist los?*" the guard asked.

Riley sneered at the man. "Nothing, Adolf, take a hike. *Raus!*"

"*Dummkopf,*" the guard muttered as he walked back down the hall to his post.

Riley waited until the guard's footsteps receded and then leaned closer to Frank.

"Listen, Frank. Can you think of any place Koenig could hide the bomb? It's three feet long, about the size of a suitcase."

Frank collapsed against the wall, suddenly overcome with all that had happened. With this new information added, his carefully built facade of strength crumbled.

"No, no, no, no," he repeated, shaking his head, his eyes squeezed tightly shut.

Angered, Riley grabbed him by his shirt and slammed him back against the concrete wall. Frank's eyes popped open in shock.

"Look, pal, I put my ass on the line for you and I expect some cooperation."

Frank stared at him, his spirit at the breaking point.

"I'm sorry, John, I can't, I just—"

Riley let him go in disgust and Frank sank back against the wall. Minutes went by while they listened to the steady cadence of the guard's boots walking his post outside the cell. The hobnails made a rhythmic clack, clack, clack, not unlike the sound of a ticking clock.

"You ever hear of *Bushido*?" Riley asked, breaking the silence.

"No," Frank said, staring into the darkness. "That your secret weapon?"

"Just shut up and listen. Bushido is the Samurai code. They lived their entire lives by it. The crux of it is you go into battle prepared to die, 'cause if you're not, you're gonna get scared. Then you fuck up and you're dead." Riley paused a moment to let that sink in and then continued. "You better get mad, Frank. You better get your blood in a boil and keep it there. Or those goddamn sons of bitches are gonna kill every last one of us. I want to get these bastards. I want to *see* their blood—I want to *taste* it. They killed a very dear friend of mine and I want them to pay. Now, goddamn it! Tell me what you know about this place or we're *all* dead. Where could Koenig hide the bomb?"

Frank recoiled at the intensity of Riley's statement, but something in his words kindled a fire inside him, scorching away the doubt, cleansing and renewing him in a way far beyond the effect of Riley's words.

In the grayish gloom, Riley saw his nephew smile. It resembled a death's head grin.

"Wait a minute," Frank said, the light of recognition dawning in his mind. He could see the *Waffenlager* as vividly as if he were standing directly in front of it. "That explains it."

"Explains what?"

"The bomb. I know *exactly* where it is. It's in their armory. Koenig goes there every morning around four thirty."

Riley grew concerned.

"Wait a minute. You said he goes there *every* morning?"

"Yeah, so what?"

"Damn. I was afraid of that."

Frank shook his head, confused. "I don't get it. What's the problem?"

"I did some checking with a military friend of mine. You can detonate a tactical nuke several different ways. It can be shot out of a cannon. Outmoded but effective. You can fly it in via cruise missile, or you can set it in place and blow it using a remote radio signal or a digital timer."

"Okay," Frank said, unsure where this was going.

"My guess is that Koenig's got himself a timer, most likely a fail-safe timer."

"What's a—"

"Fail-safe timer? A real nasty piece of work. You set it for two consecutive countdowns of whatever length you desire. The first countdown is resettable. Problem is once the timer trips into the second countdown, the sucker's unstoppable. Fail-safe. It blows."

"Can't you yank the wires or something?"

Riley shook his head. "You've been spending too much time in the nineteen forties. This stuff is all hard-wired onto microchips. There's nothing to pull. You either have the codes or you fry."

"Oh, God," Frank said, his emotions welling. "Who knows *how* the hell he's got it set."

"Maybe *we* do."

Riley saw Frank's confused look and explained.

"What you just told me suggests his first countdown sequence is twenty-four hours long, ending at four thirty a.m. The second one could be a second, a minute, an hour, who knows? It doesn't matter."

"How far away from it do we have to be when it blows?"

"If you can get everybody out to the main road before it blows, you'll be okay. The blast is confined... and clean."

Frank thought of the plan he'd outlined to the men and smiled. Now it looked even less harebrained than it had.

"Well, Captain Riley," he said, clapping the older man on the back. "Looks like you made it just in time for the fireworks."

27

Mannheim and the guards came for them the next morning, dragging them bleary-eyed and blinking from their cell. Moments later, Frank and Riley stood in front of *Kommandant* Koenig. The vast difference in the man's appearance startled Frank.

Gone was the arrogance and bravado. In its place sat a haggard man whose face bore no expression. A line of drool trickled from his gaping mouth, threatening to drip onto his tunic, and his eyes, red-rimmed and bloodshot, were set into a slack face that appeared to have aged ten years overnight.

Schmidt hadn't fared much better. Dark circles crouched beneath his eyes, and the sharp planes of his face were dulled by a night's growth of beard. He cast a worried look at Koenig, finally breaking the silence. "The *Kommandant* called you here to see if you had reconsidered your position," he said, his voice subdued.

Riley and Frank looked at each other and nodded.

"All right," Riley said. "I came to gather information on troop strength in the areas along the French border. I didn't realize until too late that my compass was haywire. The rest you already know."

The old man moved for the first time since they'd entered the room. His arms jerked spasmodically, and his eyelids fluttered, as if he were coming out of a trance.

"So," he said, his voice a hoarse rasp, "you *are* a spy."

Riley remained silent.

Koenig's mouth twisted into a death's-head grin.

"What can you tell us about the planned invasion. Will it be Calais or Normandy?"

Riley looked annoyed for a moment, then his smile returned. "Sorry, *Kommandant*, I'm fresh out of military secrets."

"What a pity," he said.

Koenig nodded to Mannheim who, in a fluid movement of surprising grace, unholstered his pistol, aimed it at Riley's head, and fired. The pistol spat a plume of flame and the roar of the report made Frank's eardrums shriek with pain. At such close range, Riley's head snapped to one side, erupting in a geyser of flesh and bone and drenching Frank with blood and bits of brain. With all his muscle control gone, Riley's lifeless corpse slid to the floor and lay there twitching in rapidly spreading pools of urine and gore.

"No!" Frank screamed. "You goddamned piece of shit!"

Ignoring the threat of Mannheim's pistol, Frank launched himself across the desk, wrapping his hands around Koenig's throat. The old man's eyes bulged, and he batted at Frank's arms, trying to break his iron grip, to no avail. Koenig started turning blue, and Frank redoubled his efforts, digging his fingers deeper into his throat.

Schmidt, panic-stricken, jumped to his feet, grabbed at Frank's arms, and began shouting.

"Guards! *Kommen-sie schnell!* Guards!"

A second later, four guards burst into the room, pulled Frank off Koenig, and clubbed him to the floor with their leather truncheons.

"Halt!" Schmidt commanded.

The guards dragged Frank, now sporting a bloodied lip, to his feet and held him, awaiting orders. Koenig coughed once, rubbed his throat, and stood, his eyes radiating triumph. "I could shoot you for this," he said.

Frank felt a stab of fear when he saw Mannheim's evil grin widen.

"Or... I could let you rot in the cooler next to the body of your friend. I am told that human flesh takes on a certain allure after two weeks without food."

Koenig laughed and Mannheim joined in. Schmidt stood apart from them, a look of horror and disgust on his face.

Frank said nothing, but only stared at Koenig, his heart and mind filled with hate. He tried to move, but the two guards held him fast.

"I'll see you burn in hell for this," he said.

Koenig nodded, a brief look of sadness crossing his features. "Then we shall burn together, my friend," he replied. "Take him to the barracks."

The two guards hustled Frank out the door, letting it swing shut behind them. Koenig stared after him a moment, then turned to Schmidt. The younger man had regained some of his composure, though a white-hot anger burned within him.

"Why, Heinrich, why?"

Koenig turned on his son, bellowing, spittle flying from his mouth. "Because their bastard fathers left me and my mother to those Russian Schweine! They could have saved us, they could have saved Germany! But those cowards halted at the Elbe. Now, for the sins of their fathers, they *all* shall pay!"

"But it was all so long ago."

"Not to me, Johann, not to me..."

"Ever since I was a little boy, you told me the past never dies. Maybe it should be allowed to..." Schmidt moved a step closer to the old man, reaching for him. "And what of *your* sins, Father? Shall *I* be made to pay?"

The old man gaped at him. "Have I taught you nothing? Have you learned nothing?"

"Perhaps I've learned too well..."

Before he could offer a reply, Koenig slumped into his chair, grabbing his head and moaning in pain. Schmidt resisted the urge to comfort him and pressed on. "This man was not one of the prisoners! We didn't have to *kill* him."

Koenig slammed his fist upon the desk. "Silence! Do not question me! The man was a spy. He got what he deserved. Mannheim?"

"*Jawohl, mein Kommandant!*" Mannheim said, snapping to attention, amusement gleaming in his vulpine eyes.

The bastard is enjoying this, Schmidt thought.

"Take the body out and hang it from one of the towers," Koenig said. "Let them learn what it means to oppose me."

❈　❈　❈

The door to the officers' quarters creaked open, letting a crack of golden light from the main room spill into the darkness. Dean stuck his head in and found Frank sitting on his bunk, staring off into space. Though he'd washed his face and hands, he still wore the shirt stained with Riley's blood. His other shirt wasn't much better, stained as it was from dirt and sweat from their aborted tunnel. But even if it had been crisp and clean, he wouldn't have changed it. Somehow that didn't feel right.

"You okay?" Dean asked.

Frank nodded, keeping his eyes on some distant point.

"Yeah."

"They're all waiting for you."

Frank looked at him for the first time and smiled wanly. "Thanks. Tell them I'll be out in a minute."

Dean nodded and closed the door softly. Plunged back into the darkness, Frank stared out his window and watched the guards walk their posts and the searchlights sweep through the compound. Camp Stalag had claimed another victim. First Blair, then Bob... now Riley. Frank thought back on that day he'd returned from the convention and felt a deep stab of pain in his heart. Riley had come to save his ass again and paid the ultimate price.

Damn you, Koenig! Damn you to hell for killing my friend.

Frank fought back the tears, as he had a hundred other times that day, and stood up. Crossing over to the window, he leaned his head against the glass, feeling its smooth, cool surface against his forehead. He squeezed his eyes shut and inhaled deeply.

I hope I can pull this off, John. We sure as hell could have used your help. But I promise I'll make Koenig pay—for everything.

Frank opened his eyes, turned, and walked out into the main room.

He found them all sitting around the one picnic table, their eyes mirroring Frank's pain. But there was also something else there: a fierceness, a resolve unlike any before. It was do or die.

"How many of you have weapons training?" Frank said, scanning the men.

Shocked by the abruptness of his question, all of them fell silent.

"Any of you ever use a rifle or a shotgun?"

Dana Webster's hand shot up into the air.

"Yes, Dana."

"I once took a riflery course in summer camp. Does that qualify?"

"How long ago?"

"About thirty years," he replied, looking hopeful.

"That's okay," Frank said, grinning, "as long as you remember which end the bullet comes out."

Everyone laughed, the tension in the room momentarily dispelled. Frank waited until they'd all calmed down and resumed. "All right, then, here's what we're going to do. Tomorrow morning at precisely four fifteen, we're going to break into Koenig's armory, arm ourselves, take out as many of the Krauts as we can, then haul our asses down that road as fast as possible."

"All right!" Freddie yelled.

"How do you know we can do it, Frank?" Roger said, his face etched with worry. "These guys aren't amateurs!"

The room exploded into excited murmuring, and the men began to argue among themselves. Some, as enthusiastic as Freddie, urged immediate action, while others, scared and unsure, insisted that it would be suicidal. Frank felt the moment slipping away.

"All right, hold it, guys! Pipe down!" Frank said. "We've got no choice in the matter. Koenig's made it for us..."

Frank paused, seeing the apprehensive looks on their faces. He didn't want to tell them but had come to realize that he had to. After all they'd been through, they deserved to know the whole truth.

"...Koenig's got cancer... He's dying."

"Cancer's too good for the bastard," Jensen said.

The men began arguing again.

Frank lost his cool. "Quiet!"

The room fell silent and Frank continued.

"Look. That's not all. He has a bomb... a nuke. And sooner or later he's going to blow this place. Why do you think no one's come looking for us, huh? I'll tell you. Because they're too damned scared! If we *don't* do this, we're as good as dead."

No one spoke for almost a full minute. Then Jensen nodded. "We're with you, Colonel," he said.

Frank nodded, his heart swelling with pride. "All right. Before

Riley died, he and I mapped everything out. We haven't got much time, so let's go over this step by step."

They spent the rest of the night studying each detail. Using blank pages torn out of his aborted journal, Frank made thumbnail sketches of various pistols, rifles, and machine guns, showing how they broke down and reassembled. It looked as if his months of research were now paying off in a far different way than he'd anticipated.

"Now, I don't expect you guys to be experts—hell, I barely know this stuff myself. But at least you'll know how to clear your weapon if it jams. If nothing else, remember this: don't panic. Any questions?"

Dean raised his hand.

"Yes, Dean?"

"After we grab the weapons, we're to attack them from several places at once. Right?" Frank nodded and Dean continued. "We've got no radios. How are we going to coordinate?"

Frank mulled over the question. After their planning conference in the cooler, he and Riley had agreed the plan needed to operate on a need-to-know basis. Everyone would have their specific job.

"Good question," he said finally. "It may not be possible to coordinate the attacks at all. We are going to have to try like hell to get into our various positions as unobtrusively as possible. As soon as Group One begins firing at the towers nearest the gate, we all come in."

"What if the goons spot one of the teams before we're ready?" Dana asked.

Frank looked at him soberly. "You take them out," he said.

A silence fell over them. Frank knew what everyone was thinking. "Is there anyone here who feels they can't kill someone?" Frank asked, scanning the room.

Again, the silence.

"Look. It's okay to doubt. I've never fired a gun in my life, and I'm scared to death."

While Frank spoke, he saw some of the men nod in understanding. Every one of them probably had the same thought: *Will I hesitate at the critical moment?*

Frank continued. "I want each one of you to look deep inside yourselves and think about this: If we don't break out of here soon, you will never see your families again. Your wives and children will be widows and orphans." He paused, letting that thought linger. "After what they've done, I, for one, am going to blow the hell out of these bastards with no regrets."

He inspected the room again. Every one of their faces held an expression of grim resolution. He knew no one would falter. He might doubt himself, but he would never doubt these men again.

"All right," Frank said, brushing the hair off his forehead. "Everyone take five."

Frank took the weapons' diagrams, stuffed them into the pot-bellied stove, and lit them with a book of matches. While he watched the embers fade to ash, he wondered if he'd forgotten anything. Everything hinged on their ability to overtake the goons guarding the *Waffenlager* and have two of the prisoners take their place. They were gambling that Koenig, in his present deteriorated state, wouldn't notice the difference. It was a calculated risk, and one he was prepared to take. He just hoped the man would show up.

God help them if he didn't.

※　　※　　※

That evening's mess was pure hell for Johann Schmidt. Koenig could still feed himself, but he took to pausing with the bite midway to his mouth and staying that way until prompted. He noticed Mannheim watching them with the cold, treacherous eyes of a snake. What might that repugnant piece of gutter trash be thinking? Whatever it was, Schmidt didn't like the feeling those small, burning eyes gave him as they stared without the slightest self-consciousness.

After the meal, Schmidt led Koenig back to his quarters, sat him on his bed and removed the old man's boots, pants, and tunic. He was like a giant doll—docile and silent.

Tucking him into bed, Schmidt found it chilling that Koenig's eyes remained fixed and unmoving. To his horror, he'd discovered that he had to close the old man's eyes for him, as if his ravaged brain were forgetting the most basic motor skills.

When might he forget to breathe? he thought. *When will this slow, rotting horror end?*

Turning out the light by Koenig's bedside, Schmidt padded out of the room, shutting the door softly behind him. He removed a key from his pocket and locked the bedroom door. No sense in having the poor wretch wandering about in a daze in the middle of the night.

He stepped outside onto the porch and motioned for one of the guards to approach.

"*Jawohl, mein Hauptmann*," he said, snapping to attention.

"At ease," Schmidt said in German. "Please station yourself outside the *Kommandant's* door. He has not been feeling well. No one is to go in or out until I relieve you after morning roll call. Is that clear, Private?"

"*Jawohl!*"

"*Sehr gut.* Carry on."

Schmidt watched the guard walk into the building, then he turned and strolled around the perimeter, checking the fence and the patrols. He saluted the *Hundführers* casually, his troubled mind churning with confusing thoughts and emotions.

When he reached one of the towers, he decided to inspect it. He climbed the winding steps, ascended into the small hut, and saluted the guards. He could tell they were uncomfortable having him so close at hand, but he was past caring. Staring out into the night, he watched the searchlights swing in their lazy arcs across the compound. He breathed deeply, letting the crispness in the air calm his nerves. Tonight, with no moon, the shadows by the barracks and the other buildings had grown deeper, more ominous.

What would he do? What could *he do?*

Every alternative was unacceptable. After Koenig's death, he would dismantle the camp. That task presented no problem. He loathed the place. Watching these accursed buildings fall was a sight he longed for, his taste for this mad scheme long since gone.

What about the prisoners?

If he simply let them go, could he expect no retribution for the horrors and cruelties heaped upon them this last month? Could he expect a hearty fare-thee-well or a see-you-next-summer?

Schmidt laughed at the absurdity of the thought, attracting a quizzical look from the guard operating the searchlight.

Goons. That's what the prisoners call us.

He'd heard them talking among themselves one day. At the time, it filled him with blind anger. He'd wanted to lash out and make them suffer. Now he saw it differently.

We have earned that name.

No. The prisoners would show no mercy. They would come after him, put him on trial, sentence him to life in prison. The horror of that image grew in his mind. He knew what to expect. He would not be accorded a prison all to himself like Rudolf Hess, nor even his own cell. Oh, no. They would put him in with thieves, murderers, and child molesters.

It didn't matter that he would inherit Heinrich Koenig's billions.

He would not inherit the man's influence, the man's *power*. They would make an example of him, an example for *everyone* to see. He shuddered at the thought.

Another, more chilling thought occurred to him. In this state, kidnapping and murders of such enormity might well bring the death penalty. He had blood on *his* hands, as surely as if he dipped them in a bucket of gore; the blood of that poor fool Neff, of the man torn apart by the dogs, and now of the man hanging by his feet from the tower across from him.

Yes, they would give him death for his crimes.

Glancing downward, he spotted Mannheim strutting about, issuing orders.

Schweine!

He looked so smug, so sure of himself.

You would know what to do, wouldn't you, my fine, loutish friend: a mass grave and a bullet in the back of the head for every last one of them. Just like the old days, eh, Hans?

Schmidt felt the gorge rising in his throat. God, how sick of it all he was.

Morbidly, he began calculating how long it would take to shoot three hundred men, how many pounds of lye it would take to dissolve their flesh, how deep to dig the pit...

He shuddered again, knowing he could never sanction such an atrocity. He could never live with the thought of all those grieving families on his conscience, a conscience that made itself known more and more every day.

Mein Gott, what have we done?

Schmidt sighed, bid the guards in the tower good night, and descended to the ground. Taking one more look about the quad, he headed to his own quarters and another long night without sleep.

28

"**H**ey, Shakespeare! Wake up!" Dean whispered, shaking Frank's shoulders.

Torn from his dream, Frank bolted awake, his eyes wide with some imagined horror, mouth open to scream.

Dean clamped his hand over his mouth. "Whoa, hold on, it's only me." He released him and Frank inhaled sharply, his heart racing.

"Jesus, you scared the hell out of me."

"You told me to get you up."

"I know," Frank said, rubbing his eyes. "But I didn't tell you to take a decade off my life, either." Now fully awake and realizing the time, Frank sprung out of bed and pulled on his clothes.

Dean glanced at Bob Neff's empty bunk, his expression saddening. "I still can't believe Koenig just shot him down like a goddamned dog."

Frank said nothing, continuing to dress.

There was nothing left to say.

It was time for action.

Pulling on his A-2, Frank moved to the door and peered into the main room. Dana, Roger, Bill Jensen, and several of the others were

307

already dressed and waiting, playing a nervous hand of poker by the amber light of a lone fat lamp.

Frank shut the door and turned to his friend. "Go check with Barracks Six and see if they're ready. And tell them we're moving out in ten minutes."

"Right," he said.

Dean left the room, passing Freddie on the way in. The raw-boned Nebraskan looked jumpy. He kept passing his olive-drab overseas cap back and forth between long-fingered hands, his hazel-colored eyes darting about the room. "I'm not sure I can do this, Colonel," he said, his gaze finally meeting Frank's.

Frank saw his own fears and apprehensions reflected in those eyes. "I know how you feel," he said, clapping Freddie on the back. "But you and Roger are the right sizes to fit in the goons' uniforms. Besides, you look like a goon."

"Oh, thanks," Freddie said, laughing. "I can't wait."

"Just remember to salute if someone of higher rank comes by."

"You mean Mannheim?"

Frank shook his head.

"Never mind. Just keep your eyes forward, your trap shut, and pray like hell no one gives you a second glance."

"You got it, Colonel," Freddie said, peeling off a snappy salute.

He followed Freddie into the main room, just as Dean slipped back in through the barracks door.

"All set, Frank. Everyone's champing at the bit."

"How does it look outside?"

Dean shrugged. "Same as always."

"At least they haven't changed their routine," Frank said. "All right, everyone, listen up. We've got five minutes till we move out. I want to go over this one last time."

BILL WALKER

✻   ✻   ✻

<u>**4:15:10 a.m.**</u>

Koenig inspected his reflection in the mirror, noting his haggard features with quiet alarm. The disease had ravaged him faster than he'd imagined. Still, he was not ready to let go, not ready to die. How long, he wondered, had it been since he'd last had these thoughts? It felt like only a short while ago, but he knew, deep down, that the black veil that periodically descended over his mind held him in its grip far more often than not.

What had gone through his mind during those times? What had he done?

It felt like two people warring inside his head, and now the real Koenig, the one staring back from the mirror, was losing the battle.

"*Nein,*" he said to himself. "I will not surrender."

Putting on his tunic and then his cap, he strode to the door and reached out with his hand to grasp the doorknob. The hand trembled, one finger curling repeatedly, like a fat, bloodless worm. Willing it to stop, he gripped the knob, turned it, and stared dumbfounded when the door held fast within its frame.

It was locked—from the *outside.*

He jiggled the handle, trying to figure out how something like this could have happened.

"*Was ist los?*"

He stopped shaking the door handle, shocked at hearing a voice outside his door. "Who is that?" Koenig demanded in German.

"Private Kesselring, sir," the voice replied.

"Why is this door locked, Private?"

Unnerved, the young guard stammered. "Orders f-from *Hauptmann* Schmidt, sir."

Koenig frowned. *Strange. Why would Johann give such an order? He must have wanted me to sleep undisturbed. God, what* have *I been doing?*

"Very good, Private. Please open the door. I have an urgent task to complete."

"*Hauptmann* Schmidt has the k-key, sir. He is to relieve m-me at roll call."

Fool, Koenig thought.

"I commend you for your attention to duty, Private. You now have new orders direct from me: open the door at once. Break it down."

The young guard remained silent.

"Did you hear me, Private Kesselring?" Koenig asked, his patience nearing its end. He glanced at the clock.

4:21 a.m. "PRIVATE! Open this door, *schnell*!"

"I am s-sorry, *mein Kommandant*, I cannot. I must wait for *Hauptmann* Schmidt." There was panic in the young soldier's voice.

"*Dummkopf!* You are dooming us!" Koenig shouted, smashing the door with his fists.

Turning away from the door, he shot an angry glance at the barred windows. What had he been thinking when he ordered them placed on his windows? What if the building caught fire?

"Idiot," he said to himself.

※　※　※

4:21:45 a.m.

With less than ten minutes remaining until Koenig's rendezvous with the bomb, Frank led the men of Barracks 2 into the early-morning dark. He felt a palpable sense of *déjà vu*. The last time he'd tried this, they'd almost made it out.

Peering around the corner, Frank watched the two goons guarding the *Waffenlager*. They stood stock still, like cigar-store Indians. Even their eyes stared straight ahead, unmoving.

Satisfied that all was well, Frank turned back to the others. "Okay, guys," he said to Roger and Freddie. "Dean and I are going to swing around behind the armory and take out the goons. As soon as you see one of us waving, get your asses over there, change into their uniforms, and get into position. There's no telling how long before a patrol comes by, so make it quick. Got it?"

They nodded, their faces taut with fear. Frank felt it too. If Dean was nervous, he didn't show it.

"Okay, Dean, let's move."

Looking around the corner again, they waited while the searchlight beams moved out of their sector, then dashed across to the recreation hall, hiding behind the rain barrel. It was another minute before they made it to the armory.

"Remember what I told you," Frank whispered. "When you grab him, make sure your left arm puts enough pressure on the windpipe to cut off his air. Then just jab straight up between his shoulder blades as hard as you can. He'll drop like a sack of potatoes."

Dean nodded, looking none too sure of himself. Frank swallowed, his throat tight and scratchy. This was the point of no return. He reached into his pocket and pulled out the spoons they'd stolen from the mess hall and handed one to Dean. He ran his thumb along the handle, now honed to needle-like sharpness. A few hours of scraping against a brick had turned them into deadly weapons.

"Are you sure these will work?" Dean asked, his fear finally showing.

"I've seen enough movies to know. Use it right and he'll go down without a sound."

Dean's eyes bugged out. "Movies?"

"Relax. Riley showed me."

"You miss him, don't you?"

Frank nodded, then said a silent prayer. "Let's do it," he said.

�֎ ✖ ✖

4:24:32 a.m.

Koenig gave up trying to cajole or threaten Private Kesselring, who, he concluded, must be descended from a particularly stubborn strain of mules. He crossed the small room to the window and pulled it open. The bars were about three and one-half inches apart and made of tough carbide steel. He saw where they bolted into the side of the building. Perhaps with the aid of a nail file... But closer examination revealed the bolts to be one-way, making them impossible to remove.

"*Scheiss!*" he hissed.

He glanced at the clock once again.

No time left for foolish thoughts; he pushed his face against the bars.

"Mannheim!" he screamed. "*Kommen Sie, schnell*! Mannheim!"

His voice echoed throughout the camp, desperate and frightened.

✖ ✖ ✖

4:25:01 a.m.

"What was that?" Dean gasped.

"Sounds like Koenig," Frank said. "Something's up. Move!"

Racing out from behind the *Waffenlager*, Frank and Dean hit the two guards. Just as Riley had drilled into his head, Frank grabbed the surprised guard, plunging the sharpened spoon up through his rib cage and into his heart. The man gave a muffled cough and collapsed into his arms. Dean's man went down a second later.

They dragged the corpses around to the back and Frank stripped them, and signaled to Roger and Freddie, who joined them seconds later.

"Was that Koenig we heard?" Freddie asked, struggling into the dead guard's uniform.

Frank nodded. "My guess is he's going to be here any moment."

When they finished changing, Frank inspected the two men. Freddie's uniform was tight, but serviceable. Roger's fit as if it were made for him. Satisfied, he said, "Get into position, and whatever you do, keep your mouths shut."

Freddie gave him a thumbs up, and both he and Roger marched to the front of the building, taking up positions on either side of the large steel door.

Dean leaned against the back wall of the *Waffenlager*. "Now we wait."

Frank had no answer for that one, but he prayed like hell they wouldn't have to wait too long.

❈　❈　❈

4:27:33 a.m.

BAM!

Koenig stood back when he heard Mannheim's first kick. The door shuddered but held.

BAM!

The door rattled again, loosened by the sergeant's savage kick. Koenig thought he saw a tiny crack appear in its center.

BAM!

The tiny crack became a gaping fissure, snaking its way toward the bottom of the door.

One more kick...

Koenig's palms sweated. So little time left.

BAM! CRAAAAACK!

The door caved in, splitting completely in two. Mannheim barged through, his pitted face reddened with effort and rage. Koenig spotted Private Kesselring lying just outside the doorway, slumped against the wall, his glazed eyes bulging with terror. No small wonder. His neck had been broken with such brutal force that his head was turned a full 180 degrees.

Koenig gave the dead guard a dismissive sneer and marched past the body, pausing at the front door when a thought occurred to him. He turned to Mannheim, his eyes two fiery coals. "Bring *Hauptmann* Schmidt to my office and hold him there until I return. This traitorous act is his doing!"

"*Jawohl, mein Kommandant,*" Mannheim said, grinning.

Koenig returned the man's salute and watched him head off toward Schmidt's, then he struck off toward the *Waffenlager*, his mind intent on his deadly errand.

⁜　⁜　⁜

4:28:15 a.m.

Frank and Dean pressed themselves back into the shadows at Koenig's approach. The old man hurried across the last few feet, his reddened cheeks puffing out with the effort.

"He's cutting it awfully close," Frank whispered.

"Maybe he gets off on the thrill," Dean offered, smirking.

Unable to see them, Frank heard Roger and Freddie click their heels and slap their rifles in the presentation of arms. Frank closed his eyes and whispered another silent prayer. Would Koenig notice the unfamiliar faces? Seconds ticked by...

What the hell was happening?

And then he heard keys jangling.

It had worked.

If everyone stayed on schedule, they stood a damned good chance of surviving. Twenty other men crouched somewhere out there in the shadows, waiting for the call to action. With the seconds ticking inexorably away, now more than ever, their fate rested on their courage. Frank waited another moment, then tapped Dean on the shoulder. "Go!" he said.

Together they dashed around the side of the armory and grabbed Koenig when he swung the door open. They shoved him into the darkened interior and followed, slamming the door and snapping on the lights. Koenig blinked in surprise, comprehension dawning in his eyes.

"You!" Koenig said, outraged. "Guards! *Kommen Sie schnell!*"

"Don't waste your breath, *Kommandant*, they're our guys," Frank said, slapping Koenig across the face. "Just the masquerade portion of our little escape party. So glad you could join us."

Dean gripped Frank's arm. "We haven't got time for this, Frank."

"That is right, *gentlemen*," Koenig said, a smile curling his bruised lips. "You have *no* time."

Angered, Frank grabbed hold of the old man's tunic, pulling him nose to nose.

"Where is it?" he said.

"Where is what?"

Koenig's calm amusement angered him even more. Dean stepped in when Frank drew back his arm to slug the old man.

"Where's the nuke?" Dean asked.

It was nearly imperceptible, but Frank saw Koenig's eyes widen ever so slightly. Then a look of sadness crept into his eyes.

"It is too late," he said softly.

"There, Frank!" Dean said, spotting the trapdoor.

Dean ran and heaved it open with a grunt, then descended into the underground chamber. The hard soles of his shoes clattered against the concrete. Following close behind, Frank snatched an MP40 off a rack on the wall and prodded Koenig toward the hole. He had no idea if the gun was even loaded.

The underground chamber was several degrees cooler than the room above it, and was constructed entirely of reinforced concrete: floor, ceiling, and walls, all of them at least a foot thick. As strong as they looked, they would be like flash paper to a flame when, or if, the device detonated.

The bomb lay, sleek and menacing, on a raised concrete platform in the middle of the room, its burnished stainless steel casing gleaming brightly in the cold light of the fluorescent lights overhead. All that destructive power in something so small.

"Open it!" Frank said.

With a confident air that chilled Frank, Koenig stepped up to the device and opened a small panel in its side. Moving behind him, Frank and Dean noted the keypad and an LED digital counter.

"Oh my God," Frank said.

His eyes were riveted on the counter, the numbers rapidly counting down.

00:00:15, 00:00:14, 00:00:13...

"Reset it," Frank said.

Koenig stood there, his eyes transfixed by the descending numbers, a tiny, wistful smile on his face.

00:00:10, 00:00:09, 00:00:08...

"Reset it!" Frank yelled, grabbing the old man.

Koenig looked at him, his smile widening. Enraged, Frank struck

Koenig a second time. The old man slammed into the side of the device and slid to the floor, his sardonic expression never varying. He wiped a trickle of blood from his mouth.

"It is easy to be cruel, is it not, Colonel Murphy?" he said. "When one's soul is stretched to the breaking point."

Frank watched in horror while the last digits ran out.

"*Götterdämmerung!*" Koenig whispered.

"No!"

00:00:02, 00:00:01, 00:00:00, BEEEEEEP! BLIP.

The sound it made almost stopped Frank's heart. And then he saw the display wink out and immediately return.

00:30:00, 00:29:59, 00:29:58...

"It's half an hour, Frank," Dean said, relief coloring his voice. "It's not much time, but we can make it."

"Enjoy the time we have left, Colonel," Koenig said.

Frank looked back at the old man, almost pitying him. *Almost.*

He was through letting some sick, old goat bait him. The time for pity and anger was past. There was only time for what had to be done.

Frank stared at him for another moment and turned to Dean. "Bring him upstairs," he said, and walked calmly up the steps.

29

Brenda tossed and turned for hours on the lumpy motel mattress before finally giving up. How could she sleep while her mind roiled with thoughts and fears that wouldn't cease? Riley had been gone almost two days and...

...nothing.

Rationally, she didn't expect it would be easy, but the waiting made her nervous. No. It made her *crazy*.

Sitting up on the king-size bed, she turned on the bedside light, revealing a room where nothing matched. Not even the chintz curtains, which were two different shades of pale lavender. She squinted at the brightness of the bedside light and picked up her watch from out of the chipped Elvis ashtray.

One thirty a.m.

And not a prayer of rest in the long night ahead. Climbing out from under the jumble of bedclothes, she trudged into the bathroom and collapsed onto the toilet. Not only couldn't she get to sleep, but her bladder forced her to get up and relieve herself every thirty minutes, sometimes less.

I can't stand this.

After finishing, she walked back into the room, parted the curtains, and looked out over Marinette Airport. Activity was minimal, but somehow the quiet pulse of the place calmed her. It also helped her come to a decision.

Returning to the bathroom, she turned on the shower and got in, letting the hot, spiky jet of water sluice over her head and down her body. Five minutes later, she packed her small valise, and turned in her keys at the front desk. It wasn't until the cool night air caressed her skin that she realized she'd forgotten to put on any makeup.

I hope I don't frighten anyone.

There was one lone cab parked at the curb in front of the motel, the driver engrossed in the morning paper and a cup of steaming coffee.

Brenda tapped on the window, startling the cabby, and causing his coffee to slosh into his lap.

"I'm sorry," Brenda said, a smile coming to her face. "Could you take me to one of the car rental places?"

Angry at first, the cabby warmed to Brenda's sunny smile and dulcet voice.

"Sure, lady, hop in," he said.

Taking a route that cut almost straight across the airport, the cabby deposited her in front of a Budget Rental Car office minutes later. She thanked him, left a large tip, and headed into the small cube-shaped building.

With glass fronting it on three sides, the office floated like a tiny island on a vast sea of Detroit steel. The glaring, cool-white fluorescent lights gave the lone occupant behind the counter a cadaverous look.

The clerk glanced up and smiled, giving Brenda a quick once-over. No more than twenty, with a mild case of acne and a small diamond earring through his left ear, he looked shy and innocent.

Brenda returned his smile. Even if she was almost twice his age, his guileless appreciation of her made her feel good.

"Can I help you, ma'am?" he said.

"I need a car, as I'm sure you could guess."

Her warm laughter made the clerk blush. Looking down, she noticed his right hand was trembling.

"We have compacts, subcompacts, mid-size and full-size. The rates are—"

"I'm sorry, uhh, Johnny," she said, glancing at his name tag. "I'm really in a hurry."

He nodded, sensing the anxiousness behind her radiant smile. "I'm sorry. I get so few people in at this hour. And none as beautiful as you." He blushed again and studied his computer screen. "What would you like?"

"Something fast and reliable."

The boy's fingers flew over the keyboard. She saw the screen change in the reflections off the lenses of his wire-rimmed glasses. "You're in luck," he said, grinning shyly. "I've got a brand-new Mustang GT with a four point six-liter V8." He leaned over the counter conspiratorially. "This beast really kicks butt. I took my girl out in one of these. We forgot all about parking," he said, blushing a third time.

"Perfect," Brenda said, smiling at his ingenuousness.

After filling out the paperwork and running her Visa card, the clerk picked up the phone. "Bring up number forty-four." He placed the phone back in its cradle. "It'll be right out front in five minutes, ma'am."

"Thank you, Johnny, I appreciate your help."

He bowed slightly. "My pleasure."

When she pushed through the glass door she paused, suddenly remembering something. "Johnny?"

"Yes," he said, suddenly shy again.

"Do you have any road maps that'll show me the way to Derleth?"

"No sweat."

Taking out a map of Marinette County, the clerk showed her the fastest way.

"Thank you, you're a dream," she said, lightly pecking him on the cheek. He turned several shades of red and stammered out something inaudible.

The red Mustang waited outside the door, its top down and engine rumbling. It sounded dangerous. Climbing inside, she clipped on the seat belt and tromped on the gas, leaving behind a patch of rubber and an astonished attendant. Normally embarrassed by such displays, she left all her inhibitions behind.

Right outside the airport she located the entrance to State Road 64, sped up the entrance ramp, and kicked the car into cruise gear.

Brenda found the sensation of the wind whipping through her hair a pleasant one, reminding her of many a Saturday night in high school. She flipped on the radio and found a station playing classic rock. Cream's live version of Robert Johnson's immortal "Crossroads" was just hitting the first guitar solo. Letting out a war whoop, she cranked the volume and mashed the gas pedal to the floor. The Mustang rocketed forward.

Judging from the distances indicated on the map, and the speed she was driving, Brenda figured she would be in the Derleth area no later than four o'clock in the morning. She recalled details of the town, remembering its tiny business district as it flew by the Cessna's Perspex windows. The camp stood no more than six or seven miles from the center of Derleth, somewhere off State Road 8.

She wasn't sure why she was doing this. Maybe, she mused, it was because she just couldn't stand the waiting. Taught since childhood to exhibit patience and ladylike behavior, those lessons remained deeply ingrained.

Yet, as she grew older, she found too many of life's opportunities passed by if one waited for them. Even the small ones. And this was no small one. It wasn't even an opportunity in the usual sense. Her husband's life was at stake, and she was not about to sit in some seedy motel like a good little girl any longer.

She trusted Riley completely, as much as she trusted Frank. She just wanted to do something, anything, and this felt *right*, somehow. She couldn't help giggling, thinking of how Riley and her husband would react.

"They'll have a fit," she said out loud.

Giggling again, she pushed the Mustang to seventy-five, and glanced in the rearview.

Nothing.

Not a soul on the road behind her. And no one in front. Just an endless ribbon of black stretching into the dark. And in that dazzling red car, rocketing along at this impudent speed, she made the perfect target for a State Trooper's speed trap. She decided that getting there a little later might be better than sitting in some jail for speeding, and brought the car back under sixty.

The junction of 64 and Interstate 141 came up faster than she'd calculated. She scooted across the other lanes, making sure to take the entrance heading north. Her pulse quickened, and she had to force herself to resist pushing the car faster.

What would she find once she got there? Three hundred men thumbing rides, or a smoking hole in the ground? She gripped the wheel tighter, her knuckles whitening.

"God, please let them make it out," she said. "Please let them *all* make it out."

An hour later she reached Highway 8 and turned east. She was glad she'd chosen the Mustang, as it took the twists and turns of that narrow, two-lane road with ease. Still, the closer she came to Derleth, the more her anxiety rose. At 3:48, she passed through Clarkville. According to the map, Derleth should lay somewhere just ahead.

She reached down and snapped off the radio, letting her ears drink in the silence. A moment later she came to a lonely intersection and braked the car at a battered stop sign peppered with bullet holes. Crickets chirped in the tall grass by the roadside, and somewhere nearby a bullfrog croaked for his mate. It was hard to believe that in this peaceful stillness, so much pain and destruction lay in wait. Like a cancer.

Pushing the thought from her mind, Brenda checked the Mustang's digital clock. It was 4:07. She'd made excellent time.

Around the next bend she spotted a diner catty-corner to the highway. The single light burning inside told her it would open soon. Brenda realized she'd never given a thought to eating since leaving Marinette. And she was hungry. Ignoring the rumblings in her belly, she pushed on, determined to at least locate the camp. It lay somewhere off this road—*she knew it*. She put on her brights then slowed down and watched the sides of the road gliding past.

By four forty-five a.m., her eyes, head, and back ached from hunching over the wheel and squinting into the dark woods flashing by. *It shouldn't be this hard to find a stupid dirt road*, she thought. That she could have passed it at any time and not seen it was another thought that depressed and panicked her. She brought the car to a halt by the roadside and stared at the winding road ahead.

"Where are you, Frank?" she screamed.

Hot tears of frustration burned her eyes. Squeezing them shut, she rubbed her temples, trying to ease the dull throbbing behind them. It didn't help. Only rest and food would.

"No sense in wrapping myself around a tree," she said.

Turning the car around, she headed back to the diner. One lone car sat in the parking lot.

Good. It's open.

Exhausted, hungry, and more than a little discouraged, she pulled the Mustang into the graveled lot and parked next to the other car, a 4x4 with massive four-foot tires.

Once inside, her stomach growled again as her nose caught a whiff of the brewing coffee.

God, that smells good.

She would rest, have some coffee, some breakfast, and think about her next move.

"Hi, can I get you something!" the young waitress said, coming out from behind the counter.

Brenda nodded. "Coffee, please."

"Sure thing, honey. Sit anywhere you like. I'll be right with you."

She chose a booth facing the road and sat down, her thoughts turning inevitably to her husband. Was he okay? Did Riley get inside? And what were they planning to do?

She pulled herself out of her musings when the waitress returned, carrying a steaming mug of coffee and a hand-typed menu laminated in plastic.

"Thank you," Brenda said, trying not to stare at the girl's gargantuan breasts. Never insecure about her own endowments, she nevertheless found herself unfavorably comparing them to her own.

"You're welcome," the waitress said, smiling again. "Do you need a couple a minutes?"

"Uhh, no," Brenda said, realizing the waitress had asked about her order.

Scanning it quickly, she found her appetite bordered on the ravenous. "I'll have a double stack of the blueberry buttermilk pancakes and a large glass of milk," she said.

The waitress scribbled the order on her pad, then took the menu and left her alone. Plenty of time for the doubts to creep back in. Maybe it *had* been a crazy idea to come up here. After all, what could she really *do*? But if anything was going to happen to Frank, she didn't want to be anywhere else.

Ten minutes later, the pancakes arrived, dripping with butter and with a tiny pitcher of *real* maple syrup. "So much for the diet," she said, taking a huge mouthful. They were soft and tender, the blueberries tasting as if someone had just picked them.

Out of the corner of her eye, she saw the waitress flirting with the owner of the 4x4, who was paying his check. Turning toward the window, Brenda spotted a pair of headlights coming toward the diner. As the vehicle drew closer, she saw the bubble on the roof and the county markings on its side. It pulled into the lot, lurching to a stop next to her Mustang.

A cop.

Ordinarily, she would be overjoyed to see an officer of the law. Ordinarily, they were people you could trust. That was before Riley told her of Koenig's far-reaching influence. Those he could not buy, he killed.

Staring down at her plate, she chewed her food mechanically, no longer noticing the taste. In her peripheral vision she watched the lanky cop climb the steps and saunter inside. She prayed the man would just grab his coffee and donut and cut out. But after seeing the waitress's eyes light up, Brenda knew she'd found trouble.

There was something going on between the two of them, and that meant the jerk would stick around, giving the bimbo the cow eyes. Probably for a lot longer than he should, judging by those spectacular breasts.

After chatting a moment with the waitress, the officer turned to take a seat in one of the booths. That's when he spotted Brenda. Her heart sank. She felt even worse when the man smiled. He had the grin of a hyena.

"Well, hi there," he said, swaggering over to her booth.

Brenda shot a glance at the waitress. The girl pretended not to listen, her lips compressed into a tight line.

Oh, great.

"You from around here? I haven't seen you before."

"Well, Officer—"

"Sheriff."

"Excuse me, Sheriff. I'm on my way to Goodman. I've got a sister there. She's just given birth."

"Well, now," he said, sliding into her booth with presumptuous ease, "I know lots of folks in Goodman. Got a cousin there myself. What'd you say your name was?"

This last question held a portent Brenda didn't like at all. What made it worse was this rube thinking he was "Mister Smoothy" with his inept interrogation.

Brenda smiled. "I'm sorry. I'm Brenda Silvers. How do you do?" she said, extending her hand.

When he didn't take it, she realized her situation had dramatically worsened. The idiot suspected something; probably suspected everything.

"I don't know any Silvers in Goodman."

"That's my *married* name. My sister's name is McCormick."

The sheriff smiled again. "I don't know any McCormicks either," he said, leaning toward her, the sleazy grin sliding off his face. "And unless you want to spend a long, lonely night in my jail, lady, you'd better start tellin' me why you're in my town?"

He stared at her with undisguised hostility, eyes glittering, his false, down-home joviality gone. Brenda's stomach twisted and the bile rose in the back of her throat. She now wished she'd stayed in Marinette.

While the sheriff's eyes bored into hers, a tiny bead of sweat formed on her brow and rolled down the side of her face. She realized, with mounting dread, that she might never see Frank again.

30

Frank rushed to the entrance of the *Waffenlager* and pounded on the massive steel door: twice fast, then three times slow. The noise resonated inside the concrete structure, sounding like thunder. Outside, he knew, it would be barely loud enough to hear. It was the prearranged signal. Five groups of five prisoners waited anxiously, stationed in the shadows of barracks throughout the camp.

One at a time these groups would sneak into the armory. Once there, Dean and Frank would equip them and send them to their attack points. Four of the groups were assigned to hit all eight of the guard towers. It was essential they neutralize the lights and machine guns. If not, they stood little to no chance of making it. The fifth group would wait outside the guards' quarters. Once the shooting started, it would be up to Group Five to kill as many of the guards as possible.

Turning from the door, Frank saw Dean and Koenig emerge from the secret room. Dean kicked the trapdoor shut.

Just then the steel door swung open and Group One entered. Their confident mood became subdued when they caught sight of Koenig.

Frank tied the old man's hands behind his back with a length of rope found in the corner, then placed him in a spot where he could watch his every move.

Starting with the machine guns, Frank bypassed the MP40s in favor of the Uzis. They used the same ammunition, but were newer and more reliable, had larger capacity magazines, as well as a higher cyclic rate of fire. He gave each man one gun plus five fully loaded magazines. As a backup, he broke open a case of Glock 17s and distributed them with the Uzis. Seventy-five percent plastic, the Glock held seventeen rounds in its magazine and provided deadly accuracy.

"All right," Frank said as he saw the men readying themselves to leave. "There's something you need to know..."

※　※　※

T-minus 00:24:17

It is taking much too long, Mannheim thought, his beetled brow furrowing with impatience. Always awake before dawn, he'd seen Koenig's furtive ritual many times, and often wondered what it was the old man checked on every morning. Regardless, the *Kommandant* never stayed away longer than a few minutes... until now...

He scowled, glancing at his watch. *Much too long.*

He turned his attention to Schmidt, who sat stiffly in one of the leather-covered chairs near the *Kommandant's* desk. The young *Hauptmann* looked more than a little unnerved with a guard standing over him and an MP40 pointed at his head.

Good. Let the self-righteous bastard squirm.

How he hated these aristocratic university types. Always had. They did nothing but keep men like him from going anywhere in life.

His mind returned to Koenig. No doubt the *Kommandant* had a large sum of money stashed away and could not resist playing the king in his counting house.

Yes, that was it. Koenig had a pile of cash ready and waiting for when this foolish charade ended.

No doubt he also had some plan to escape over the border into Canada. The stocky sergeant leered. He would beat the old bastard at his own game. After all, why should he rot in prison after all this was over? Why not take a piece of the pie? Better yet, why not take the whole pie and get out while he could?

"You realize that the *Kommandant* is ill," Schmidt said, breaking into Mannheim's thoughts. "His perceptions are distorted, his judgment cannot be trusted."

"Silence!" Mannheim said, striking him with the back of his hand. "It is you who cannot be trusted."

He turned back to the window, watching for the old man. The problem was the *Waffenlager* wasn't visible from the *Kommandant's* office.

Enough of this idleness! Time to act.

* * *

T-minus 00:23:15

Bleeding from the corner of his mouth, Schmidt tried to control his rising emotions. Everything had finally gotten out of control in a way he'd never expected.

Heinrich turned on me.

His father now placed his trust in this hired killer, this piece of worthless trash who would not hesitate to sacrifice them all for his own gain.

Mannheim turned from the window. "What is it that the *Kommandant* finds so important about the *Waffenlager*?" he said, approaching Schmidt like a cat stalking its prey.

"I do not know. The *Kommandant*—"

"Liar!" Mannheim screamed.

Schmidt recoiled, expecting another blow that did not come.

"No, my good *Hauptmann*." Mannheim chuckled. "I am not going to strike you. We are going to take a little walk. *Kommen-Sie!*"

When the other guard made a motion to follow, Mannheim ordered him to remain.

A moment later, Schmidt was propelled out the door and into the quad. All of his fear evaporated while they marched toward the *Waffenlager*. He no longer cared what happened to him.

All this must end.

※ ※ ※

T-minus 00:22:48

Group Three had just gathered inside the *Waffenlager* when Frank heard a frantic knocking on the door.

Trouble.

He pushed through the knot of men still loading their weapons and cracked open the door. His eyes widened when he saw Schmidt and Mannheim heading their way.

"What is it, Frank?" Dean asked.

As commander of Group Three, it was Dean's assignment to take out one of the towers farthest from the gate. Frank shut the door, his mind already formulating a solution

"Listen up, everyone," he said, yelling over the chattering men. "Schmidt and Mannheim are coming. Hide yourselves as best as you can. This is *our* show. Let them come to us."

The men fell silent, flattening themselves against the wall, their weapons gleaming in the dim light.

Frank took up a position behind one of the ammunition crates, his heart hammering against his rib cage. Would Roger and Freddie pass muster again?

Hearing voices, Frank's fear reached fever pitch. They were speaking German. No way would Roger or Freddie be able to answer back. Grabbing a Glock lying next to its open crate, Frank raced to the door and flung it open.

"Come in and join us, gentlemen," Frank said.

Schmidt's jaw dropped, and Frank thought he saw relief dawning in the young German's eyes. Mannheim glowered, momentarily speechless.

Frank checked the quad, then beckoned them with the Glock. The two Germans moved into the building, the door slamming shut behind them.

"Hold them," Dean said.

Four of the men, including Dean, grabbed Schmidt and Mannheim and pulled them toward the spot where Koenig sat.

"Well, well," Frank said, his mood improving vastly. "Looks like we're going to have ourselves a grand 'ol time. Dean?"

"Yeah, Frank?"

"Have your men deploy. You stay here with me until we arm everyone. That clear?"

"Yes, sir," Dean said, smiling ear to ear.

Dean turned to his men. "Everyone, move out, except Clancy," he said. "Clancy, tie up Schmidt. I'll deal with 'Handsome Hans,' here."

The other man moved toward Schmidt to secure him with the rope.

Frank breathed an inward sigh of relief while he watched the men from Dean's group file out. What just happened could have resulted in disaster. Instead, they had the Hydra's heads in their hands.

Turning back to their prisoners, Frank waited while Dean and Clancy finished securing them. Schmidt remained impassive; Mannheim's eyes smoldered. The sergeant's stare never wavered from Frank's face while Dean tied his hands. Suddenly, quick as lightning, Mannheim had Dean in a chokehold, a small dagger at his throat.

"You learn a few lessons in prison, Colonel," Mannheim said, tightening his hold on Dean. "'Never be without a weapon' is one of them."

Frank remained calm, though Dean looked terrified when Mannheim pressed the dagger to his carotid artery. A small drop of blood oozed from his skin where the blade had nicked it.

"You will untie the *Kommandant* and then myself," Mannheim demanded.

"What about Schmidt?" Frank asked.

"He is of no concern to me," he replied.

Frank didn't know what to do. Nothing he thought of came without a risk to Dean, and that he could not accept. He couldn't gamble with his friend's life.

"Do it now, Colonel, or I shall cut his throat."

Jensen, who stood near the door, began creeping up behind Mannheim. But the wily sergeant must have had eyes in the back of his head, for he pivoted sideways, dragging Dean with him. He glared at Jensen, pushing the dagger harder against Dean's neck.

"Tell the *Neger* to keep his distance," Mannheim said.

Jensen bristled. "Who're you callin' *Neger*?"

"Bill!"

Jensen turned to Frank, his dark eyes flashing with anger.

"Collect your weapons and join your group," Frank said, nodding toward the steel door.

"I can *take* this peckerwood," Jensen said.

"I know, but we need you out *there*."

Grumbling, Jensen grabbed a Glock, an Uzi, and the requisite magazines and left, casting an evil glance at Mannheim. The sergeant ignored him, keeping his gaze locked onto Frank.

"The *Kommandant*... now."

Frank nodded toward Clancy, who began untying Koenig's bonds.

Schmidt broke the silence, speaking for the first time since entering the *Waffenlager*.

"Heinrich," he pleaded. "You have to end this now. Everything has gone too far."

"Shut up, *Dummkopf!*" Mannheim said. He turned to Koenig. "*Herr* Koenig and I are going to take the money he has secreted here and take a little trip, are we not, *Herr Kommandant?*"

Koenig stared off into space, having once again lapsed into a catatonic state. Even freed from his bonds, he stood immobile, like a zombie.

"What is wrong with him?" Mannheim asked.

"He is ill, you fool," Schmidt said, his voice trembling with emotion. "Just like I tried to tell you. He has brain cancer. He's dying."

From the expression on Mannheim's face, Frank concluded that it made little difference. "Then he won't need his money," he said, smiling again.

"What money? There is no money here!" Schmidt said, incredulous.

"Do not trifle with me, *Hauptmann*. I have seen our *Kommandant's* daily journeys to this building. Where is it?"

"Tell him, Schmidt," Frank said. "Tell him he's welcome to what's hidden below."

Schmidt stared at him, a look of bewilderment crossing his features.

Oh my God, Frank thought. *He doesn't know!*

Mannheim pushed the knife into Dean's neck again, drawing another fat drop, which became a steady trickle running down into his shirt.

"No!" Schmidt screamed, charging Mannheim. He ran toward the sergeant's outstretched hand, headlong into the dagger's blade. It buried itself to the hilt slightly below his sternum. Staggering backward, he stared at the dagger and the rapidly spreading stain on his tunic before collapsing in a heap.

Using the momentary confusion to his advantage, Dean elbowed Mannheim in the stomach, spun him around, and landed a haymaker that laid him out cold.

"Get the others in here now!" Frank yelled to Roger and Freddie.

※　※　※

<u>**T-minus 00:15:19**</u>

Koenig awoke from his catatonia, his head aching as if he'd been kicked by one of his father's prized horses. *My God, how long has it been since I thought of them?* Shaking his head to clear his vision, he frowned when he spotted a body on the floor lying in a spreading pool of blood. His rheumy eyes widened in horror.

"Johann!"

Whimpering, he scrabbled across the concrete and took his adopted son in his arms, gently cradling the younger man's head in his lap. He saw that Johann's blood now stained the expensive tailored uniform in which he'd taken such pride. To the devil with it; it didn't matter now.

"I am sorry, Heinrich..." Schmidt said, coughing between words. "For everything. I failed you..." A small pink froth edged out of his mouth.

"Hush now, Johann. Do not speak."

The younger man's eyes pleaded otherwise. "What was Colonel Murphy talking about? What did he mean? What lies below?"

"It is nothing," Koenig said, the tears coursing down his face. "All will be over soon."

Schmidt smiled, and then grimaced as a horrible fit of coughing shook his body. It sounded as if he were tearing himself apart internally. Mercifully, it subsided a moment later, but it left him visibly weaker. He tried to speak again but appeared to have lost his wind. Leaning closer, Koenig barely heard him.

"I love you, Father," Schmidt said, his last breath escaping with those final words.

The old man suddenly felt as if his entire world had caved in.

"I love you too... *Son.*"

With nothing left, he wept, and waited for the bomb to do its work.

✷　✷　✷

T-minus 00:14:23

With Koenig, Schmidt, and Mannheim no longer a threat, Frank made sure everyone had their weapons and had moved into position. He also saw that the perimeter guard was changing. He waited until the new guards began their sweep, and the earlier shift was inside the guards' barracks.

Grabbing his own Uzi and as many magazines as he could carry, Frank moved to the door and looked out. The eastern sky had lightened. Daylight approached.

"Change in plans," he said, after closing the door once more. "When we move out, the three of us stay together and form the point. Dean? You and I are going to start shooting at the towers. When everyone hears us, they'll let it rip."

"What about the gates?" Dean asked.

Frank moved over to another pile of crates, lifting off one of the tops.

"You know how to use these, Freddie?" Frank said, pointing to the LAW rockets inside the crate.

"No, but if you hum a few bars I can fake it," Freddie said.

Frank smiled. "All right. Take three of 'em. You get to blow the gates and anything else that gets in our way. Let's do it."

He flung open the steel door and walked outside.

31

Outside the *Waffenlager*, the three men hugged the side of the building, waiting for everyone to move into final positions. Less than fifteen minutes remained before the whole place became a smoking crater, and Frank's entire body trembled with terror and the heady anticipation of imminent freedom. Would they have the time to get far enough away before the blast? He didn't know. One thing, however, was abundantly clear...

"We've got to move, now," he said to Dean. Turning to Freddie, he held out his hand. "Give Dean and me one of those LAW rockets."

Dean's eyes gleamed when Freddie handed him the fiberglass and aluminum bazooka.

"We haven't got much time, so we've got to make every shot count. Freddie? You aim for the gates, while Dean and I take out the two towers. On three we step out, aim, and fire. Got that?"

Dean and Freddie nodded, quickly reviewing the firing instructions printed on the rockets' side.

Moving to the corner, Frank peered at the gates and the towers, gauging the wind and the distance. He fell back, pressing himself against the wall, and looked at Dean and Freddie, nodding once. "All right, boys, let's give 'em hell. One... Two... Three!"

On cue, the three of them ran into the center of the quad, extending the rocket tubes to firing length, automatically raising the sights.

"Achtung!" someone cried from the towers.

Frank raised his LAW rocket, aiming through the sight directly into the heart of the east tower. He saw the guards scrambling to turn the searchlight toward them.

"Fire," Frank said.

"*Was ist los?*"

The guard's final words cut off as the three guided rockets struck their targets. The ground shook with the resultant explosion, sending debris flying in every direction. Racing to avoid the falling wreckage, Frank, Dean, and Freddie scurried back toward the armory.

When they reached their previous position, Frank looked back at the gate.

"All right!" he said, slapping Dean's hand.

Both towers lay in a heap on either side of the gate, completely decapitated. The gates, smashed and twisted, yawned open.

Freedom beckoned.

The sounds of small arms fire intruded on his thoughts as Groups One through Five began attacking their assigned targets.

"Let's go kick some butt," Frank said, pulling back the bolt of his Uzi.

He ran toward the fighting, taking down two guards who came running around the corner. Turning the same corner, he came face to face with a panicked guard trying to clear the breech of his MP40. The man's bulging frightened eyes spoke volumes. When he saw Frank, he shook like a rabbit frozen in front of a pair of oncoming headlights.

Not waiting, Frank grabbed the man's gun, throwing it as far as he could. "Go!" he said.

The guard, still scared, looked bewildered.

"*Raus! Sie sind frei! Raus!*" Frank yelled, pointing toward the waiting gates.

The guard, though skeptical about his good fortune, took off running in a mad dash for freedom. He kept glancing over his shoulders every few yards to see who might be drawing a bead on him.

"Why did you do that?" Dean asked, watching the young German disappear down the road. "Given the chance, he would've killed you."

"Didn't want to be like *them*."

Before Dean could offer a comment, they heard a horrifying scream followed by the chatter of machine gun fire. They ran toward the noise, discovering most of Group Five dead or dying, and both Bill Jensen and Dana Webster pinned down between a squad of guards hiding behind Barracks 9 and a lone guard sniping from the last remaining guard tower. The sniper had a direct line of fire to the gate. The tower had to be taken, or none of them would get out.

Out of the corner of his eye, Frank spotted an unfired LAW rocket clutched in the hands of a prisoner missing most of his head.

The sniper fired, and Frank heard the whine of the 7.92mm slug as it tore past his head. Scrambling back behind Barracks 7, he rejoined Dean and Freddie, who'd appeared moments before. Freddie looked dazed.

"You okay?" Frank asked.

Freddie nodded. "Yeah, I think so."

"We've got to take out that tower. Dean, you and Freddie make a flanking maneuver and join up with Dana and Jensen. It looks like they can use all the help they can get. One of you keep an eye on me, and on my signal, lay down a blanket of covering fire. Keep that sniper and that squad of goons occupied."

Dean looked doubtful. "Frank, you haven't got a prayer. You'll be a sitting duck.

"We're *all* sitting ducks if we don't get out of here in about ten minutes. So, if you have any brilliant ideas, I'm listening."

Dean shook his head.

"All right, then," Frank said. "Get moving."

He watched Dean and Freddie move off, then set about the task of setting up the LAW. He pulled the pin, snapped off the caps at either end of the tube, then telescoped it to firing length. The sights popped up and he took a practice aim, careful to keep his hand away from the ultra-sensitive trigger. He closed his eyes and said a final prayer for all of them.

※　　※　　※

T-Minus 00:10:15

Bill Jensen slapped another magazine into his Uzi and pulled back the bolt, feeling it slide back into place with a satisfying *ca-chunk*. The heat wafted from out of the receiver and the barrel. Back home in Texas, he'd seen too many semi-autos jam when they grew too hot from some yahoo who decided to show off his rapid-fire technique. But this Uzi was different. It was a real peach, designed to operate in desert heat—even half-clogged with sand. Still, he had no idea if it would hold up in the long run. Assuming he even *had* a long run. But that wasn't the worst of it. He had only two magazines left, and the goons were laying down some wicked suppressive fire from two directions.

He snapped off a burst and turned to Dana. The wiry little actor was firing deadly accurate three-shot bursts and hitting goon after goon. The kid was okay. It wasn't the first time he'd misjudged someone. And in a perverse way, he hoped it wouldn't be the last.

"How you doin', Webster?"

Dana dropped down behind their makeshift barricade. "My agent told me I'd never make it as an action hero—too small and too sensitive. 'Too small,' I said. 'Stallone's practically a midget.' Anyway, screw him. Screw 'em all. I'm sure as hell showing him, aren't I?"

"You sure are, kid, you sure are."

Grinning, Dana raised himself to his knees to pull his last remaining magazine out of his back pocket. Jensen's eyes bulged. "No, stay down!"

The shot from the tower sounded as if it were fired from miles away. And for a brief moment, Dana looked surprised. Then he pitched forward, blood gushing from his mouth.

"No!" Jensen screamed, throwing himself over the body. He turned Dana over and saw the blank look in the man's eyes, the stunned expression, and shook him violently.

"Don't you die on me!" he cried.

Tears streamed down Jensen's face, carving tiny rivers in the dust coating his ebony skin. He clutched the body to him and wept. "Oh, goddamn you bastards!"

Dean and Freddie joined him then, keeping a respectful distance while the black man grieved for his newfound friend. Jensen stared at them through his tears. "I told him to stay down. The little bastard wouldn't listen. I—"

Just then the Germans counterattacked. Both Freddie and Dean began firing their Uzis. Jensen gently laid Dana's body back on the ground and closed his eyes. Then he snatched up his Uzi, along with Dana's. And then, as if willing the gods to strike him down, Jensen leaped to his feet with an Uzi in both hands and screamed, "Eat lead, motherfuckers!"

Laughing maniacally, he fired at the guards, mowing them down like weeds. In his zeal he'd forgotten all about the sniper at his back.

❋ ❋ ❋

T-minus 00:09:32

From his position behind Barracks 7, Frank saw Jensen's brave but foolhardy move, and forgot all about his orders. Up in the tower, the sniper busily reloaded his Mauser rifle. Any second and he'd draw a bead on Jensen, and it would all be over for the big Texan. He was thankful, at least, that the guard was not using the MG34 machine gun.

It must be out of ammunition.

Cradling the LAW in his arms, Frank belly-crawled out from behind Barracks 7, taking refuge behind the body of one of the guards. The man had a nice neat hole smack in the middle of his forehead.

Suddenly, the firing ceased, and Frank realized that Dean, Jensen, and Freddie had run out of ammo. Jumping to his feet, Frank saw the sniper put the rifle to his shoulder and take aim.

"No!" he screamed in his loudest voice. The ploy worked, distracting the sniper for the nanosecond it took to pull the trigger and fire the LAW. It streaked out of the tube with a loud *whoosh*! A split second later, the tower disintegrated in a shower of splinters.

And then... silence.

With all his antennae raised, Frank walked out into the quad, his Glock held at the ready. Aside from the prisoners, nothing moved. All the guards were dead. Dean, Jensen, and Freddie joined him moments later.

"What time is it, Frank?" Dean asked, breathless.

Frank glanced at his watch. "We've got eight minutes," he said. "And we've got to be at least a mile away when this place goes." He paused, coming to a decision. "We'll split up right now. Freddie, you take the east end of camp. Dean, you take the west end. Bill and I will cover the rest. Tell as many of the men as you can to make a run for it and not to stop for anything. Got that?"

Dashing toward their assigned areas, Frank and Jensen beat on the doors of the barracks, screaming at the tops of their lungs. "Everyone out! Run out the gates and don't stop until you've reached the main road!"

Frank grew hoarse as he screamed the words over and over. The other prisoners, timid from all the shooting, moved slowly out of the barracks, shocked at the carnage. Moments later, the trickle became a torrent as men poured out from all the barracks and dashed out the gates.

When Frank reached the center of the camp, Freddie came running up to him. "East end's all clear, Frank. If there are any others, they've already gone over the wire."

"Anyone in the cooler?" Jensen asked.

Freddie shook his head. "No, I checked."

Frank's watch struck 4:55 as Dean joined them.

"If any of you ever wondered whether you could run a four-minute mile, now is the time," Frank said. "Move it!"

The three of them took off without another word, passing through the gates and never once looking back. Joining the two hundred-odd men in front of them, they each felt their backs warming in anticipation of the blinding flash to come.

* * *

T-minus 00:04:03

Mannheim awoke, groggy and disoriented, his eyes swimming with bright-colored spots. What had happened? Where was he? And then he remembered. Swine! Filth! He would show them all! He spotted the *Kommandant* across the room cradling Schmidt's head in his lap. The old man cried softly and was singing some nameless lullaby.

Feeble idiot!

Scrambling to his feet, Mannheim went to the door, registering mild surprise as it swung open at his touch. He stared into the quad, viewing the slaughter with indifference. Bodies lay everywhere. The guard towers were smoking ruins, and the gates nothing more than twisted bits of wood and barbed wire. The most notable aspect of the destruction was the silence. Absolute and total. Not even the crickets chirped.

The prisoners had left. Good riddance to those pieces of garbage. Let them rot somewhere else. Hans Mannheim had other plans. Returning to the *Waffenlager*, he grabbed an Uzi out of an open crate, smiling when the magazine snapped home. So much better than those ancient MP40s—always jamming. His smile took on an expression of bitter irony when he recalled the Uzi was Israeli made.

He grabbed an empty satchel and went to the old man's side. "Where is it, Heinrich?" he said. "Where is the money?"

The old man turned, his eyes glazed. "Johann? Is that you?"

Mannheim's eyes took on a predatory gleam. "Yes, Heinrich, it is I. It's time to go home. The game is over."

"*Ja*," he said, nodding like a little boy minding his mother. "I am tired, Johann. So very, very tired."

"Then let me help you carry our money, Heinrich. Where is it?" he said.

The old man's head cocked to the side, his eyes closing for a moment.

"Where is it, you old fool?" Mannheim hissed.

"Downstairs," Koenig said, his voice turning sing-song.

Mannheim frowned. Downstairs? What did this crazy, old man think he was, stupid?

Then it hit him.

A cellar.

Of course!

Getting to his feet, he looked around for the trapdoor, seeing nothing at first. Then he spotted it, peeking out from underneath an open gun crate. Grunting with effort, he dragged the heavy crate away from the trapdoor, looped his hand through the ring, and heaved it up. It was heavy steel, like the door to the *Waffenlager*, and Mannheim wondered how the old man had managed it all by himself. He let it slam to the floor with a dull *clang* and descended the steps until just his head appeared above the floor. "I'll be right back, Heinrich."

The old man smiled vacantly and began singing in a weird, off-key voice as the sergeant disappeared below.

"Who's afraid of the big, bad wolf...big, bad wolf... big, bad wolf—" Koenig halted in mid-verse, his eyes turning hard and steely. "*Gute Nacht*, Sergeant."

When Mannheim reached the bottom of the steps, he saw a massive concrete block with a large metal container the size of a small steamer trunk resting directly on top of it.

A safe!

Mannheim smiled. One of his many talents and pleasures involved safecracking. He could open anything.

Walking around to the front, he frowned when he didn't spot the usual dials and handle. Shrugging, he reached out to the metal panel and flipped it open.

Strange.

All he saw inside was a keypad, a lock, and a digital readout. He looked at the numbers:

00:00:10, 00:00:09, 00:00:08...

What kind of a safe was this? No dial, no handle, nothing familiar. *00:00:05, 00:00:04, 00:00:03...*

Somewhere in the back of Mannheim's egotistical and stunted mind, something long forgotten fell into place.

00:00:02, 00:00:01—

He stumbled back, his eyes widening in fear.

"Oh *mein Gott—*"

❊　❊　❊

T-minus 00:00:02

They were in sight of the main road when Frank looked at his watch one last time.

"Hit the deck!" he screamed.

He landed in a belly flop, the wind knocked out of him. But before he could react, the world turned a blinding white. He clenched his eyes shut and clamped his hands over his ears. And yet, Frank still saw bright golf balls dancing in the dark behind his eyelids. The ground heaved, and the noise, even through the skin of his hands, threatened to burst his eardrums.

Seconds later, he dared to open his eyes. He sat up, gasping at the sight of the mushroom cloud, dark and roiling with flame and debris. Some of the men started to get up.

"Stay down!" he screamed. "Shock wave!"

Almost before the words left his mouth, the wind whipped up by the blast tore through the trees, bending them nearly to the ground. Through the ringing in his ears, he could hear pieces of debris falling around them.

That's all I need, he thought. *After everything I've been through, I get killed by a falling searchlight.*

After another five minutes, when it became apparent that nothing was going to fall on their heads, Frank sat up and looked around. From his point of view, everyone looked disheveled, but otherwise okay.

"Jesus Christ!" Dean said, eyeing the mushroom cloud. "That was one hell of a bang."

Frank heard Freddie yell from a couple of feet away.

"Hey, Frank? What about radiation?"

"Not a problem. They designed these tactical nukes to blow very clean. No one would march through a battlefield if they weren't."

Freddie nodded and climbed to his feet.

"All right, you guys, let's move out!" Frank yelled.

Running toward the front of the line, Frank realized all the men looked a little dazed, but whole.

They were alive.

They were safe.

They were going home...

32

"So why don't you tell me who you really are and why you're in my town?"

The sheriff's eyes took on a hard glint, not easy for a man who looked more at home in a high school computer club. Brenda's stomach growled again, this time from fear rather than hunger. What could she do? If she ran, gangly as this nerd was, he would certainly catch her. Running solved nothing. Telling another set of lies appeared equally useless.

Glancing out the window, she spotted someone walking up the road. About to turn away, her eyes widened when she realized the man wore a World War II German uniform. Something had happened at the camp!

"Are you gonna answer my question, or do I have to run you in?"

Noticing her wide-eyed stare, Toby Lennart looked out the window and froze. "What the fuck?" he said.

And then the room whited out, as if a giant strobe had gone off in their faces. The diner began to shake, sending dishes and glassware clattering to the floor where they shattered into a million pieces. Light fixtures wobbled, and the jukebox fell over with a resounding crash.

"Frank!" Brenda screamed.

349

Lennart ducked under the booth's table. Hilda, the buxom waitress, screamed hysterically, the diner disintegrating around her. The cook yelled something unintelligible and grabbed a fire extinguisher as a large grease fire threatened to engulf the kitchen.

As quickly as it came, the shaking stopped, leaving a silence that terrified Brenda more than the noise.

"Oh, God, Frank!" she whimpered.

"What did you say?" Lennart said, pulling himself out from under the table, his lean body trembling.

Brenda gasped, realizing her mistake. "Nothing," she said, trying to brush it off.

"I heard you. You said Frank. Frank who?"

"It's nothing," she said, heading for the door. "I was scared. I didn't know what I was saying."

Turning to go, she reached for the door.

"Freeze, goddamn it!"

Halting in her tracks, Brenda turned around and saw the sheriff's massive .357 Magnum pointed right at her head.

Instead of feeling the fear she expected, her anger took over.

"What right have you to point that gun at me? I haven't done anything!"

"Well, now, I don't know about that," Lennart said, his jocular air returning. This time there was nothing funny about it. "I can think up several very *serious* violations," he continued. "Most obvious being leaving a restaurant without paying your bill..."

Ripping open her purse, she pulled out a twenty and threw it on the table.

"...and bribin' an officer of the law."

"What?" she said, not believing what she heard. The man either had cast-iron balls or no brain. Brenda bet on the latter.

"Yes, ma'am, we sure do have ourselves a *nasty* little problem, here."

Before she could say anything else, the sheriff grabbed her wrist and slapped handcuffs on. Twisting her arm behind her, he laughed when she cried out from the pain. He clamped the cuffs on, clicking them extra tight. Sadistic bastard. Then he leaned over her shoulder, his mouth next to her ear. She smelled stale onions on his breath, and it made her want to puke. But it was what he said next in his tight whisper that made her shiver. "Got you now, baby. And we is gonna have ourselves a party. You, me... and Hilda." He turned to the waitress. "You all right, Hilda?"

The waitress nodded, a dazed look in her eyes. "I'm fine, Toby, don't mind me." She waved him off and began picking up the mess on the floor while Lennart pushed Brenda out through the door and down the steps. Outside, Brenda scanned the area. The man in the German uniform had disappeared. Lennart dragged her to the cruiser, opened the rear door, pushed her in, and slammed it shut.

"Didn't your mother ever teach you any manners?" Brenda snapped.

Ignoring her, he climbed in and started the car. The engine roared to life, its overworked valves chattering noisily. Slapping it into reverse, he backed out of the spot, turned, and headed back toward the source of the explosion.

"Fucking Krauts," he muttered. "This goddamn shit's gotten way outta hand."

He knew about the camp!

Somehow, this revelation didn't surprise her. However, she wasn't sure which was worse, having this guy take her to jail, or handing her over to Koenig's security force.

Sighing, she sat back against the seat, wincing at the awkward position of her arms, feeling the muscles in her shoulders pulling with the strain.

Making herself relax, she reasoned that no matter who this hick was in bed with, she was in a world of shit.

***

With Frank, Dean, Freddie, and Jensen in the lead, the huge pack of men moved down Highway 8, making for a sight few could ignore. Their somber mood lifted with every step that took them farther from what was left of Camp Stalag. They began laughing and joking, and someone in the back started whistling a jaunty tune. Recognizing it, other men smiled and joined in. The song grew louder and stronger, and Frank smiled with quiet satisfaction. The tune was the "Colonel Bogey March," the theme from *Bridge Over the River Kwai*. It struck the perfect chord in the aftermath of all they'd experienced.

They'd beaten a man who'd tried to take away their dignity, who'd tried to take them all down in the blaze of his madness. Frank's smile faltered when he remembered Bob Neff, Blair, Riley, and the score of other men who never made it out.

Feeling a slap on his back, he turned and saw Dean grin and give him the thumbs up sign. He laughed and took up the tune himself, his heart swelling with pride.

***

"Where the hell are you taking me?" Brenda demanded.

The sheriff glanced in the rearview and smiled, his piggish eyes undressing her for the umpteenth time.

"You don't wanna know. And I ain't tellin'," he chuckled, proud of his clever humor. Christ, he was such a clod. How could any town entrust its safety to such a man as this? Brenda shook her head. Obviously, they couldn't.

Turning her attention to the passing scenery, she tried to keep from thinking about Frank. She almost laughed in spite of her maddening anxiety. That was like the old saw about not thinking of pink elephants. How could she think of anything else? That explosion could mean only one thing.

Stop it!

The cruiser bounced when it hit a pothole, causing the cuffs to dig into her wrists. Damn, that hurt. But the pain in her hands was far more welcome than the ache in her heart. Shifting so it relieved the pressure, she found the only way to be comfortable was to perch herself on the edge of the seat. The problem was staying there.

The cruiser rounded a curve and Brenda spotted black smoke billowing up into the sky.

Oh, God, Frank!

Hot tears stung her face. How could anyone have lived through that? How could they— She shook her head. No. Frank had to be alive! He had to be! Uncle John had been so resolute, so confident about their plan, so adamant about her staying behind. Now, she wished she'd left sooner. Maybe then, she'd have made a difference.

Stop it!

The plan *had* to have worked. But where were the men? Goddamn it, where were they?

The sheriff whistled tunelessly, trying to carry the country tune warbling out of the cruiser's tinny-sounding radio. The happy song only made Brenda angrier.

"Will you turn that shit off?" she snapped.

The sheriff smirked and turned it louder. Shouting in anger, Brenda began kicking the partition.

"You are a feisty one, ain't ya?" he laughed, turning his attention back to the road.

They rounded another curve, and his happy expression turned to horror. "Oh, shit!" he screamed.

Panicking, the sheriff stomped on the brakes, causing the cruiser's bald tires to lock up and slide. The sheriff screamed like a woman when the cruiser rocketed toward a large boulder at the side of the road. Barely missing the huge stone, the cruiser came to a rattling halt, sitting halfway into the ditch. Unable to prevent it, Brenda catapulted forward, banging her head against the Lexan partition.

Dazed, she wormed her way back onto the seat and gasped. Right in front of the car stood hundreds of men wearing World War II American uniforms.

✻ ✻ ✻

The cruiser plowed into the ditch barely ten yards in front of them and Frank grinned when he saw the frightened eyes of Toby Lennart peering out through the windshield.

"Well, guys," he said, glancing towards Dean and Freddie. "Looks like we have a late arrival."

Looking beyond the paralyzed sheriff, Frank noticed someone in the back of the cruiser, but the shadows inside were too dense to tell much. When he moved forward, Frank heard the person screaming from the back seat.

The sheriff slammed the car into reverse, but the cruiser stayed where it was, rear tires spinning uselessly.

"Hold it right there!" Frank yelled.

Immediately, every weapon still in their possession came to bear on the hapless sheriff, who put the cruiser in park and dropped his head onto the steering wheel in abject defeat.

"Frank!" the person in the back screamed.

"Brenda?" he said, his heart skipping a beat.

Rushing to the rear door, he saw her, tears streaming down her face, laughing hysterically. He yanked the door open and pulled her out and into his arms.

"Oh, God, Frank! I thought you— I thought..." Her words dissolved into a flood of tears, and she buried her head in his shoulder.

"I was afraid I was never going to see you again, sweetheart," he said, his own tears coming unbidden. "I missed you so much."

Jensen, watching the tearful reunion with a big grin on his face, stepped up to the driver's door and waved the sheriff out with his Uzi.

Like a frightened deer, Toby Lennart appeared unable to move. Jensen wrenched open the door and dragged him out, letting him spill onto the road like the dregs of a cold cup of coffee.

"Don't! Don't hurt me!" he blubbered, hiding behind his scrawny hands. Hauling him to his feet, Jensen pushed him toward Frank and Brenda. "Take the damn cuffs off her," the big man said, his tone leaving no doubt what he'd do if the sheriff didn't obey.

Fumbling with his key ring, the sheriff managed to get them off after a few clumsy tries. With the cuffs off, Brenda's arms locked around her husband's neck. To Frank, it was the moment that almost washed away all the horrors of the previous month.

Finally breaking the embrace, Frank looked into her eyes. "What on earth are you doing here?"

Smiling, she said, "I couldn't just stay in some dumb hotel room, Frank. I had to do something. Where's Uncle John?"

Frank looked to Dean, then back to Brenda, an ineffable sadness in his eyes. "I'm sorry, sweetheart."

Brenda's eyes welled with tears and she collapsed against Frank, sobbing uncontrollably.

Furious, he handed Brenda off to Dean, went up to the sheriff, and grabbed him by his shirt. "I ought to let these guys tear your goddamn head off. What do you say, guys?"

All of the men began yelling, and Lennart looked as if he might faint.

"Frank!"

Everyone, including Frank, turned to Brenda, who wiped her eyes and sauntered over to the sheriff. Lennart relaxed, shuffled his feet, and smiled. "I sure am sorry about the inconvenience, ma'am. Hope we can part as friends."

He stuck out his hand and his smile widened. In a flash of movement, Brenda hauled off and slugged the sheriff with a roundhouse punch that would have made Mike Tyson proud. With his eyes crossed, Lennart staggered forward, then collapsed on the ground, out like a light.

"My wife, the commando," Frank said, holding up her arm in victory and laughing.

When everyone joined in, Brenda, slightly annoyed at first, started to giggle. She threw her arms around her husband and held on, never wanting the moment to end.

"Hey, Frank," Dean said. "What'll we do with 'Handsome Harold' here?"

Frank bent over the sheriff, who began to moan as he came around. He pulled Lennart's pistol from its holster, emptied the bullets into his hand, then tossed it into the woods. "So, Toby? How are we doin'?"

Lennart's eyes bugged out when he saw Brenda. "You keep her away from me," he whined.

"Don't worry, Toby," Frank said, taking his wife by the hand. "You've got no more to fear from us. But not too long from now some guys'll be along to help you clean up the mess back there. You can't miss 'em. They all wear identical suits and sunglasses. And they'll be looking for you."

Lennart blanched as he puzzled over Frank's meaning.

Turning away from the sheriff, Frank yelled, "All right, men! Let's go home!"

Locking arms with Brenda, Dean, Jensen, and Freddie, Frank strode toward town. The men cheered and followed.

As they marched down Highway 8, Frank gazed down the long ribbon of asphalt toward Derleth, wondering what lay ahead, wondering if the FBI, or Koenig's people were even now on their way. And even if they were, Frank wasn't afraid—not of anything anymore.

He had no idea what lay down that road, but he knew, without a moment's hesitation, that he would never forget the brave men who stood by his side.

His father was right. It was something special...

EPILOGUE

The line to the table at the back of the store snaked around and through most of the aisles. And although Brad had been waiting more than half an hour, and had missed most of his karate class, he resolved to stick it out. Only two people now stood between him and the reason he'd come. One, an obese matron of indeterminate age, giggled when she left the line clutching her prize to her ample bosom.

Christ!

He couldn't believe the reaction. You'd think it was some Holly-wood big shot who sat there, or some tattletale starlet gushing about her naughty affairs, rather than the unassuming man who smiled pleasantly and signed his name to the title page of his book.

The last person in front of Brad, a short, balding, middle-aged man, smiled at the man seated at the table and said, "I got to tell you this is the most amazing story I've read in a long time. I don't know how you did it, but I would sure be proud to shake your hand."

The balding man extended his hand, which the other man, slender and graying slightly at the temples, grasped and shook with muttered thanks and a kind smile.

Now it was Brad's turn. "Hi," he said, feeling a little silly.

"Hi there," the man said, smiling amiably. "What's your name?"

"Brad. But it's not for me. It's for my Dad—for his birthday."

The man nodded patiently.

"What's your Dad's name?"

"Alvin. Just write it to Alvin," Brad said.

The man took a book from the stack next to him, quickly wrote on the title page, and handed it to Brad.

"Thank you," Brad said.

"No," the man said, his gaze level and somber. "Thank *you*."

Stepping away from the table, Brad got into the long line for the register.

This line promised to take as long as the other.

So much for karate, he thought.

Staring at the book, Brad studied the inscription: "To Alvin," it said. "Give 'em hell..."

He smiled, closed the book, and checked out the cover art:

Superimposed on a striking, blood-red sunset, a man hung from a barbed-wire fence, his bare, sinewy arms dripping blood, his face in shadow. Immediately behind him, perched like some odious, carrion-eating bird, loomed the dark profile of a guard tower. A lone guard stood within its sinister confines, watching... waiting...

Brad smiled, shivering with delight. He could *feel* the drama and the desperation in that potent, Dantean image.

Wow!

Dad was going to *love* this. He was always reading stuff like this. Caressing the dust jacket, Brad let his fingers fondle the slightly embossed Gothic-style letters forming the title. He smiled again.

Great title...

CAMP STALAG

A True Tale of Courage

by

Frank Murphy

ABOUT THE AUTHOR

Bill Walker is a graphic designer specializing in book and dust jacket design who has worked on projects by Ray Bradbury, Richard Matheson, Dean Koontz and Stephen King. Between his design work and his writing, he spends his spare time reading voraciously and playing very loud guitar, much to the chagrin of his lovely wife and two sons. Bill makes his home in Los Angeles.

Other Books by Bill Walker

Titanic 2012

A Note from an Old Acquaintance

Abe Lincoln: Public Enemy No. 1

Abe Lincoln On Acid

D-NOTICE *(Coming 2021)*

Starring... John Dillinger *(Coming 2021)*